Consequence of Choice

Also by Slovie Solomon Apple:

They Were Strangers

Consequence of Choice

In Life, Love, and War

Slovie Solomon Apple

VANTAGE PRESS
New York

This is a work of fiction. Any similarity between the names, characters, and places in this book and any persons, living or dead, is purely coincidental.

FIRST EDITION

Published by Vantage Press, Inc.
516 West 34th Street, New York, New York 10001

Manufactured in the United States of America
ISBN: 0-533-14650-X

Library of Congress Catalog Card No.: 2003093781

0 9 8 7 6 5 4 3 2 1

Contents

Acknowledgments

To the Reference Department at the Roseville Public Library in Roseville, Minnesota, for their untiring assistance in acquiring needed materials.

To my dear friend, Jeanne Nagel, who made numerous trips to the library for pick-ups and returns, and was always ready to help in so many ways.

To my son, Dr. Martin Apple, for his help and encouragement, and always being available for discussion, input, and inspirational critiquing.

To my granddaughter, Stephanie Gimble Dillon, her husband, Reilly Dillon, and my great-granddaughter, Shelby Dillon, for their love and support.

To my grandson, Nathan Apple, and his wife, Tamara, for their art contribution, which made the cover special.

To Jodi Meyer, for her assistance with the manuscript.

To Betty Habrman Struebing, special thanks for help on the manuscript with her incomparable computer skills.

To all of them, special appreciation and sincere thanks for their contributions that made the book a reality.

Finally, I wish to acknowledge the invaluable learning experiences and help I received from the distinguished books listed in the bibliography.

Consequence of Choice

Prologue

On the 50th Memorial for Pearl Harbor, some young adults, offspring of the "Baby Boomer" generation, were asking questions about WWII. Most of what they learned was from books, movies, and television. They knew the wonderful stories of our men in service fighting in that terrible war. In 1939, Germany attacked Poland; this was the beginning of WWII. The war came about, the result of the seeds of hate rooted in the Germans at their treatment in the Versailles Treaty at the end of WWI.

There were questions wanting to know details of all that occurred when a citizen volunteered or was drafted into military service. There was also interest in what those at home, family of the Baby Boomers, were doing on the home front as the war went on. The book, then, is intergenerational, and chronicles the stories of the other characters, living their everyday lives, caught in the war.

The history of the six key people is traced to see what events were important to each to mold them to who they were when they met each other. Over the years, just before WWII, they are taking charge of their lives with the innocent belief that they have control of their lives.

They have noted at times, but not too seriously, the war in Europe, which is too far away to be important. They become three couples who go through carefree days of youth and innocence, fall in love, marry, and expect to live happily ever after. Then December 7, 1941, happens, and there's the sudden shock of war. Everything is never the same again. Now the war isn't just "over there," it is right where they are in St. Louis, Missouri.

The war impacts the three loving couples. Death, destruction, and betrayal surround them. When the men return, there are problems adjusting to civilian life and their marriages.

Thousands come back with serious physical injuries. Thousands had injuries and scars buried deep within them that couldn't be seen, but were taking their toll. How the couples coped with it, is thought-provoking. Were they right? Were they wrong? How would others have dealt with their problems? What choices would have been made, and with what consequences? Who can say? Who can judge?

As the years slip away, there are fewer of us—of the dwindling generation of World War II to tell some of the story. We were there!

Part One
Remembering

I
About the Varnars

Serena lay there wonderfully outlined under the cool satin sheets. The sun's rays slanting through the opened windows and the increasingly warm air were already claiming their territory. Today would be another unbearably sticky summer day, as only it can be in St. Louis, Missouri. From outside, the noises of an awakening neighborhood were slowly stirring the woman's consciousness, and her eyes opened, then shut, and gradually opened wide. Her attention now drawn to the bedside table, where the calendar there indicated the beginning day as July 1st, 1966.

Serena's mind began to race as if on "Reverse Fast" when trying to adjust the time change on a clock. It came to an abrupt halt at July 1, 1941, the date of her wedding.

Twenty-five years ago, she thought, *twenty-five years. Where has the time gone*?

She turned, and slowly, lovingly, her hand moved over the indentation of her Max's head on the pillow next to hers.

Max was an early riser, and she could hear him showering in the adjoining bathroom. A wonderful excitement enveloped her as she pictured him showering—robust—still quite handsome with his shock of curly hair—formerly a chestnut brown—now turning into a silvery gray mane.

"Distinguished looking!" was how everyone described him. She inhaled deeply the slightly cooler air of a wayward breeze. A contentment filled her, and it was good. Max came out, a bath towel wrapped around his waist. When he saw her awake, he greeted her with "Morning, Beautiful!" It was a custom he had started the morning after their wedding. For a long time, it had thrilled her to hear him. Like a schoolgirl it made her blush and feel tingly all over.

Serena didn't think she was beautiful. She had taken stock of herself a long time ago. "Nice looking? Yes, Nice figure? Yes!" And others were constantly confirming this. None of this really mattered. She was quite comfortable with herself—how she looked—and who she was. She was herself, and not in competition with anyone. Independent though she was, Max's love gave her assurance, a security, and she loved him with all her being. That she knew from the first moment she met him.

Max was vigorously using a towel to dry his hair—then came over and stooped to kiss her. She put her arms around his neck and pulled him down. They locked in a longer more passionate kiss and embrace. "Happy Anniversary!" they began in unison and both laughed, their thoughts in harmony on this, their special day. He bent to kiss her again. "Max! Max!" Gently she put her hands on his chest to back him up. "I know, Siri" (his name for her). His voice became a little husky as it did when he was deeply moved.

"This is a great day, you know!" *God,* he thought; there was a seriousness now about him. *God has been good.* He felt humbled, almost a disbeliever. He shook his head. "Incredible, I don't know how I got so lucky to have you, Serena."

He began to dress and turned in time to catch a glimpse of Serena as she dashed nude to the shower. It always excited him to see her. Beauty is in the eyes of the beholder, and to him she was beautiful not only on the outside, but the inside of her was the astounding part to him.

"She's warm and considerate of others," as he said so many times when speaking of her. To him, "she was a wonderfully caring human being," as he put it so often. She was all that and more—proof of that was their having reached this significant milestone day.

Serena was a petite woman. Her light brown hair had silvery threads in it, matching Max's, and her face was round from which two laughing blue eyes held your attention, for she looked straight at you when she spoke. It wasn't very long before he heard her singing happily in the shower and began whistling her tune. Smilingly she emerged a short while later, her face a rosy pink, hugging her robe around her. Max was putting some papers in his briefcase.

A glance at her watch as she put it on, elicited a verbal concern. "I have an appointment at the beauty shop, and I don't want to be late. I'm meeting Carole for lunch."

Max gave her a peck on the cheek. "I'm off, too. I have a lot of last minute things I have to attend to." He grabbed his suit coat and left. His voice came trailing from the stairs. "See you later."

Serena ran into the hallway to remind him. "Be back early, Max. Rabbi will be here to go over some things with us before the guests arrive."

Tonight they were celebrating their 25th wedding anniversary and had chosen to renew their vows. Max wanted it desperately, and Serena had agreed. It meant a great deal to both of them. It would be a simple affair with family and a few friends, among them two of their closest, Carole and her second husband Dave. In making out their guest list, Serena and Max had been saddened because in the past twenty-five years, so many of their friends had passed on. They missed them and had reminisced often and had become more aware of their own mortality.

Serena came out to the yard where a few tables were being set up. It was July, a lovely time of the year especially in St. Louis. The earth bursting forth with its new beginnings for spring, had become alive with soft rains, and sunny days. Now, the flowers and shrubs were outdoing themselves in competition, and the blending delicate fragrances of lilacs, lilies of the valley, and roses mingled in the summer air. Serena took a deep breath, and stood there, silently taking in the home she loved and its surroundings. She walked slowly down the hill to the brook where water gurgled over stones and rocks of different sizes and colors, and the cascades of weeping willow branches, fell gracefully—some almost touching the ground.

This space was hers. She had come here numerous times to sit on the marble bench with its inscription—"My Love Forever," a gift from Max, a long time ago. There had been happy times celebrating good things in a family, and there were many sad times. It seemed for every pleasure, there was an occurrence of sadness. Life couldn't be too good or the fates were tempted—then there would be tears, many tears that came from unbearable pain—as if to balance out one's life! Always, too, there had been prayers, so many prayers!

Serena would come here to think and reflect—to speak her worries and thoughts out loud, heard only by the willow tree. She remembered the happiness and promise when they planted the small sapling—now grown to its full majestic splendor. It had been like a good trusted friend, with whom she shared what she couldn't share with anyone else. She saw its leaves golden in the fall—then in spring renew itself, always giving her a pledge of hope.

Today, she felt the need to be here. She was happy with her life—all of it! Sitting there with her hands touching her lap as if in a prayer—a serenity about her—softly she murmured, "Thank you, God, for all my blessings!"

Her blessings included her son, Robert, and his wife, Judy.

"How many times," she wondered, "do people travel back in mind to choices made where Providence, alone, would know what the consequences would be?"

Today she was thinking about it—what she knew of the beginning of her existence, who she was, and how she came to be where she was now. This would take her back five generations. She had missed a great deal, not knowing many members of the first two. It happened because of the horrible World War I anti-Semitism, causing the deaths of millions of Jews. She and her family were Jewish. As she was remembering it all, she realized that because of choices that were made in overwhelming circumstances, she was here by the narrowest of chances.

Serena Warner lived with her parents, Robert and Ann, and an older brother, Saul, in Madison, a college town in Wisconsin. For all her nineteen years, this middle-class Jewish neighborhood had been home. There were families from many other ethnic groups, and everyone knew who you were. They all lived together as good neighbors—like a close-knit family. Growing up she had often heard her father reminiscing with his friends, and she listened to their discussions on how and why they had come to be in America. They had been refugees, escaping from oppression and violence, had come immigrants from Eastern European countries—some from Russia and Romania—some from Austria-Hungary—and many from Germany and other countries. Her father had come from Poland.

Their stories were different, harrowing experiences of long treacherous journeys across many lands, but in one aspect of their lives, there was a sameness—they had come to escape the religious persecution—the anti-Semitism that plagued them and made their lives unbearable. The simmering hatred, which began centuries before, was always there—lying dormant for short or extended periods of time—then suddenly awakened and unleashed with such fury against them—for one reason only—they were Jews!

They became the recipients of torturous crimes committed against them. They were pressured to convert, suffering unspeakable hardships to preserve their birthright. They were born Jews, and no one had the right to take that from them! They endured the terror of pogroms and revolts, with the burnings, the killings and the suffering. As a result of the changing political conditions by governments in different countries, they were used as scapegoats, blamed for everything that went awry. The hate manifested itself in many different diabolical ways, depending on the perpetrators. Steadily, conditions worsened from those brainwashed with a hate that consumed them.

Serena had learned some of the family history, which because of the brutal conditions could only be traced back a few generations. With forced evacuations, and expulsions from their homes and countries, where could they be? From those in charge, there were denials, contradictory reports, and often refusal to answer questions of where loved ones could be found, those trying desperately to learn—became cognizant of the fact—they would never know. The enemy had taken them, prisoners, slaves, and those left behind were prisoners, too, of their minds. Their loved ones were never forgotten—and always remembered in their prayers. They were haunted day in and day out. Where were they? How were they? Were they still alive?

Her father, Barak, was born in Bialystok, Poland, near the Russian and Polish borders. He lived there with his parents, Misha and Ressel, and a sister Seren. Their home was in back of a small brick factory owned by the government. Misha and his son were makers of bricks used by the government, to build and repair bridges, and roads, and places needed by the military. The work was hard and deemed important enough that Misha had not been pressed into the military service.

Poland, located in Central Europe, was tied to its neighbors, Russia, Prussia, and Austria-Hungary. Poland was often overrun by her neighbors. It was a crossroad and its boundaries changed many times because of wars and occupations by outsiders. These aggressions would lead to new attacks on the Jews, with more restrictions imposed and harshly enforced.

Misha lived with a constant nagging in his brain. Any day now, things could change and he and his son would be taken and conscripted into the dreaded military service—with years of extraordinary hardships, cruelty deliberately calculated for soldiers who were Jews. He sought help from the under-ground organization to get Barak away. "We are working on it," they told him. There were so many others waiting to escape the oppression. Misha prayed and waited.

The family was looking forward to visiting with friends. It was a way of sharing whatever news they gathered—important to their lifelines. They left unaware of the happenings that day in another country on their side of the world, far away, and yet, not so far away. The date was June 28, 1914. It was a day that would change their lives forever!

At a parade in Sarajevo, Bosnia, an incident took place. Archduke Francis Ferdinand, heir to the Austria-Hungary throne, and his wife, Sophie, were assassinated by Gavrilo Princep. Princep belonged to a patriotic group of young Serbian students who had been fighting to unite all their people and free them from Austrian rule.

Austria-Hungary blamed Serbia for the assassination. War had been threatening Europe for more than a decade. Rival European nations had engaged in an arms race for years and had also been busy making protective alliances among one another. They were designated to prevent a general war. They were set up, however, that an attack by one nation upon another would trigger just such a war! Their hopes were in the patriotic alliances. It took the Princep murderous deed in the Balkans to spark and set the smaller nations aflame, and so began World War I in 1914.

Poland's borders to the east were in conflict with Russia, to the north with Germany, and to the south with Austria-Hungary. Troops from these countries were now constantly crossing Poland's borders. Six months later, the winter of 1914, Misha was taken to serve in the Russian army. New borders had been imposed on Polish territory overrun by the Russians. He had to leave immediately. It was heart-wrenching for Misha and the family to say their good-byes as he left for war. Ressel's worries compounded as Jewish soldiers were always put in the front lines—the first to get the brunt of the fierce battles—a death sentence for certain.

With the war on, news traveled slowly. The Germans began using poisonous gas in attacks on the Russians. Thousands of soldiers suffered horrible deaths. Misha was there, if he was still alive. Ressel thought of him, and for a fleeting moment, her soul was uplifted, then remembering where he was filled her with despair. She prayed, "Please, God, don't let him suffer."

It was sometime before the family learned of Misha's death—killed in one of the major battles. When? There was no way to know for sure. Serena's father recalled, "It was one of the saddest days for us all. Mother was inconsolable and Seren wept. I didn't say much, but he was on my mind, and at night I would dream of him. We had good long talks and we were happy. Then I'd awaken to the sad truth. It was that way for weeks. We were together, but there were the lonely, forlorn days for each of us. My father was never coming home to us. It was a difficult realization to grasp. Why did this have to happen to him? Why to us? It was unbearable to have to think of life without him."

Every day brought new rules and restrictions. Ressel heard a new Russian officer had arrived to take charge of their area. Ressel knew it meant trouble. Anguished, she made contact with the Underground. They came late one night. She begged for help to get Barak away. They came and listened, sympathetic, and promised they were doing all they could and help would come soon. Meanwhile, she was given directions to a safe place if there was an emergency and she had to get away quickly.

The area's new commanding officer rode in with several officers. Gruff and fierce in their manner, they struck terror in Ressel. She stood there, pale, trembling, worrying and wondering what he had come for. The children, hearing the sound of horses' hooves, had hidden.

In Russian, he began, "We are not satisfied with the arrangement here. The government wants the factory to produce twice as much bricks. The place would be taken over by the military. You have until morning to leave," he informed her.

"Leave here? To where?" she questioned.

He strode up to her and in a loud, ominous voice, threatened, "Go, it will be better for you to go!"

They ransacked the place and took the little food they had. One officer took Misha's clothes. She had kept them; she couldn't bear to part with them. They left making rude remarks and laughing boisterously. She watched them ride off, then called the children and tried to calm their fears. After they had gone, Ressel shut the door quickly. Worried, she made the decision to leave that night. It was imperative to make contact with those who would help her escape. The ultimatum had been given, and her perception was "the family's situation made it too dangerous to wait until morning." The children had to be smuggled out immediately.

There was very little to take with them—just a few clothes and very little food. She rushed to make small bundles, one for each to carry—small enough not to arouse any suspicion. In the side seams of her skirt, she sewed a few pieces of gold jewelry given to her by her parents. Living in these unstable conditions, most families tried to have a little something saved for an "emergency move." It was something Jews had to live with.

Ressel looked around at what had been her home. Now, she was forced to leave it. Then there was her Misha, buried somewhere in a strange land. Her pain was so great she couldn't hold back the tears. She prayed for courage and strength to get her family to Misha's parents in Warsaw. They owned a construction company, and she knew they could help her get to

America, to her brother Dave. He lived in a place, called Wisconsin. She had always been so proud to receive his mail marked U.S.A.!

Over the years, he had written glowing letters, asking them to come, but Misha decided to stay. He couldn't leave his parents and a sister and her husband, and they refused to go. After much contemplation, their decision again was to stay. They made the choice and were oblivious of what the consequences would be.

Ressel, Barak, and Seren walked out of their home. The night was dark, and a cool wind blew across their paths. Ressel shivered. Frightened, though she was, she stepped forward with a boldness of spirit and led them carefully—quietly to the designated area. There would be someone on watch, nearby.

Ressel had written to Misha's family telling them of his death, but she didn't know if they had gotten the heart-breaking news. Sending or receiving mail in a war-torn country was almost impossible, but she had hoped by some miracle the letter had gotten through.

She had worried about them—the shock of learning of the loss of their beloved son, and what it would do to them. So many times Ressel's anger filled her heart—anger at Misha and his family for not leaving when she wanted them to make the change to America. It was a time the government was allowing travel. Her Misha would be alive, and all this would not be happening. When the anger subsided, she felt a great guilt for haboring these thoughts and feelings. She would pray for forgiveness. Every day, for a long time, she would pray.

Misha had made the decision—his choice to stay—and he thought it was the right one. His parents in their declining years—couldn't see the advantages in making the change. Ressel had been trying to accept this but couldn't. She didn't know if she ever would—she lived with the new reminders every day brought.

The refugee organizations were sometimes difficult to contact—so many needed their help. They succeeded in securing a safe passage through many parts of Poland for Ressel and her family. They had to stay in different homes during the day, leaving at night, always fearful of being caught. They traveled in all kinds of weather—sometimes stayed in barns—with horses and sheep. Seren became ill with a raging fever, and they were scheduled to leave that night. Ressel couldn't see taking her sick child. The person waiting, insisted, they had to leave. It was dangerous for them to stay. They traveled a long way to the next safe house. It was in a town called Torun.

Through the Underground, they managed to get a doctor. He shook his head after examining Seren. "The girl is gravely ill," he said. Reluctantly, those in charge made changes—other arrangements with new people, who would help the fleeing family at a later time. The doctor stayed, trying to help a very sick Seren, but it was too late. Three days later she succumbed to the illness. Ressel couldn't believe this child she loved so, could be taken from her.

She blamed herself. Somehow, she was to blame. Maybe she shouldn't have come this way going to Warsaw. In torment she questioned, "What should I have done differently? How could God let this happen? He had taken Misha and now Seren. Why?" she asked, wanting to know, and cried, not succeeding in stifling her sobs.

"Oh, God, what have I done to be punished this way—my child to die before me?" She questioned, full of pain, and heartbreak at its greatest depths.

She wouldn't let Seren be buried. She sat with her dead child's body. "I can't go and leave her." Over and over in constant repetition, she spoke, not listening to their pleas to let them take the girl. It was becoming a situation full of danger for all of them—fearful of being discovered, Ressel had to finally relent. They came to bury Seren. She had contracted meningitis. "How? Or where?" They didn't know.

The next night Ressel took Barak to the small grave—they were slated to leave in another hour. Their tears fell onto the small unmarked mound.

Seren's brother didn't want to leave her. They had been playmates, companions, and friends. What would he do without her? His heart ached and he, too, questioned, "Why? Why were all these bad things happening? Seren was a good, kind sister. If you were good, bad things weren't supposed to happen."

He didn't understand. "Why? Why his father had to go to war and die, and why they had to leave their home and travel in fear to so many places. What would happen next and where would it all end?" He wondered.

All these things to think about, but now Seren wasn't there to talk to him, and his mother was so sad, he couldn't talk to her; she would begin to cry. All this had to stay inside Barak. His life had become so changed. So much was missing from his life. He wished he could go back to feeling how he did before—when Seren and his father were alive and they were a family.

His world was all mixed up. He grasped the finality of it. He could never go back to how it was! There was this emptiness, and he didn't know if it would ever go away. For a young man faced with this seriousness of life, there was much to ponder and question. To the "Why?" of everything, there was no answer.

Serena would cry whenever she heard her father tell this part of his story. His voice would break. "That's so sad, Dad." She would come over, put her arms around his shoulder, and kiss him gently on the cheek.

Ressel and Barak were taken to Warsaw, through many dangerous areas, many times with little food, or water, and always bone-weary! They learned the Germans had taken the construction company and home of the elderly Varnars. They were living in a restricted area where the Jews had been sent—an impoverished area—a ghetto. Their daughter, Misha's sister, and her husband lived there too.

The elderly woman escorting them quietly informed them they were in danger. "Follow me. I will take you to them. Quick, we must hurry." Ressel was surprised as the escorts spoke little.

Ressel looked around. She didn't know if she could trust this person, but she followed her. There was nothing else she could do. She was taken to the Varnars. Ressel thanked her. "Don't thank me. We have to do for each other. Be careful, Shalom!" And she was gone in a flash.

The Varnars had gotten the mail telling them of Misha's death. They shed tears together. They had expected their son to outlive them, to be their "Kaddish," the one to say the Memorial Prayers when they were gone.

"Now I say the Kaddish for my Misha," the father cried. "It shouldn't have been this way." He wept for his son, Misha.

The Varnars listened as Ressel recounted the happenings in Bialystok and the surrounding area, now ruled by Russia, and how Misha had to go into the Russian Army. The parents felt a great guilt about Misha's death. "We were foolish and stubborn. We should have gone when Misha and you wanted us to go, but we stayed. We never thought the country we call home and love, would turn against us. Now Misha died because of us. We're to blame and Seren, our beautiful granddaughter, is gone too. This would not have happened if we had listened to both of you. Forgive us. We ask God to forgive us. Every day we live with this heartache."

Their faces were sad with a haunted look that told of sleepless nights and no peace in their hearts.

"Oh, God," he said—and with a clenched fist beat his breast.

Ressel tried to calm them, with a handkerchief over her mouth, the grandmother shed her tears trying not to make any sort of noise.

From outside there came several explosions, just a few minutes apart. The old man went to the window—he could see smoke billowing up from the square in the center of town. Then he saw people running in different directions. Before the next hour was up, a woman came, out of breath—she had been running. Saboteurs had bombed a German truck with gasoline drums on it. Trucks with German soldiers were entering different areas cutting off exits, looking for those responsible.

"It is necessary for you to leave right away. Every minute counts. Arrangements are being made. Hurry!"

If they were found, Jews from Russian enemy territory, they would be shot in the square as spies. The grandfather disappeared for a few moments, then came back and gave Ressel some necessary things for her trip. Grandfather Varnar took his daughter-in-law's hand and placed a gold watch and chain and two gold rings in it. "This will get you to America." Ressel didn't want to take them, but they insisted. "It is necessary to save you and our grandson." For Ressel it was heart-wrenching to think of leaving these aging parents and the younger sister-in-law, Nedda, and her husband, Herschel, in these dreadful circumstances.

While they were readying to leave, they became aware of a commotion in the yard. Always alert, Grandmother Varnar hurried to the window. She turned, her face white and frightened. "There are Germans soldiers downstairs. They are coming up." They could hear them running up the steps on the first floor.

The grandfather opened the window and motioned Ressel and Barak to follow him over the roof-top to the next building. The grandmother shut the window, pulled the shade, and lay down on the bed. It didn't take long and soldiers were up on the third floor. The door was locked, and immediately an officer followed by four soldiers pushed their way in.

"Where are the strangers?" The officer was angry. He didn't see anyone. This could be another false report.

"There's no one here," she said slowly. Frightened, it was an effort for her to speak. She started to get out of bed. The officer motioned her to stay, then pushed her down with the butt of his rifle.

They checked everywhere, running their bayonets through clothes in the closet and looking under beds. They ran the window shade up and beamed the area on the roof-top with a piece of equipment that looked like a huge flashlight. Satisfied there was no one else in the place, they left, angry and disappointed. They had hoped they would find the saboteurs and were loud in their verbal condemnation, certain they had been misinformed.

Hidden on the roof-top next door, the grandfather waited for a long time before he ventured back. It wasn't too long before a member of the refugee organization appeared, anxious to get them away, after such a close call.

Serena would often say to her father, "I'm so glad you got away, Dad. Just think how close we came to not being here. We're here by chance!"

She would go to where he was sitting just to be close to him.

II
The Escape Journey

Footsore and weary, they entered Germany on a miserable chilly night. It had rained and the ground and grasses were very wet. They had managed to escape the guards, stationed at various points along the borders, and forewarned—to be especially careful, to listen for sounds of danger—people talking or moving about near them. The order then was to stop where they were, so the guides, more familiar with the area, could investigate. The area they reached was wooded, one with homes off in the distance. They had to make it across to that point and headed in that direction.

The guide waved them on in five minute intervals. Barak went first—stopped at what appeared to be a pile of newly cut logs. Ressel came next. She reached Barak, and they both waited, until the guide, checking cautiously, joined them. They traveled in this time-consuming manner and had almost reached their destination, when someone's dog began barking furiously. Lights in several homes came on.

"Follow me and run," the guide ordered, and made a mad dash forward. They ran stumbling and sometimes falling. The guide ran back several times to help Barak get his mother up.

"Keep running." The guide kept pressing them onward. "We're almost there."

They made a desperate effort to keep up with him. Finally, he said they could stop. Exhausted they collapsed on the ground.

"Shhh!" They were quiet and listened for a long while for any sound of danger.

"We have a little way to go and we'll be in a house—safe for a day," their guide informed them.

It was crucial for them to go on. Their lives were at risk. They had to be safe before the break of dawn. They came to an area of homes and followed their guide into what appeared to be an alley or road. Suddenly out in the darkness, they heard the "Stomp! Stomp! Stomp!" of many soldiers' boots. Ruthless and menacing, they came nearer. It was a sound they had heard often enough to recognize as German soldiers. Panic-stricken, they flattened themselves against the wall of a house and waited as the troop of soldiers marched by.

"German guards going to relieve others at one of the check points," their guide whispered to them. No one else spoke.

He groped his way into a dark hallway, to a door where he stopped. They waited as he tapped ever-so-lightly, then tapped again—just twice. The door opened immediately and they were ushered in—almost pulled in. The door was quickly shut and bolted. There were blackout shades on the windows, and all in the room were of a serious mind. Everyone began quietly helping the newcomers.

First they brought dry clothes and blankets as they were chilled from the damp night air. Then they were given hot food. They were hungry and ate with relish. There wasn't any conversation—names were never mentioned—if they were caught, they couldn't give much information that would endanger the network of people, sacrificing, and courageously helping refugees to escape. Barak fell asleep almost immediately, but Ressel lay there thinking, worrying, thankful to have come this far through dangerous, enemy country. She heard planes droning off in the distance, and then machine-gun fire as they became engaged in an air battle. Ressel heard the people in the kitchen talking. "Allied planes were in a confrontation with the Germans, but they didn't know if they were French or British." Barak and Ressel slept late the next day. They ate—then slept again. By late afternoon, they were up and readied with food packages for that night's journey.

It took two days and two nights to get through the next lap of their journey. They slept in forested or wooded areas during the day—waiting for darkness to continue on. They were nearing the sea and fog was rolling in over the hill. The weather was always colder near the water. Their guide paced back and forth between some of the tall pines; the person to continue with them was late, so they had to stay in a rundown hut for another day. The cause of the delay—they didn't know. They could see German sentries, with their rifles, positioned at check points, walking in their goose-step back and forth—watching the sea and coastline.

That night when it appeared to be safe, a dinghy came close to the shore. Ressel and Barak hurried out into the cold water to reach the small craft and were helped in. Almost immediately, the two men, one at each end of the dinghy, began paddling in even strokes to get to the vessel waiting for its passengers. They climbed the rope ladder over its side and came aboard, but before it could take off, searchlights came on. Ressel and Barak were hustled below as machine-gun fire came over the deck of the ship. Luckily it got away, but it had been hit. The captain assessed the damage. With careful maneuvering it would get to the next port, Nykebing on the eastern coast of Denmark.

On the vessel Ressel and Barak learned why there were so many German soldiers patrolling the coast and sea. It seemed there had been a most important naval battle fought here, the battle of Jutland, between the Germans and the British, which began May 31st and had ended June 1st. The sea battle had been a huge victory for the Germans, and the defeat, a somber one for the British. The German naval and military were everywhere along the coast, expecting retaliation from the British.

The vessel sailed to Nykebing where the Underground got them transportation across Denmark to the seaport of Esbjerg on the western coast of Denmark. It was a frightening situation. Ressel worried someone would stop the vessel. She was resigned to the fact traveling in these dangerous territories, they would be caught and there was nothing she could do about it. She was doing the one thing she had set out to do—get Barak to America with a chance for a safe life. Ressel could breathe easier about Barak's situation.

She knew if they had remained in Bialystok he would have been taken into military service by the feared Russian conscription laws and would have perished.

At Esbjerg they embarked on a larger ship that took them across to England to London. There were more passengers escaping like the Varnars. They were told to stay below deck and to come up for a while in the evenings. They were told to be silent, as U-boats were about in the North Sea.

Barak hoped when they got to London, they could stay in one place for more than just a few days. He was tired, bewildered at all that had taken place in his life, all the changes. So many times he thought about Seren. How she would have loved the different places, and the travel, and the boats. She could have liked it even though the trip had been fraught with danger.

He would have felt better, too, if she had been along to share the adventure. Then, he wondered, "Was it bad of him to have wished she was along?" He thought about it. He wouldn't have liked for her to go through the long difficult journey with the strain and terror, but she would have been alive! The lump in his throat choked him and his eyes misted up. He wiped away the tears he wasn't ashamed to shed.

His mother never talked about his sister. Several times he started to say something about Seren and his mother's tear-filled eyes—so sad—made him feel he was hurting her. He didn't want to hurt his mother. He loved her. He thought about his sister to himself. He pictured her with him as they played together, laughing, always laughing. Now he hadn't laughed for a long time—not since Seren died. He wanted to—needed to think of her. He didn't want to forget her!

They arrived in London, spring 1915, by train. Ressel's eyes were already taking in her surroundings as she descended the train steps. The porter put down her bags.

There were numerous offices, with signs in many languages promising help to newcomers. Ressel and Barak headed for the Polish office. It was a busy place. They went in and sat down on a bench where a woman and a man were sitting. Ressel listened to their conversation. It seemed they were upset at having to wait and decided to leave.

A young woman at a desk up front motioned for them to come forward. Ressel explained her problem. She was to meet someone who would help her get to America. She wanted to leave as soon as possible and thought that wouldn't be a problem here in England. The woman rang a bell on her desk and another woman came and took them to a room where they were to rest and wait.

Ressel talked to Barak of the miracle that they were there. She couldn't believe they had made it through so many dangers, crossing so many lands and waters, which would have been impossible without the God-given help they received.

They were there, but she had left so much behind. A day or night didn't pass when she failed to think about her life's losses. So much had happened to them. They had traveled in terror and fear, with not much time to think. Now the reality set in and had to be faced.

They were still waiting when another person, a woman, probably in her fifties came to get them. They sat together and Ressel answered her many questions. They would be helped to get to her brother and family, but she would have to wait before they could leave.

"No! There was no way of knowing how long it would be." This in answer to Ressel's questions.

Ressel became visibly shaken when told, "It isn't safe to cross the Atlantic Ocean to America at this time." German U-boats were on the prowl—operating there and Britain was at war with Germany. Its ships—hunted-targets!

Britain had been at war with Germany since the beginning, August 4, 1914, when Germany attacked Belgium. Belgium was a neutral nation, and all nations were pledged to respect. Germany crossed Belgium's borders, and England honored its guarantee of Belgium's neutrality by going to war with Germany.

The British had suffered greatly from German U-boats, almost succeeding in starving England into submission by cutting off her lifeline of food and supplies. The American President Wilson sent warnings to the Germans, and they restricted their attacks for a while.

Then in 1915—a U-boat torpedoed the *Lusitania,* a British passenger liner, which sank in half an hour, and about 1,200 people drowned; 124 of them were Americans. This act brought the United States to the brink of war, but President Wilson wanted to remain neutral and was elected for a second term. He won with his campaign slogan, "He Kept Us Out of War!"

In 1917 Germany announced it was resuming unrestricted submarine warfare and began the destruction of ships carrying food and supplies. Ressel and Barak found themselves once again in a country at war!

The Varnars were once more living under war conditions, with shortages of food and supplies needed for everyday living. There were blackouts—dark hangings in windows to keep light from shining through. This was one of many war restrictions enforced so as not to give aid to enemy pilots.

The Germans in this war had developed many death-dealing machines. They had a balloon, a rigid-bodied, motor-driven, lighter than air, craft that dropped bombs on London. It was frightening to hear sirens going and to see people running to escape the death and destruction falling from the sky.

The explosions lit up the black sky, as pieces of brick, concrete, and wood spiraled into the air and downward. They fell mostly at night, but often during the day. Ressel and Barak were caught in several raids.

They would follow the people running for underground shelters where they could wait until the all-clear signals sounded. In the crowded shelter, the explosions could be heard and sometimes debris and dust would come down.

People were brave trying to comfort each other. When the all-clear sirens came on, it was time to get back to their homes. They walked over fallen brick from buildings, glass from broken windows, and debris of every form and description.

There were fires of burning buildings that had been hit, noises of firemen and their fire engines, and the wailing of people returning to their bombed-out homes. Then there was the panic of what to do? Where to go?—And the savagery of the mounting casualties. The British were brave and suffered day after day of relentless bombardment.

Days and nights like this worried Ressel, when Barak would question, "When do you think we will be able to leave?"

Together they would visit the Jewish refugee organization where there were always long lines waiting to ask the same question, "When can we leave?"

The answers were always the same. "We don't know, but we are working on it. We will let you know."

Everyone talked about the dangers crossing the Atlantic Ocean to America. The German U-boats were everywhere, it seemed. Each day brought news of a ship or two sunk. This was very bad news indeed! By February 1917, U-boats had sunk more than a half million tons of food and supplies needed by Britain and other Allied countries.

Ressel and others worked out ways to stretch their food rations. They baked and cooked, and shopped and shared. Barak helped in a small shop and was able to bring a few things home that were needed. Then, wonder of wonders, Ressel was notified she could leave the second week of March. Her brother in America had been sent notice of their arrival. Soon she would be in America with Barak. The journey had been a long one. There were many times when she didn't think they would survive the many dangers that had confronted them.

Ressel reflected on the changes that had taken place in her life. So many times at night when she couldn't sleep, her thoughts had been of Misha, how much she missed him. She was saddened that she would never know where his final resting place was, but she prayed for him. He would always be in her heart with her beautiful Seren! How wonderful it would have been if they were all together, going to the new land America, where there was so much promise, *but life is not what we wish it to be,* she thought.

In retrospect, reflecting on her life—what had been—life's sweet moments in Poland with Misha and their family. Yes, there had been sweet moments, in the midst of hate and fiendish horrors, that lived in her heart—that couldn't be taken from her. It would sustain her all the rest of her life.

The few weeks passed quickly. Now there were sad farewells to say to those who had become part of their lives. They had been kind and caring, and helped her in so many ways. She thanked them.

"Ressel," they said, "you did the same for us. We were there for each other."

That night before they were to leave, she was nervous and excited. She and Barak talked about leaving London, going to America where he would meet his Uncle Dave. He had always heard so much about him. Now he would meet him.

They were taken to the station at Charing Cross and got on a train to Liverpool. At the pier they saw their huge ship and stood in line to get checked before they could embark on it. There were military police everywhere. They were on the alert for spies.

The Varnars passed inspection and boarded. The ship finally got under way. The sky was an English gray, mist falling, and a fog, thick and heavy, hung low. Everything was wet adding to the discomfort and bewilderment of passengers.

A British warship escorted the liner all through the Irish Sea to some point in the Atlantic Ocean. Ressel felt a bit easier in her mind, seeing the British naval escort and prayed there would be no incident involving a German U-boat.

At night the ship was in darkness with windows and portholes covered—a blackout and everything had to be quiet as the liner worked its way through treacherous mined channels.

The German U-boats were busy in the Atlantic. On March 27th, the Germans had sunk four American ships. President Wilson called a special session of Congress to declare war on Germany. War was declared, April 6, 1917!

On board the liner crossing the Atlantic, the Varnars knew nothing of these latest developments. They had a few restful nights—maybe it was knowing they were on the last lap of their journey to freedom and family.

It was where Ressel's heart had wanted to be for a long time. "Oh, God," she prayed, "We're on our way to America!"

Six days after America declared war on Germany, the Varnars arrived in America. The date was April 12, 1917.

Tired, but happy, they came to Ellis Island, a welcome haven for those who made it through the many examinations and endless questions and paperwork. "It was quite an intimidating process," according to Ressel.

They questioned Barak about his name. They said it should be changed. "Barak is too foreign sounding." It would be better to call him Robert (Bob) and Varnar became Warner.

Ressel thought, *If that's the way it has to be in America and the people in charge must know, this is the right thing to do.* She became Ressel Warner.

In New York, there were no delays; the "Jewish Immigrant" organizations were under pressure to move the Jewish refugees out quickly. They had promised American authorities, the Jewish immigrants would be taken care of and would be no burden on the government.

Ressel's brother, Dave, had been notified of their arrival time in Wisconsin, and he was to meet them. They were put on a train going west. Ressel was excited to see her brother after long years of separation. She talked about him to Bob. Of course she hadn't seen him for such a long time. Would he be changed? Bob wondered too. He sat up looking out the window. So many different things to see. He noticed the houses and streets, and sometimes people. He wondered how it would be at his Uncle Dave's. What was he really like? How would their lives be? What would they be doing? There would be much for him to learn. He had very little schooling. He worried. His life was full of uncertainties.

Well, in a few more days, his questions would be answered. He so wanted things to be good for his mother. So much had happened that saddened her. She had always been loving to her family, and he felt a great responsibility toward her. That he promised himself. He knew his father would have wanted it so.

A few days later, they arrived in Madison. Bob had seen Wisconsin through his window. He liked what he saw—a clean green with grass and trees place. They got off at the station. Ressel didn't see anyone resembling Dave, and for a moment there was a concern.

Then she heard, "Ressel! Ressel!" She turned and saw Dave hurrying toward her. She knew by his voice, he was glad to see her as she was, now watching him as he came nearer. He grabbed her tightly and there were tears. Dave embraced Bob. "Where was Seren?" Ressel had not written. It would have been too dangerous on the continent if the mail was somehow confiscated and their whereabouts known.

On the ride through the city to Dave's home, she spoke to her brother in Yiddish pouring out her heart about happenings to Misha and Seren. All because of the hate in their world.

Dave listened, repeating over and over again, "Oh, my God, Ressel. Oh, my God, You've gone through so much. I wish I could have been there to help you!"

His sister was crying—they drove on in silence, lost in their own thoughts.

"No," Ressel said. "It's better you're here. We don't always know why certain things are done. You came here a long time ago—and because of that, we now have a place halfway around the world to come to.

"Life with its twists and turns—how do we manage it? I live with anger at the happenings—and frustration to deal with them. Over and over in my mind, I go to blame someone. Sometimes I blame God and know I shouldn't. I believe in Him and have faith. He knows what's best, and there must be a reason for it all—but it's hard for me to see it."

"I understand what you're saying, Ressel."

"Am I wrong?" she asked.

"We have to find our own answers, Ressel."

After another long silence, she asked, "What about you, Dave?"

She asked questions—to his sister's question about his wife—"No, he wasn't married."

They drove down a quiet neighborhood road and Dave stopped in front of a nice house.

Bob helped his mother out, and she kept saying in Yiddish, "Oh, Dave, it's wonderful. You have your own home—America is the Promised Land!"

They went into Dave's home, and he showed them around. She wanted to see it—the wonder of it! Dave put his arm around his sister's shoulder. He had missed her, for so many years he had missed family. Now, they would be together.

"Ressel," he said his voice sounding very emotional. "This is yours and your son's home—here in America with me. We are a family again!"

III
Americans in World War I

The next few weeks were busy ones for all of them. Ressel, Robert, and Dave exchanged stories of how life had been for them since Dave left Poland for America. There was much catching up to do, and in remembering, there were tears for the sad times; some too painful to remember, but there was also laughter, talking of the happy memories of family get-togethers.

Ressel and Robert acquainted themselves with their new home and neighborhood. Life was different here, but they soon fell in love with America. Dave did his best to make them feel welcome. He was so happy to have them share his life here.

But life in America was changing and going down a road it had tried to avoid—the war in Europe! America was grossly unprepared. The United States Army numbered only a little over 100,000 in the spring of 1917.

As soon as war was declared, many patriotic men volunteered. Robert wanted to enlist, but there were problems with papers to prove who he was. It would take time, but his goal was to become an American citizen.

A draft bill was signed June 5th. All men in the country between ages 21-30 were to register. It was expected close to 10 million men would register. There were discussions, speeches, and rallies protesting the war. That didn't change anything. America was at war! Ressel worried and wondered what would be happening. Again they were in a country at war. She never imagined the war in Russia and Poland, and the countries she had escaped through, would involve America.

Every night, Dave read the papers to her. They told of meetings with President Wilson and Secretary of State Newton Baker, trying to decide who would lead American troops in

France. There were a few to consider, and they made a choice. They chose General John J. Pershing to command the American Expeditionary Forces. He was a graduate of West Point, served on many Army posts, and fought in the Spanish-American War. He had lived in France and could speak French. The president and the secretary felt he was the one for the important American role in the relentless war raging in Europe. The papers gave all the details. Americans hoped it was the right choice.

In Madison and in the rest of the country, families were attempting to cope with sons, fathers, and brothers called into service. The whole nation had to be mobilized for war! This included food, fuel, factories, transportation, means of communication—telephone and telegraph, and the press—a gigantic task, but all were gradually mobilized to meet the needs of the world's first total war!

Housewives, in Madison, did the same as housewives in all cities around the country. They joined the war effort in the many ways they could. They gave up sugar, a mainstay in any kitchen, saved fat, which was collected and used in the vitally important manufacture of explosives. Special heatless, wheatless, and meatless days were observed. They were willing to deny themselves the kinds and quantities of food they had been used to eating, if their sacrifice meant the boys "somewhere in France" would get more and better food as a result. There was never a prouder moment in Ressel's life then when she brought a can filled with fat, saved drop by drop, and handed it to the butcher. Then Ressel walked out proudly—so happy in her heart—she had done something good for her America.

These were times of serious fuel shortages, munitions plants were forced to shorten their hours of operation, and some had to shut down altogether. This meant a shortage of essential supplies desperately needed by the servicemen. Americans worried about their soldiers in battle with no ammunition for their rifles or cannons. Their efforts continued in any way they could help on the home front to benefit the fighting men. To save more fuel and electricity—and to provide more daylight hours in the evening, the government decided to try having everyone move his clock forward one hour. The plan was called "Daylight Saving."

Wives and their children, in Madison and around the country, moved to live with parents; friends helped friends—situations on the home front were critical, gravely critical! Businesses were suffering, feeling the shortage of manpower. Uncle Dave owned Kahn's Emporium, a retail business that stocked women's, men's, and children's things. It employed many Madison citizens, who were now being called into service. Many changes had to be instigated because of the draft. Women, in all walks of life, were called to help in any way they could, then men could be released for war service. The patriotic women responded. Those who could, took the jobs, while others and family, cared for children and homes. Ressel and Robert went to work in the store to help.

Every day the headlines in the newspapers told the story of the casualties, the sinking of ships by German U-boats, and the successes of the German Army, that left devastation everywhere in Europe. Ressel worried at the report in the news, wondering about Misha's elderly parents; she had said "good-bye" to them in the ghetto in Warsaw. The "not knowing" frightened her. So many times she thought of Misha's sister, Nedda, and her husband, Herschel, who had chosen to remain in Warsaw. She wondered where they were and if they were alive. She had written letters and received no answers. Then thinking she might be a source of trouble for them, "letters from America," she stopped writing, waiting for the war to end, hoping to try to locate them. Sometimes when she was eating, she'd stop, couldn't eat, wondering if they had food. It made her sad—they weren't here safe in America!

One morning the papers announced the first of six medical contingents of the American Army had gotten to England—physicians, nurses, and many hospital corps enlisted men. They had been sent secretly. After a brief stay in England, they were sent to France to take charge of a base hospital behind the British front. They were desperately needed. Casualties were running high. Pershing thought it was due to how the war was being fought. The Allies and enemy soldiers were fighting trench warfare, and there was a stalemate with great losses. He wanted to change the style of fighting, but the French and the British disagreed with him.

Pershing believed the American troops could make the change—the British and French did not. In spite of this, Pershing saw to it that American soldiers were trained in open warfare with rifles and bayonets. The draftee had six months basic training in the United States—the training was for offensive, not defensive fighting! They were given training to make them physically fit for combat, then shipped overseas. Newspapers kept America informed—General Pershing was in France in 1917!

Convoys carrying American troops landed in France and brought hope to the Allies at a time when they were terribly bogged down. Things looked desperate, at their worst since the start of the war in 1914. The French and British had suffered tremendous losses. By the end of 1917, thousands upon thousands of American men and officers were in France.

The Germans began a campaign to separate the British-held front from the French front farther south. They drove a battle line between the two armies and began an attack at the British in Flanders. The Allies were facing one of their greatest crises. The next few months saw setbacks and losses, and some successes, but the casualty lists became longer and longer. In Madison, and across the country, the lonely homes without their loved ones became lonelier with the dreaded news their loved ones would not be returning.

The Germans failed in some of their drives, but they were successful in others and had come to within a few miles of Paris. America and the Allies hoped and prayed. It seemed the French capital would fall. Citizens fled, and the government made plans to move. The state of panic became worse. Paris was being bombarded by artillery shells fired from a gun of long range. The Germans had planned on bombardment of Paris to destroy civilian morale. They thought they could win the war before American troops could go into battle.

It was at this point American fighting men dug in and held their ground. The Germans had built defense positions of barbed wire, machine gun nests, and concrete artillery bunkers, which the Germans thought would hold. Hundreds of thousands of

Americans had to be moved to the area between the Meuse River and the Argonne Forest. Heavy equipment and thousands of heavy guns had to be transferred. It was done at night so the enemy was unaware an attack was being readied. The battle began and lasted over a week. The Germans put on a desperate resistance on their last line of defense. It was fierce, brutal with an enormous tragic loss of life.

The German High Command requested terms for an Armistice. The war ended on November 11, 1918. Bitter negotiations gave the world "The Versailles Treaty."

Under the treaty, Germany had to pay one billion dollars for damages, but Germany was in serious financial trouble.

They had to surrender their fleet, and were to deliver coal to Belgium, Italy, and France. They were allowed a tiny army and navy to defend themselves.

They could not build subs, military air-craft, tanks, or any other weapons. There was to be no re-arming.

The Emperor Kaiser William had to abdicate, and he left with General Von Hindenburg—exiled to Holland.

The Americans didn't want to be involved in anything with Europe, and the U.S. Senate refused to approve the treaty. They took a simple way out and just declared, "The War in Europe is ended."

After President Wilson, the new administrations under President Harding and President Coolidge were sure they had left Europe and its problems behind. Unfortunately, the negotiations were bitter medicine to the Germans, and the hate festered. The Treaty was the forerunner of troubles to come. Germany lost World War I, but the peace set the seeds of World War II.

The cost of the war was staggering: almost 20 billion dollars. Thousands of men lost their lives, and thousands more were wounded. The troops came back to a country devastated and financially encumbered. They came by the thousands, descending on their hometowns unprepared for the returning. Reunited families needed places to rent. The men needed employment. Factories and businesses that had changed almost overnight for the war effort, now had to convert to making goods for civilian use. The country was struggling to recover.

In Madison, the Kahn's Emporium continued as it had during the war. Dave and Robert worked through the store helping people, especially those who had family members in the service. They were given credit to get things needed for their families, and those having a difficult time were told not to worry—they could take care of it when they were able to. Many times the store encountered difficult times, but Dave and Robert continued to help in any way they could. It was a powerful hard time for everyone!

Three nights a week, Robert attended classes at the local high school. The young man took his classes seriously and enjoyed them. The cause of this was twofold. He had been denied schooling in Poland, and the freedom to get an education here—to learn—was important to him. Secondly, he liked the young woman, Ann Kanner, a pretty, soft-spoken volunteer, who came to school to help the struggling students, many of them immigrants like Robert. Finally, the long-awaited day arrived. He saw his mother and uncle beaming as he stepped up to receive his coveted high school diploma. He felt he had accomplished something of importance. He had set a goal and reached it. It felt good!

Ann, too, had been greatly impressed by this eager young man. They became friends. She liked the way his brown eyes looked straight at her when he spoke. They had discussions on many levels—one of them was higher education. It was a challenge to him. He wanted to try, and she encouraged him. It may have been because of Ann that Robert enrolled in evening classes at the University of Wisconsin, pursuing a degree in Business Management. She was in his thoughts a lot, and no matter the explanation, quietly cupid's endeavors were on the road to fruition.

Working at the store and going to classes kept Robert busy, but he finally got up the courage to call Ann to ask her out. He was a little nervous, not sure she would accept. This asking for a date was something new to him, but he had thought about it—and knew—nothing ventured, nothing gained. She accepted. They went to a movie the following Saturday night. It went so well—lived up to both their expectations—and thereafter became a steady date night.

To Ann, Robert was different from some of the other fellows she had dated. He was of a serious mind most of the time, talking about coming to America and how much he had wanted to come. Sometimes, he would tell her stories of his father and sister—funny stories and things he remembered. They would laugh together—they were sharing his life. She derived pleasure from things that made him happy. Then there were the times she could see the talk was painful for him and she felt his pain. He was a sensitive human being. He endeared himself to her through his stories and she learned how much he loved his family. It was something special to her. She liked being with him, and their friendship blossomed.

Ann would tell him about her family. It was the same for him—he wanted to learn whatever he could about this young woman who was a new part of his life—a very important part. His thoughts of her were many. He knew he loved her. There was a happiness in his heart, but there was also a sadness. He thought of his father and Seren and wished they could have been here. He missed them! That part of his being held a large emptiness—filled somewhat, now, with Ann in his life.

Dave and Ressel invited Ann's family for a Friday night dinner. The table conversation was most sociable. It was a happy gathering, with lots of laughter and merriment. Later Robert and Ann slipped away to the porch swing. They sat in silence with his arm around her shoulder, their heads close together, looking up at the indigo sky, a bright half moon, their only company. He held her hand and spoke. "Ann," he said, as he had said before, "I love you." Only this time he finished with "Will you marry me?"

They came in, after a while, to tell their families and received congratulations and embraces; both families happy at the good news. Not too much time went by, and Ann and Bob became engaged. He gave her a gold ring with a small diamond, "But you can see it without a microscope," is the way she described it. "Someday," he promised, "I will get you a bigger one."

Ann laughed at that. The ring meant so much to her. "I don't ever want another ring. I love it, Bob. I love it!" Giving the ring represented his love for her. That was all that mattered.

Ann's parents planned the wedding, and it was a wonderful one, held in the Shaare Emet Synagogue. Standing there under the wedding canopy, Robert looked out at the new friends and family gathered to witness this happy event. Missing were his father and Seren. The couple settled into a small apartment and into being married. That meant being busy, Ann helping students, and Robert working in the store. Dave had discussed future plans for the store with Ressel and Robert.

"After you've finished school, I'm giving you a partnership in the business." He was very pleased with how his nephew had handled responsibility. Ressel and Robert were overwhelmed. Dave had been a tower of strength to both of them. They had told him so many times. "You've done so much for us. How can we ever repay you?"

Dave waved that away with his hand. "I missed my family. Now, you're here with me. It's good to see you safe, and I'm not alone." He came over and put his arms around his nephew. They stood there for a few moments, locked in a big bear hug, the kind men give when they care about each other. Ressel received a few responsibilities—reluctantly relinquished to her—grocery shopping, cooking, and caring for Dave who got his favorite dishes—for which Ressel received constant praises!

After receiving his degree, Robert got several offers for different positions—one was at the local bank. He discussed this with Dave.

"You have to think about it and decide for yourself. Whatever you want to do will be all right with me!"

Dave meant it. Above all, he wanted Robert to be happy in whatever he chose to do. Robert was like the son he never had. Robert kept his appointment at the bank. He listened carefully to their business proposition and was quite impressed with what they offered.

"You can think about it, and let us know by the end of the week."

They shook hands and parted. At the store he thought about the position at the bank. There were many enticing factors to consider. One—he wouldn't be working all the late hours and could be home more. Then, it was a new challenge, and something he would be starting on his own.

He liked all of it, but he felt an obligation to Uncle Dave, a deep obligation. He thought of the future. He could be of help when Dave grew older and couldn't work anymore. He could be there for him. That meant much to Robert.

The next day he stopped at the bank, told them he could not accept the position, and thanked them for considering him. "I'm sorry you won't be with us." The gentleman seemed genuinely unhappy about Robert's decision.

At the store he told Dave of his plans to stay. "Are you sure, Bob?"

"Yes, I've thought about it and this is where I want to be."

Dave was pleased, "If you're sure, I'm glad."

Months went by and at a dinner with the family, Ann and Bob made the happy announcement that they were expecting their first child. Their son was born and was named Saul Misha, after Ann's grandfather and Misha, after Bob's father. A year later they were blessed with the arrival of their daughter, Serena, named for Bob's sister, Seren. Both sides of in-laws were happy—a child named for a beloved deceased family member.

In his heart Bob was happier. He and Ann had their beloved children. He hoped somehow his father and sister knew how happy he was. He wished they could have known Ann and her family, and Uncle Dave, who loved them all and had tried to get them to come to America. *If only they could have come to be here with us*! His heart cried silently. *If only*! *If only*! He thought, *By what twist of fate did all this happen*?

For the next few years, beginning with the year after the war, Dave had made numerous inquiries of authorities in charge of locating missing persons in Europe. It seemed like an impossible task to run down any lead. The Jews had been herded from so many places, but—still the family kept hoping. Finally, the family received word, Herschel had been taken with men to be used for slave labor. There was no way of knowing where he was sent to, or if he was alive. Jews in slave labor were shipped to other countries by the Germans. Most of them succumbed to the harsh brutal treatment. The Varnars and Nedda had been murdered in a pogrom in the ghetto. The Germans left destruction, fires, and the killings of the Jews. Partisan fighters from many countries helped wherever they could.

This Partisan group came upon the burning ghetto and went in to see if they could save anyone. They found a few injured who were taken where they could be helped. One French Partisan found a small child covered by Nedda's body. The child was Nedda's, a little girl named Tova. They were lying in a shallowly dug grave, and the fire, fast approaching, hadn't reached them yet. Hastily, he covered her with his vest and took her to safety. There had been no further word of her whereabouts. The search for her would continue, and the family lived with that flicker of hope. Ressel thought about that little girl very often. The parents weren't there to suffer the pain of a child lost, but Ressel knew the pain. Every night, the child was in her prayers, wherever she was. She prayed for the child's safe-keeping and hoped someday she would be found. Ressel kept that hope in her heart.

IV

Problems—Good Times and Tragedy

In the day-to-day living, time has a way of slipping by and so it was in America. Warren Harding had been elected president in 1921, served two years, then became ill and died. The country was struggling with its economy and the problems that were the aftermath of war. Calvin Coolidge came into office in 1923 to 1929. The fateful stock market crash came that year, adding to the misery of what came to be known as "The Great Depression."

People in every walk of life in Wisconsin and the rest of the country were mired with its disastrous effects. Thousands lost their jobs. Family providers suddenly cut off from earning any income didn't know where to turn. People were frightened and bewildered. There was no help forthcoming for their desperate situations.

It was strange to see people trying to earn a few cents selling apples and oranges on street corners. Often customers didn't have the few cents to purchase them. Others stood there begging for a "nickel" or a "dime." It was impossible to imagine the pain and futility of a former family provider coming home to a hungry family waiting—knowing he was returning empty-handed.

In Madison, and all over the country, heads of large companies and businesses who lost everything, deeply in debt, committed suicide—jumping out of windows in tall-storied buildings. Every day the sad news was printed in the newspapers.

Banks foreclosed , and people who had savings in them, now found they had nothing. People stood in long lines, pounding hysterically on the doors of the closed banks, but to no avail. The bank doors remained closed, with those inside trying not to hear the panic-stricken voices yelling and crying. There was the agonizing torment of knowing their life savings were lost. Something never heard of before.

In desperation people went door to door looking for any kind of work to earn twenty-five or fifty cents. Day in and day out they walked, and with time, clothes became threadbare. Bits of newspaper and cardboard replaced shoe soles worn thin looking for employment.

Keeping a family warm in cold weather was another problem to be dealt with. Adults and youngsters walked miles over railroad tracks and bridge trestles, looking for pieces of coal that sometimes fell off of railroad cars as they whizzed by. They were carefully gathered and brought home, and thankfully gave an hour or two, of warmth in a stove or furnace.

Some people were lucky to live on relief, but it wasn't enough. They walked around hungry, and went to bed hungry. One small box of macaroni and one meatball cut into five pieces fed five or more in many families who counted themselves fortunate to have that. There were thousands of protestors walking, carrying signs telling the world "We Want Food!" The country was on a continuous downward slide—in a calamitous situation.

It was heart-wrenching to see the faces of the down-trodden, honest faces full of despair—no smiles—dark-circled eyes that told of sleepless nights and tortured minds. The whole country was lost in a hopelessness. People went to bed with it, and woke to try again for another day.

A frustrated Herbert Hoover was elected in 1928 and served until 1933. A conscientious man, he labored to overcome the country's problems, but couldn't cope with the situation no matter how hard he tried. Nothing worked!

In Madison, Robert and Ann struggled along with the rest of the country. The Kahn Emporium had almost gone bankrupt. The name was changed to Kahn and Warner Emporium, and Robert worked with Uncle Dave, trying their best to save the store. Many businesses did go bankrupt, adding more people to the unemployment rolls.

The business like many in the country did make it through difficult times. Dave and Robert devised a system whereby everyone took a drastic cut in salary. Workers at the store split their work week, working only two days, but no one lost a job, and the store limped along.

It more than satisfied those who worked there. At least they were bringing home a pay check, smaller, but they were working, and they knew Dave and Robert were doing the same, sacrificing to help them through troubled times. The town never forgot!

Ann, like the rest of the housewives in the country, was busy raising the children. Robert tried to be there for the family, but these were troubled times, and there were days when he couldn't be home—much was left to Ann.

Like most parents, they were inexperienced at parenting, and children were raised by trial and error. Sometimes things were right, and sometimes they were wrong. Every family thought their way was best.

The Warners gave their family of their hearts, giving them love and understanding, and above all made every effort to have their home a secure place, in spite of all the daily uncertainties.

The children, growing up, saw the problems facing their parents and friends, and they learned the importance of being supportive of each other.

Franklin Delano Roosevelt ran for president, and the country weary, having lost faith, listened to him, put their hopes in this man, who said he could help the country. Many politicians had said the same thing, but this man was different.

In 1933, he was elected thirty-second President of the United States and millions were heartened with his new policies, which he called "The New Deal."

Under his leadership, banks reopened, and Congress passed the "Emergency Relief Bill" to spend 500 million dollars on different projects aimed at helping the country.

FDR was the instigator of many new programs, which put millions and millions of men to work. He worked tirelessly, introducing the "National Recovery Act" or "N.R.A.," which got better pay and better working conditions for people.

In the winter of 1933, the "Civil Worker Administration" started putting millions more people to work, paid for by the government. People received government checks.

Then Roosevelt began what was known as one of the "greatest construction programs, the Public Works Administration." Its projects built buildings, bridges, roads and highways, all financed by the government. It was called the "P.W.A." It put millions to work, the Depression started to die down, and a new age began to develop.

Scoffers and Republicans against the "New Deal" called it the "Alphabet Government." They could scoff with their disrespectful, disparaging remarks, but he was the only one who knew what to do when the country was in a crisis!

When it was announced Roosevelt was going to speak on the radio, millions stayed home waiting to hear what he had to say—it was so important for them to listen to his "Fireside Chats," as they were called.

He came on with his wonderful, warm voice, and spoke genuinely. Everyone felt as though they knew him personally. He became their friend. Those listening felt so much better when he was through. They put their trust in this man.

Americans believed in him, in the future again, and lived with hope because things were better. Everyone was singing, "Happy Days Are Here Again!" The radio blared the song all day long—into the late evening hours. No one cared—their moods had changed—they were happy!

While America led by President Roosevelt was dealing with life during the Depression and Crash, news from abroad in the newspapers, on radio, and news reels in the movie theatres began telling about a German named Adolph Hitler, "an upstart" they called him.

Hitler had been in prison and when he was released, he couldn't believe Germany had lost the war. To him, Germany was invincible! He began to make speeches against the Versailles Treaty, espousing maniacal hatred for Germany's enemies.

He continued his fiery speeches, blaming those who signed the Armistice, calling them "criminals," and said Germany was stabbed in the back by Jews, politicians, and profiteers. He blamed them for Germany's problems—people out of work—food shortages, and inflation. Over and over he stressed these points.

He had a deep hatred for the enemies of Germany. He lived on hatred, and he used it repetitiously in speeches in Germany. He joined the Worker's Party and became a politician. When he joined the party, it was so small—only seven members. Money was lacking, work was hard to get, men in crowds went to the beer halls to hear speakers offering solutions for Germany's problems.

Hitler took the stage quite often and thrilled them with his speeches, telling them Germany's problems would be solved by aggression, power, and violence. He hated democracy. He called it a "Jewish domination." He organized the "Nazi Party."

He had great success as an orator and was given the job of putting out propaganda for his party. His speeches began to draw crowds. He blamed Jews for everything wrong in Germany.

Leaders of German industry were having problems with the semi-communistic workers who demanded they be allowed to regulate industry to their advantage. The German business world backed Hitler. To them he was an anchor against Communism.

German unemployment rose to over 2 million. Hitler's countrymen looked to him. In his fiery delirious speeches, he stressed Germany and her future. He always spoke against the Versailles Treaty. He presented himself as a bulwark against Russia and Communism. His nationalism was magnetic and got him 13 million votes.

General Paul Von Hindenburg, hero of the victory over Russia, was President of the German Republic. His advisors kept after him to listen to Hitler. Hindenburg did not approve of Hitler but finally agreed to appoint him Chancellor. Hitler now had more power.

He knew America and other countries were busy with problems of the Depression and Crash to pay too much attention to Germany. Secretly he began to re-arm Germany.

In 1945, Hitler declared Germany would have universal military training. Nineteen countries, including Russia, France, and Britain protested mildly but didn't act on it. Thus began the brazen violations of the Versailles Treaty. He started the Hitler Youth Movement, which enlisted millions of German boys aged fifteen to eighteen for labor service. There was another for the younger boys.

The young maidens had to join the "Bund Deutscher Maidel." They had to wear white blouses, blue skirts, brown short jackets or vests, heavy socks and shoes. Hitler pushed this Youth Movement into various services. All were backed by ceremony-loving Germans, and they had to support Hitler. The few who didn't found it was not good to cross him. They marched and saluted him at reviews, were loyal supporters who listened and believed the hate he delivered in his speeches.

In secret German soldiers were training in Russia where military experiments were held. The army was enlarged, almost tripled in size. He took more power, by a decree, that the Nazi Party was the only political party in Germany. Still secretly the work sped on to make Germany stronger—submarines were built, sub and airplane factories sprang up all over Germany. While President Roosevelt's programs building roads and bridges and highways were putting millions to work and helping the country's economy, in Germany, Hitler said the highways he was building were to open the way to the beautiful Alps. In truth, they were highways that were valuable to him, for he could quickly move an army over them. In theatres in Madison and around the country, the newsreels showed the workers in Germany, supposedly, doing exactly what millions of American workers were doing—improving the economy and the country—but the ultimate goal of Hitler was secret.

There were those in America and around the world who were beginning to feel an uneasiness in what they saw and heard.

America in 1936 elected President Roosevelt to another term. The economy still struggling, but the Depression was slowly losing its iron grip on the country. It lasted through much of the '30's.

The different seasons came, and soon were gone. It didn't seem time was passing, but the years sped on. The years of hard work and worry had taken their toll of first Dave, then Ressel, both suffered with ill health.

For many years after leaving Poland, Dave had missed his family. Now, knowing how ill Ressel was, he chose not to go to the store anymore. Instead, he spent much of his time sitting with her, talking to her when she was up to it. Anguished, he saw her life slowly ebbing away.

Robert, too, was greatly concerned about his mother. They had come through that long journey together—lost loved ones, and were survivors!

Ann and Robert visited and did everything possible to keep both Ressel and Dave happy and content. Robert was now in total charge of the store. He would come and discuss different aspects of the store, listening to what Dave had to say. This was a wonderful way to let Dave know he was still a vital part of the business even if he couldn't be there.

Saul, while growing up, going to school, had worked at the store just as his father had. Now, almost through with college, he had more responsibilities relegated to him. After graduation, he would be given more, and he looked forward to the challenges and making this his life's work.

Saul had grown tall as his father—looked a lot like him too—with the same medium brown hair and brown eyes—a nice-looking chap and well-liked by those who knew him. He had dated a few young ladies, but didn't think seriously about any particular one, until he met Jennifer. He remembered their first date. He had called to tell her he would be a little late. When he came, he was apologetic and a bit upset that he had kept her waiting. He had been delayed at the store.

"It was something that couldn't be avoided," she told him. She had understood and it made him feel better. This hadn't happened with a few other women. That night she had found a special place in his heart. He found her to be a kind, warm-hearted person, with the virtue of being patient.

They became good friends. Jennifer liked his sincerity when he spoke with her, and she saw a young man who cared about his family. Their friendship turned to more—and they became engaged that Thanksgiving and planned to be married the following year. The Warner family was a close-knit one. Ressel and Dave had done their best to keep the family together with Ressel, the grandmother, and Dave, almost like a grandfather. Ann and Robert had continued with love and caring as the next generation, and now both the grandparents and parents could derive pleasure because Saul and Serena with their emotional attachment fit into their special place in the family. Life and family were precious to all of them.

Serena almost nineteen, a student at the University of Wisconsin, was beginning her second year in Journalism in the fall. "Pretty as a picture" was the description by those who knew her. Her light brown hair, with its golden glints, turned many a head. Her laughing blue eyes and shapely form elicited many a whistle from young men of the campus. She was pleasant to be with and had friends galore. She took it all in stride. As far as she was concerned, she was "just average," and that was good enough for her.

Spring came. It was a lovely time of year anywhere, but especially in Madison. The holidays had ended, and everyone was looking forward to the dance held annually. Saul was going with Jennifer.

For weeks, at the female gatherings, the topic of conversation concerned Michael Cotler, a new young man on campus. All they knew about him was he came from Michigan and was good looking! There had been much talk and speculation, and fantasy, and hopeful yearning among the young ladies, wondering who he would be taking to the dance. Serena had been introduced to him by some of her friends who were always in a group.

"He was a quiet person, didn't say too much," she noted, and he seemed very nice. She had stopped once to say "Hi" to him after running into him at "The Raven," a favorite campus hangout. He was always pleasant, and she liked him.

It was on a Wednesday, after a lengthy conversation on the phone with her friend Sherry. Sherry knew all the gossip on campus. Serena had just hung up, when it rang again. Thinking it was her friend again, she laughingly answered, "Yes, now what?"

She was a little shocked, but pleasantly surprised when she heard, "Hi! This is Michael Cotler."

Apologetically, she explained she had answered the phone thinking it was her friend calling back. She wondered what he would have said if he knew the interest in him had dominated most of the conversation with Sherry.

After a few minutes of the usual banter between a boy and a girl, he asked her to go to the dance with him. That was so totally unexpected, she didn't answer right away. She caught her breath, then answered, "I'd love to, Michael."

It made him feel good to hear her enthusiastic acceptance. He had wondered whether to ask her. She was so popular and had probably been asked a long time ago, but he took a chance and she was going with him.

"That's wonderful!" She loved the way he said it.

"I'll pick you up around seven?" He put it in a question.

"Fine!" she answered.

Happy and excited, she ran to tell her mother who for weeks had heard all the discussions about this young man Michael.

"I'm so glad for you, dear." For the things that made her children happy, she was pleased.

We are young for such a short while, she thought.

It was wonderful to see Serena so happy to be going with Michael; she knew Saul was feeling the same going with his Jennifer. The days flew by, and with much anticipation, the great day finally arrived. Serena was busy for hours getting herself ready. Her mother came to do the zipper on her new gown.

"You look wonderful, darling."

Mrs. Warner was so proud of her daughter. "The dress you chose is perfect for you. Come down when you are ready. Dad will want to see you."

She skipped down the stairs and circled around before her father. He echoed her mother's comment.

"Wonderful, Siri." He liked the color blue. "Like a summer sky," he said.

Serena was on cloud nine.

Saul was leaving a little earlier. He came down to show Serena the corsage he had gotten Jennifer, and he was eagerly looking forward to the evening with his Jennifer. He was all smiles when Serena told him the corsage of tiny pink roses was exactly what Jennifer would love.

He kissed his mother, and she said proudly, "You and Jenny are going to be one of the handsomest couples there tonight."

He waved to Serena. "I'll see *you* at the dance."

His dad got up. "Have a wonderful time, Son. Wait. I'll walk you out." They walked out together.

Michael made his appearance a short while later. He felt a little awkward meeting the Warners for the first time—then he handed Serena the box with the dainty corsage of purple violets.

"They're just beautiful, Michael. I just love them."

He helped her pin them on and whispered in her ear, making her blush. Serena went to get her wrap, and Michael had a few moments with her parents. He was a little uncomfortable answering questions from her father, knowing the Warners were sizing him up. He didn't blame them. He was a stranger to them—came from a different state—taking their daughter out. They had a right to know all about him.

Serena reappeared and he got up to leave. He bid them "good night" and "glad to have met you both."

The Warners voiced the same sentiment, then ended with, "Have a wonderful evening!"

At the dance everyone was in high spirits. The couples were lovely—cocktails from the bar, and lovely music from a wonderful band created a fun-filled atmosphere. It was clearly a night for youth—for romance—and revelry.

Saul and Jennifer sought out Serena and were introduced to Michael. Later they exchanged dancing partners, then met back at their table. Saul ordered—the ladies had cocktails. Michael wanted a martini, and Saul ordered wine.

They talked and laughed, Saul answering Michael's questions about the store, and Michael answering Saul's questions about his future plans. Saul had succeeded in making Michael feel at ease. He liked the young man. There were more dances and soon—much too soon, came the witching hour—midnight.

Many had left the dance earlier, going to private parties. Serena and Michael had been invited but decided not to go. Saul was taking Jennifer home.

Once outdoors, Serena and Michael walked to the car. It was a breathlessly beautiful evening with a dark navy blue sky and millions of glistening stars in an absorbing solitude. The night air was cool. Serena shivered as she drew her wrap around her shoulders. Michael drew her a little closer to him, and they walked a little faster.

Michael drove her home and parked. Michael put his arms around her and kissed her gently. She had been thinking of this while they danced, and wondered how being kissed by him would feel. Now, here it was—an emotion enveloping her that was new—strange.

I like him, she thought. I like him a lot! It surprised her to admit this. She hadn't known him very long and here they were kissing. His kisses began slow and gentle—every once in a while, he would stop a bit to tell her, "I've been thinking about you since the first time I met you." To herself she thought, *that's just the way I've felt about him.*

His kisses were becoming more passionate. At times he held her so tight, she could hardly breathe. He kissed her again and again, murmuring how much he really liked her.

She turned her head to avoid his searching mouth, and he reluctantly released her. They were both silent for a few moments. Then he began, "I wanted to call you so many times."

"Why didn't you?"

"I wasn't sure, I saw you with so many friends. I"—he hesitated.

She interrupted him. "I'm so glad you did call." She wanted him to know.

He kissed her again. His touch quickened her pulse, and she could feel the flush rising from her neck to her face. She felt uncomfortably warm, but there was the ecstasy of the moment, which could not be denied. The kisses came—more passionate—longer—his hand began groping for her bra. Her mind was sending out "caution" signals. She had been told and warned often enough about, "what girls won't allow."

In this situation a feeling of uneasiness became more focused. Nervously, she pulled away and moved closer to the door. "Michael." She cleared her throat, her voice was hoarse. "It's getting late. I have to go in now!"

"Oh, all right!" His voice took on an irritable tone. Serena sensed he was angry, and she made an attempt at conversation, but he said nothing.

There was an awkward silence as he walked her up the steps. She thanked him for the lovely evening and the beautiful corsage. He didn't kiss her and left hurriedly saying, "I'll call you." She heard the abruptness in his voice and felt he was chastising her. It was almost 2:00 A.M. on the clock in the hallway. Quietly, she made it past Saul's room with its opened door. He hadn't come in yet.

She couldn't fall asleep, tossing and turning—restless, thinking about the evening. Some of it had been exciting and she felt good—wanted to be with Michael. It worried her when she thought about it. Somehow, she was at fault—had failed in handling the situation of the kissing, the tight embraces that seemed to be going in directions she wasn't comfortable with. How did other girls manage it? There were discussions.

Serena now realized, most of them didn't know anymore than she did, and sex wasn't discussed at home! She remembered the subject brought up a few times—a sentence or two in the discussions—then turned off as if more would come later. She could see it had been totally inadequate.

She wondered if Michael would call her again. If he did, what would she say? Would she go with him? Would he call because he respected her letting him know they had to stop? She had no answers, only more questions!

Maybe he would call and that would put an end to it. She hoped he would, because she liked him. Then she hoped, he wouldn't call. She fell asleep with new worries that accompany the innocence of crossing over from girlhood to young womanhood.

Serena and Saul slept late—the parents had breakfast together, commenting on "The children must have had a good time to sleep so late!"

At lunch Serena talked to her parents about the dance, who was there, and answering their many questions. Yes, she had been with Saul and Jennifer and they met Michael and had a good time. Her mother gathered from the short answers and tone of Serena's voice that things had not gone as well as she would have them believe. Serena excused herself. She had some schoolwork to finish up.

Saul came down early afternoon for a snack, read the paper, and then fell asleep on the living-room sofa. It had been a comfortable relaxing day for the Warner family—they were together.

At dinner Robert spoke to his son. "You're tired, you don't have to go in with me to open the store. I'll open up and you can come in later—say around ten."

There was always much to do before the help came in to ready the place for business.

"I don't feel right about that, Dad." Then Saul questioned, "Are you sure? Will you be okay?"

His dad nodded, "I'm sure when you come in, there will be time enough to do what has to be done."

Mr. Warner was at early breakfast when Serena came down and joined him. She had an early class with the spring vacation ended and was anxious to be off.

"Can I give you a lift?" he asked.

"No." She was meeting some friends.

She pecked him on the cheek with a, "Bye, Dad," and out she bounced.

Mr. Warner drove off thinking of Serena and the family. He thought how fortunate he was—his wife—his children—his work at the store, and how wonderful his Uncle Dave had been to all of them. Yes, he was quite proud of his family.

He had worked hard, and his life was a happy one. There was one thing he found he couldn't forget. It gnawed at him—in the back of his mind. If only his father and sister, and the rest of the family could have come to America. How many times he had wished that, the family being together.

There was always the remembering of the unfortunate cruel circumstances that occurred and brought him and his mother to Madison. *Funny,* he thought, *to be thinking about that this morning.*

He drove into his parking space and saw Dan, the security officer's car. Dan was waiting at the door. He was a big man, over two hundred pounds. He had been with the company for many years. He had started as a young man and now was a grandfather. Dave and Robert always enjoyed talking with him.

They exchanged, "Good mornings," and comments about the almost summer-like weather, even though it was fall.

Robert opened the door, and Dan went in to disengage the alarm system. Before Robert could close the door, two masked men with drawn guns forced their way in. Dan was coming back and saw the men. He started for them; one shot Dan and hit him in the chest. He fell, heavily hitting the floor.

Robert tried to reach him and to set the alarm off. One of the men became enraged. He wanted the door to the vault opened, now here was Robert trying to get the alarm again. He fired point blank at him, and Robert went down.

The two men failed in their robbery attempt and took off before the few on the street realized what had happened. Some heard the shots but didn't know what they were. Things like this didn't happen in town. Robert managed to crawl to the alarm and set it off. They found him there near Dan, both dead.

Mrs. Warner and Saul were having late breakfast. The conversation was about the dance and Jennifer. Saul relating some of the things his mother wanted to hear.

"Yes, we had seen Serena and met Michael." He had made a good impression on them. "Seemed like a nice chap," was the way Saul described it.

The doorbell rang insistent rings, meant to summon quickly. Mrs. Warner opened the door to a police officer. She knew something was terribly wrong when he asked, "Mrs. Warner, are you alone?"

Frantically, she called, "Saul! Saul!"

"What is it? What happened?"

The officer relayed the sad news and as Mrs. Warner broke down, he kept repeating how sorry he was to have to be the one to tell them. He stayed awhile, asking if there was anything he could do.

"Mr. Saul," he added in a lowered voice, "you're wanted at the store."

Saul called his Uncle Dave and left it to him to tell his grandmother, Ressel. He called a friend of the family to come stay with his mother until he could get Serena. On the way to the store, his thoughts were of his father. "Oh, God," he prayed, "I hope he didn't suffer." He had to pull over, he couldn't see, his tears blinded him. He felt sick. He waited for a minute and started off again. He wanted to get to the store. He had to see for himself. He couldn't believe his father was dead.

"Poor Dad, I should have been there." He pounded the steering wheel with both his hands. "I should have been with Dad!"

He was angered that this could have happened to his father. His imagination ran wild—how terrible it must have been for him. What was he thinking?

"I should have been with you, Dad." He had to stop again, pulling the car over to the curb. He put his hands on the wheel and bent his head. The tears started and he sobbed—sobs from deep down—filled with unbearable pain and unbelief.

Questions again. "Why? Why did this happen?"

The week was a hectic one, making funeral arrangements, caring for his mother and sister who were trying to deal with the shock of the tragedy.

His Uncle Dave dealing with his loss of Robert, who was like a son to him—and Ressel couldn't accept this last blow, the loss of her only child. Saul had to be strong for all of them. He wouldn't cry anymore. He had shed his tears.

For days the town papers were full of the "horrible crime" —of the bravery of both Dan and Mr. Warner. Each day told some bit of news—how he had come as a young man from Poland and its anti-Semitism. He had overcome so many obstacles, working hard, and was known and well-respected for his dedication to the community.

The funeral was held on Sunday in the synagogue he loved. There was a very large crowd. People from all walks of life came to pay their respects. They all had wonderful stories to tell about the many things he helped them with during the "Depression Years." It was like losing a family member!

"He was always there for us," so many reiterated sadly, "He was always there."

So many would miss him, this man of integrity—a kind man who had been their friend.

These were some of the words of the editors and columnists of the Madison papers and in papers in other cities around the state.

And what of his family? In shock and disbelief that this could happen, suffering their loss, they were strengthened in hearing the many heart-warming out-pourings about this man-son-husband and father, they loved.

Their world had suddenly become one with tragedy. They were shocked, then angry. They questioned, as people do, when bad things happen they can't come to grips with—can't understand. Their prayers gave them no answer. There was only bewilderment and a deep despair. Their lives would go on, but this tragic event would manifest itself on each of them, in different ways.

Saul felt a deep sense of guilt. Why didn't he go with his father as he usually did? He was tortured by the thought that maybe if he had been there, he could have done something to help.

He felt a deep regret—he and his father had talked together about so many things, but he realized there was so much more he hadn't said. Now the time was stolen from him. He could never tell him he loved him. He blamed himself—couldn't shake off that feeling. For him it came down to that alone. It would bring changes in his life.

Serena took the loss extremely hard. She had loved him—taken for granted that her father would always be there. Each day brought a new remembrance of him—a reminder of how much he was missed. She felt a great sorrow, wishing she had spent more time with him. A sadness filled her heart when she thought about it now—when it was too late.

Sometimes in her room, feeling alone, she would speak her feelings out loud.

"Oh, Dad," she would say, "I miss you so." How she wished she could tell him she loved him. She had said it many times, but wished she could have said it that last morning. If only the clock could be turned back to the day before the murder when all was well with their world.

Friends and neighbors came to pay their condolence calls. Some of Serena's friends came with Michael. It was late when the last few had gone and the Warners were left with their sadness.

Saul left to take Jennifer home—the others went to bed. Serena heard her mother sobbing, went in to comfort her and stayed, helping her to bed—then sat bedside holding her hand until she fell asleep.

Her eyes wandered slowly around the room. There on the vanity she saw the oval gold-framed wedding picture of her parents. They were both smiling.

"It was such a happy day, their wedding day." They had said it many times to their family.

Back in her own room, she was grateful for her 'quiet space.' There were so many things to give thought to.

Serena dozed off and then awoke. She had slept less than a half hour and was quite tired. This happened a few more times; exasperated, she got out of bed. The night was endless—she sat in the chair near the window and watched day breaking—gray clouds hung in the sky, and the wind was blowing the leaves off the trees. It was fall. Serena shivered, then got up to dress. It was pretty early. She thought, "*What difference does it make*? *The day has to start. Let it start early.*" It was another day to get through to its end.

V
Coping with Change

The tragedy of losing her husband in such a violent manner had a devastating impact on Mrs. Warner. She suffered a heart attack.

Saul, dealing with his father's death, now had to face his mother's mortality. What if anything happened to her? His thoughts were of Serena—how difficult it would be for her. It seemed there was one worrisome problem catapulted on top of another that had to be dealt with.

He felt keenly his responsibility to care for his mother and sister—and there was his Grandmother Ressel too! He knew his father would have expected it of him. It had to do with family—caring for each other—close-knit!

He was busy with the store, meetings and conferences, busy with people around him, but in his heart felt deeply the absence of his father. He missed the easy ways he and his dad could converse and discuss so many things. The tremendous loss was a constant, always there in the back of his mind, and in his heart. He was thankful for the store. There he could go and lose himself in the work.

Saul put his personal life on hold. For a long time he had loved Jennifer. They had met at the University of Wisconsin. She was pursuing a degree in Psychology while working part-time at a clinic.

Jennifer, a little over five feet tall, was a pretty young woman with light brown hair and fair of face, from which danced her sparkling brown-flecked green eyes.

She was attracted to him, and they dated off and on at first, dating others in between. She loved his sense of humor that made her laugh and forget some of the sad situations she encountered at the clinic.

He loved to be with her—she was a warm, caring human being who always greeted him with her engaging smile that was special to him. There was a mutual need to be with each other and soon, there came the realization they were in love.

Their togetherness headed toward the eventuality of all committed relationships—they became engaged and had planned to marry the following year.

But they discovered life is not predictable. Events just happen—some so senseless—their interruptions empowering your world as it was—as you knew it, to suddenly stop!

The resulting discussions and heartbreak for both Jennifer and Saul happened over a period of time. Saul, after much soul-searching, had made up his mind to discuss postponing their plans for a while. He had argued it over and over in his mind. There were so many times he had to change plans to see her because of a problem at home or at the store. There was much to take care of that required his attention. She had been understanding, but he thought, *It isn't fair to Jennifer*. And he couldn't come up with a solution for the two of them.

For at least a few years, he would have to devote time to his family—to try to help them over this critical period in their lives, his mother's illness and helping Serena. Then there was his grandmother. She had lost her husband in Russia and lost her daughter, Seren, in Germany while escaping the horrors of war. Her son, Robert, and she had gone through so much danger in Poland, Germany, Denmark, and London to get to America. They had survived led by her will and courage.

With Robert's death, she seemed to have lost the will to go on. There was nothing anyone could do for her, except keep her comfortable. The doctor wasn't hopeful. "She could be gone any day," was what he told Saul. This was a sadness they all had to deal with.

Jennifer had waited patiently—weeks passed and then Saul called wanting to see her. When they met, there was this strange feeling of distance between them. There was an awkwardness as they talked, and Jennifer knew nothing had changed since the last time they were together.

Disheartened and unhappy, she asked again as she had before, "How much longer is a few years?"

She felt she was losing Saul, the love of her life. It was affecting her school, her work, and her health.

They sat close to each other, but they were miles apart in thought. The pain was there to see in his face, and it was there in his voice when he answered truthfully. "I don't know, I wish I did, but I don't."

"We'll see each other." He started to say more, but Jennifer got up. She knew it wouldn't be the same anymore. She understood or tried to understand, but there was a hurt there—sometimes resentment, which she couldn't help feeling. It resulted in arguments. They decided it was best not to see each other for a while—for how long, neither one knew.

Jennifer had thought about it too and determined it was best to terminate the relationship. Waiting for his calls, hoping to hear from him. Then seeing him once in a while, her hopes rising again, only to have them dashed by the uncertainty of the situation, had become very wearing. She took off the ring and handed it to him. He wouldn't take it. This was a breaking up. He hadn't wanted this. He thought they could both wait—he loved her—but there was his family.

"Keep it, Jenny," he begged her.

But she said, "No, you take it!"

Her heart was racing—she found it difficult to breathe as she handed, what had been a joyful part of her life, back to him.

Her parents were shocked and in disagreement over the break-up. Her mother thought she should have gone along with Saul and acquiesced to the postponement, but her father was angry and told her she was wasting her time. "Forget him and go on with your life," was his advice to her.

Up in her room, she paced back and forth and cried. There was an emptiness—sadness where before there had been joy—the joy of loving and being loved. She didn't feel that anymore—not today!

Her thoughts were of her parents, like so many others, when they are caught up in the void of seeing the suffering of their children, witnessing the depths of their despair and having to stand by brokenhearted, helpless to resolve any of it.

The choice she and Saul made ended with unhappiness. She tried to lose herself in school and work, but found she couldn't really lose herself—her feeling and dissatisfaction with her life. It had to be dealt with in the after hours—the later evening hours, trying to cope with it all until morning—then her mind would be somewhat relieved by concentrating on work again. It was a vicious circle she rounded day after day.

For Saul, too, the treadmill of his day-to-day existence was hopeful, watching his mother's recuperating progress. His spirits were elevated as he saw her regaining her strength—optimistic that it was just a matter of time.

He missed his Jenny. So many times he wanted to call her, to hear her voice, but the break-up with its pain was too fresh. He ached to talk to her but didn't want to hurt her anymore than he already had.

He had no way of knowing how much she had wanted him to call, had prayed he would, so she could hear his voice. She loved him so! She had come so near to calling him, but then pride would come into the picture, "He didn't call, so I won't call," manifesting itself into no solution when each one thinks his way is right and the suffering then goes on.

Serena went back to school, spending time with her friends. Michael would be there. He didn't have much to say and would leave suddenly with Marcia, one of the girls in the group.

The girl talk was "They had become quite chummy."

The boys discussed Michael and Marcia as "having something going."

Serena felt hurt; she had liked Michael and he had not called her as he had promised after the dance.

The gossip began a few weeks later. Michael and Marcia had eloped. He quit school and was working in his father-in-law's clothing store. Marcia was pregnant.

Some of the boys stopped to see him and sometimes went to lunch. Michael didn't have too much to say—they didn't have much in common anymore. He was out of school, and the friends said he wasn't a happy young man.

It was a devastating new set of circumstances for the group of Michael's friends. The girls went shopping for a wedding gift for the couple and sent it with a card signed by all, wishing them "much happiness."

Mrs. Warner had made great strides in improvement in her health, which made them all feel better. Serena didn't go out too much, spent a great deal of time in her room. Mrs. Warner knew it was her father's death, her daughter was dealing with—but thought it was this "Michael" thing too. She knew Serena had been hurt.

So many times she wanted to go up to comfort her—it took all her strength not to, knowing this was something private she couldn't help with. She knew her daughter had shown strength many times before and prayed this would be another.

It was something Serena had to face and deal with. It was one of the "depths of misery roads" most travel in the process of maturing. It would take time, and if there was one thing the young had on their side, it was "time."

Saul made frequent business trip for the store, visiting markets in the different cities around the country. One of the cities he went to, on numerous occasions, was St. Louis, Missouri. There were vendors there dealing in a variety of items that the Kahn store featured—fashionable women's hats, and shoes with matching handbags. Customers came from everywhere to get them. The demand was great, which helped business.

St. Louis was considered one of the leading places in the world and had numerous large shoe-manufacturing plants. Saul had made many friends and always enjoyed his visits there. Mrs. Warner had some serious discussions with her son concerning Serena. She thought a change of scenery—another place would be good for Serena. She exacted a promise from him that he would take her with him on his next visit to St. Louis. He agreed to broach the subject to Serena.

"When?" his mother questioned.

"Soon. Soon. Don't worry, Mom. I will very soon."

The "soon" was several weeks later. At dinner, Saul mentioned his forthcoming trip. "How would you like to come with me, Serena?"

They had spoken of it many times before, but the time was never right. Serena was involved with Michael and busy with school. This trip seemed perfectly timed. For a long time, Saul wanted her to accompany him. There was a young man, Maxwell, son of a friend of his, he wanted her to meet. That he didn't tell her. As an added incentive, and knowing the female penchant for shopping, he reminded her of something.

"Remember that new Maryland Shopping Center I told you about? It's now open. It's the newest in town, in fact, in that part of the country. It's a new development—a Mall—a new experiment in Shopping Area Phenomenon," he told her.

The talk was, they would open all over the country and eventually, the world—depending on the interest and investments in these new business projects. As in everything else with new ideas, some believed in them, and then there were the proverbial skeptics, the scoffers who predicted, "an experiment bound to fail." Saul with his business acumen had been greatly interested and supportive. "Someday," he said optimistically "we'll have a Kahn and Warner store in many of the malls. This Maryland one is something to see."

Serena, like all normal females, was born with this little part of the brain that activates and lights up at the thought of "shopping."

"Think about it and let me know in a few days if you're interested, okay?"

"I'll leave it up to you, Serena."

Serena considered her brother's invitation. Actually it had helped make up her mind. *Why not?* she thought. *A break before school in the fall.*

At the end of the week, she broke the news to her brother. She wanted to go, but "would it be right to leave Mother just yet?"

Knowing his mother would welcome Serena's decision to go, Saul assured his sister their mother would favor her coming with him.

Whenever Saul came to St. Louis, he was invited to stay with the Kellers. Mr. Keller owned several shoe stores one in St. Louis and one in the new mall. There were many giant shoe manufacturing plants in St. Louis, conducive to the success of the Keller Shoe Company. Having business vendors in town saved shipping and operational costs increasing profits. Mr. Keller was a much valued business associate and friend.

Saul set up an appointment with Mr. Keller, saying he was bringing his sister. He had often spoken of her with such affection. "We're going to stay at the hotel downtown," he told Mr. Keller.

Mr. Keller insisted they stay at his home, but Saul wouldn't think of it. "Too much of an imposition," he argued.

After a discussion that seemed to be going nowhere, Mr. Keller turned the phone over to his waiting wife, who had been listening.

She reasoned with Saul. "You should plan to stay here and give us a chance to meet Serena," and added, "Max would introduce her to some of his friends. She'll have a great time, and it will be good to see you both."

So it was decided, Mrs. Keller handed the phone back to her husband. "It's all settled."

On Friday of that week, the two left by train for St. Louis. It was an all-night trip. Serena was wide-eyed and was enjoying this new experience of having dinner in the Pullman dining car.

The atmosphere was elegant, with lovely velvet fringe trimmed drapes on the windows. Each table had a small dainty lamp on it, the dishes were pretty, and the service was something special. The waiters in spanking white jackets and white gloves were so nice and attentive, Serena loved it. It was something she would share with her mother and friends.

Serena wanted to know about the Kellers, and Saul enthusiastically assured her, "You'll like them!"

Later they played "Hearts," the card game, and each won a game. "We'll play one more for the championship."

Serena knew full well that Saul would win, as he usually did. They were having such fun laughing together. It had been a long time since this had happened. Saul spoke, "I'm so glad you decided to come, Siri." Every once in a while he called her that.

"I'm glad, too. This is great!"

"We better turn in. We have to get up early." They said their "good-nights," and Serena went to her Pullman bedroom. The bed was already made up. It looked comfortable enough, and she hopped in and turned off the light.

In the dark, she pulled up the shade and watched the towns as they flew past, but it was the train that was rushing ahead leaving the towns far behind. Noisy train wheels rolled along the tracks—metal on metal making contact, and soon it became a monotonous "hum and click—hum and clack," and it was to that sound Serena fell asleep.

A knock at the door awakened her. It was the porter telling her they would be in St. Louis in a half hour. She thanked him and quickly scrambled out of bed.

Saul knocked. "Are you ready?"

"In a minute!" She rushed—checking to be sure she had everything. The train had stopped and she followed Saul out, into the hustle and bustle of the busy station and she saw St. Louis for the first time.

They were met by Mr. Keller. The men shook hands, so glad to see each other. Saul admonished him saying, "Sam, you shouldn't have gotten up this early. We could have taken a cab."

"Don't worry, Saul. It was my pleasure." He turned to Serena, "I know you're Serena." He took her hand, saying, "We've heard so much about you. It's really good to finally meet you."

They walked together, Saul conversing with Mr. Keller. Serena listened. It seemed these friends had much catching up to do. Mr. Keller had found a parking space not too far off—soon they were on their way.

Serena, sitting in back, leaned against the window, studying the neighborhood areas they passed—with children's wagons, tricycles, and swings waiting for their sleeping playmates to awaken. Serena wondered who the people were living there. It always fascinated her trying to imagine what they looked like—who they were—what they did, and how they managed their daily lives. Being in journalism, people always interested her.

They came to the Keller home in the East End of St. Louis. It was an area of gracious homes that stood proud. Mrs. Keller came out hearing the closing of the car doors. She stood on the top stair, smiling as she greeted them. Taking Serena's arm, she escorted her into the foyer as she inquired about the trip. Saul brought up the luggage, and after a few exchanges, Mrs. Keller said she had breakfast.

"Do I have a few takers?" she wanted to know. Saul wanted toast and coffee and Serena too. "Follow me." She led them into the dining room where a table was already set. A plate of blueberry muffins and a plate of bagels waited there. Mrs. Keller brought in the hot coffee, and soon all were eating and talking, Serena, answering questions between bites of the muffin and sips of coffee.

Serena had been observing Mrs. Keller and liked what she saw—fair-faced, her hair worn short, about five foot four, nice appearing, with a warm smile, and very pleasant. Mrs. Keller interrupted her thoughts with, "We're so glad to have you come. Saul told us so much about you. We felt it was time to finally meet you, Serena."

"I'm glad I could come this time."

"When you're ready, I'll show you to your room." Mrs. Keller volunteered.

A little while later, Serena followed Mrs. Keller up the stairs and was shown into a sunny yellow and soft blue room.

Serena loved it and said so, adding, "These are my favorite colors."

"Mine, too! Take your time settling in."

She put her hand on Serena's arm. She liked this young woman. She was like a breath of fresh air.

"Our son, Max, will be home later. Come down whenever you feel like it and have lunch. We'll have dinner at six."

Before she left, Mrs. Keller told Serena again how delighted she was to have her here. She had made Serena feel welcome.

Serena paused at the window, which looked out on a large garden area—bound by lovely trees and bushes. She thought how comfortable she felt here. Just yesterday she was home in Madison; today it seemed so far away, like the many reasons that led to her decision to come.

Sometimes this "Michael thing," would intrude her mind. It still pained her to think of it, but purpose and will had helped stem the hurt that now had subsided.

There were some magazines on a shelf. Serena checked them and took the *Readers' Digest*. Folding the spread back, she took off her shoes and dropped into bed. She was going to read—but set the magazine aside.

Her thoughts mingled with school and friends, good times and bad, her loving mother and dad. She thought of him a lot. There were so many things that had made her sad—vulnerable-loving-hating, and the frustrating life consuming anger!

Serena knew how much of her heart and will it was taking to overcome them—to become a caring, loving part of the human race again—but most of all to believe again. It hadn't come easily—because of her father's death. People said, "It will take time. Time was the ultimate healer!"

Serena must have fallen asleep. When she awoke, it was late afternoon. Leisurely she showered and dressed. Coming down she met Mrs. Keller in the hallway and apologized for coming down so late.

"I knew you were tired."

"You look lovely." She complimented Serena on her dress.

Saul and Mr. Keller were in the living room smoking and discussing business. They seemed so involved, Serena slipped through the French doors on one side of the living room that led to the patio.

A garden of beautiful flowers surrounded the area. On the patio stood a wonderful bird cage, a replica of the Eiffel Tower. It housed two parakeets, with exotic hued feathers—one bright blue and the other lime green. Serena stopped at the cage, and one parakeet began speaking to her, "Hello! Hello!" Then the other began too. Serena answered, "Hello! Hello!"

Someone had come into the living room. She heard Saul and the Kellers—then a new voice, which she guessed belonged to the son. Then she heard Mrs. Keller calling, "Serena, Serena, dear," and out she came all smiles, her son in tow. "Serena, this is our son Maxwell—Max to everyone." She turned her mother's loving face toward him. Serena gave him her full attention—he was a handsome young man—chestnut brown curly hair, dark-dark brown eyes, fair skinned and nice teeth when he smiled, and he was smiling at her.

He held out his hand. Soft spoken he said, "I'm so glad to meet you!"

She could see he wasn't disappointed in seeing her. "I feel I know you. Saul always talks about you, but I couldn't picture you. I'm glad you came."

Mrs. Keller, conveniently, had to check something in the kitchen.

"I saw you talking to the parakeets."

"They're so beautiful. What are their names?"

Max walked over to the cage.

"What's your name?" he asked the one in the corner whose feathers were blue.

The parakeet answered, "Boy Blue! Boy Blue!"

"That's right, Boy Blue," Max said softly.

Then he looked at the other one.

"And what's your name?"

The bird ruffled its feathers and hopped from one foot to the other. This one's feathers were the lime green.

The bird answered, "Limey! Limey Girl!"

"You're right, Limey."

Max opened the cage door and mixed the birdseed, then he offered a tiny hoop to Boy Blue. "They're Mom's pets. She loves them." He said it so caringly.

They started across the yard. Over on one side was a tennis court, on the other quite a large pool.

"Do you play tennis?" he wanted to know.

"I play at it. I'm not very good."

"I'm not too good either, but if you'd like, we could play tomorrow. We can struggle through, at least have some fun chasing the bad hits. You'll have lots from me. What do you say, Serena?"

"I'm game, if you are."

"Okay, tomorrow morning."

"What else can we do?" he wanted to know.

"After dinner what would you like to do?"

"I don't know. What do you usually do?"

"I have some friends. I could call and see if they can come over. They'll like to meet you."

He looked straight at her in such a way that she could feel herself blushing.

"That would be nice."

They were on their way in when Mrs. Keller made an appearance on the patio.

"Time for you young folk to come in. Dinner is ready."

"In a minute, Mom. I'm going to call Carole and Charlie." And he left his voice trailing. Then it was quiet.

"Can I help with anything?" Serena asked Mrs. Keller, who was hurrying toward the kitchen.

"Thank you, dear. You may bring in the rolls." Serena sniffed the many wonderful aromas coming from the kitchen. "It smells delicious!"

"I hope you'll like what we're having tonight." Mrs. Keller looked at Serena and paid her a compliment. "I just know you are a good cook."

Max came in with the news that Carole and Charlie were coming over about eight o'clock. "Then we can decide what we're going to do." He seemed so pleased—quite exuberant.

Mrs. Keller led the foray from kitchen to dining room with a platter of baked chicken, Serena followed with a bowl of mashed potatoes, Max followed just giving Serena support. He held the chair for her and soon the room was filled with happy voices talking and lots of laughter.

Max had Serena's attention, saying something none of the others could hear. Saul noticed Serena was rapt in whatever it was he was saying to her. It was plain to see, the two were comfortable with each other. To this he could breathe a sigh of relief. It could very easily have gone the other way—young folk so critical of each other.

Max's conversation turned to Washington University, what a great school it was and how much he liked it. Everyone was in a jovial mood, enjoying dinner and being together. After dessert, Serena helped Mrs. Keller clear the table. Mrs. Keller noticed Max helping—she smiled to herself.

At eight o'clock Charlie and Carole came and were introduced to Saul and Serena. The young adults had hurried out to the patio where Charlie and Carole had monopolized the swing—leaving Serena and Max to settle on two wicker chairs nearby.

The discussion of 'what to do' ended with the decision to take a ride to the university campus and to show Serena around. Max sat in the back seat with Serena, and they were talking about school.

"At first I wasn't too keen on school here. I wanted to go to some school out of state. I thought about applying to Harvard, but my parents insisted Washington University was a good school. It's my father's Alma Mater!

"So," Max said, "I relented and now I'm so glad I listened. That was the time when Charlie's family came here from Michigan. Charlie's my best friend. We love it here. Don't we, Charlie?"

Carole's answer was to move closer to Charlie, which wedged them in pretty tightly to each other.

"There's the football field," Charlie announced, as they neared the campus.

"Let's go up to the bleachers, there," Charlie pointed.

Carole and Charlie started walking. Charlie had his arm around Carol's shoulder. Every once in a while, he nuzzled her cheek and neck and they stopped frequently to kiss. Max and Serena were back about eight or ten feet.

"Hey—stop it, you two." Max sounded embarrassed. He looked at Serena.

"It's okay, Max." She let him know it didn't bother her.

They reached the bleachers. Max took her hand to help her up one step, "How about here?" he asked. Carole and Charlie moved so they formed a close foursome—talking and laughing, innocent youth at its best.

A half-moon hung in the dark sky shining clear and bright over the huge field; and they were the only ones there—in a different world—almost apart from the rest of the universe.

They talked of many things, Carole questioning Serena about school, friends, and her plans for the fall. They listened intently as Serena responded with such enthusiasm about her—to receive her degree in journalism.

The proverbial light bulb sparked in Max's brain. "Serena, if you could transfer here, we have a really fine school in Journalism. Just think the fun we could all have. Of course, we'd study, but think of all the good times!"

Carole jumped in. "Max, that's a brilliant idea."

Riding over to the campus, Carole and Charlie had detected something different in their friend Max's voice. Carole, a romantic, had whispered to Charlie, "Max likes Serena." Charlie said nothing—just kept driving. Max had dated so many girls. He was, "a top of the list date" to many sororities—always invited to their dances, but hadn't gotten serious about anyone.

Charlie always wanted to know "Why? What was wrong with that girl last night?"

"She was okay—a nice girl." Then Charlie knew to drop it.

Tonight was different. He was giving Serena his full attention, not just being polite as he usually was whenever he found himself in a boring situation from which he couldn't extricate himself. His friends were quite cognizant of this fact, so Carole did her best to help in any way she could. They had just met, but she liked Serena, too.

"Think about it, Serena. It would be so wonderful for all of us if you could. Right, guys?"

Max answered right off, "Oh, boy, would that ever!"

Charlie agreed, but didn't say too much. Sometimes he seemed to have other things on his mind. Carole, knowing this, would try to "jolly him out of his mood," as she called it. Sometimes he responded quickly, and other times it was a more gradual progression, depending on the how and why of the mood.

Serena liked the group, but about changing her plans—she knew her mother would object strenuously and then there was Saul.

Out loud she countered with, "I couldn't possibly change schools, but listen—we can write and maybe see each other again. We can still be friends."

She saw the disappointment in their faces.

"Can't we?"

Max spoke, sounding more than a bit deflated.

"Sure, but it won't be the same."

Charlie interrupted the changed atmosphere, "What about having some ice cream?"

In the car, Carole brought up the subject again. "You know, Serena, that wasn't a bad idea of Max's. I wish you could come here. I know for myself I'd like that a lot."

The malt shop, frequented by the young crowd, mostly college students, was in a neighborhood not too far from campus. The place was noisy with talk and laughter and a blaring radio. After about an hour, Charlie wanted to leave; he had to be at work the next morning. Back at the Keller home, Serena thanked Charlie and Carole. She hated to see them leave. They said their good-nights and drove off.

"You must be tired, Serena. Do you still want to play tennis in the morning?" His voice was full of concern.

"I'll be fine," she assured him.

At the top of the stairs, he kissed her, a friendly kiss on the cheek.

"Good night," he said, "I'll see you tomorrow."

Serena undressed slowly, thinking of the wonderful day spent with Max and his friends. She smiled as she rubbed her cheek where he had kissed her ever so gently. She thought, *I like Max,* and it surprised her. She hadn't figured on anything like this happening to her.

I really like him! It made her feel good to acknowledge that to herself.

Charlie and Carole had been a happy part of the evening, too. She remembered that they all expressed their feelings about her coming to Washington U. They were so sincere about wanting her to be with them. The more she thought about it, it began to make some sort of sense. It didn't seem as impossible as it did at first when Max, excited, broached the matter.

She knew there was much to think about. Drowsily, she turned toward the window and watched the drape being moved by the cool evening breezes. For the past weeks, she had been nervous—had to keep herself busy. The nights were troubled. Tonight, she felt a calmness she couldn't explain. This she knew—she was glad she had come to St. Louis.

VI
Rose-Colored World of Youth

Max was waiting to play tennis. After a few sets, punctuated with banter and laughter, they decided they had enough, chasing well-aimed shots that had them chasing balls from one end of the court to the other. They discovered this—each played more than a fairly good game.

"That was fun!" Serena was panting as she wiped her perspiring forehead and face.

Max had enjoyed the tennis game with her. He admired her good sportsmanship, and found he wanted to spend as much time as possible with her.

"I'll get in touch with Charlie and make arrangements for tonight. How does that sound?" he questioned.

She was all smiles. "Wonderful!"

An hour later, coming down the stairs, she saw Max—handsome in cool summer slacks and a yellow knit sport shirt. The sight of him made her heart skip a little. The gods of love, Cupid, Venus, and Eros, must have all descended to the space of Max and Serena. There now was Max trying to catch his breath at the lovely sight of her in a white linen sun dress—with a blue scarf around her brown hair and her blue eyes shining and happy—an unforgettable picture to be sure.

"Gee, Serena, you look," he hesitated, "so wonderful!"

She liked the feeling of knowing he approved—was attracted to her, but it was more than that—it was his sincerity. It seemed to come from his heart. They drove to the Keller shoe store in downtown St. Louis and met Saul and Mr. Keller. Both seemed quite pleased, and one could conclude their meetings that morning had been beneficial and productive.

"Let's get going, Serena, I promised you the Maryland Shopping Center and I mean to keep my word."

Max couldn't join them. He had responsibilities in the store. "I'm still learning," he laughed. Mr. Keller, the proud father, assured the little group, "Max is doing a terrific job. I don't know what I'd do without him."

He had come over to Max's side and had his arm around his son's shoulder. Serena tried to hide her disappointment of not having Max along.

The tired shoppers returned quite late in the afternoon. It had been good to have time with Saul, and "The Mall" had been a positive experience.

At lunch she thanked Saul for bringing her to see it. He asked about Max and his friends.

"Oh, yes, she was glad she had come and met them all."

Max was waiting, eager to offer his news.

"Charlie and Carole are coming later, and we're going to the Park Plaza for dinner and dancing. We're going to have a fun evening."

Charlie and Max took turns driving, so Max drove, and Serena sitting in front could hear Carole and Charlie arguing. Charlie was in one of his "moods," as Carole characterized it.

A valet parked the car, and the two couples soon mingled with others entering the beautiful Park Plaza. The maitre'd showed them to their wonderfully situated table right on the edge of the mirrored dance floor.

Tiny lit lamps at each table added to the romantic atmosphere. The place was dimly lit. The lighting was brighter around the bandstand, and a huge crystal chandelier, rotating with tiny lamps reflected like stars on the ceiling, the guests, and the mirrored dance floor. It was a most spectacular sight, and an overwhelmed Serena kept repeating over and over, "Oh, this is so nice."

Max was so pleased that she appreciated his efforts to make this a memorable evening.

They ordered wine and on the dance floor, couples were joining those already dancing as the band played the favorites of the forties. Max asked Serena to dance and led her there. He held her tightly, and it felt glorious to be in his arms.

Carole wasn't getting through to Charlie. They sat, not talking, looking at the guests on the dance floor, sipping their wine. Serena felt badly for Carole and said so to Max.

"I know he has moods, and he won't talk about them. I know he has problems; he's my friend and I like him. He's troubled and I'm there for him whenever he needs me. He knows that and I don't like to talk about him."

Serena thought, *Charlie is lucky to have a loyal friend like Max.* She decided not to ever say anything about Charlie again.

She liked Carol and Charlie and didn't want to jeopardize her friendship with any of them. Serena didn't know if their friendship would continue after she left St. Louis. Promises are easy to make, but it takes commitment to keep them. She hoped so; in her heart she hoped.

She wanted it to continue with Max, that she knew, although it was difficult to believe that she could feel this way just having met him, but there it was. This was different. She couldn't explain it. Her thoughts caused her to misstep.

"Oh," she said, "I'm sorry."

Ever the gentleman, Max said, "It was my fault," and he held her closer.

There they were in the middle of a crowded room, but it was as if they were the only ones—so engrossed were they in each other—in their private world.

The band took a break, and they headed back to their table. For the rest of the evening, Charlie made attempts to be his old self again with jokes and stories, making them laugh. He could be very entertaining when he wanted to, and Serena was sure Carole had done her part to change his mood.

They ordered their dinner, and this time Carole and Charlie got up to dance. Serena could see Carole was in a happier frame of mind. It gave her a sick twinge to think the hold Charlie had on Carole and how much Carole loved him.

Serena took a deep breath—she knew what that was like. Max interrupted her with, "A penny for your thoughts. You looked so serious."

"I'm sorry." She smiled. "You'd be paying too much."

Max took her hand; just then the dinners arrived and were set down. The waiter fussed a bit. Then they were alone again.

"I've never said this to anyone, Serena. I think I'm in love with you! I know it sounds crazy, but it's true!"

She looked down, and he gently lifted her chin upward. Her blue eyes glistened with unfallen tears.

"You're beautiful, you know!" And he kissed her on trembling lips and then kissed her again. "I do love you, Serena."

She tried to compose herself. This new feeling, an impelling force that quickened her senses. The wine may have been a bit of a contributing factor, but she knew it was because of Max!

"I love you, Serena." Max said it again in all his simple sincerity, and she knew he meant it.

Charlie and Carole came sauntering back, and Serena was grateful for the interruption. Charlie took inventory of the dinner.

"Wow, that looks good. I don't know about you guys, but I'm hungry," and with that he plopped himself down beside Carole. The conversation was mixed.

Carole, with her woman's intuition, felt she and Charlie had arrived back at an inopportune time. From the looks on Serena's and Max's faces, something serious had been going on.

Seeking to bridge the awkward gap, Carole asked, "How did you like the Mall, Serena? Did you find anything?"

"Yes." She described the gift for her friend, Sherry, and the ones for her mother and grandmother. The talk of shopping kept the girls busy for a while.

Charlie's favorite subject these days was what the newspapers and radio were saying about "this guy Hitler." He was always betting Max, "I'll bet Hitler's going to do this," and he'd talk about what he thought would happen.

"Did you hear anything on the radio today at the store?" he asked.

Max worked at one of his father's shoe stores, and the radio was on all the time.

"Yes." He explained, "The morning news had a special report. Germany had signed a treaty with Russia."

"What do you suppose that means?" Charlie questioned.

"I don't know. I haven't thought too much about it, Charlie."

"Why not? I think it's important. No one knows what that guy is going to do next."

Max and Charlie had many discussions on what was transpiring in Europe. Charlie thought somehow America would be involved, and it was of grave concern to him. Carole could see Charlie was getting upset. She interceded, "I'd like one more twirl around the dance floor, then let's call it a night. We can see you two tomorrow."

Max drove Charlie to Carole's and after a few "good-nights," Serena and Max were on their way home.

They sat on the patio swing, the night was cooling down, and Serena shivered a little.

"Are you cold, Serena?" Max took off his suit jacket and put it over her shoulders. He moved closer and put his arm around her.

Serena was saying how much she liked Carole and Charlie. He was pleased about that. Again he told her how he felt about her and wanted to know how it was with her. Did she care even a little?

There was a silence, then Serena spoke up. She didn't want to say something that wasn't true. She wanted to be sure.

"I like you, Max, but we've just met. We don't know each other very well!"

She was speaking from her previous experience, which had made her more cautious. "What good are experiences if we don't learn from them?" she wondered.

He didn't know about it, and she didn't feel she had to share what was past. That was part of her private life he had nothing to do with. Michael's rejection had hurt.

He felt a little exasperated in her not letting him continue with what he wanted to say.

"Okay." He said it quietly. He hoped he hadn't offended her. "I'm sorry, Serena, but that's how I feel. I've gone out with other girls, and I know I never felt like this—like I feel about you." He looked so serious speaking to her.

"We'll wait and see," she voiced her concern. They went in quietly whispering their "good nights." She gave him his jacket and said, "Thanks." It was then he put his arms about her and kissed her.

The stood close for another few minutes—Max reluctant to let her go. "See you tomorrow," he whispered as they parted.

All were at breakfast when Serena came down. They greeted her warmly. Max got up to help with her chair.

"So you're all going to the park?" Mrs. Keller questioned. "You have a glorious day for it!"

The breakfast talk was cheerful. Mrs. Keller inquired of Serena, "Have you been enjoying your stay in St. Louis so far?"

"Oh, yes, everyone's been wonderful."

"That's good, my dear, and I'm sure Carole and Charlie have been entertaining. They are such a nice couple and good friends of Max's."

Max spoke up, "If we go early, we may avoid the hot humid part of the afternoon."

"We're ready when you are!" Saul was quite enthusiastic—having wanted, for so long, to visit Forest Park, especially the zoo. He loved animals.

As they were leaving, Mrs. Keller came out. "I've fixed you a picnic lunch, and you can get your cold sodas at the park."

Both Serena and Saul voiced their appreciation simultaneously.

Max took the basket and on his way out stopped, as he did every morning, to talk to Boy Blue and Limey Girl. In her stay there, Serena had learned how much he cared for them and they reciprocated his feeling, chattering away, "Bye Max! Bye Max!" It was always a cheery morning in the Keller household. Everybody was happy.

Mr. Keller kissed his wife and left. Serena remembered it was much the same at their house when her father was there. She was glad to see life that way again.

It wasn't too long a drive, and soon they arrived at Forest Park. Max found a parking space not too far from the lake. People were out paddling canoes and youngsters sat relaxed at the water's edge dangling their bamboo fishing poles, eternally optimistic they would soon have a catch.

"What would you like to see first?" Max asked.

"Let's start at the beginning and walk through," was Saul's suggestion. It was early, but already, there were many visitors. Some were standing in front of different exhibits. Others were sauntering. In the summertime, people in St. Louis walked at a slow pace, because of the heat.

The sun was attempting to climb higher in the sky, and it was warm. It seemed the sun's collected heat rays had stopped just outside the zoo's gates—for inside—they found an oasis—cool with tall trees and bushes and plants from all over the world—flourishing—shading the walks.

Here and there were groups listening to tour guides. Serena and Max stopped to listen. Many were carrying binoculars. They were looking at birds and their nests. This was an Audobon Society group—people of all ages. They were looking at orioles, and the guide was explaining how they built their strange-looking nests. Serena looked so interested. One member let her use his binoculars and pointed her in the direction where she could see the nests hanging there—feats of bird engineering and ingenuity.

Saul, meanwhile, was busy taking pictures of the primates in their habitat—one of the most popular tourist stops. The zoo had earned the reputation as one of the finest in the world.

There were signs, "Do not feed the animals," that were unheeded. People were throwing peanuts and bananas, and the animals would jump and run to pick them up. Lions and tigers walked in and out of the stone caves. They were all so majestic and beautiful.

Max voiced his concern that some of the animals were rapidly disappearing.

"Isn't it a shame, Serena? We should do all we can to save them."

Saul was in his element, busily snapping with his camera. He heard Max, and he was in total agreement.

"They are magnificent, just magnificent."

"Hard to believe," he said it slowly, "that these could be gone someday."

By this time they had covered quite a large area of the park and zoo, and Max was feeling a few hunger pangs.

They managed to catch one of the park's vehicles to their car. With the steady stream of people converging on the park, they were fortunate to find a table and benches.

Serena set it with the checkered cloth Mrs. Keller had provided. The food and water in a thermos were in the cooler, and soon they were enjoying a feast of fried chicken, and potato salad. The dessert was cookies and watermelon, so sweet and juicy as only can be found in St. Louis.

The conversation was light and happy, and there was laughter, much laughter. It was the innocence of youth, an innocence of the times, and hearts were light. It was a moment captured, set aside in the mind to be remembered and brought forth again and again.

Saul may have been busy, but the chemistry between Serena and Max had not escaped him. The concerns for his sister and why he had wanted her to come were uppermost in his mind. He hoped he had done the right thing introducing these two. Too late for post-mortems. Time and time alone would tell.

Saul, changing the subject, asked Max about his plans for the future. He thought awhile before answering.

"Dad wants me to come into the business with him."

"And what do you want?"

Max wasn't sure if that was what he wanted to do.

"Well, my friends and I are thinking of that war in Europe, Saul. No one knows what's going to happen, so how can we plan anything?"

This had become a national predicament. Young men entering college, those already there, and young men from every walk of life were confronted with this uncertainty.

"I graduate next year, 1940. If we don't have a war, I'll probably be with my dad."

"Good idea!" Saul agreed.

"I don't think there's going to be a war. Some people think there is, but most of our people don't think so. It's not our war." Serena was voicing the discussions she heard.

"We can't let it upset our lives. Isn't that right, Saul?"

Serena had been to several gatherings where the young women had spoken of their concerns about the war. They didn't want their young men taken away, so the war situation was discussed and dropped as if that would make it disappear.

"The government wants us all to have the year of Compulsory Training," Max explained to Saul. He didn't know it was a concern to Saul, too.

Max continued on, "Charlie graduates next year, too, wants to enlist in the army, and 'be ready' he says. I kind of agree with him. I've been giving it a great deal of thought. You get that year in—and it's out of the way and you can plan your future. Of course it's an interruption in your life, but lots of guys are seriously thinking about it."

Max was thinking of Serena. He cared about her and hoped they could further their friendship. One thing he had come to realize in the past few days, he desperately wanted to pursue this relationship. Serena, over and above all else, was the cardinal point in his future. He couldn't see a future without her.

Saul had addressed a question to Max and gotten no answer. Max was thinking his own thoughts. Serena gently poked him, "Max?"

"Oh, I'm sorry. I didn't hear you."

"I was asking if you could show me some good fishing spots the next time I come."

"You bet." Max was thinking, *He'll probably—no most likely, bring Serena again.*

After taking up the remnants of the lunch, Max offered to take them to the area on the Mississippi River he thought they might like, but Saul decided they had better head back.

Because the day was getting quite warm, Mrs. Keller had come out to check on the water situation for the parakeets, then sat down on the wicker sofa to wait for Max and the guests.

It wasn't too long before she saw the car coming up the driveway. The tourists and Max got out, not as bouncy as when they left in the morning. St. Louis summer heat could zap you! She brought out a pitcher of icy cold lemonade and filled tall glasses.

Saul took his and kept drinking until the glass was empty. When he could come up for air, he thanked her. "You always know what hits the spot, and we all enjoyed the picnic lunch." Saul's compliment was sincerely given.

Serena offered her thanks. "It was so good of you to do that. It was such a wonderful day. I'll never forget it!"

"My pleasure was to do that for you." Then turning to Serena, she said, "My dear, I'm so glad you could come. We had looked forward to meeting you for such a long time!"

Mrs. Keller liked this young woman. She found there were many things she approved of—her warmth—her sincerity—a most pleasing personality, and she was a "down to earth" person.

The visit was coming to an end. Saul and Serena had mutually decided they would spend the evening with the Kellers, providing they were not interfering with any previous plans of the family. The Kellers were most appreciative of their thoughtfulness and said so. Max wanted to know if Carole and Charlie would stop by for a few moments to say their good-byes, and so it was all arranged. Their energy at low-tide from the St. Louis humidity, the guests retired to their rooms to rest and freshen up before dinner.

At dinner, toasts and good wishes for good health and continuing friendship came from Saul, Mr. Keller, and Max. Then Serena expressed her thanks for their hospitality, and added, "I felt so welcomed. I loved being here."

Mrs. Keller extended the invitation. "Please, Serena—promise you'll come again. We'd love to have you."

This was important to Serena because she liked Max's mother, and she was pretty sure she liked Max. Yes, she knew she liked him!

The door bell rang, and Carole and Charlie came in.

It wasn't too long before the men were discussing the St. Louis baseball teams, the Cardinals and the Browns. Arguing about sports wasn't too exciting to the women, and they made it out to the patio.

Soon their talk was of shopping for school in the fall, Mrs. Keller asking about their plans. Just then Charlie and Max came out and asked if the girls could be excused for about an hour. They left in Charlie's car and drove to campus where Max had taken Serena her first night here.

Carole and Charlie were both sorry to see Serena leave. They promised to write to relay news. Carole held her hand up as if she were swearing on a Bible. She looked at Serena, her face so serious.

"I promise to write." Her voice almost cracked, she was so emotional. She really liked Serena and would miss her. She asked Serena to consider the transfer to Washington U. She went on, "Charlie had never seen Max care for a girl as much as he does you, Serena. We're happy for him. He's our best friend!"

Charlie beseeched her to take seriously their need. "We need you to be here with us."

Charlie was speaking for all of them, most especially for his friend, Max. He knew Max. Serena, in just a short time, had become very important to Max.

Both Charlie and Carole told her again they were happy to have met her, spent time with her. They liked her. She could feel their honesty—real friends, and she was so glad she had come—so much had happened, and she had a mixture of other feelings—a little sadness, and she couldn't say why.

Carole hugged Serena, and Charlie, so unlike Charlie, hugged and kissed her much to the amazement of both Carole and Max. They delayed their departure, time and time again. They really hated to leave.

It was when Carole took charge and said, "We better leave and give Max and Serena some time together." Charlie finally took the hint and drove them back.

The heat of the day had relaxed its hold, and it was cooler out. They were on the patio, and Max asked if she would walk for a bit around the yard. She knew a little of what he wanted to say. He would begin it at some point of every evening he had spent with her. "I'm so glad you came, Serena."

Tonight he added, "I hope you enjoyed being here with me."

"You've all been wonderful, Max, your folks, Carole and Charlie, and you. I'm glad I came."

Max stepped in front of her. "You know I like you a lot." His voice got stronger, he had his arms around her. It felt good when he did. He was taller than she was, and he stooped a little to kiss her. She kissed him back, and his arms tightened about her.

They stood there, two new lovers, totally engulfed in their emotions. There they were adrift from the rest of the universe once more, in their own little world, with the sky—their company and twinkling stars on this wondrous evening, with promise for the future.

As they made their way back to the patio, he held her hand. It was getting late and Serena had to finish packing. Max kissed her good-night again before she went up. He looked so sad. They found the parting difficult.

Serena got to bed, but not before she had written a note to Mrs. Keller and left it on the dresser. Saul was to waken her at 3:00 A.M. He had ordered a cab. Their train was due to leave at 5:00 A.M.

She didn't sleep much, tossing and turning and dozing, and she was up when Saul came in. They came down quietly with their luggage to the patio. Boy Blue and Limey Girl began stirring. Not wanting to awaken the Kellers, they waited outdoors for the cab and it was on time.

The drive to the station was quiet. Saul could see Serena was tired and looking out at the passing city—lost in thought. Saul got the tickets, and the porter helped with the luggage. He informed them the train would leave in fifteen minutes. Soon the train was rolling along—the wheels rattling on the tracks—a little noisy but soothing. Saul sat back, his eyes closed. Serena tried to relax, but couldn't—chronologically, her mind was going over all that had happened in her life in the past week.

They had dinner in the Pullman Dining Car. It gave Serena a chance to talk to Saul. "What would you say if I told you I would like to go to Washington U. and get my degree there?"

"Why?" he wanted to know, and then he listened to her enumerate the reasons.

She liked St. Louis—had made friends, with Carole and Charlie, and she was sure after listening to them expound so many positives about the school, that she would like it there. Then there was the Keller family too.

"You like Max. Don't you, Siri?"

Sometimes he called her "Siri"—his pet name for her.

"Yes, I think I do, and I'm sure the change will be good in other ways. What do you think?"

Serena had great respect for her brother and listened to what he had to say.

"If you're sure, we will talk to Mom. You know she didn't want you to go to school out of state before."

"I know, but promise you'll talk to her." Serena knew now—talking about it—this was what she wanted to do.

"Promise?" she questioned.

What she was asking was important to her.

Saul nodded. "Yes."

In his mind, he knew he would worry, but he knew the Kellers and Max and he knew Serena. He had cared for her since his dad died. Serena had come a long way. She was a good person, and he loved his younger sister. How would it be for her if she went? Only time would tell.

Part Two
Life Goes On

VII
Happenings in Madison and Europe

Summer in Wisconsin is a most pleasant time of the year, situated as it is between two of the largest lakes in the country. There is the beautiful Lake Superior, part of its northern border; Lake Michigan, bordering most of its eastern side, and the Father of Rivers, the mighty Mississippi, enclosing its western edge. The totality of all this combined, results in the atmosphere of an almost air-conditioned state.

Of course there were many warm days, but usually with comfortable breezes. In summertime tourists came from all over the world to the popular Wisconsin Dells. The resorts had everything tourists could ask for, to make their visits memorable ones—proof of that was the many times they came back with their families or friends.

There, also, were the multitudes who came to visit the different cities of Milwaukee, Sheboygan, and Green Bay, among others. Then of course, there was Madison, the college town. Students came from all over the country because that's where the pride of the state, the University of Wisconsin, was located. Wisconsinites were known to be most friendly and well-liked as visitors would tell you. To Serena and Saul, it was a wonderful place to call home.

"It's always good to go away, but it's wonderful to come back." Saul was referring to the warm pleasant days of Madison, in contrast to the hot humid days of St. Louis, and the cool wonderful nights there, instead of the many unbearably humid ones in Missouri. Serena had to agree, but St. Louis, even with its abominably hot weather, now held other attractions for her—principal among them—Max!

Serena and Saul had been back for almost a week. The trip, in all its phases, was discussed. Mrs. Warner questioning the glowing accounts of events that had taken place. She could see a change in her daughter. Her eyes sparkled and there was a lilt in her voice when she spoke of "Max." In private, there had been talks between mother and son about the move to St. Louis, and Serena transferring to Washington University; fall, and the new school semester, were not too far off. Mrs. Warner listened.

Saul was keeping the promise he had made. He thought it was a good idea and after detailing the situation asked, "How do you feel about this move, Mom?"

Naturally there was deep concern for her daughter—a new school—new friends, and being away from family. Even with Saul's assurances about the Kellers, Max and his friends, who sincerely wanted Serena to come—there were some feelings of apprehension and anxiety.

"Am I being selfish in wanting to keep Serena here?" Mrs. Warner questioned.

Saul argued, "This would be an excellent learning and growing experience in many ways."

"If you think it's time, then we'll do it." She was agreeing, but not altogether really sure in her heart. Still she knew Saul would only suggest what was best for his sister.

"I guess all parents feel the way I do when it's time to let go. It's a difficult choice."

Mrs. Warner looked downcast and Saul came over to put his arm around her shoulder. "I understand, Mom. You have to remember Siri *is* a fine young woman." He emphasized, "is."

"She'll be all right, you'll see." He said it with such certainty, she began to feel better about the idea.

After her husband's death, Mrs. Warner, on several occasions, had spoken to Saul about resuming his relationship with Jennifer. She felt guilty, that the blame was partly hers, because she had been ill. She didn't know exactly what had happened, or what had been said between Saul and Jennifer, but when the subject of Jennifer came up, Saul made it clear, "this was best!" It had been on her mind for a long time.

Now, Serena would be on her own. Mrs. Warner would attempt to speak to Saul again. He was always sure. "It wasn't the right time." And the subject was always deferred. "Not right now, Mom." She was not a meddlesome mother, just a devoted one and her concern was for her children. Saul was a grown man, an important man in his business and in the community—to her he was all that—but he was her son—hurting—and she wanted to help in some way, if at all possible.

She remembered parents in a group discussing "parenthood." One woman said in a voice of certainty, "When your children are grown, you should stop worrying about them!" Another, perhaps a little wiser, answered, "You never stop worrying—because you're a parent until the day you die." Mrs. Warner, right or wrong, was one of the latter and wondered, "If King Solomon were alive, what would he have said?" She hoped a more opportune time would soon present itself for her to speak to Saul and she prayed he would listen.

In the weeks that followed, Serena received endless letters from St. Louis. Carole wrote, "We all miss you, especially Max. You are all he talks about."

Serena read and re-read the letters. She couldn't wait to receive the next mail. It was Max's letters that made her heart pound with each word of his love for her. In the last few letters from Carole, there was always the question, "Are you coming?"

It was Serena's birthday, and she had received cards from her friends in Madison and family. Carole and Charlie sent theirs, and Max sent red roses with a card. "Hope I'll see you soon" and signed it "My Love Forever." Her thoughts were of Max, and she was happily humming as she arranged the flowers in her mother's special crystal vase.

That afternoon was spent with friends at lunch. They wanted to hear more about her trip to St. Louis. "Did you meet anyone special?"

"Yes," and she told them about Carole and Charlie and Max, the good time she had, and how she liked St. Louis.

Then the talk turned to school in the fall. Some were looking forward to it—to get through; those engaged to get married, and some anxious to find work. They all agreed there was much to think about. Serena listened and said little. She didn't know for sure what her plans were.

The family had taken Serena to dinner at her favorite restaurant to celebrate. Saul proposed a toast. As they lifted their champagne glasses, he said, "Serena, we love you." He paused, "Mom and I are going to miss not having you around." He stopped at Serena's bewilderment.

Serena looked at him—then her mother.

"What do you mean?"

"Well, I kept my promise, and talked to mother. If you still want to go, we'll help with your move to St. Louis."

"You know how much I want to go." She was all smiles—then became serious, "Not because I want to leave you. I'll miss you two. You know that."

They discussed it a bit further—then the music began. Saul interrupted, "Let's dance, Siri," and he led her to the dance floor where a few couples were already dancing.

Saul, questioned her, "Siri, tell me the truth. Is that what you really want to do?"

"Oh, yes, Saul, you know I do. I've thought about it a lot, and I decided, this is what I want to do!"

"If you're sure, and are happy, then I'm happy for you!"

Back at their table, Serena found two gift packages. At her mother's urging, she undid them. From her mother, a lovely gold ring with a pearl in the center. She loved it and took her mother's hand across the table, "Thank you, Mom."

The two had always been together—close—and would be separated shortly, one to taste the fruit of adventure—the other would stand by praying for the fruit to be sweet!

"Open mine now, Siri." Saul was anxious to see if she liked it. It was a gold bracelet engraved with, "To Sis with love—Saul." He fumbled with the clasp as she held her hand out for him to slip it on her wrist.

"It's just beautiful. I'll treasure them both forever."

There were a few brief moments of quiet. Saul had been thinking how strange their lives would be now that Serena was going away. "It'll take some getting used to, little sister, not having you around."

"I know. I've been thinking the same about you and Mom. I promise to write often and call. You'll see it won't be so bad, and who knows, you might find you even like not having me around to pester you!"

Saul detected a slight quiver in her voice. "That'll be the day." He kidded her.

"Do you mind if we leave a little earlier tonight? I want to write to Max and Carole."

"No problem," Saul assured her. "We understand."

"You're both so wonderful—no wonder I love you."

She knew, to her mother, it was a sacrifice to let her go, and though she was happy, she wondered, "Was I doing the right thing?" She didn't think of herself as being selfish, but "if she went away for her own happiness, wasn't she?"

Over and over absent-mindedly, she turned the bracelet around her wrist, thankful she was sitting in the back of Saul's car so they couldn't notice the tears. It was difficult to explain—she was happy and still there were tears.

Serena back-tracking in her mind remembered how she had made the decision to go with Saul on that trip to St. Louis that was resulting in so many changes for her and her family—because now there was Max in her life.

Later that evening after she had sent off the letters to St. Louis, thoughts of Max were interludes on her mind. They were happy thoughts and would probably be a source of dreams into the night—and daydreams in the coming weeks. All in all, it had been a most wonderful day!

In St. Louis, when they received her letters saying arrangements were being made for her move in the fall, Max was overjoyed, and Carole had written, "That's putting it mildly." Mail from Max with plans, full of hope for the two of them telling her how much he wanted her there, were always bright moments in her day. Even Charlie, usually in a low-ebb attitude, got on the bandwagon and wrote, "I'm so glad you're coming!"

Charlie, busy with a part-time job, classes in the evening, and trying to maintain good grades wrote, "Because when you come, I'll be able to get to my studies without so many interruptions from Max when he wants to talk about you—which is all the time!" Charlie, making a point, had that all underlined.

Serena, noted too, that Max's mail mentioned the war in Europe. "Everyone is talking about it. There are more news flashes and reports on the radio every night. It's disturbing, and many here think there's more to this war in Europe than we are told."

Carole's letters came with the news, "Charlie talks about the darn war all the time." She wrote, "I told Charlie, I don't want to hear about it anymore. He's so serious and worried. Confidentially, I'm saying that to Charlie, but I'm really frightened. School will resume in the fall, and then Charlie and Max will forget the war overseas." Carole and the rest of America hoped.

In the summer of 1939, President Roosevelt in one of his "Fireside Chats," having heard the concerns of Americans, promised, "We're not going to fight!" Then a German sub torpedoed *The Athenia,* a British passenger ship they had mistaken for an armed ship. It was bound for Montreal and had sailed before the British declared war on Germany. Twenty American citizens lost their lives. President Roosevelt, again was emphatic when he broadcast to the American people, urging "no man or woman to thoughtlessly talk of America sending its armies to European fields." He assured them a 'proclamation of neutrality' was being readied at that moment. People's fears were calmed.

Mrs. Warner arranged a farewell party for Serena and her friends. Sherry was losing her best friend. They had grown up together, never thought they'd be parted. The two sat off in a corner, each promising to write, to keep in touch. Sometimes the room rang with girlish laughter recalling happy times; then hugging and embracing brought tears. One of the group was leaving them. Late, in the evening as they started to go, they wished her well—but they knew even with all the promises things would be different for all of them.

Serena and her mother arrived in St. Louis the first week in the sweltering month of August. Arrangements had been made, and Serena would share a room with Carole in one of the dormitories at Washington U.

Then came the pleasant meeting with the Kellers and Carole and Charlie. She liked them. They were easy to like. She reflected, "Sometimes we meet people and our instincts and intuitions tell us immediately we want to know them better." Mrs. Warner felt this strongly about all of them. She understood Serena's whole-hearted acceptance of them and she approved.

Charlie, she could tell, was a little more difficult to know, but she liked him.

Now having met them, her concerns for her daughter were alleviated. They treated Serena like family, and Mrs. Warner felt their sincerity when they assured her, "We'll look after Serena here."

The next few days were busy ones, and it didn't take long to get unpacked and Serena settled in with her friend, Carole. By the end of the week, the heat had been quite wearing on Mrs. Warner and she felt since Serena was all set, she would leave. The Kellers insisted on having a dinner so they could all be together before Mrs. Warner, or "Ann" as they now called her, went back to Madison. It was a lovely family dinner and Mrs. Warner was glad to have had the chance to be with them all again.

She listened as Max told her some of his plans. He would graduate in 1940—the next year. She could see how much he cared for Serena. It was the way he looked at her when she spoke. He was always looking at her—couldn't keep his eyes off of her. It made Serena blush, when she looked up and saw him.

After dinner Max asked if he and Serena could be excused for a few hours, Carole and Charlie were coming about 7:30. The two came in to say their 'good-bye' to Mrs. Warner, then they were off. Max and Serena sat in back. They would all begin talking at the same time. Everyone had so much to say and tell her and question her about. One thing was abundantly clear—they were all happy to have her back.

They asked Serena where she would like to go—she wanted to go to the campus. That's where they first took her. It was exactly what they all wanted to do. They got there and walked up the few steps to where they sat the first time. Max had his arm around her shoulder. Carole and Charlie sat behind them. They talked about school, acquainting her with some of the things she needed to know. Her grades and all necessary papers were being sent to Washington U. She hoped they would be there on time so she wouldn't miss any classes. They were all bubbling with joy. It made her feel welcomed and good inside.

They went back to Max's home, then all went to the station to see Mrs. Warner off. They waited until she said her good-byes to the Kellers and Max—to Carole and Charlie—and stepped aside so Serena and her mother said their farewells. Mrs. Warner was at the window waving at them as the train pulled out. It wasn't until that moment that a little sadness set in and there were tears as she sat down; she couldn't see them anymore. She would miss Serena. *Another adjustment in life as it goes on. There are always new adjustments,* she thought.

Beset by the many crises in the past few years, she relinquished her thoughts with, "We'll take a day at a time. It'll be fine!" She was assuring herself. Slowly she put her head back on a small pillow and turned to look out the window at the landscape of Missouri as it whisked by. It was late and time to retire; she sat a bit longer. Tomorrow she would be home.

The all-night ride was long; she was up early—dressed and waiting to step into home territory. Her eyes quickly found what she had been looking for—there was Saul smiling. It was good to see him. Those standing nearby could guess they were happy, by the way they greeted each other. He helped her with a few packages and luggage to the car. Now, they headed home to contend with the many changes. They had come to know, "In life there is no permanence—there is always change!" After her mother had gone, Serena spent the rest of the week making those last-minute purchases.

Saturday night, Max and Charlie came to take the girls out to the Tivoli Theatre. There was low talk and whispering during the showing of the picture, but when the news reel came on, it suddenly became very quiet in the theatre. The news was sobering. The patrons walked out visibly disturbed by what they had seen and heard.

Max drove to the Shanghai Café for "the best Oriental food in town." There was talk about the school—about work, and then Charlie started a heated discussion about the news shown in the theatre. He was upset by pictures of thousands of German soldiers in their uniforms marching—marching—headed for somewhere. After the heated discussion died down, the group left. The girls went back to their dorm. "No!" They couldn't see the boys on Sunday. There were things to do before Monday—the beginning of school.

On a Monday morning—September 1939—Serena went to her first class, a new beginning. She sat there with opened notebook and text waiting anxiously, quietly observing the students as they arrived. Classes began when "Professor Comstock," that's how he wrote his name on the blackboard, began talking—lecturing for almost an hour. She didn't mind, for he had a most pleasant voice, and enunciated clearly, making the material easy to comprehend. She hoped her other classes would be comparable to this, her first class. The next assignment was handed out and class was dismissed.

In the hallway, she breathed a sigh of relief. Not knowing what to expect, she had met her first challenge, and motivated herself with, "I'll be fine!"

She met Carole waiting patiently on the library steps.

"How did it go?" She had been concerned about her friend's first class.

Serena was full of excitement and enthusiasm, relating thoughts on the class and teacher.

"I knew you'd be okay, Serena. I gave you my full vote of confidence, and that's what I told Charlie and Max."

"Thanks, Carole. You are a friend!"

"What's next on your agenda?" Carole wanted to know.

"I have reading to do before my next class, and I better get to it."

Carole had to leave. "I'll meet you back here after classes." And off she hurried.

She was concerned for Serena—her first day at a new school and away from home. She was sure Serena felt a bit of homesickness. Carole wanted to be there for her friend, and so had taken the walk back from the library, to their room.

That evening, they had barely settled down to studying when the phone rang. Serena, the closest to it, picked it up. It was Charlie. After a few pleasantries, she handed the phone to Carole.

"Was it okay for dinner Saturday night?" he wanted to know.

"We'll be with Max and Serena."

Charlie seemed a bit flustered. "I'll have to go." He was calling from work and added, "We're really busy. See you Saturday!"

Charlie worked part-time in a drug store, and went to school evenings. He would graduate the spring of 1941. He was disappointed, having wanted to graduate with Max, but Charlie had financial problems. His goal was to get his degree in Pharmacy. His father had died young, and Charlie lived with his widowed mother. She was a seamstress and had supported herself and her son. Charlie had a deep love for her. He hated to see her work so hard—as she did—often so tired. It had worried him and growing up with that, gave way to his "moods."

Now, Charlie working helped, but she insisted he graduate. The going wasn't easy, and the "moods" happened often. Charlie counted himself "lucky." Carole loved him, even with his many "moods." He was a good guy. She knew it and told herself that many times.

For a long time, Charlie never talked about his problems. He had opened up once to Max, first—and later, to Carole—and then clamped up. But Max learned when Charlie was in one of his "moods," his friend was in deep pain and couldn't talk about it.

One day Charlie was in one of his "moods." He came over to see Max, and Max sensed his friend needed to talk to him. Max listened, never interrupting, never offering advice—just listening to the pain his friend was letting go. Charlie told him later, "Thanks, Max. I needed you and you were there." Their friendship grew. Max was always there caring—just being his friend—and Charlie and Max were closer than brothers. Charlie, a plain down-to-earth person was someone Max could confide in.

Carole, too, who had fallen in love with Charlie, who was funny and kind, learned to jolly him out of his "moods" when she could. Sometimes his mood was too dark and wouldn't go away. When this happened, Carole and Max were affected by his mood swings, but they were loyal. Most of the time, he was fun to be with and interesting to listen to. He would talk about the different medications and how they helped people. He loved his work and always had some new drug to tell about. "Doing for mankind." That was important to him. He knew a lot about many things and read whatever he could lay his hands on. When people asked when he did his reading, he jokingly laughed, "In my spare time, of course!" It was obvious to those who knew him, there wasn't much spare time in his hectic schedule.

A little before eight, Max called. He was anxious to know how classes had gone for Serena. Then about Saturday night, "Was it okay?" He gave her a little rundown of their plans.

"I'm looking forward to it, Max." Before he hung up, he said softly, "I love you." Serena always felt a sort of elation after talking with Max. With pulses throbbing, she thought of him close to her, his warmth, and the wonderful smell of him—and she could feel herself blushing.

By the middle of the week, Serena found herself inundated with assignments. Max called several times and missed her. When she finally got to speak to him, she explained the research she was busy with and the many visits she had made to the Reference Library Department. It was for a paper due the end of the week. She was determined to get it done and done well. She reminded him, she had promised her mother and Saul, "School will come first." For both of them, wanting to be together, the promise was sometimes difficult to keep. This often meant a bit of tension between them.

Added to this was the disturbance and interference into their lives of the continuing war news from abroad. At first a little concern to Americans, who went about their everyday business, seemingly oblivious to what was happening, now listening intently, trying to digest what they were hearing—the ominous reports of an escalating-spreading war in Europe.

During that September of 1939 when Serena started school at the University of Washington, Germany invaded Poland. Hitler gave as one of his reasons for the invasion—an attack by Polish troops on a German radio station. The "bizarre" Polish attack was faked by the Gestapo.

Hitler's method was "Blitzkrieg"—a lightning war. First, air attacks without warning destroyed most of the defender's air force still on the ground. Second, bombers hit rail and road communications, munition dumps and civilian centers, causing confusion and panic. Third, planes, diving looked for marching men, and bombed them. At the same time, the planes machine-gunned the refugees as they tried to escape from the enemy soldiers. This caused crowded roads, which prevented the moving forward of the defending soldiers. As this war came out of the sky, it was also on land—with tank, artillery, and infantry moved in motor vehicles. After damage was inflicted by bombing, the soldiers came in, occupied the area, and dealt with whatever resistance was left.

Hitler's aim when he invaded Poland was to regain land lost in 1918, to put it under German rule. He ordered S.S. Death Head regiments to go behind infantry advance to conduct what was called "security measures" behind German lines.

These "measures" were explained to assembled officers at one of the concentration camps. They would have to kill or put in prison every enemy of Nazism. They were to be dealt with most severely, which the 'Death Head' regiments had learned in the concentration camps. The first enemy was Jews!

These words were soon translated into the most evil of deeds. Jews and Poles were to be the victims of this war—behind the war on the fronts. The 'Death Heads' were ruthless, and atrocities were widespread. Soldiers fought on the fronts while the civilian population was being killed behind the lines. This was the beginning of the Second World War, one of the most destructive conflicts in history!

With Hitler's Blitzkrieg in Poland, Warsaw and other cities fell. Homes, churches, and synagogues were filled with people from the cities—then set on fire. Those trying to escape were machine-gunned down. Mass executions took place. Thousands were sent to harsh labor camps where they were worked to death, but there were always enough replacements. The program was one of "racial extermination!" All Jewish properties were to be handed over to Aryans! While some Jews waited to be sent away, they were kept in certain areas and forbidden to be out after five o'clock. Many were shot for being even one minute late.

Both Britain and France, allies of Poland, helped with bombing raids, but Germany was well prepared and a strong enemy. In one month, in October, Poland was defeated! Germany was in complete control of the country.

Hitler now set the date, November 12th, for the attack on France, Belgium, and Holland, but it had to be postponed because of bad weather—but the killings, atrocities, executions of Jews were carried out by men who were anti-Semites, appointed by Hitler as trustees of the German cause in Poland—"to Germanize it fresh."

Jews expelled from these regions, conquered by Germany, were relocated in other places where they would be for a short period and then sent to concentration camps or labor camps where death awaited them. The month was November.

Inmates of the camp did not count the days. There were other things to think about. "What would happen as the hours of the day moved on? Who would live or die that day? Would there be water or a piece of stale wormy bread? Where was the family? Where was God? It was hard to pray to God. Had He forgotten them? What had they done? Why were they here?" Their tragedy lived in their minds—tortured minds and broken hearts in weakened bodies. Why?

That November in America, Thanksgiving holiday was approaching and Serena went home to be with family and then came back for Christmas and Hanukkah.

There were letters, lots of calls and gifts exchanged between Serena, Max, Carole, and Charlie. In the letters, as always, Max honest, direct, and straightforward about his feelings for her, told her he loved her. Serena could tell Max she loved him, too. The more times they were together—the more sure each became of the importance of their relationship.

His letters questioned if she could spend New Year's Eve in St. Louis. They would be with Carole and Charlie. "Please come," he pleaded. "I miss you!" Saul and Mrs. Warner gathered from Serena's conversations with them, she wanted to be with Max. She had shared the fall and winter holidays with them. They had many family conversations, knew Max had become an important part of her life, and were happy for her.

Mrs. Warner had been thankful. Max was a splendid young man—pleasant—a warm person, and she was sure they would be good for each other. In her heart she hoped, listened, but she didn't say too much. Both she and Saul could see the happiness in Serena's eyes and face when the subject was "Max." In the end, the choice would have to be Serena's.

VIII
Age of Innocence Maturing

The New Year came with so many changes. The "foursome" were planning to spend the celebration at the Park Plaza with dinner and dancing. On the way there, they talked about their future. Max was graduating in June getting his degree and was going into his father's shoe business. Serena would get her degree in journalism and hopefully get a position on a magazine or on the *St. Louis Globe.* Then she thought awhile, *I might find something in Madison. I'll have to wait and see.*

They drove about a mile down the highway, and Max pulled over to the curb. "I have something for you and I want to give it to you now."

He turned on the light and put a small black velvet box in her hand. Her heart almost stopped beating—or was it racing. She couldn't remember—when she told the story later.

"Open it!" he urged. "Open it, Siri."

Serena's fingers trembled and fumbled, and he had to help her. Finally it opened to reveal its lovely contents—a gold ring with a small sparkling diamond.

"Oh, Max, it's so beautiful!"

He took it and put it on her finger. He held her hand. "Will you marry me? You know I love you. I've said it often. I love you!" He said it simply and with sincerity. "I'll try my best to make you happy."

"Yes. Oh, yes, Max. I do want to marry you, too."

"I promise you my love forever," he said. Then Max took her in his arms. They were strong and she felt safe there. He held her for a while.

"We better get going. Charlie and Carole will wonder what happened to us." Serena thought they should go. "We're late picking them up."

She was so happy. She couldn't explain it, but this whole thing of dating was like a game—played haphazardly by many, with no thought of real connected feelings—of truly caring—they knew none of that. It was often filled with untruths and falsehoods. It went on and on, with hope in trying to reach the 'mountaintop,' then the hopelessness, that comes from no real commitment, sets in. Once more there are one or two players, and the game begins all over again.

Only couples truly in love know they will be together at the top of their mountain. Max and Serena had climbed to their mountaintop—now there was the safe feeling—a secure feeling—they belonged to each other. They were embracing again, and he held her tight and passionately kissed her. When she could catch her breath, she asked, "Can we stop and call Saul and my mom, and your parents?"

They stopped at the drug store and first called Charlie and Carole, apologizing for being late. "Something came up. I'll tell you when we see you," Max explained to Carole.

They called the Kellers first. They had been nervously waiting at home, knowing Max was going to give Serena the ring. They congratulated the couple and thanked them for letting them know.

"We've grown to love you, Serena, and we're so happy to have you in the family. We'll see you tomorrow."

"Thank God, Max made a good choice. He loves her and they'll be happy." Mrs. Keller was weeping. "Why are you crying?" he asked. "You should be happy." She tried to explain it to him.

"*Men,*" she thought. After all these years of togetherness, he still didn't know when she was happy or not.

Mr. Keller, on the other hand, saw it from a different perspective. "Women, they cry when they're happy, and they cry when they're sad. Go figure them out!"

In Madison, Mrs. Warner and Saul were ecstatic, congratulating the new couple and wishing them many happy years together. Later, Mrs. Warner took her turn at crying; but hastened to assure Saul. These were tears of happiness.

"Oh, my." She clasped her hands together, "Just think Serena's going to be a bride." That was something every mother hopes and prays for. They called Dave to tell him and Ressel.

Serena and Max took off, smiling from ear to ear. They found Carole and Charlie waiting. The minute they got in the car, Serena said, "Put the light on—we have something to show you."

She put her hand out so Carole and Charlie could see it.

"Oh, Serena, it's just beautiful!" Carole was genuinely happy for her friend. If there was a twinge of envy, she didn't show it.

The couples talked back and forth as they neared their evening's destination.

As they parked, Max, his voice emotion-filled, said, "We're going to celebrate tonight!"

There was silly, happy talk as they were being shown to their tables, decorated with colorful streamers and silly little hats the revelers would wear later. Charlie, however, had other ideas; he insisted they put them on right away. Carole picked hers up and found a small box under it. She looked a little startled.

"Open it up, Carol." Charlie sounded so excited.

You could tell he was nervous. He accidentally tipped one of the water goblets on the table.

Serena was getting goose bumps. She loved her good friend and was getting fidgety. Max already knew what was going to happen. Charlie had confided that he was going to ask Carole to marry him. Charlie knew Max had the same idea about Serena. They decided to do it New Year's Eve, and they didn't want to do it together.

They wanted their girls to savor their big important moment individually—then together. Charlie put Carole's ring on and told her how much he loved her. "Will you marry me, Carole honey?" He asked.

Carole began to cry—Serena, too.

"I know, I know," Max told Charlie. "They're crying because they are happy!"

Carole, with sobs, answered Charlie's big question. "Yes, Charlie, you know I love you."

Both couples were embracing, and people at other tables were sensing something out of the ordinary was happening and began applauding them. Someone asked the band leader to play

Irving Berlin's "Always." The two newly engaged couples began dancing.

Serena said chokingly, "I'll always remember this moment, Max."

He held her tighter. "Me, too, Siri!"

At the table, before they sat down, Charlie and Max hugged each other—and Serena and Carole were hugging and laughing, and holding up their hands with their beautiful rings.

Carole and Charlie went to call Carol's father and Charlie's mother. Both parents were very happy, congratulating them. Charlie and Carole promised they would see them the next day—New Year's Day.

The evening was so fun filled—before they knew it, the crowd was counting down to midnight to celebrate the incoming new year. All stood up and sang "Auld Lang Syne." There were wishes, handshakes, and kisses from strangers—happy for these lovers—newly engaged. All agreed—"What a night to remember!" The couples in love—friends together—life looked good with promises—promises of futures bright!

Max dropped Serena and Carole off, then took Charlie home. The two were so happy—they couldn't get over they were both engaged. "Wow!" Max said, "I can't believe it!" Before Charlie got out, they hugged each other.

"See you tomorrow!"

Back at the dorm, it didn't take Carole long to get to bed. "I want to dream about this wonderful night." But Carole didn't fall asleep, she lay there late, later into the night, and in her mind envisioned mail addressed to her, "Mrs. Charles Schwartz." She fantasized how wonderful that would be. Tonight there was a feeling of relief. She knew she and Charlie would be together always. She loved him and knew life with him would not be easy, but tonight there was a sort of closure to all her uncertainties about Charlie. There was a calming feeling about her, and she fell asleep thinking of Charlie.

Serena, too, had been mulling over the day with its magical ending. She put her arms together in a self-hug and lay there wide-eyed and content.

She smiled to herself. "Isn't life wonderful?"

And in the quiet of the night, wrapped in dreams—the wonderful dreams of youth in love, she was transferred to her own Eden.

It was New Year's Day. Max went to pick up Charlie, then to the dorm to get Serena and Carole. They were invited to the Kellers for breakfast. The Kellers were so happy to have them all there. There was talk and laughter and congratulations, again.

Then Charlie and Carole were going to see her father. She remembered her father's many comments and anxieties about Charlie's moods. Like a caring parent, he worried, his mind not at ease. She would try to assure her father. "He's okay, Dad. Charlie's okay."

Many times he wished his wife had lived—maybe she could have talked to Carole in a different way, a woman's way. Would that have made a difference? It made him sad when he thought of it and that was often. They came in and he congratulated them telling them how happy he was for them. He could see Carole was happy, so he supported her and wished the best for them.

He talked to Charlie. "I know you'll be good to Carole, Charlie." It sounded almost like a prayer.

They were at lunch as Carole's father talked to them about their plans. He spoke to Charlie and asked him if he would consider coming in with him in the drug store after he got his degree.

"If you would like, Charlie, we could be partners. Someday this would be yours. If you'd like that. I'd like nothing better than to have you here."

Charlie was overwhelmed. Mr. Berg had never discussed too much with him; all the time he was dating Carole. This made him feel good. It meant Mr. Berg accepted him.

"You can think about it. We'll change the name of the store to both our names. We'll be partners. If you think you'll be happy here." Charlie got up to shake his hand, but Mr. Berg hugged him instead. It felt good to Charlie—Mr. Berg hugged him like a father. That was something Charlie had missed all his life. It was new to him. Carole thanked her dad and hugged him. She was thankful—he was finally accepting Charlie.

They left to meet Charlie's mother. She had seen the ring. Charlie had shown it to her the night before when he went to pick up Carole. She was happy for Charlie. She knew he loved Carole, and she knew him to be a good-hearted person and would be good to Carole. She had loved Carole for a long time and had hoped Charlie and Carole's relationship would grow into something permanent.

Carole, through tears, smiled. "You will be like a mother to me."

They stayed for refreshments and then left—driving to the campus—walked around, then sat in the bleachers, talking about their future. They would both work hard. There was hope and promise, and they could see light at the end of the tunnel and they would reach it—they were young—and in love and the world welcomed young lovers!

The St. Louis winter had been a warm one—rain and cool mornings gave way to climbing temperatures in the mid-seventies. This was a pleasant change for Serena who was used to the Central Plains weather of freezing temperatures and lots of snow blown about by cold northerly winds.

"It's nice," she had remarked to Carole, "not to have to wear snow boots and heavy coats and jackets." Carole couldn't imagine it!

The spring quarter at school began—hectic months for all of them with school and work. Then there were the pleasant get-togethers of the families of the engaged couples. Having the same circle of friends meant the couples were usually together. Serena and Max managed to attend a few parties given by friends of the Warner family. As always, it was a source of enjoyment for Serena to visit Madison and be with family. It was a fun time, and yet there were serious moments—serious thoughts for both of them. They were slowly being introduced to what would be part of their future lives together.

Young couples in love have their optimism to guide them through this stage. Everything is upbeat. They look at the world through rose-colored glasses and time is forever.

Graduation came on a perfect St. Louis summer day and exercises were held outdoors. For Max, it was a culmination of four years of hard work. There had been moments of discouragement and frustrations, but he had made a commitment to his goal and had accomplished what he had set out to do.

Max's parents were so proud and all of them—Serena, her mother, and Saul sat together. Charlie and Carole sat in the row behind them. They all looked for Max and finally saw him in the long line of graduates marching up to receive their degrees. What a wonderful moment to treasure and remember.

Everyone came back to the Kellers for a little celebration. It was exciting to receive the congratulations of family and friends, and Max had a feeling of overwhelming satisfaction. He was proud of himself and that felt good.

Later Max and Charlie drove the girls back to the dormitory. Serena wanted to walk a bit and set out with Max. Charlie and Carole stayed in the car, busy with saying their "good nights." Max held Serena's hand as they walked. He told her of the plans his father had discussed with him. He was to be given more responsibility. He would help with the buying and would be given one of the stores downtown. The plans were for the store to support Max and Serena when they were married. Their wedding was planned for July of the next year, a month after Serena's graduation.

"Oh, Max," Serena was so pleased. She had great respect for his parents. "That's so wonderful of them to do this for us. We're lucky!

"Just think, we have all these exciting things to look forward to, my graduation—our wedding—and your own store!"

He agreed with, "We have a busy year ahead of us. We'll do it together."

They had started back and were almost at the stairs of the dorm. Max stopped to embrace her. "Hold me tight, Max." He kissed her and she returned warm loving kisses on his face and lips.

"I love you, Serena. Love you so."

"I know, Max, and I love you!"

Carole came out of the car followed by Charlie. It seemed he needed to give her one more kiss.

Max went to work at the store and found the new things he was learning about running the store were exciting. His father was teaching him the know-hows of being a buyer. One thing he found was that it wasn't as easy as it looked. There was much to learn, what to buy and how much. It had to be merchandise the customers wanted. It was a huge responsibility, and Max was determined to shoulder it all. He learned by trial and error. Sometimes the errors were a bit costly, but Mr. Keller, a patient man, would explain the problems and encourage his son.

"Don't worry," he would say. "We all make mistakes, but benefit only if we learn from them!" Max found that to be true and validated his father's trust in him by seeing to it—the blunder was never repeated. Max had a close relationship with his father. Working with him now, his respect and admiration grew even more.

That June when Max graduated, the news from overseas became more worrisome. Max had met with different groups and there was discussion with customers about the situation. Some talked about joining the Reserves. Some thought the Navy was best. "You're on a ship and can sail around the world!" A classmate of Max's had been thinking of doing that. The discussions went on and when they left, the perplexing question of "What to do?" was still up in the air.

At the same time Max was graduating, the news from Europe was that the Germans, using their "Blitzkrieg" method, had successfully invaded and swallowed Poland, Norway, Denmark, Belgium, Holland, and France—a country at a time! They had met with fierce resistance in the defending countries. Thousands perished. The countries overrun by the Germans, had forces, now training in Britain and were given American rifles as soon as they arrived from America. America was sending the much needed armaments.

President Roosevelt, constantly in touch with Prime Minister Churchill, received correspondence telling of the 'drastic need' for planes and ships to halt the Germans. Roosevelt gave Britain, American destroyers, and got the use of British bases in the Caribbean and Western Atlantic, for the American Fleet. The country was concerned that America would become part of the war. Roosevelt, in one of his "Fireside Chats," explained that U.S. naval ports would see to it that the help Britain needed so urgently, would get there. That was a priority because things in Britain were getting worse.

Roosevelt, in another speech, told Americans we were going to build up defense and armaments to help people abroad who were battling aggression and by so doing were keeping it from our country. The situation was very grave. He told the country of the need to mobilize all citizens—men and women—property and money to help make American defense work. The Allies were constantly hit with bad news—Germany, Italy, and Japan signed a ten-year agreement. This alliance was called "The Axis!"

That same June 1940, a bill was proposed that called for peacetime military conscription, unheard of in American history. In Washington, hearings went on while German planes and British Air Forces battled over Britain. In St. Louis and around the country there were protestors.

The bill came before the Senate in August, and in the House of Representatives in September while German bombers were smashing and destroying England and thousands were being injured and killed.

The country did not want a peacetime draft and for a while forgot the bill, but on September 16th, Roosevelt signed the bill and it became law. The Selective Service Act—"The Draft" became an important factor in dealing with the lives of millions of American males between the ages of 18–64.

It limited the term of service to one year, and the Army was authorized to take up to almost 800,000 or so from those aged 21–35. This was the first draft—"The Compulsory Training Act." American Youth's Age of Innocence was maturing. Max and Charlie, and young men in college—had wanted to finish their schooling. They did not object to a year in military service—if they were to fight, they would rather know how.

There was to be a national registration on October 16th. Max and Charlie registered. Through a complicated lottery system, the men were called as their numbers came up. Max and Charlie weren't too worried because the first monthly drafts were small—about 10 men from each 6,000 Selective Service

Boards or "Drafts Boards," and each board had a pool of over 3,000 registered men. Many felt they wouldn't be called for a long time.

For Max and Charlie, and the young men around the country, suddenly the everyday mail was of great interest. Sooner or later their mail would come with their orders to report. They called the notice their "greetings," since the letter began with "Greetings."

Charlie had graduated at the end of the spring quarter. He had done well and received congratulations from family and friends who understood the struggle it had been for him. Carole's pride in Charlie's accomplishments was something wonderful to see. She had a party—with Max and Serena, the Kellers, and Charlie's mother at her home. She was so pleased her dad wanted to do it. He entered in the festivities and had become more supportive.

Charlie had joined Mr. Berg in the drug store after more discussion of his future plans. The two seemed to work together—just fine. Carole's smile broadened every time she came into the store and saw Charlie and his white coat with the name plate that read: Charles Schwartz, Pharmacist. The atmosphere in the store was different—customers couldn't put their fingers on it. They came—stayed a bit longer—talking and discussing daily situations. They told Mr. Berg they really enjoyed talking with Charlie—Charlie's moods became more infrequent.

Serena and Max saw each other only on Saturday nights, but they talked on the phone. Serena was busy with school, preparing for graduation and their wedding in July. They managed a few weekends in April, looking for an apartment. Places were at a premium. There were very few "For Rent" signs on buildings. They found one at 707 Westgate in a part of St. Louis called University City. The buildings were mostly red brick, all looking pretty much alike. Here and there a few single homes divided the triplex or six-plex buildings.

They were met by the caretaker, Tony Lombardo, a man in his early forties. He spoke with an accent. Max asked him where he was from. "From Italy," he said. He had been here a few years. He told how glad he was to be here in the United States and not in Italy where the dictator, Mussolini, was head of the Italian government that had now joined the Axis with Germany.

His face became serious as he expressed concern about his family that he had hoped to bring to America. But arrangements couldn't be made now for their departure, and he agonized about their welfare. Max's empathy for Tony's situation was evident by the questions he asked, and Tony felt he was one who understood—and had opened up to him. It was a telling sign of how deeply most Americans felt about the war situation now engulfing most of Europe.

"Two apartments had been burned out by a careless tenant who had fallen asleep with a lit cigarette. They were being renovated," Tony told them. It was night but he could show them the apartments if they liked. They wanted to see the one on the second floor. They climbed the stairs, Tony shining his flashlight until they got to the landing. He opened the door to the apartment. It smelled clean, of fresh paint. It was dark; the electrical work had not been completed. They were shown through the front rooms quickly, Mr. Lombardo leading with the flashlight. The rooms looked good, as much as one could see at night with the beam of the flashlight moving around quickly. He then opened the bathroom door; there was no window in it and two pigeons, roosting on the tub, with a flutter of wings flew out noisily, frightening Serena. Mr. Lombardo apologized, "They won't hurt you," he said. "We'll have the window in this week."

Serena and Max liked the apartment and wanted to see it in the daytime. Mr. Lombardo was nice, but firm. They had to decide or forfeit it. "There was a long list of would-be tenants." By the time they came back down the stairs, Serena and Max had decided to take it. They had been disappointed so many times. Downstairs near the cars, Max handed him the deposit and Mr. Lombardo made out a receipt. The two men shook hands. Max asked about the other apartments. The third floor wasn't rented. There were many who wanted it, but a decision had not been made. The first floor apartment was rented to a couple who had been there for a few years. "They're nice!" That was Tony's assessment of them.

Driving home Serena snuggled close to Max. "That's one worry settled. We have our own apartment. Won't that be wonderful—our own place?"

Max agreed. "Do you really like it, Siri?" She answered by putting her hand under his arm and nestled her head on his shoulder. They stopped at the Kellers to tell them the good news. Then Serena called her mother and Saul. Both families were excited and pleased to hear things were going forward. Tony had called when the apartment was finished, and Serena and Max, anxious to see their apartment again, brought a lamp, two bridge chairs and an end table. They sat in their living room—full of hope, making plans.

On Sunday they invited Carole and Charlie to see it. Carole stood staring longingly around the apartment. Serena noticed, came up, and put her hand on Carole's shoulder. "Someday soon you'll have your own place too."

Charlie and Max had been discussing different aspects of their work when the girls came back into the room. They got up and gave the chairs to the girls, then sat down in a semi-circle.

Charlie surprised them by opening the conversation with, "Would it be a problem if we moved close to you guys?"

"Problem?" Serena and Max were delighted.

In love, content with life, Max said "Wouldn't that just be the tops?"

Max told them about Tony.

"If you like, I'll speak to him about an apartment. I don't think the one upstairs is rented. Maybe he can show it to you!"

"That would be just great, Max!" Charlie was so appreciative.

The girls were ecstatic. "We might be neighbors." To them, in their minds, the wonderful possibilities of that were endless!

Max called Tony the next day—the third floor apartment was rented, but Tony would keep them in mind.

Summer was in full swing—warm days with high humidity, as preparations for another graduation forged ahead.

The crowd of parents and friends and families began gathering—waiting for the commencement exercises. Programs were put to use as fans, waving back and forth trying to move the stubborn hot air without much success. Every once in a while, a few clouds moved in and then it didn't seem so warm, but the weatherman had promised, "There would be no rain." Then the movement of the white program sheets could be seen again.

Max and his family and Serena's family sat together—eager and full of anticipation—happy at this auspicious event. Serena and Carole sat in the front rows reserved for the graduates—but in different sections. Charlie was there with his mother and Carole's father. The university band struck up, and people, last-minute arrivals, hurried to their seats. Speeches began, some a little too long for this warm afternoon, then finally the graduates came up to get their degrees. The audience applauded and whistled as family members came up. There were tears and smiles as Serena and Carole received theirs.

The Kellers had open house for both Serena and Carole. Friends came and the evening sped along as it does when people are having an enjoyable experience. Today had been special—and tomorrow was another day. One by one the guests began to leave. Charlie, Carole, and their parents were thanking the Kellers again for wanting to give Serena and Carole the open house for graduation. The families had become close friends. There were hugs and embraces and kisses enough going around—then it would start again.

Mr. Berg took Charlie's mother home, and Charlie and Max took the girls back to the dorm. The girls were giving up their dorm apartment.

Saul and his mother were staying with the Kellers. They were leaving early in the morning—back to Madison! They had a busy few days going over wedding plans with the Kellers. They were anxious to get back, as there was much to do.

So the evening—a wonderful, memorable one—ended.

Serena and Max spent the week fixing up their apartment. They had gotten a few new pieces of furniture with money the families had given them for wedding gifts. Like all couples in love, the thought and pleasure of putting their own place together, gave them an almost unbelievably new feeling of independence—their own first home. Max, struggling, fixed the curtain rods for the bathroom. Serena was so proud of him as he put up pictures in the spaces she had designated for them. Then they would step back and admire his handiwork. It was wonderful and they loved everything they put in their apartment.

Serena's mother had sent a few pieces she had wanted from her room, and the Kellers sent some of the things Max wanted. They spent the following Sunday setting up the furniture—then moved it around again. When they were satisfied with the changes, they sat looking around and enjoying their own private haven. They were thankful for everything. They knew they were lucky and said it.

Max took her in his arms and kissed her, nuzzling her on the neck and ear—holding her—not wanting to let her go. "I love you, Serena. I'll always love you!"

Serena stepped back and looked at him, "I love you, too, Max!"

She couldn't believe how much she had grown to love him during the past year. Her love for him was so strong. Every time he held her or kissed her, she felt goose-bumps. They were the thrill of him near her. She didn't discuss this with anyone; this was private. She loved him—this was the way he affected her. She was happy to be with him. He loved her. He had told her she made him happy. They were good together.

Max took Serena's arm. "We don't have too much longer to wait."

The wedding was only three weeks away.

IX
Love, Weddings, Beautiful World

Serena came home to help with some of the wedding plans, and she found her mother and Saul had done a very thorough job in getting almost everything organized.

Being a bride put her in a special category, according to them. Saul began to call her "Princess." Nothing she could say could dissuade them, so she finally let them do the things they wanted to do for her. She loved the way the attention they gave so lovingly, made her feel, and made them happy doing it. Wedding invitations had been sent to family and friends and that included one to Jennifer. Gifts began arriving at the home in Madison and some to the Keller home. They waited for answers to the invitations. Saul was especially interested in the one from Jennifer. She answered she was 'happy to come,' and Saul was ecstatic—didn't say much—didn't have to. His mother knew.

Serena had shopped with her mother and Saul for her wedding dress. When she came out with her first choice for them to see, her mother began to cry and even Saul became misty-eyed. After two others, they decided on the first one. Serena loved it!

Carole was to be maid of honor and Charlie, Max's best man. Saul was taking what would have been his father's honor—Saul would give Serena away. Max and his family came a few days before the wedding date and were staying at a nearby hotel. Carole and Charlie and parents arrived two days earlier and were staying at the same hotel with Max and his parents. There was a wedding rehearsal, and everything went fairly well that night. The wedding was to be held in the Shaare Emet Synagogue at three o'clock Sunday, with a dinner after the cocktail hour to be held in the dining room.

The beautiful morning of the wedding day arrived, and Serena, who had not slept much, was up early. The date was July

1, 1941. "Today is finally here!" She lay there thinking happy thoughts. She would remember this day always.

There was much to do. She, her mother, and Mrs. Keller had appointments for their hair at the beauty salon. Then Carole and Charlie's mother were coming for theirs. It was a very busy morning. After the ladies left, the house was quiet for a few hours.

Saul had been mulling over Jennifer's coming to the wedding. He had this feeling of wanting to talk to her since receiving Jennifer's answer to the wedding invitation. He wanted to call her. He hadn't spoken to her for a long time, but she had never left his mind or heart. He wrestled with, "Should he call or shouldn't he?" That was the question. He finally decided, "He would!"

They would meet for coffee. He would pick her up in half an hour. "Is that enough time?" he asked.

"Fine!" was her answer. She tried to sound low-key, but inside she was apprehensive. "Why?" She wondered. "What would he say?"

She had debated about answering the wedding invitation, thinking she shouldn't go. She didn't want to hurt Saul's mother or Serena, so she wrote that she would be happy to come.

At the restaurant, when he saw her, his heart did a big "Loopy De Loop!" He, now, knew for certain what the ache and loneliness in him meant. He had missed her so much and had lived with denial for so long. For Jennifer, too, the blood came rushing to her face and neck, and there was a throbbing in her head. He was older—not in years, they were few—but there was a little gray at his temples, the result of all he had been through. She wondered, *how he thought she looked.* A little of her woman's vanity hoped he didn't find her too changed!

Saul's thoughts were, *How good it is to see her.* To him, she would always be lovely. The kindness was there in her face—and yes, a little of the pain they had both experienced by the separation, that almost destroyed both of them, had left its mark. He blamed himself. They sat almost like strangers. He began asking non-consequential questions and then they came tumbling out—feelings pent-up for a long time—being released, waiting to be said, wanting to be heard. "I love you, Jenny. I'll always love you. I'm sorry—so sorry." He said it over and over. "Can we begin again?"

Jennifer's eyes were welling up full of tears—that finally fell. She reached for a handkerchief. She was overcome with emotion. So much time had gone by—been lost. She didn't answer. He got up and moved to her side. He clasped her tightly with a kiss to her cheek, then his hungry mouth found her lips, and they were locked in each other's arms. His next words to her were, "Forgive me, Jenny. Can you ever forgive me for taking all this time out of our lives?"

She told him, "Answering the wedding invitation had not been an easy decision for me. We can try, Saul. I've never loved anyone but you."

He took her hand and looked intently into her eyes. "Jenny, will you marry me?"

She hadn't expected this. "Are you sure, Saul?"

"I'm sure, Jenny."

She couldn't say anymore. He was again smothering her with kisses. "Let's not wait too long to get married. Let's do it before the end of the year. What do you think?"

"We can try." She looked happier then when she had come into the coffee shop.

"Jen, let's go tell your family and tell mine. I know they will be happy for us."

They got up to go—their untouched coffee cups forgotten. They left in a hurry, happy at the change of events—because one chose to answer an invitation, and the other could say, "I'm sorry," and ask for forgiveness. Their love was a more mature love now—made stronger by the test of youth and decisions—loving and waiting with pain and hurts that were forgiven. The forgetting—would that take longer? Their love would decide.

The photographer was waiting, and for a few hours, the scene was a hectic one. It seemed hundreds of photographs were taken of the bride and groom, pictures of different family groups and friends. Pictures were taken of the bride and groom under the "chupa," the bridal canopy, as is customary in Jewish weddings. It had been beautifully decorated with white roses and greenery. There were pictures of Charlie and Carole with the bride and groom, and one was taken of Dave and Ressel. They were not well, but they had made it, so happy to be at their granddaughter's wedding. It was all a wondrous getting together, a beautiful sight to see.

Rabbi Golden came, and signatures were taken on the "most important document of their lives" as Max would later remember it. It was almost time for the ceremony to begin. Ushers had been busy seating guests in the sanctuary, and now all was ready. The bridal party lined up ready. Ted Weiss, the violinist, and a friend of Max's, began to beautifully play, "The Wedding March." Saul escorted his mother, and she was seated in front.

Mr. and Mrs. Keller escorted their son down the aisle to the steps. Max was nervous and looked very serious. Carole, very pretty, dressed in a pale green gown came down escorted by Charlie. Saul now escorted Serena. When she appeared, everyone turned to see her—beautiful in the lovely white gown—short veil encircled with a wreath of orange blossoms. Slowly, they came down and everyone commented on the breath-taking sight. They stopped at the steps, and Saul put Serena's hand in Max's. They went up together to the canopy where the Rabbi, maid of honor, and best man were waiting.

Rabbi began the wedding service with prayers—then explaining to the bride and groom the Judaic laws of marriage. Then Max and Serena entered the service with their pledges to each other, "to care for one another, forsaking all others—be true to one another," as they exchanged wedding rings. Ann's tears fell but she didn't call attention to herself by wiping them away. Her thoughts were of Robert. How proud and happy he would have been to see Serena married.

During the ceremony, Ted softly played, Irving Berlin's, "Always." Rabbi blessed the couple and Max was asked to stomp on the napkin-covered glass, smashing it. "A symbol," the Rabbi said, "that even in the midst of happy occasions, we remember the destruction of the Temple in Jerusalem."

The couple and attendants followed the parents out—almost dancing down the aisle to the music of "Bride and Groom—Mazel-Tov!" The receiving line was happy with the congratulations given to them. It seemed everyone was talking at the same time. There was a heart-stirring excitement in the air. It seemed everyone was delighted to be there and all agreed—it was a beautiful wedding!

The guests entered the dinner hall that had beautifully decorated tables and as they were finding their seats, the band played. When all were seated, the bridal couple was announced: "Here are Mr. and Mrs. Max Keller." Everyone applauded as they found their way to the bridal table, where the parents, Saul and Jennifer, Dave and Ressel, and Carole and Charlie were sitting.

Saul and Jennifer were in earnest conversation. Carole's head was bent downward, and Charlie was talking to her. The music was loud and the room was noisy, but Carole heard him: "We'll be next, honey!" Their wedding was to be August 20th, Serena would be the matron of honor, and Max best man.

Saul had given Jennifer a new engagement ring and two wedding bands. They wanted to be married soon. Theirs would be a small wedding.

After dinner, the young couples were dancing. The bride and groom appeared before leaving. They were staying at the hotel in Madison for their honeymoon and were planning to leave for St. Louis in the morning. The Kellers had to be back for the stores. 'Good-byes,' embraces, and kisses went the rounds, and then the bride and groom left amidst applause. Guests began leaving, and the caterers and staff began to clean-up.

The Kellers thanked Mrs. Warner and Saul for the beautiful wedding. They said their 'good-byes' as they too, were leaving in the morning. Carole and Charlie were leaving that night. Charlie had to be back at the drug store.

At the hotel, the newlyweds did some of their packing. Max left an early wake-up call at the desk. Their train would leave at 6:00 A.M. They couldn't be late. Max had to be back. Serena seemed to take a long time in the bathroom and when she came out in a lovely off-white, satin, lace-trimmed gown, Max's voice became husky as his eyes devoured the loveliness of her. "You're beautiful, honey, so beautiful!"

In a few minutes, he followed her to bed—turning off the lamp on the table near him. He put his arm around her, and for a while they spoke of the wedding—confessing to each other they had been nervous and worried something would go wrong. Now, they were more than satisfied—their families had given them a beautiful wedding that left them with wonderful memories.

Max turned to her and kissed her. She snuggled closer. "Are you happy?" he asked. "Oh, yes, Max." She loved him. So many times she had pondered the wonder of it all, that by chance she had met Max—fallen in love and married him. She was with her thoughts while his lips were seeking hers and found them, opening and closing in more passionate kisses, as his arms enclosed her. All the hungry wanting and waiting, the love within them now exploded into the bliss of the union of their bodies, their hearts, and their souls. In their intertwining they were locked safely as one. Here was ecstasy!

After the lovemaking, they lay there, each with his own thoughts. Serena with her thoughts of the moment. Max was her first. She had given herself wholeheartedly to her husband. They had never talked about it, so she didn't know if she was Max's first. She hoped so. Max's thoughts were of Serena and how much he loved her. He had known other girls, but in Serena, he had found someone special. Remembering the wedding ceremony, he would love her always! They fell asleep—his arms about her.

It was late, late afternoon when they arrived at the station in St. Louis. Max hailed a cab to their apartment. It was good to climb the stairs to the second floor. Max put down the luggage and opened the door, then turned to Serena, swooped her up, and carried her over the threshold. "I didn't think I was going to be able to do that," he kidded her as he set her down and embraced her in a lingering kiss. "We're home, Siri! We're home!" He had a broad grin on his face. Her voice, too, was full of gladness.

"Yes, it's wonderful, Max, to be here in our own place." They were tired—so much had happened in the weekend—but their faces reflected the joy and delight of that memorable moment.

The beginning of their married life in their own surroundings—their first home!

Carole and Charlie had thus far been unsuccessful in locating an apartment, but they decided to go ahead with their wedding. They were going to stay at Carole's home, and had hopes that something would turn up before too long. On August 20th, they were married. Max was Charlie's best man, and Serena was Carole's matron of honor. Mr. Berg was to escort his daughter down the aisle. When he saw her in the bridal gown and veil carrying a lovely bouquet of miniature white roses, his eyes became misty and the lump in his throat was hard to swallow. She looked beautiful, like her mother!

His thoughts were of his wife. She had been on his mind so often, during the wedding preparations. He wished with all his heart she were here beside him to share the happiness, their daughter's wedding.

He whispered to Carole, "I know your mom is with us—happy and proud of you."

Mr. Berg held her arm going down to where Charlie waited before the altar.

It was a small gathering of friends, and as you would expect, Charlie was a little nervous—especially when Max forgot which pocket held the rings. After a few minutes, actually it was really only a few seconds, he finally produced them—much to Charlie's relief. After the ceremony, the couple received the many wishes for happiness. Everyone was in a festive mood, and there were more congratulations. The newlyweds were beaming.

The table holding wedding gifts was overflowing, and Carole couldn't believe how wonderfully generous friends and family were. There was a lovely dinner at the Park Plaza and about ten o'clock many had gone. They had been there from almost three o'clock that afternoon. The couple slipped off for their one-night honeymoon at a hotel, but they wouldn't say where it was. They didn't leave until all the guests had gone. Max and Serena promised to see the parents of the bride and groom home safely.

Both Carole and Charlie wanted to stay at the Park Plaza, the place that held so many wonderful memories for them. This special night, their wedding night, would be another. Carole, a little nervous, asked Charlie if they could go out for a little walk. Charlie, understanding, said, "Sure." It was a wonderful evening out, the lights around the area made it a special place. There were not too many out walking at this hour, but they didn't notice. Charlie held her arm and listened as Carole talked about their lovely wedding. Charlie was quiet for a while, thinking his own thoughts. His thoughts were of Carole. "I'm so glad we're married, Carole. I love you, honey." He put his arm on her shoulder and they stopped walking. He kissed her. Then they stood locked in an embrace. A few folks walked by and turned to look. Carole and Charlie were unmindful of them. It was as if they were the only two people in the world.

Later, Carole came to bed after brushing her teeth for the "umpteenth time," as Charlie later explained to Max. Before Charlie came to bed, he pulled back one of the window drapes and turned off the light. Looking out over the city, most of it still lit up, he remarked, "It's beautiful out there, Carole. It's a beautiful world." Then he came to bed. He turned to face Carole.

"You're so beautiful, Mrs. Schwartz. What are you doing here with this guy?" He was kidding her as he put his arm around her. Carole had been a little nervous, and Charlie had taken the edge off of that.

She entered into the spirit of it and answered, "He's my husband and I love him." Charlie kissed her gently on the lips. "And I love you, Mrs. Schwartz!" he whispered.

His mouth was soft and warm on her neck, then moved down to her breasts, then to her neck and then up—hungrily to her lips. This sensation was new to Carole as she felt the warmth of his body. His arms held her tightly and his mouth pressed hers. He was young and strong. She had waited for the one love of her life. Charlie was that to her.

She abandoned her being to his love-making—soon they were lost in the fast beating of their hearts—the sweet warm passionate kisses, and the rush of all of it to their heads. The beauty of the moment stayed and they lay there, resting in each other's arms.

"You're mine, Carole!" He said it with such pride and wonderment. They lay there silent and content. He with his thoughts, she with hers. There was no need to talk—they were as one. She turned on her side, and he settled in close to her. Tired and happy, their day of days ended, the memory of it set back in their minds to remember time and time again.

The honeymoon couple were home the next day and soon settled into the everyday life. Charlie worked in the drug store with Carole's dad. Carole had gone on several interviews for a job she was pretty well prepared for. In her junior year at Washington U, she did student-teacher training under supervision, and then again in her senior year. She had received her certification in Elementary Education and wanted to teach at one of the schools in University City. It was in the area Max and Serena lived, and there was the hope Charlie and she would find a apartment there.

The end of August, Carole was called and advised she would be teaching the second grade class at Delmar-Harvard Elementary, which was located in University City. School opened the first week in September. Carole was so excited. It was what she wanted most—to help children. It was so important to her. Charlie and her dad were quite proud, and Charlie teased her calling her "Teach!" Serena and Max were invited to a dinner celebration to honor the new teacher.

The months hurried by, then Tony, the caretaker, called Charlie with good news. The apartment on the third floor was being vacated. The tenants were being transferred. Young men were enlisting for overseas assignment and some were being transferred to other states where companies needed replacements. Charlie and Carole came, that same night Tony called, to see the apartment. It was much like Serena's and Max's, so Mr. and Mrs. Charles Schwartz, happy with it, paid the deposit, and could move in—the first week in November.

Max was busy at the shoe store and its problems and would come home and find Serena disappointed; job hunting had been unsuccessful. She visited many newspapers, magazines, publishing companies, and came away with promises of calls that didn't happen. She told Max she didn't see too many women in these places and wondered why. Max would encourage her. "Don't worry. You haven't found the place for you, but it will happen. You'll see."

Max was right. It had taken time, but Serena's efforts to find her place in the world of journalism came to fruition. She received a letter asking her to call for an appointment to see a Mr. McGrath, the assistant editor of a local newspaper in one of the suburbs. Her appointment was for 9:30. She arrived a bit early and walked in exuding an air of confidence that belied the proverbial "butterflies in her stomach." A young woman at the reception desk showed her to the personnel department. There she filled out the necessary employment forms and then followed the discussion of the job requirements and salary. She listened but didn't care about the salary. She wanted the job.

She was sent to Mr. McGrath. For a few moments, she was ignored. Then he looked up and began questioning her about several aspects of the work. He wanted to know what she was most interested in writing about. He explained there were many aspects to this job—many things she would be called on to do.

"I want to try everything," She emphasized "want." "I am willing to learn to gain different perspectives on many things."

Mr. McGrath had stopped checking the papers he had, and he was looking at her and listening to what she was saying. He was thinking, *We can use this young woman. We don't hear enthusiasm like this very often.*

Mr. McGrath gave her a sheet of paper that had a title of a topic typed on it, "The Importance of Our Zoo." He asked her to do a column on it. She sat at a desk, thought for a moment—wasn't sure how she would tackle it. Then she began writing how she felt about the topic. It was very important to her. She had loved it from the first time she visited St. Louis. She thought St. Louisans were so fortunate to have it—a most enjoyable and learning experience.

She finished it—re-read it—then typed it on the "Royal" set to the side of the desk, and brought it to Mr. McGrath. He read it, nodding his head as if in approval. He liked it and so would the paper's readers. He asked could she start working the following Monday. She said, "Yes." Her heart was beating so fast, she thought he could hear it. He took her around and introduced her to some of her fellow workers. They were all men. She would have the desk "over there." He pointed. She thanked him and said she was looking forward to working there. He walked her to the door and shook her hand.

Out on the sidewalk, she leaned against the building and took a deep breath. It would be a learning experience, and she was determined to make the most of it, to do her best for this man who had put his faith in her and given her a chance. She hoped she would never disappoint him. She couldn't wait to tell Max the good news.

Charlie and Carole were planning to move the following weekend. Mr. Berg knew he would miss them. It was good having young people there, but he knew young people need their own place. The night before they were leaving, they spoke to Carole's father, letting him know how much they appreciated their stay with him. It had been good for all of them—living together. Charlie witnessed the love Carole and her father had for each other, and his father-in-law had treated him like family. Charlie had a great respect for him. Carole's father's concerns were alleviated when he saw how happy the couple were. He liked Charlie and thought of him as his son, even when Charlie was in a "mood," but the moods didn't come too often now.

With Carole working, it was taking longer to get settled in the apartment. There were boxes everywhere. Carole described it as "chaotic." They emptied a few boxes every night and worked like beavers on the weekends, but didn't seem to be making a dent in the situation.

Serena, discussing it with Max, decided to have them for dinner, thinking this would help Carole and Charlie. This being their first company, they also invited the couple in the first floor apartment, Bill and Elaine (Lainie) Hoffman. It would be a chance for Charlie and Carole to meet them.

Serena had spoken to Carole about the neighbors. She said they were very "likeable, cheerful, fun to be with." Carole and Charlie were anxious to meet them. Bill and Lainie came up, bringing a box of Fannie Farmer chocolates, which the host and hostess accepted graciously. Serena saying, "These milk chocolates are our favorites," then added, "This is also the first sort of house-warming gift given to us, which makes it something special."

This so pleased Bill and Lainie.

About ten minutes later, Charlie and Carole showed up. Charles brought a bottle of wine. Max was going to get glasses and serve it, but Charlie said, "No, save it. We got a few holidays coming up—like Thanksgiving."

"And what about the holidays in December and New Year's Eve?" Bill questioned.

Max and Serena had told them about the holidays the past two years and the good times they all had. Bill and Lainie had listened and so enjoyed the stories, they hoped they could be with the group on the next New Year's Eve.

"Okay, that's settled. We'll put it aside."

Max went to help Serena bring the food out, and soon they were enjoying a tasty dinner of hamburgers, mashed potatoes, and peas. There was soda pop to drink and ice cream and cookies for dessert. They were laughing and each one telling stories—Max about shoe customers or salesmen—Charlie about funny things in the drug store—children coming in to get five-cent ice cream cones, but only having one penny. They would look so disappointed at the thought of not getting their cones—they would start to cry. Carole's father told Charlie—to give the children the cones. Charlie told how quickly the tears would stop, to be replaced by smiles.

Carole told stories about the children—the funny things they said—sometimes blurting out secrets about their parents. Carole would be embarrassed. Then Serena told of different things that happened in the office of the newspaper. "There are a lot of arguments. Everyone has a different opinion about everything and there's a lot of discussion. I enjoy listening to all of it."

Charlie, talking to Bill, was telling that he worked in the drug store with Carole's father. When he asked Bill about his work, he found out that Bill worked with his brother, Joe, in their appliance store. It was a small place located in downtown, the older part of St. Louis that housed several fine department stores, Famous Barr and Stix, Baer and Fuller. Bill was telling how the war in Europe was affecting many businesses.

Max told of his problems in the shoe stores, and Charlie, very serious, couldn't put too much in business losses. He was concerned because drugs and medical supplies were short here, because they were needed for fighting men overseas. Drugs and supplies were needed home, but more importantly needed in Europe, Africa, and the Middle East where soldiers were wounded and dying.

The girls were sitting off by themselves talking to Lainie. Lainie had dropped out of college in her first year. She had to go to work. This was before she met Bill. She worked in one of the fine department stores in the downtown area. Lainie sold lingerie and loved working in the department that carried so many beautiful things. The department was always busy—men came into the department for birthdays, holidays, or anniversary gifts for wives, sweethearts, or girlfriends.

Lainie, a bubbling personality, was the perfect associate for that department. She made them all laugh when she related the many funny incidents that occurred when men, embarrassed, came in to buy. They very seldom knew the sizes they wanted. After they had come in a few times, Lainie was quite helpful. She kept a notebook with information such as sizes, colors, and dates to be remembered. Her customers depended on her, and she said, "We do our best to make them feel at ease. I love being there. They are so nice and appreciative!"

Charlie and Bill got up almost at the same time—it was time to go—but not before they planned to get together—after Thanksgiving to make plans for New Year's Eve.

They were saying their "Thanks" to Max and Serena. Charlie and Carole were grateful—they had been able to unpack a few boxes. One thing they all agreed on, "We're glad we're neighbors! Think of all the good times we can have next summer," Max was saying, as he put one arm around Charlie and one around Bill. The evening ended on that optimistic note.

The families in Madison and St. Louis had been in touch—making plans for Thanksgiving. The Kellers had invited Serena's family, Carole and Charlie, and their parents. Serena's family called with disappointing news. Travel for Ressel and Dave was not feasible because of their deteriorating health. Ann was having them and Jenny and her parents. They were all looking forward to spending the holiday together.

Serena had so wanted them to come. She missed them, and she had waited for them to see the apartment. They assured her there were other holidays and they would come. There had also been numerous calls—important ones. Saul had called—he and Jenny were to be married in the spring. Serena had accepted to be Jenny's matron of honor, and Dave was to be Saul's best man. There had been much excitement that week on the phone.

The holiday, the first Thanksgiving in their marriages, Mrs. Keller had made special gifts for the apartments of the two couples. "Just a small remembrance," she said. Of course, this was so unexpected, and Serena and Carole hugged Mrs. Keller. She was always so unassuming—so thoughtful. They agreed she was a warm, loving person.

Serena, talking to Carole, said, "Max is a lot like his mother and takes some other qualities from his dad!"

The table was beautifully set with a fruit centerpiece. They took their places and when they were seated, Mr. Keller welcomed them. They bowed their heads and he led them in prayer.

"Overseas," he said, "our brothers and sisters are suffering." He asked God to watch over them. He thanked God for bringing them together, for their blessings, and then asked for peace to come to the war-torn countries. They had listened silently and the prayer for peace was uppermost in their minds, too. Then they started on the holiday dinner, and little by little the mood became more jovial!

The food was very tasty, and they ate with such relish, enjoying every mouthful. There was talking, listening, and laughter, as in all close-knit family gatherings. Now, there were many, "No, thank-you" answers to questions of "Would you like some more?"

They finally had to admit, they were "stuffed!"

The young brides had contributed to the bounty—Serena with a "super pumpkin pie," and Carole with her "delicious cookies." Everyone complimented them and made such a fuss; the new husbands were bursting with pride.

The men adjourned to the living room to discuss business and of course, "the war overseas" and what was happening in St. Louis and America.

The ladies moved to the kitchen to "clean up!"

By the time they were finished, the men were ready to leave—there was work the next day. The host and hostess bid them all "good night." There were warm embraces and a feeling of contentment for a holiday spent with loved ones.

X
Candles and Bombs

It was the Saturday after Thanksgiving. Serena had come downtown to shop for a few gifts. First on her list was a gift for Max's birthday, December 6th. The large department stores, "Stix, Baer and Fuller," and "Famous Barr," in downtown St. Louis, were busy decorating windows and departments, for the approaching Christmas and Hanukkah holidays.

The shops on Delmar Boulevard were doing the same. Colorful wreaths of gold, red, and green were being hung on light poles. At intersections, high up on wires, stretching from one side of the street to the other, artificial garlands sparkled with small colored Christmas lights.

It all looked mighty festive, but folks couldn't seem to get into the holiday mood, so Serena planned a party for Max. She had invited the Kellers, her mother, Saul and Jennifer, Carole and Charlie, and the parents of each, and Bill and Lainie. They had all accepted with such eagerness and spirit. Serena hoped it would be a fun-filled evening. Serena stopped at a jewelry shop and found a silver chain with a Star of David. She was having it engraved and would pick it up during the week.

Max was working late, decorating the store with red-and-green crepe paper along the moldings on the wall. Then he put a few well-placed artificial poinsettia plants around and finished the windows. He stepped outside to check it all and was satisfied with the results. Tired, he closed the shop and headed home.

Serena was in her robe waiting for him. "You shouldn't have stayed up, Siri." He admonished her, but inside he felt a contentment. It was good to come home and find her there.

Max was getting ready for bed, but he came into the living room and turned on the radio. "Anything new on the news?" he called out to her.

"I was out shopping and didn't have time to listen," her voice came back. She came in carrying a tray with two cups of steaming hot tea. His favorite cookies she had picked up at Schenberg's market looked very tempting. They sat together, cozy, sipping slowly and listening intently to the late, late, evening news.

Max and Serena, like other young couples in St. Louis and around the country were busy dealing with everyday life. Everyday life now unfortunately included concerns over the Selective Service Act and how it would affect their lives. Serena and Max had discussions on what was the best thing to do. The news mentioned how many men had signed up. The total count for Missouri would be announced later. Max got up and turned the radio off. The news had disturbed him. He glanced through the newspaper and became engrossed in reading one of the detailed reports about the war news.

Max and Serena discussed part of it. He was always eager to hear her take on some of the news, and what they thought about it down at the paper. The discussion was short, and Serena knew there were many aspects troubling Max. He kissed Serena "good night," and after the lights were out, he lay there in bed, tossing and turning frequently going over it in his mind. He would have to discuss it with his father. If he took the training now, he wondered what was best to do with the store. He was an American and wanted to go. The country needed everyone to be prepared.

President Roosevelt had called on all. He addressed them, "My Fellow Americans"—and told them in a somber, worried tone, the need to do everything we could to help Britain who was fighting for her survival. If Britain fell—so would we. That was a point brought home forcefully to all Americans.

The Soviets had launched an attack on Finland. The country's small air force fought against the Russians—putting up a tremendous effort to fight back. Britain and France sent airplanes to help. Thousands perished in Finland—their cities were on fire. The Allied countries had great admiration for this small country—fighting valiantly against the military strength of Russia, but were finally defeated. The Soviets then took Lithuania,

Latvia, and Estiona. Germany now was planning to concentrate on taking Great Britain.

Hitler ordered his army, navy, and air force to prepare detailed plans for the invasion of Britain. German planes attacked Britain. The battle for Britain was fought in the skies. They pounded Britain night after night. Hitler's plan was to weaken the British in the air—to be able to claim superiority in the air before an invasion of the land could begin. Hitler made that his priority. The British, courageous and unyielding, took the unrelentless bombing and lived through it during the night—and saw the destruction and devastation at daybreak.

The week that followed was hectic for Serena. The company from Madison were due in Thursday evening. Serena's mother and Jennifer were to stay with the Kellers. Saul was coming in that night, Tuesday, and Max was to pick him up after work and bring him to the apartment. Serena was waiting—she as happy to see him as he was to see her; she rushed to hug him. "You look wonderful, Siri. I can see married life agrees with you." They all laughed. She took him by the hand and showed him around the apartment. He kept saying, "M-m-nice! Very nice!"

Later they sat in the kitchen and had a late dinner, Saul reporting news from Madison about her friends, her Uncle Dave and Grandmother, Ressel. Serena waited for him to speak of Jennifer—and when he came to that subject, his face lit up. "I think you know, Siri, how much I love Jenny. We're busy with plans for our wedding."

"Is it still in March?" she asked. "I'll talk to Jenny when I see her on Saturday, we have to discuss a few things."

Serena's mother called to talk to them all on the phone. It was late, but they each chatted a little. "Mom, I can't wait to see you!"

Saul told her how much he liked the apartment. Serena was working on Friday, so her mother wasn't going to see her daughter's place until the night of the party. She sounded a little disappointed; she had so wanted to see the place Serena had talked about so glowingly—the place where she knew her daughter was happy. She consoled herself, saying to Serena, "I guess I'll have to wait."

Saul then spoke to Jennifer, made plans to pick her up at noon, and take her to see Forest Park and the zoo he had so often talked about. Serena and Max stayed up late, getting things ready for Saturday night. It was called for 6:30. Saul had gone to bed, anxious for tomorrow to come so he could show Jennifer around.

Serena packed a picnic lunch for Saul and Jennifer, and he left in a happy mood to pick up his Jenny. He had Serena's car. Max took the afternoon off to help Serena with the last-minute details.

Jenny sat snuggled close to Saul as they drove along the scenic route to the park. Saul found a spot and parked near a grassy knoll. The sun was out, but the weather was fall-like. Saul took the basket, and Jennifer carried a blanket. They had gone a short way when Saul decided to go back. They definitely needed the sweaters left in the car. Jennifer waited and soon Saul came hurrying back, "Oh, yes," Jenny said. "This feels much better."

She thanked Saul. They walked—sauntering, looking for a "good spot."

Jennifer kept pointing to some breathtaking views around the lake and the changing colors of the shoreline foliage. Saul stopped at what he thought was a perfect spot. There was an abundance of trees for shade, and the sun's rays slanted down through them warming the spot—just enough.

Jennifer spread the blanket. "Are you hungry?" she asked. It was past noon.

"What a question," Saul answered. "You know, Jenny, I'm always hungry!"

They sat opening the basket. Serena had enclosed a note addressed to both of them. "This is the same menu Max's mother packed for me and Saul and Max when I came to St. Louis for the first time. It was lucky for us, and I hope it is for both of you." She signed it, "Love, Serena."

They began removing the goodies that they were anxious to savor. There was chicken, salad, fruit and pop.

"Wasn't it wonderful of Serena to prepare this for us?" Jenny was filled with admiration. "She had so much to do, yet thought to do this. She's amazing, Saul. I'll be so proud to have her for my sister-in-law."

She bent over to kiss Saul. "You're all so wonderful!"

Her voice broke a little as it did whenever she spoke of something that had an emotional impact on her. They discussed their approaching wedding.

"I can hardly wait, Jenny." Saul was holding her hand. "It's just a few more months!"

"I know. I feel the same way. It will be wonderful! We'll have our own place, Saul."

"And, we'll be happy, Jenny. I love you, so."

They lay there on the blanket and watched lovers strolling on the walks, others on the lake paddling their canoes, their laughter coming softly over the water, like a delayed echo. Saul asked Jennifer if she still wanted to see the zoo. She wanted to see it, but thought they had better get back. "There will be other times," Jenny said. "If it's okay with you. Let's go home." Saul agreed. They drove back, both quiet.

"Are you happy, Jenny?" Jenny's answer was to snuggle closer to Saul. There was an air of happiness about the two of them that was evident to everyone.

The Kellers, Jennifer, and Mrs. Warner came earlier so Jennifer and Serena's mother could see the apartment. Mrs. Keller brought a bouquet of flowers from the garden, put them in a vase, and set them aside so Serena could put them where she liked. Serena was showing the apartment to Jennifer and her mother.

"It's lovely, Serena." They both complimented her on her creativity in fixing it in her special way. Serena pointed out the things her family had given her and the wedding gift from Jennifer. Jennifer was so pleased. "I'm so happy you like it!"

Carole and Charlie and their parents came in and wished Max "Happy Birthday!" Charlie brought their gifts and set them on the table Serena had arranged. Bill and Lainie had been watching the guests arrive and came up about ten minutes after Charlie and Carole. Serena served a buffet dinner, and everyone said it was beautiful—and wonderful—and tasty. The guests sat on the sofa and bridge chairs (borrowed from Carole and Lainie) set around in a semi-circle.

They ate, talked, and laughed, and every once in awhile got serious discussing changes in St. Louis. They lit the candles on the birthday cake. Serena brought in the gifts. Max opened them, thanking each person for their gifts. Then Serena gave Max her small box. "You know what they say about small packages," she said. Max opened it and was really surprised. Serena had remembered he had said he wanted one.

"It's just beautiful, Siri."

She said, "Read the inscription on the inside."

He looked at it and then looked at Serena. He read it out loud. "My Love Forever, Siri!" Max came over to hug her. "I love it. I'll wear it and treasure it always." Everyone wanted to see it. It was passed around. They "ooh'd and aah'd." They all loved the silver chain and the Star of David.

Serena put it around Max's neck. He took off his tie and wore it with his shirt opened at the neck. She loved the way it looked on him. There was laughing and humor. Bill and Lainie enjoying hearing how Saul and Serena grew up—the trials and tribulations of siblings. Max and Serena told about how they met. Max and Charlie talked about their friendship. Everyone was having a good time.

It was late, and as the guests began to leave, Serena and Max thanked them all for coming, and their gifts. The Kellers, Serena's mother, and Jennifer said their farewells. Ann hugged her daughter. She had missed her but was glad as parents are to see their children happy.

Carole went along with Charlie, who was taking her father and his mother home. Then Bill and Lainie left saying how much they had enjoyed meeting everyone.

Saul and Max were ready for bed but sat in the living room listening to the late, late news. Serena in her robe joined them. Max turned off the radio. Saul began the conversations wanting to know about Bill and Lainie. He thought they were an "interesting couple," as he put it. Max filled him in. "Everyone likes them," he offered.

"We have a group of nice friends, with Carole and Charlie, and Bill and Lainie, we have some nights just sitting around and talking. There are so many things we discuss—things we are interested in or are problematic. We trust each other."

Saul listened. "That's good. I'm glad for all of you." He felt a twinge of—*not envy,* he thought. But things had been different for him since his father's death. There hadn't been time for normality in his life.

They talked into the wee hours now frequently interrupted by "yawning"—first Serena, then Max, and finally Saul succumbed to them.

"I think we're tired—we better hit the hay." Saul said it as he slowly got up—off the sofa. Serena and Max agreed.

"Don't forget we're going to my parents for brunch and spend the afternoon there, then I'll take you all to the station," Max volunteered. They were taking the five o'clock to Madison.

Serena hugged her brother and Max and left them. Saul put his arm around Max. "It was a wonderful party. Congratulations again."

"Thanks Saul. I'm so glad you could come!"

"I am too! Wouldn't have missed it!"

Saul put one arm around his brother-in-law's shoulder, as men do when there is a close relationship. He was smiling at Max as they said their "good nights." Max shut the bedroom door. The place was dark except for the night light from the bathroom and silence claimed the apartment.

They slept late but managed to arrive on time for brunch. There were the welcoming hugs and kisses, and Saul and Jennifer were certainly happy to see each other. Their embraces "were like those of lovers on the screen." To Serena, seeing her brother happy was a wish come true.

Saul and Jennifer were leaving to see the zoo for a few hours, if it was okay with everyone. Max and Serena begged off the invitation to join them. They knew the two lovebirds wanted to be together.

"Be sure you're back in time to get to the station!" Ann reminded them. The two started out when they got to the first step on the patio—they turned and smilingly waved good-bye.

Then they hurried to the car. Before noon there had been a few clouds in the sky, now the sun was shining, the temperature had climbed to almost 60°. "Wouldn't it be nice if weather in Madison were like this?" Jennifer couldn't believe this was winter weather here in St. Louis. She sat close to Saul. It was so pleasant riding like this. When they got to the zoo, she almost didn't want to get out—but Saul insisted. "You'll love it, you'll see!"

He started near the primate exhibit. He knew Jenny would like to see the mothers and their infants that looked so human. There were some of the younger ones already putting on a show—pushing one another, then running up the trees, like children romping. Jenny loved it. "Look, Saul, look over there," and she pointed where an older male, probably the leader, was playfully cuffing some of the younger ones who then knew to stop their playfulness.

They sat on benches, after visiting the tigers and lions, and talked, Jenny so thrilled for Serena and Max in their apartment.

"I know, Jenny, when we get home, we should start looking." He took her in his arms and held her tightly. Passers-by looked and walked on. They were used to seeing young lovers in the park. There were many very young men in uniform, now a common sight, walking with their girls and not thinking too much of what was ahead. Invincible youth. Then there were many with their girl friends who were a bit more serious going off—unsure of any future, because the world wasn't sure.

Jenny and Saul talked about the Kellers.

"They're such nice people," Jenny said.

"Yes," Saul answered contentedly. "They like you a lot, Jenny."

Jenny sat up; she had been leaning against Saul, "It's wonderful here. I could stay here forever." Jenny voiced a thought she felt so keenly while sitting here—relaxing. Saul agreed. It was a little noisy with voices and animal sounds—but to them it was a quiet place and they didn't hear it at all. Saul glanced at his watch. "We'd better be getting back. You won't believe it, but it's past 2:30."

They got back to find their suitcases on the patio waiting to be put in Max's car. Saul got out to help Max.

Jenny apologized, "I hope we've not delayed you too much."

"No, there's plenty of time. We'll leave about a quarter to four. That will give you time to settle in. The train will already be there on track."

Jennifer and Saul went in to thank the Kellers. Mrs. Keller hugged Jennifer. She liked the young woman, and Saul she knew. In her heart she wished them happiness. Later when they were leaving, she voiced her wish out loud to them, "Be happy. We wish you much happiness."

Ann came last—she waited until the rest were in the car, then she thanked them again. "If all is well, we'll see you at the wedding in March."

"We'll be there." Mr. and Mrs. Keller stood there together—waving them all off.

The train was on track and waiting. The porter helped them with their bags, and they were shown to their Pullman bedrooms. Later they met in the dining car. They had the 6:30 sitting. The waiters in their crisp white jackets and white gloves brought their orders. It all looked so good and they ate, finding themselves ravenously hungry.

Looking out, the sky was dark with a bright moon shining down. "It's so beautiful out there." Jennifer couldn't believe how lovely. "This is all so wonderful. I can't thank you two enough."

Ann took Jenny's hand as she continued, "You made this a most unforgettable weekend. Everyone was gracious and it was good to see the Kellers again and Max's friends. They are such happy people. It's wonderful!"

Ann answered her future daughter-in-law. "It was a pleasure for all of us to have you and Saul along, especially for me!" She was quite sincere about that. A wish of hers had come to pass. Saul and Jennifer were together again.

They took turns playing a few rounds of "gin-rummy." Then tired, they turned in. They fell asleep, blissfully unaware that at those very moments, across the Pacific Ocean, in a quiet peaceful harbor in Hawaii, events were happening that would shake the world. Their lives would be changed forever, and the history of the world would be reshaped. But for a few more hours, the train would carry them along on its way to Madison, as if they were far removed from the impending tragedy.

XI

Americans Deal with Japanese Treachery

The train pulled in early the next morning. Madison, blanketed in newly fallen snow, greeted them. The air was crisp and clear, and gusts of a brisk north wind swooped up the snow depositing it in drifts. They had come back to winter in Wisconsin.

A newsboy at the corner was waving a paper and shouting, "Extra! Extra!" Saul couldn't hear the rest of what he was saying. He ran to get a paper, then hailed a cab. When they were on their way home, he unfolded the paper and couldn't believe the headlines. He read it in a question. "Japan declares war on the United States and Britain? Makes sudden attack on Hawaii? Heavy fighting at sea reported?" It was unbelievable and shocking. The cabbie had been watching him in the mirror.

"It happened yesterday," he informed Saul. "We're going to be at war now—like it or not!" He sounded worried. "I'm too old to go, but I have two boys who will be going!" He shook his head. "Those damn Japs!"

A chill went through Ann, who was stunned into silence. Her family, Dave and Ressel, and Robert had talked of horrors of war many times, and she had learned to fear war and all its consequences. Her children, Saul and Serena, had grown up hearing the tragic stories from their Grandmother Ressel, Uncle Dave, and their father. She had tried to allay their fears and concerns. They had questioned many times, "Would it come here?"

"No," she had answered confidently. "No, it wouldn't come here!" Now, it was here! Ann worried for Saul and Jennifer, for Max and Serena, her children, but there was more—'the country.' *God help us all,* she thought. Her eyes closed for a second and to herself said again. *God help us all*!

Saul read more of the news out loud. "In a surprise raid that hit with such fury, it was early morning those aboard the warships couldn't understand what had happened. There were over 90 navy ships anchored in the harbor. The Japanese went after at least six great battleships, the *Oklahoma, Utah, Arizona, West Virginia, Nevada,* and *California.* They were torn apart by torpedoes and explosives. The *Arizona* went down with over a thousand American sailors.

"The sneak attack came early as the sound of Sunday church bells was lost in the machine-gun fire and scream of bombs. Most of the planes were lost and over 2,400 servicemen lost their lives."

Ann asked him not to read any more. Saul finished with "President Roosevelt was meeting with Congress to ask them for a declaration of war against Japan. He was going to speak to Congress and the country at noon.

"We'll listen!" Saul's voice had taken on a somber tone. The rest of the ride home was mostly in silence except for the cabbie, who every once in awhile offered a sentence or two of how the news had been taken in Madison. "Everyone's worried and very angry!" he said.

Saul got his mother settled in at home and was taking Jenny to hers. She didn't want to stay for breakfast. No one seemed to be hungry. The news—not so good—had taken their appetites. Saul took his car out of the garage and picked up Jenny waiting in front. They drove along in silence for a short distance, then Saul stopped the car by the side of the road. The sun was shining, sparkling the snow that had not yet been disturbed by shoveling.

Saul turned to her. "Jenny," he said, "if we're going to war, I want to enlist. If we have to change our wedding date—get married earlier, do you think we could do it in February if we have to?" This had been worrying him since reading the news. He didn't want a postponement again.

In the cab, while Saul had read the paper, her heart had been racing, and her mind had questioned. "What now? What was going to happen?" Their lives were taking another turn. She was glad he was thinking about it too.

"We don't have to have a big wedding. Don't worry," she told him, "We'll work it out."

Somehow it didn't seem right to have a big wedding when so many sad things were happening in the country. So many people were being killed.

Saul loved her for her way of "calming matters," as he explained it to his mother later.

Saul had questioned, "How could it happen? What would it mean to them—to their families—to the country?"

He felt angered that this could happen to the country—to America!

He thought, "Because of yesterday—our world—it's changed." It was unfathomable!

At Jenny's house, he took her traveling bag—and held her arm—helping her through the snow. When her parents greeted them, he could tell they were worried. He spoke to them for a few minutes, then left, saying he was going to see Uncle Dave. "I'll see you tonight, Jenny," and he hurried off.

At Dave's, he had another concern. He could see his uncle's health deteriorating and his grandmother's too. He cared deeply for these older members of the family, his father's mother, and uncle. They had all gone through much in another war. He had listened with awe to what they had come through, and yet, they were always there with their love and support. Now, they needed him, but their America needed him more. They understood that's where he wanted to be.

Dave and Saul discussed the store. He knew Saul wanted to join up and was proud of him. Worried? Yes, but proud. He was telling Saul, "The attorney would take care of everything." If anything happened to Dave, the store would revert to Ressel, Ann, Serena, and Saul, to do with as they saw fit. There would be competent people managing the store. Dave didn't want Saul to worry while he was in the service. Saul was going to see the local draft board to see what his classification would be—and where to go from there.

Ann and Saul were having a cup of hot tea and a muffin while waiting to hear the president's speech. The commentators were speaking in lowered voices. They were describing how President Roosevelt came in on the arm of his Marine captain son, James. Supported by steel leg braces, he stood before the lectern to deliver the historic address to the emergency session of Congress.

He spoke slowly—his words being broadcast coast to coast, live—by radio network. He began, "Yesterday, December 7, 1941—a date which will live in infamy—the United States was attacked deliberately by the naval and air forces of the Empire of Japan." He told the people, "We, and our nation are in grave danger." He ended his speech asking Congress to declare war on Japan and predicted that "America and our people with determination will gain the victory." It didn't even take an hour, and it had passed in the Senate with only one dissenting vote. At four o'clock that afternoon, President Roosevelt, wearing a black armband of mourning, signed the Declaration of War against Japan.

That night in Madison and all across the country, American streets were dark—a nationwide blackout went into effect. Soldiers were now outside the White House and Washington government buildings, on high alert!

Saul and Jennifer set their wedding date for March 7, 1942 and while Jennifer went ahead with wedding plans, Saul was to see about his draft status and volunteering. Saul went down to the recruiting center where he was to report for his physical and was sent to a room where a number of young men were in various stages of undress. Saul did the same, put his clothes in an assigned locker, then stepped in line to receive his file and marched out with the others. They were on a floor with various offices—and lines as men waited for their turn for entry.

Saul's first examinations, by doctors with specialties in nose and throat, eyes, etc., were finished when they put their checks in red or black ink, signed their names, and sent him on to the other doctors.

He was being checked at the cardiac office and was detained and asked several questions. Did he have pain? Was he often short of breath, etc.? To all of these, he answered, "No." He began to feel a bit uneasy. The doctor had checked that examination with a large red check. He was told to step out of line and get dressed. He was through and could go home. He didn't do that.

Saul took his file and went into one of the other lines where he saw some of the men he had come in with. He waited his turn for further examinations. His feet were checked. "No arch here," the doctor remarked.

"Feet hurt?" he was asked. "No," he emphasized. "No!"

The doctor opened his file.

When he saw the red ink check, he looked at Saul and inquired, "Young man what are you doing here? You have already been discharged!"

Saul answered that he wanted to join. "I feel fine!"

The doctor, exasperated and tired of these "want-to-be" recruits, called an orderly. He gave him explicit instructions and handed him Saul's file. "Be sure this gets to the office and see that this young man gets dressed and is shown out."

Saul, dejected, followed the orderly to where the lockers were. He dressed quickly and was taken to the section where the bus was waiting. All the way home, he thought about what had taken place at the induction center. He had been certain he would be accepted. He wondered how Jenny would take the news that he was rejected for military service because of his health. He became defiant. He would see the family doctor during the week—and get this all cleared up. He was sure it was all a mistake.

Saul had wanted to do his 'share' for America—for his great-grandparents and family, his grandfather, Misha and Aunt Seren, whom he had not known. He wanted to do it for his grandmother and Uncle Dave and his father, especially his father. Now, he felt cheated—not being able to do this for them. It had been of great importance to him.

Saul tried to console himself with, "I'll have to find other ways to help!"

The next week he received his card notifying him of his 4-F Classification, and a letter stating he was "deferred for a physical impairment"—a heart condition and suggested he "consult with his family physician as soon as possible." The family called Serena and Max. When the news was relayed to Serena, she was greatly saddened and worried. She couldn't accept that her brother, Saul, could be seriously ill. He had always been the strong one.

The families in Madison and St. Louis insisted Saul see the family doctor. After a thorough examination, the doctor confirmed what those in the military had found. There was an abnormality, and arrangements were made for Saul to see a cardiac specialist. "There could be serious problems," Saul was told. There were things he could start doing—a new regimen of exercise, nutrition program, medications, no stress, and he could live a normal life. This was a great relief to Ann and Jenny. Saul thought it was all foolishness. He felt fine and said so. He had never been ill and didn't like being "fussed over," as he put it. Max and Serena called every night to learn how things were progressing. On hearing the latest that Saul would be all right, Serena burst into tears. She had been filled with despair. Max came over to her as she set the phone down—and he held her as the tears fell—releasing the torment and anxiety she had felt for her brother.

Saul went back to work—trying to deal with problems—directly or indirectly caused by the war. Young men were being drafted. Many had enlisted—having to leave their jobs. It was difficult to find replacements. Men were deferred because of physical disability and women went to work in defense plants and factories because the pay was higher. Saul found this to be true at the store. It was hard to keep employees. There were also constant changes in the age registration for the draft. The call was for more men, and as the war went on, the need continued for—more men.

In Madison and around the country, there were other changes taking place. Families were changing—young fathers were now going to war, leaving wives to deal with family members. The new experiences were making them more independent. Saul had hired several. They worked part time and proved to be very dependable employees.

Saul treated them "like family," the way they described their boss. He was their friend; sometimes when they had problems they could come to him and he helped in any way he could.

He organized a Savings Bond club. The country was asked to save bonds. Each person at the store put in a certain amount of money in their own account. When they had enough—they purchased a Savings Bond. Savings Bonds helped pay for the war. They were all so enthused and felt it was one good thing they were doing to help the country.

Holidays and Christmas were sad—with husbands in the war. It was nearing Christmas. The decorations and lights were turned off because of the black-out. There were no Christmas or Hanukkah lights in home windows. Mothers and family tried their best to make the children happy at holiday time. Saul and Jenny decided to make a party for the children of their employees. It was held in the back room of the store with small rugs covering the bottom of the doors so no light shone through. There was dinner, gifts and toys for the children, and a bonus for the mothers trying to make ends meet and cope with everyday living. At the end of the evening, everyone was in more of a holiday mood. The mothers were thankful for the children's laughter, which gladdened their hearts, and Saul's and Jenny's too. The families never forgot how "caring and wonderful" they were. Among themselves they spoke that way about them.

Saul had joined the Civil Defense—needed to help the citizenry in Madison. Their jobs were many. They walked the streets at night to be sure no lights were on—they watched the traffic and did countless other jobs. They were a most welcome presence on the street. People knew who they were, and if help was needed, they did whatever they could. They kept the streets safe. Saul took his job quite seriously.

Saul and Jenny went ahead with their wedding plans. It was impossible to find apartments because of the war. Rentals were frozen by the government. The wedding date was set for Sunday, March 7th, and still no apartment. In February, a friend of Saul's was called into service. He and his wife had to vacate their premises. The wife was going back home to live with her parents for the duration of the war. There was so much sadness and sacrifice that young people and families were making. The landlord, after much persuasion, let Jenny and Saul have the apartment. Jenny was proud of everything she put in it. Her parents gave her things she treasured from their home, and Saul's mother and grandmother gave them some of the things the couple loved and cherished. They finally finished it—ready with everything and couldn't wait to be its occupants. They visited their home the night before the wedding.

Serena and Max and the Kellers came in on the 5th. The wedding was held in Jenny's home, with family—Grandmother Ressel, and Uncle Dave. Serena was matron of honor and Max was best man. Jenny made a beautiful bride as her parents escorted her down in front of the fireplace where Saul, Max, and the Rabbi waited. It was a beautiful, solemn ceremony. The group was a happy one, but there was also sadness. The times were uncertain times, that touched every home.

The Rabbi spoke of the sacred bonds of marriage, the commitment to each other, and lastly offered a prayer for "our president, our country, and our fighting men." Then he added, "Let us not forget our brethren, all over the world—but especially in Europe, who are suffering untold horrors," and to that, softly—everyone said "Amen."

There followed the wonderful dinner and the wedding cake and lots of wine. About midnight Saul and Jenny left for their new home. Saul took top honors for the happiest groom to carry his beaming bride over the threshold. Once inside, he kissed her again and again, repeating after each kiss, "I love you, Jenny! I'll always love you!"

To Jenny, too, he had been the only one for her and she answered, "And I love you!" Now, they were together. It was late when they got to bed. He held her and cuddled. He was warm, and in his arms she felt safe. His lovemaking was soft—gentle—caring. She loved him for his quiet ways—yet strong.

Saul would always be there for her, and she would be there for him.

In their own place, a new beginning. They began their married life full of hope—in a chaotic world at war. Those who questioned—could never imagine how the turmoil and chaos would resolve itself—touching so many. Monday, before noon, they met Serena, Max, and the Kellers, to take them to the station. In Madison, as in cities all around the country—sights were the same. So many servicemen—soldiers and sailors in uniforms, leaving on assignments, to all parts of the globe. "Many looked so young!" Serena noted as she looked about her. And she understood the pride of the wives, sweethearts, and families—but also the unspoken fear for their loved ones. There were smiles to cheer those leaving, but the lengthy embraces were eloquent in their meaning.

Jenny and Saul waved their farewells to the Kellers standing on the train platform. It was always sad to see loved ones leave. A light snow began falling. Jenny drew her coat collar up, and snuggled her nose in its warmth. Saul took her arm and they headed to the car and home.

XII
You're in the Army

On the morning of December 8th, Serena and Max awoke to the news of the Japanese sneak attack on Pearl Harbor. Max, listening to the destruction that had taken place, was shocked—then angered—at the dastardly, cowardly act, with the resulting loss of innocent lives. He and Serena had often discussed his wanting to go to war to help Britain and the Allies in the war in Europe. That war was with Hitler and Germany. America was neutral, hoping to stay out of the conflict, but helping with military supplies and whatever was needed.

The attack on America was a wake-up call for the country. The devastation on Pearl Harbor was timed with several attacks on other American islands—Guam, Wake, Midway in the Pacific; Japanese troops also landed in Malaysia, the Philippines, Hong Kong, and the small island of Bataan. In schools, maps came down on blackboards to find these places—most Americans never knew existed. America, now declared war on Japan in what came to be known as the 'Second World War!' The Second World War was really two wars—the German War and the Japanese War.

The day he had to report, Max, not wanting to be late, had arrived quite early. The group he joined was transported to the induction center. It was usually a one-way trip. If found acceptable, he would already be in the Army with a two-week furlough to wind up his personal affairs.

Max went through an exam with a psychiatrist, then was fingerprinted. These had to be checked with the F.B.I. files. He was then given a questionnaire to fill out. What he had experience in? What he would like to do?

He had learned much in the store about managing—bookkeeping and inventories. He had always been interested in machinery (as a hobby). He thought he could work in maintenance with planes, jeeps, etc.

Max signed his induction papers, was given a serial number, and told to memorize it. Then Max, and the rest of the inductees, were to assemble for the administering of the oath. An officer spoke to the men for a few moments—then asked them to raise their right hands. For everyone who did so, it was indeed, a solemn moment. The ceremony over, Max and the rest headed home. Max was now a soldier on furlough to wind up his affairs. There was much to do—and not too much time to do it in. He visited his parents and friends, but most of his time was spent with Serena.

When the Selective Training Act became law, Max, like other young American males, registered and were given a card, a DDS-Form 2, which they carried with them at all times. The local draft boards used the mail to communicate with the registrants. The everyday mail became most important in their young lives. Max, classified 1A, waited anxiously to be called. He finally received his "Greetings" from the local draft board—with the date and time to report. Patriotism swelled his heart. He loved America—had grown up hearing his parents talk of how much it meant to their parents and grandparents to be in America—the land of freedom. He, like others of his generation, had taken their freedom for granted. Now, it had been brutally attacked and threatened by Japan—almost unbelievable, and this generation was being called to take on the world in its defense!

Serena and his parents had known for a long time how Max felt. In their hearts they suffered the misgiving of his going into harm's way. Outwardly, they were brave for him, and said nothing. They were Americans first. When Max thought of leaving Serena and his family, there were terrible twinges in his heart and so many stirred up feelings. Serena had taken time off from work, which was given wholeheartedly. Everyone was doing their best for men answering the nation's call.

People bought flags. Flags of all sizes hung from buildings and houses and cars. The radio blared the national anthem, and the country was trying to cope with the war and the uncertainty of the times. The country, divided on so many issues, was coming together. They were united.

There were discussions on the radio, and articles and editorials in the newspapers. Opinions—opinions—so many opinions. There was fear—fear spoken, and fear unspoken and President Roosevelt spoke to them, and it would be faced and had to be won—to save us and the world. Americans believed in him and our country.

The last day of Max's furlough came too soon. Serena hid the fear in her heart, her fear for Max. She was brave, waking trembling many nights from nightmares. Max's thoughts were always of Serena. He wondered how he could make it through the days away from her. Of course, he knew his parents and her family would be there for her. He knew the nights would be long without her beside him.

The night before Max left, their lovemaking was first long embraces—just being close together was fulfilling for the moment.

Later, their love, so intense—so complete, soared to new heights. They nestled under the covers—her back to him—his arm around her.

"I love you, Siri," Max said softly in her ear.

Her hand took his and kissed it. "And I love you, Max!"

They had talked much—spoken their thoughts of, hopes and fears, for their future, but there was more—so much more they didn't voice. For now, there wasn't anything else to say. They couldn't stop the tomorrow from coming. They would face it—a day at a time!

Serena drove Max to the station. There were soldiers and sailors leaving. Parents, wives, and sweethearts embracing—saying their farewells—so many in tears—afraid for their loved ones. *They had all wanted to be brave,* Serena thought, *but emotions are emotions*! She was brave until he hopped up the two steps and turned to wave at her. The tears started when she couldn't see him anymore.

The quick mobilization of men, after Pearl Harbor, found them pouring into training centers and camps. They came by the thousands, only to find them still under construction—unfinished. Max's orders were to report to Camp Funston, Kansas. He arrived at the training center and found it was almost like a city. It would be his home for a while. He didn't know what the length of stay would be. There wasn't much time to explore the new area outside. He found his way to the barracks, a two-story building that seemed to have room for at least a hundred men. (He learned later it was over sixty.)

Max laid claim to one of the beds—more like a cot, covered with a khaki-colored army blanket and a pillow. He plopped on the bed—tired—a lonesome feeling in his gut. He lay there, his eyes taking in the new surroundings. Many had come in before him. He saw their bags set on the beds and on the floor. There was a steady stream of young men coming in and quickly leaving, bewildered expressions on their faces entering this new unfamiliar world.

An announcement over the loudspeaker said, "Chow is at 1800 in the mess hall." Max got up to check where the men's room and showers were. He found them and washed up, looking at himself in the mirror. He nodded his head talking to his image. "You're in the Army now, soldier." He gave himself what passed as a salute.

He found the mess hall with long tables and benches for seating. Soldiers were hurrying in—they found the lines, took their trays, and after they received their food, found places, but had to hurry—everyone was rushing to sit.

The soldier next to Max began speaking to him—introduced himself as "Jerry Olson from Iowa" as he extended his hand. Soon, they were talking to the one across the table, Jim Danielson from Sioux Falls, South Dakota. The talk was of the war. The anger they felt of the Japanese attack—their hurt for the men who lost their lives. They all voiced the same theme, "they were glad to be in the Army."

Max went back to his own spot in the barracks and started a letter to Serena. Some of the fellows went out for a walk. Some were playing cards on the beds. Many were sitting on cots, looking around. Max finished his letter, then went to shower.

He had to wait his turn. There was quite a line-up. Jerry Olson came in and the two talked about home. Jerry was lonesome.

"Everyone feels that way I'm sure," Max told him.

After the showers the two walked back together—feeling better—having found a friend. Max's first day was ending. Lights went out at 9:45. The men were still talking—cracking jokes—then little by little, their masked attempts at joviality let up, and it became quiet. Max lay there in the dark. He turned to one side, then a few minutes later to the other. It didn't take long for him to find out this wasn't like the bed at home. He was anxious for the morning to come, to begin the training. He fell asleep thinking about how much he missed Serena.

Basic training began early the next morning. The first call came at 5:55 reveille, and roll call ten minutes later. By 6:20 Max and the others had washed, dressed, made their bunks and fallen in for the five-minute march to the mess hall. They were there twenty minutes, then marched back to the barracks.

Max and the others prepared their equipment, then made the forty-minute march to the training site where scheduled training activities took over from 8:00 A.M. to 5:00 P.M. nine and one-half hours. They had one break for the midday meal. Now they marched to the Barracks for supper and back—it was almost seven o'clock.

There was more than one complaint about being tired, but there was an exhilaration too. They were learning what the Army was all about. Their day wasn't finished yet—there was mail call, an announcement, a few housekeeping chores, and of great importance—the cleaning of their equipment. The schedule went on, thirty minutes for showering and preparing for bed, and now the time went quickly, it seemed, 9:45 and lights went out. The first training day had taken almost sixteen hours. Sore muscles and aching feet welcomed, "hitting the hay," that night.

To Max, and the others, the training schedule was a full and rigorous one. They learned practical things—like caring for clothing, how to pitch a tent, read maps, and aerial photographs, fortifying places on the fields and camouflage. Most found the physical tasks most grueling; the marches, hikes, and obstacle courses took some getting used to. Max, and the others kept up the pace, no matter how much blisters on the feet pained them.

They were determined to make it through. Guard duty, drill, and inspection were also part of the training. They learned the school of soldiering—fired rifles, pistols, threw grenades, learned about booby traps, and aircraft identification. This was all very important when they went on maneuvers in which war games were staged. A learning experience for many was the instruction in "dirty fighting."

Max and his company didn't treat basic training lightly. They were all determined to make it through and kept boosting the morale of those who had tough days. The group had bonded into a proud unit at the end of the training period.

There was a close group of two fellows and Max, who hung out together. Jerry Olson, twenty-three, from Cedar Rapids, Iowa. Max liked him a lot—a down-to-earth chap. He had a girl, Mary. He carried her picture in his wallet. The boys told him, "how pretty she was and how lucky he was." He hoped to marry when he got out and have a farm of his own.

The other young man in the group was Jim Danielson, twenty-five, Irish, married and had a son, one year old, Timmie. He had his pictures of Timmie and his wife, Peggy. Jim and Peggy grew up together in Sioux Falls, South Dakota. His plans were to buy a house when he got out. Now they were living with Peggy's parents. Jim couldn't wait to get his own place.

Max wanted a home of his own so he and Siri could raise their family. They talked about their plans a lot there—three buddies. They were all optimistic about their futures. Some nights after they read their mail, the three would sit around and discuss their situations at home. One thing they all agreed on. They "wanted to get in the fighting—get the war over, and go home to their families." Talking of home made them a little homesick. With all the people around them, they could still feel lonely. Max often felt that way. Jerry said it, "You guys are swell, but I miss Mary and the folks!"

In the evening, before retiring, Max always wrote home to Serena and his parents, and tried to get mail out to Charlie and Bill at least every other week. Many times at the end of the day, he was too tired to write to anyone, but he knew his letters were as important to Serena as her letters were to him, and he got them out.

Training had gone on for months, and with it the Army Service Forces stressed the training of a soldier's specialty. It was important to develop their skills. Max had gained his experience at the shoe stores. He had been helping in the Quartermaster department and was doing well. He was to be sent to the Quartermaster Officer Candidate School at Fort Warren, Nebraska, for seventeen weeks. He had been quite pleased for the opportunity to work at something he liked doing.

Max received mail regularly from Serena, and his parents and Charlie. Mail call always made him feel good to read about home and how much he was missed. They could never know how much he missed them.

Charlie had written that he had gone through training at Jefferson Barracks, had been home on furlough. "It was so wonderful," he wrote, "to be with Carole and to see Mom!" Now, he was at a Medical Corps center at Camp Grant in Illinois. He liked what he was learning. He had written to Max in some of his letters about the war—about the 'learning to kill.' He wanted to save people, but he knew—"The enemy deserves to die!" He had said, and Max agreed with him.

"The enemy had attacked us on our grounds—killed Americans and wounded all Americans, in their hearts and souls. They had shattered the tranquility of the country. Everything had changed—nothing would ever be the same again."

It seemed like a long, long time—and it was. The training had taken forever, but at last Max received his furlough. His friends at camp were happy he was going. They kidded about Serena.

The next morning, he was on his way home—so anxious to get there, he couldn't sit—kept getting up roaming through the different cars of the train. The porter came to tell him they would be in St. Louis in another twenty minutes. Serena was waiting at Union Station, nervous and excited to see him. She watched as the train came in, then stopped. Passengers were hurrying off—then she caught sight of her soldier husband, handsome in his uniform and her heart began racing.

Max almost jumped off the platform when he saw Serena. *God,* he thought, *I've missed her.* His army bag dropped to the walk and he swooped her up, holding her so tight—smothering her with a long, long kiss. He put her down to look at her as his eyes hungered and caressed her.

"Oh, baby. Oh, baby," he kept saying over and over. "I've missed you so!"

When he released her, she put her arms around him and returned his kiss. It was good to have her arms around him. "I've missed you, too, Max." She was saying it through tears. She had missed him—her letters to him said so—but seeing him—she realized just how much she was happy to have him home—even for a little while.

Max drove the car and Serena sat close to him. He wanted to drive faster, but she cautioned him.

"I want to be home with you, Siri."

"Soon, Max! Soon we'll be home!"

Max walked around the apartment—his face all smiles. He had missed this—being there with Serena. Coming back to the living room, he sat down on the sofa and Serena came over to be with him. His arm went about her and he held her close. "It's so good—so good to be home, honey, here with you."

She had dinner—but he didn't want to eat. "I just want to be with you," he told her. They sat that way for a long time talking together. She gave him the news about their friends. Charlie had been home. Carole was pregnant.

"Isn't that wonderful, Max? Charlie and Carole are going to have a baby!"

Her voice was wistful, but so were her thoughts.

Max talked about his new friends at camp. He had written Serena about them. He was looking forward to going to Officer Candidate School—a new challenge for him.

"I'm so proud of you, Max!" He could see it in her eyes.

"Aren't you hungry?" she asked. "I think I'll fix us a little something."

Serena got up to leave. He pulled her down gently.

"I want to make love to you, Siri. I've missed you."

Max took her hand and led her to their bedroom, their special place. He had thoughts about this room and her so many times. Now it was a reality. He was here with her.

Serena undressed and went into the shower. Max followed and they showered together. Their happy laughter rang through the wet walls and through the apartment—a most welcome sound. The place had been too quiet for a long time.

Their lovemaking was the culmination of two lovers—lost in two different worlds, who searched for each other. They finally found themselves together again with their longing and passion that erupted into a sudden storm. Then came the beauty of the rainbow, arching over their perfect world, and for a while—making it perfect again.

They lay there—their hunger for each other completely satisfied. It wasn't late—but they dozed off. Serena, safe in her Max's arms and Max content with his arms about Serena. This was real—not a dream as it had been so many nights for him.

It was fall and early evening. Dusk was creeping in. Usually, the street lights were on at this hour, but with the blackout, it seemed later than it really was. Serena had been up for a while. She sat in the living room—shades drawn, with only the light of a small, scarf-covered lamp. She was listening to the radio, that was turned low, getting the news of the day.

In the bedroom, Max stirred and stretched, and not finding Serena next to him, he came down. She reminded him to call his parents. They were so glad to hear his voice, he felt a twinge of guilt that he hadn't called them when he just got home, and he said that.

"That's all right, Son. We understand." His conversation with both his parents was short. His father had just gotten home.

"Good to talk to you, Dad. We'll see you tomorrow. Can't wait to see you and Mom."

Max's parents were having early Thanksgiving because he would be away at school for the holidays. Everyone was looking forward to being together. It would be a celebration, but a cloud hung over everything. There was a heaviness on everyone's heart. Try though they did, it couldn't be entirely hidden—but on the morrow, they would put forth a herculean effort to be happy and thankful.

Part Three
Freedom's High Cost

XIII
Home News

Serena and Max were leisurely breakfasting in their robes. The phone rang. It was Carole. She wanted to stop and see Max for a few minutes "if it was okay!"

It was a happy, pregnant Carole who came in breathless. Max greeted her with a hug, saying how good she looked.

She countered with, "You don't know how much you and Charlie are missed around the place."

Max was anxious to hear the latest news about Charlie.

"Charlie thought he would be using his pharmaceutical knowledge in the Army and had chosen to take up the challenges of the Medical Corps School. He didn't know where he would be sent after that." Carole sounded quite concerned.

"Oh, Charlie will be okay." Max said matter of factly. "You know Charlie!" They talked of the baby. "Charlie is so excited and can't wait. He mentions it in all his letters," Max told her. With the conversation—they shared tea together, Max inquiring about her father and Charlie's mom.

Carole was going to see them both that morning, and with a little help from Max, she got up from the sofa.

Looking at how happy Max and Serena were, Carole put her arm on Max's. "Take care, Max," she said, as they walked to the door.

Serena was busy taking up the remnants of breakfast, and Max came to help.

Lainie called, "Was it okay to come up and see Max?"

She came in bouncy and happy. Lainie had always been bubbly and fun-loving, and seemed to be even more so now. At least that was Max's impression. He hadn't seen her for over a year.

Lainie gave Max a run-down on her work. She was so enthusiastic. So many young men from the company had gone into service. She had just gotten a promotion—made buyer of the women's wear department, "probably until the war is over and the fellows come back." But that was fine with her. It was a learning experience. She loved the job—went to New York on buying trips. She raved about how she enjoyed meeting with different salesmen who took her to dinner.

Then Max wanted to know about the latest news from Bill.

"Bill was through with his training at Fort Leonard Wood. You knew that?" she questioned.

"Yes, Bill had written that."

Bill had worked with radios in the store—was quite familiar with them—got to be pretty proficient at repairing all makes. It was the specialty he was working on in the Army. He was learning and working on something quite important.

"In communications," Lainie called it. "He loves it!" Bill was sure his work would be helpful, but he couldn't say much more to Lainie or to anyone. His letters to all of them said how much he missed Lainie. To Lainie—his letters were constant reminders of their love life.

"I can't wait to be with you. I dream of you every night."

The letters made Lainie miss him more every day. She needed their love-making. She craved it. That was a constant for both of them. In one letter he reminded her of the last wonderful love-making event.

Lainie had called him at the shop to come home for lunch—she had a surprise for him. It was Valentine's Day. She met him at the door, nude, except for a sheer heart-shaped G-string.

"Do you remember," he wrote, "that wonderful Valentine's Day Celebration we had?

"I think of it a lot especially when I feel sad being away from you."

Lainie remembered those special times, even when he didn't write about them. She couldn't stand the thinking and missing of his love-making.

Lainie was answering Max, who was anxious to know how Bill was feeling. She said, "He's fine but sometimes he sounds so lonely."

She had to leave—was meeting with a representative from a Chicago firm. It was quite important for her job.

"Be sure to give Bill my best when you write," Max called after Lainie as she hurried down the second floor steps.

Max closed the door and stood with his back to it, leaning there for a few seconds. He thought about Lainie. There was something very different about her. He couldn't say what it was exactly. All he knew, it left him with an uneasy feeling.

Max called to Serena. When she came in, they talked about her work. He asked how she felt about the handling of war news at her office. Then he asked about Lainie.

Serena looked troubled. She didn't want to talk about Lainie, but he wanted to know. Serena said, "When she goes out like this, she comes in very late—almost near morning. Then we don't see her for a couple of days. She won't answer the door or phone. I've tried to talk to her, but she won't say anything. I decided it really was none of my business then."

Serena didn't know that Lainie would hear the knocks at the door, and the phone, but she was in bed with a hangover from drinking and filled with remorse; she had gotten drunk and had sex with one of the men. She came home upset at what she had done. How could she have done this to Bill? She didn't want to see anyone and waited until she heard Serena leave.

Max, shocked at hearing this about Lainie, changed the subject and began talking about Serena's work.

Serena told how the news had been heavily censored after too many military facts had been carelessly given out, putting the servicemen and country in grave danger. The papers, radio, and movie news were constantly reminding the country of the absolute necessity of keeping quiet about war news in their conversations. It was important to keep any helpful information from the enemy. Couldn't say where a family member in the service was stationed. There were many German spies in the country, living and working in neighborhoods—friendly but sending back information to Germany.

It was said over and over, "A slip of the lip can sink a ship!"

"Censorship is everywhere!" Serena told him.

Serena showed him letters he had sent that had been checked, and there were spaces where words or sentences had been censored and cut out. Max couldn't believe it. "I'll be even more careful," he told her.

Later they dressed and left for the Thanksgiving celebration.

Serena noticed Max looked a bit worried. She wanted to know, "Are you okay?"

"Sure," Max answered, "but I've had some uneasy vibes about Lainie. She seems so occupied with her job. Is everything all right with her?" he asked.

Serena didn't answer.

They arrived at the Kellers, who were out on the patio waiting to welcome them.

Max's mother, after embracing him, said, "You look so handsome in your uniform, my son. We're so proud of you."

His father shook his hand, then grabbed him in a big hug—soldier or not—Max was his son. Max had missed them. "It is so good to be home again—to be here with all of you."

Thanksgiving dinner brought good memories, and they talked about them. This early holiday was good to a point—they talked, saying things out loud, but in each of their minds, an interlude interrupted their thoughts. *It was good,* Serena thought, for Max to be here now—but her mind worried.

"When he leaves, where will he be going, and what will happen?"

She was actually an optimist and told herself, "He'll be okay," but inside she was far from sure.

Mrs. Keller, her voice attempting to be cheerful, said, "Next year when the war is over, we'll be able to have a nice turkey. Then we'll really celebrate."

With rationing, she was lucky to have gotten a chicken. In her mind, there was a prayer: "Please, God, watch over our son and our country."

Mr. Keller looked at his wife, smiled at all of them, and with disciplined self-control, said, "We'll have a toast." He offered it as he lifted a small wine glass, and the family did the same.

They were all smiles. "We're happy you could make it home to be with us, and we give thanks to God!"

They all answered, "Amen!"

Max's father, with lowered voice, prayed, "God watch over him."

Dinner progressed and outwardly a cheerfulness prevailed, but inwardly, a torment on each of their minds remained—"the worry!" Serena, happy to have Max home, teased, "I'll bet he's the handsomest soldier in the whole army!"

Every day at work, she heard the news about the Allies and it had not been good. Now, there at dinner, she alone heard her mind whispering over and over, *Please, God, bring him safely through this.*

At one point, Max got their attention and smiled as he spoke, "It's so wonderful to be home with you all." He said it again—his voice emphatic. The smile disappeared from his face, and as he sat down, he thought not about himself. "God, it's a big favor I'm asking. Keep safe our country, our men," then added, "and my family. Please, God!"

Dinner over, Serena and Max called her mother and Ressel, and Saul and Jennifer. Everyone in Madison was in a jovial mood. The Kellers knew it was for Serena and Max. The Warners, like all Americans, were concerned for the country so courageously waging war with its enemies.

Max and his father were listening to the news broadcast. Mr. Keller was optimistic. "We were attacked, caught off guard, but eventually America and her Allies will prevail. The enemy will be driven out, Max, because right will win!"

Max agreed. "We'll do our best, Dad!"

"I know you will, son. That's why I'm so proud of you!"

They got up and Mr. Keller put his arm around Max's shoulder as they headed for the kitchen.

Serena and Mrs. Keller got up when the men came in.

"It's getting late, Siri."

Mrs. Keller agreed. "You two, better get some rest."

Max had two days left on his furlough.

Max was going to the store with his dad in the morning—then he and Serena would be together. He kept asking what she would like to do. Go to a show? Dinner?

"No—just dinner and then could we just be home?"
"Perfect!" he answered.
"I wanted to be home with you, Siri!"

Their time together flew. The last night they had dinner, then they walked around University City, before the curfew. Lights were out. Sometimes they met Civil Defense Security Officers. They wore hard hats and had arm bands identifying them. They were walking around, watching different areas, streets, and stood on corners. Serena had written Max about it, but seeing it was another matter. Lights dimmed for security. "It makes us feel safe," she told him.

St. Louis had three ammunition plants. They could be targets for an enemy—any one of the Axis members—therefore it was necessary to take precautions. Blackouts were necessary and security was very strict.

The evening was lovely, as it usually was in the fall of the year in St. Louis when the stars were out. In the darkness, they made it safely back to Westgate Avenue. At the apartment, their shades were drawn and the one small lamp was lit. Max began packing his bag. Serena showered and got into her robe, waiting for Max to finish his. She had fixed a salmon-salad snack he loved, and the radio was on playing softly.

When he came out, they each had a small glass of sherry, ate the snack, and talked about his visit home. Max put his arm around her and kissed her on the cheek. "It was so wonderful to be home with you, Siri, honey." His voice was low and loving.

"I know, Max. I'll miss you."

He put his arm about her, and it was a most wonderous feeling. She felt safe. Serena sat on the edge of the bed—dropping her slippers. Her mind elsewhere. She began with, "I can't wait for it to be over. It will be so wonderful when we can be together for always." Then she added, "Please, Max, take care of yourself."

Max helped her take her gown off, and kissed her gently—holding her close—close to his body. She felt warmth and she smelled the wonder of him. She loved his talc—she loved her Max.

"Oh, Siri," he said in awe. "I can't believe how lucky I was to marry you."

Their love was a wonder to each of them—a promise of their future. He kissed her warmly—embracing her, feeling her, touching the beauty of her body that sent joy through his being. They were soon lost again in their absolute love.

Morning came, and there was the rushing and so many last-minute reminders. Max walked around the apartment, came into the living room, sat for a few minutes on the sofa, then went into the bedroom. He was holding their wedding picture when Serena found him. Setting it down, he took another look around. Serena, in the doorway, didn't say anything. He followed her and they left for the Union Station.

The sight of soldiers and sailors rushing about, the shouting—the noises and farewells, people arriving and people departing were becoming all too familiar for St. Louisans, and people all across America. Max held Serena locked in his arms while his lips brushed her lips and cheeks, and hair. He didn't want to let her go. The porter announced, "All aboard!"

Reluctantly his arms let go of her. He got on the platform—pushed by those behind him. He waved a final farewell, and he was gone. She caught a glimpse of him in his seat looking out the window. When he saw her, he threw her a kiss and waved again. She waved back and watched as the train pulled out rolling along, leaving St. Louis—leaving her—standing there alone.

Serena made her way through the mulling crowds to where the car was parked. She didn't feel like going back to the apartment. It would feel so empty now with Max gone. She didn't want to be with her friends; she just wanted to be by herself. The car, like an old horse that knows its way back to familiar grounds, had turned into Forest Park.

This was just the place for her to be. Early morning made it simple to find parking. Slowly she walked to some of the spots she and Max had visited so many times. Near the lake she chose a bench that looked out over the large expanse of water and saw the trees in dress of various colors of fall. She sat there for a long time, remembering happier days and felt much better. An inspiring thought came to her. Spring was not that far away and with spring came hope, "Things will be better!" A little more composed she started for home.

Serena tried to keep her mind from thinking about Max—with fruitless results. For her—work was a saving grace—that is, up to a point. It was the evenings that were hardest to bear.

Carole had given her the information of first-aid training classes by the local Red Cross chapter. Classes were to be held once a week in the evenings at school. Serena and Carole volunteered. They would be working together—a team. They worked hard, learning many life-saving techniques. They mastered the bandaging of supposed arm and shoulder injuries, and every imaginable kind of leg injuries, using limbs and branches of trees and pieces of wood as splints.

Their first efforts were disasters and the instructor made Carole and Serena do them over and over until they got them right. With time they got to be good enough to pass, to get their Red Cross Certificates. They had taken classes seriously, knowing what they were learning could save lives if the enemy attacked. They rolled hundreds of bandages that were sent overseas.

Serena wrote Max. "I'm so glad to be of some help. That's so important to me." Max was proud of her efforts and told her so in his letters. Coming to one of the classes, one night, Serena read on the bulletin board, the Red Cross had need of women who could knit. Serena's grandmother, Ressel, had patiently taught her to knit. Serena volunteered. She was told there was a great need for wool sweaters for the men in service fighting in the cold freezing climes in Europe.

Serena took a kit home to see if she could do it. There were several styles. Each kit contained enough soft wool yarn to make a long-sleeved turtleneck, or a long-sleeve V-neck sweater or vest to keep a sailor's or soldier's chest or back warm. There were kits with navy-colored yarn for men in the navy, khaki-colored wool for men in the army.

There were kits for children's clothes, too, sweaters with pants for boys, and sweaters with skirts for girls. There were scarves and hats, and mittens and socks. They were sent abroad for the children in the wartorn countries of England and France, and others. As she knit, Serena's thoughts were of the youngsters. Her heart was sad that they were innocent victims suffering—cold and hungry somewhere overseas.

Serena had written Max that she was doing well with the knitting. She could now take one kit home every week, knitting in the evenings after work. It kept her busy. The articles, when finished, were marked with "size tags." She helped getting them folded and boxed and sent prayers with them—that those wearing them would be safe.

Max had been gone a little over a month when Serena's next letter brought good news. "We're going to be parents."

Max wrote back, "I can't wait to finish up here so I can come home."

Even though he was tired at the end of the day, he had been unable to sleep for the past few nights since hearing the good news from Siri. He called Sunday afternoon—so excited at the prospect of being a father. He told Serena, "I think about it a lot. I wish I could be home with you, Siri. I miss you!"

Charlie got the news from Max. "We're going to be fathers—you and I, Charlie! Wow! Our kids will grow up together. We have a lot to look forward to, pal!"

Carole was kept busy with programs and involved the school children in the war effort. They wrote letters to the men in service who had no families. They became Pen-Pals. The men were so glad to receive mail, and answered, saying how wonderful it was to receive letters at mail call; they didn't feel so alone.

Often Carole brought schoolwork down to keep Serena company while the knitting needles clicked away and another sweater progressed. They would discuss wonderful plans for when their men came home—when the war was over.

Lainie saw them, but not too often. She was busy trying to get merchandise from companies in St. Louis. Because of the war, stores were having more difficulty than ever before. Once in a while, she again had to meet a representative from out of town, if other girls weren't available. She was careful not to drink. At the dinner now she had an excuse—couldn't drink she had an ulcer.

She worried about her transgression. She fought herself pro and con. She thought about it again and again. She made excuses sometimes. She was lonely and had missed Bill for a long time. When she thought that way, it didn't seem so terrible to her. Then she felt a loathing, that she could think that way, when what she did was so terrible and she knew it.

Lainie hoped Bill would be home soon, but the war news from the Pacific wasn't too good. Sometime when she couldn't stand to be alone downstairs—thinking of her troubles, she would come up to visit Serena and Carole who were always happy to see her. They would listen to the news.

Later, downstairs, Lainie wished Bill was home. She wondered how she could be with him. She wouldn't tell him—couldn't tell him. Bill, jealous, would never stand for that. That would be the end of their marriage. She felt she had already ended it.

Bill always said, "We were made for each other." It became painful for her to write Bill. It was an everyday war she waged with herself. She hated herself for what she had done.

Carole and Serena had discussed Lainie's situation. They worried about her. They could see she had changed in so many ways. She was restless and tired. Lainie was beautiful, but she was looking pale. She didn't talk about Bill. Serena wondered to herself, how it would be when Bill came home?

There were nights when Serena couldn't sleep—thoughts came that worried her. It wasn't just Bill and Lainie she worried about. There was Charlie and Carole, and herself and Max, and how things would be for all of them.

There were so many changes taking place—many women working in jobs that once were for men. Women were different now—more independent. This was causing problems.

Serena heard it in so many discussions, in the articles written in the paper, and in the news reels in the movies. She worried about herself. When the war was over and Max came home, would he find her different?

XIV
Uncle Sam's Nephews

Max was finished at school. He was to come home again, but his leave was cancelled. Movement of the troops, of course, was top secret. Serena and the family were disappointed at this turn of events and wouldn't know for weeks where he was stationed. Mail from Max came from a P.O. Box number in New York. Serena's letters went to that number and were forwarded to wherever Max and his company were located.

The war in Europe had been on since 1939 when Hitler's Germany attacked Poland. Many Germans living in America were tied to their "Fatherland" in various ways. There were many German organizations, the members living here in America enjoying America's freedoms. They had marches, voiced their hate, and were protected by American laws.

In the country, they infiltrated into companies, living in communities, even marrying spouses here while spying for Germany. They searched out places of employment where they could operate—some working in banks where hundreds of customers came in. They ingratiated themselves with the customers—learning where members of the families were in service—offering condolences if a son or husband or brother was killed, when and where it happened, etc.

Americans were constantly warned on radio talks by President Roosevelt, and in movie news reels—to be careful, in conversations, not to say anything that could be helpful to the enemy that would put servicemen in harm's way. Everyone tried to do the right thing, but every once in a while, there were slip-ups. Mail was sent out, but censors checking the mail would have to cut out certain parts of letters they would not pass through.

From Max's letters, Serena thought she knew where he could be, by his writing about the weather. He had written her "to be careful—not to go out in the rain or when it was foggy. That's not too good for you and our unborn child."

She guessed he was in England.

Sometimes on Sunday afternoons, she would walk down to the Tivoli Theatre—not caring about the movie—just to see the news reels. The papers carried reports of the bombing on England in attacks by the German Luftwaffe, but in the movie reels, she could see the devastation and hear the noise of the bombs as they hit their targets. It frightened her to think Max could be there, and her assumptions were correct—that's where Max was. She had learned that, accidentally, one day in a letter from Max. He had been out to dinner and had delicious "pasties." It had passed the censors!

Supply ships crossed the Atlantic in a convoy escorted by naval ships to try to protect them from German submarines. There were more supplies coming into England every week. When the ships were unloaded, Max and his company worked in an elaborate system of allocating, distributing, and transporting food, clothing, equipment and ammunition to meet the demands for the armed forces of the Allies at the various theatres of war. The job for each area was a new venture. There was a problem getting it all together—new convoy routes for naval escorts and transporting it safely by motor, rail, or ships. Most importantly too, he was taking care of matters pertaining to morale—things like movies, educational programs, and newspapers, etc. It was an utmost necessity for the men to have these.

Quite often Max went along on flights to different areas to check out the supplies and the condition they arrived in, were more needed, and how to get them there. It was dangerous and they were often at risk—with the Germans firing at their planes. Sometimes they had plane escorts, but the planes were usually needed elsewhere.

Coming back from France, on one of these trips, two German planes swooped down—out of the clouds, pursued them with gunfire, diving on them from different directions. They were near the English Channel when their tail gunner was hit. Max had to scramble quickly to man the gun. They left the French coastline and were crossing the Channel—the Germans kept coming. The plane had been hit, but the pilot maneuvered it as best he could. The plane was needed. He had to get it back to the air field. This was his primary concern.

Max had been injured, but he kept firing at the enemy. Suddenly, the German Luftwaffe turned away. It was then the pilot saw a squadron of "R.A.F." (Royal Air Force) planes approaching. They engaged the Germans in a battle over the English Channel.

Max saw one of the enemy planes on fire as it hurtled downward in black smoke, then hit the water below. The squadron continued on to the coast of Europe to hit planned targets in Germany.

The pilot had great difficulty, but he succeeded in landing the plane. An ambulance, already waiting, took Max and the pilot to a military hospital.

There Max underwent surgery for back and leg injuries. He didn't write the family that he had been hurt. Later he explained to them, "It wasn't life-threatening and the care was first-rate!"

The nurses there liked "the American." He didn't complain even when in "terrible pain," was the story told by those on duty on the floor where his room was.

"He's sick for home!" One young woman, telling it, shook her head, "Poor chap!"

One young lady, in particular was very glad to have her shift on that floor. She would drop in even when off duty. "Just to see how he was doing." She would tell friends who teased her. When he was better, she volunteered to take him out in the wheelchair and helped him with the crutches. It took months for recuperation and therapy, and "he was lucky" she said. Before he was released, she invited him for dinner "if he'd like to come." He had her phone number. Her name was Leslie Hodges, and she lived with her parents. "Ring me up," she said, "whenever you want to come."

Max was out of the hospital and back at his job. A few weeks later on the weekend, he called and was invited to come. He met Leslie's parents. They were very hospitable and kind to him. They spent many hours talking about America, Max answering their many questions.

He talked about his family and Serena, and the child they were expecting "any day now," he would say proudly.

He felt very much at home; they kept inviting him and he liked being with a family. Food was scarce and Max would bring small gifts of food, which delighted them.

After dinner, Leslie and Max usually went walking around the neighborhood. London had been in a blackout for a few years now.

Sometimes when Max's trips took him across the Channel to France and other countries in Europe, he didn't see Leslie for weeks.

When he came back and visited, she told him how much they all had missed him.

"I missed you and your family, too," he said.

Usually he stayed for a few hours, tonight he left earlier. "I'm expecting news from home," he told Leslie.

At camp, he did have a letter from his mother. Serena's grandmother, Ressel, had a heart attack and died. Serena had gone to Madison for the funeral. This was a shock to Max. Ressel had become close and important to him. He went to a synagogue in London and attended memorial services, saying the prayers for departed loved ones. He came for Ressel, the only grandmother he had known. He planned to come again soon.

That night he was restless. His thoughts were of the family. From the back of his brain, somewhere, came memories he had forgotten. So often growing up, he had heard his father discuss how his parents had sent him away to America to escape the wars of hate, the pogroms in Russia. They had wanted a safe life, with freedom for him. However, they had been unable to escape and were killed for no reason except they were Jews. Max lost grandparents he never knew. Tonight he thought about them. His heart was saddened. *Now, so many years later*. Max thought, *We're here in Europe fighting the hate of the evil-doers* led by this maniac Hitler, who was concentrating on killing the Jews. His hate spouted false propaganda—and what was astonishing was how so many were brainwashed into believing it and entering into it, becoming perpetrators killing millions of innocent victims. He began to understand what his grandparents and father had gone through. He had often heard Serena's grandmother tell the horrible experiences. He had listened but his mind couldn't accept that hate—but now he had seen some of it.

Every year since America had entered the war, troops from America were coming in more and more ships to England. Every day in America, new recruits answered the call and were in training camps learning to be soldiers, then when ready, they were sent to the different war fronts from England.

The war in Europe with the Germans, Italians, and Russians had gone on in 1943 and 1944. It had become a world conflict, embroiling almost every country on the globe. Germany, of course, was the principal aggressor that had brutally conquered them all.

The Resistance groups in each country were gathering strength and against great odds were becoming a force of invaluable assistance to the Allies in a rumored invasion of Europe.

The problem was getting supplies to them. Munitions were desperately needed to blow up bridges and roads and airfields the Germans used.

Max and his Quartermaster Corps were kept busy sorting, preparing and sending supplies where needed. They accompanied the supplies to the different fronts. On one trip, they had landed in a huge cargo plane carrying machine guns, and other desperately needed supplies. They were in an area near forests and hills. Nearby, soldiers and Resistance fighters waited for their arrival.

They worked quickly, quietly, no one speaking, unloading, so the plane could take off before being discovered. The many trucks driven by Resistance fighters, waited to be loaded.

All of a sudden, from behind a hill to the left of the plane, a flare went up illuminating the whole area. One of the machine guns was immediately readied and fired. The Germans retaliated. The battle was fierce, the enemy unyielding. Partisans came back to help keep the enemy busy, with gunfire whizzing back and forth. The plane had to be fully unloaded, then it would take off. Soldiers, and Partisans, and the enemy lay wounded and dead, scattered over the field. The plane got off the ground and amidst heavy gun-fire came back to be sure the Partisans with trucks were hauling the remaining supplies away. Max watched. He knew the courageous Partisans, at great risk to themselves and their families, would help the wounded escape to a safe place.

In the plane, Max was helped by the medic. He had been hit. One shot to his thigh and the other hit the right side of his face into his jaw. It was a painful injury. He was flown back to England and was in the hospital. This time it would be a longer stay. Leslie was there—sorry he was hurt, but she was glad for one thing—she would be near him. Max received a medal for "bravery."

Letters from Serena became more important to Max. He hated being in the hospital—wished he were home with his wife. He missed her. He worried. This latest injury left him with a three-inch scar running down his cheek to the jaw. "Would it make a difference to Serena?" He wondered.

Serena wrote almost every day. Sometimes he didn't receive mail for a few days, then there would be three or four letters from her. Mail delivery was dependent on ships crossing safely. The German U-Boats torpedoing ships sent plenty of mail to the bottom of the ocean. Serena tried to keep Max abreast with all she knew about Charlie and Bill. Max was always inquiring. He worried about his two friends.

"They were both on islands in the Pacific," she wrote. "We don't know much else about that."

Carole read the St. Louis newspaper accounts, and from the radio broadcasts, she learned, like the rest of the country, the battles with the Japanese, were not going well for the Allies. The Japanese military were cold-blooded—merciless. Their bombers struck at Singapore causing heavy loss of life and much damage. One report told of troops trapped who tried to get through jungles and swamps, to get to their lines. Before leaving, they left their wounded safe under trees, calm and unafraid. Captured by the Japanese, the wounded men were taken to a place nearby where they were shot or bayoneted to death. They were found this way by returning Allied troops.

One night Walter Winchell, in a somber voice, came on the radio telling of the advances the Japanese had made on Bataan, in the Philippines, and landed near the American defense lines. The Japanese, well prepared, were victorious in all these battles.

American troops fought to reach their objectives; they came through dense jungle but behind were mountains providing good observation points for the enemy. The battles with the Japanese were savage.

Lainie didn't know, but Bill was in a cave—high up in the mountains, and at great risk was sending messages to headquarters informing them of Jap movements. The Japs were receiving great numbers of new reinforcements and munitions. They wondered how the Americans got the information. Planes bombed the ground troops and then Allied troops arrived to do battle.

The Americans suffered great losses. Captured prisoners were mistreated—starved—dying of illness—and often left on beaches or in the jungles—their bodies mutilated. It was through Bill's reports that the world learned of the atrocities. Bill and two other soldiers kept moving from cave to cave, so they wouldn't be discovered.

The Japanese were trying to locate the source of the radio communication they were certain was somewhere up in the hills. Their planes came in every day, bombarding the places they were sure contained the radio apparatus.

The bombs exploded all around the cave, but Bill kept up his transmitting and reporting of how many Jap ships were passing, and aircraft carriers, and troop carriers. He finished up his broadcasting—saying he was moving that night. They packed and waited for a villager who was to take them to a safer place. On the islands many of the natives were helping the Allies—at great risk to themselves and their families.

They left quietly. They stopped many times when they saw Japanese soldiers slashing through the bushes. At times gunfire erupted and shells fell exploding near them. One soldier was killed and Bill was hurt. The soldier and villager carried him, zigzagging across the hillside. They made it to a makeshift hospital after two days of travel.

Bill had been in great pain, but he had urged them to go on. Exhausted, he tried to impress upon the captain to report to headquarters so another radioman could be sent out to set up the radio-transmitting station. This was a very productive spot since the Japanese ships and troops moved through this area.

Tired, he fell back and the medication of morphine was administered. He was taken to surgery. His wounds were serious. He was flown off to a military hospital in Hawaii and then flown to the States.

Lainie received notification that Bill had been injured and she would be contacted as soon as he arrived. Lainie, hysterical, ran up to Serena's and they set about calling the hospitals, the draft board to inquire where they could get more information. Lainie, later with a headache, consoled herself—telling Serena, "Thank God he'll be coming home!"

Bill was sent to a Jefferson Barracks Hospital. He was there for many weeks. Lainie visited him every weekend. The doctors talked to both Lainie and Bill. He would get better, but they couldn't say yet what the prognosis would be.

Bill was then transferred to a convalescent camp that had an occupational therapy program, the first in the country. Bill in a wheelchair was taken to the sessions, but after weeks with no improvement, he became depressed. He was paralyzed and wouldn't walk again. He might get use back of his arms, but doubtful at this point. Bill would be confined to a wheelchair.

The doctor spoke to both of them. Bill would remain at this level. Their lives were changed forever. After the doctor left, Lainie held him and they both cried. Lainie left and told him she would be back on the next weekend. When she left, Bill felt alone, of no use to anyone. His depression became worse. He thought about Lainie; she could leave him. He wouldn't blame her if she did.

At home, Lainie couldn't go to work, staying in, she thought about their life before this happened. Before Bill left for war, they had discussed and made such wonderful plans. She began to cry, thinking of what she had done to their marriage. Was

God punishing her by doing this to Bill? She cried a lot—but crying didn't help—only made her feel worse.

Serena and Carole called her—went to see her and talked to her. Lainie wasn't the same person who had loved life before the war. The next week she went to see Bill. She tried to be cheerful and helped in the way the doctor said she could—talking to him about coming home—life would be better. She stayed her allotted time. There seemed to be improvement. Bill wasn't so depressed. Lainie felt hopeful. There were changes that had to be made if Bill was to come home. There was much to do.

For Carole, the reports of the war in the Pacific, brought more concern for Charlie. There were so many nights she had frightful nightmares, and awoke—her heart pounding—covered with perspiration. She got out of bed, thankful it was a bad dream. Yet, Charlie was out there helping the wounded, fighting in this war. She worried—"Were the nightmares some sort of messages that Charlie was hurt?"

When she received a letter from him, he never said much about what was going on in the war. He missed her and "the gang," and "couldn't wait for it all to be over so they could all come home."

Carole gave him good news, "what she was doing, school and keeping busy—waiting for him to be with her."

The letter came telling him, "We're parents of a beautiful baby girl born in May." Charlie and Carole had decided if the baby was a girl, she would be named Judith, "Judy" for Carole's mother. She sent a hospital picture of the baby.

It was wonderful news for Charlie. He and others had just come into camp having slashed their way through the jungle. It was raining, but warm. Still after the soaking rain, the chills came on. They had come in for a rest period.

For a couple of days, they had battled their enemy, the relentless Japs. There had been savage fighting, hand-to-hand combat on the island. The Japanese, defenders of their positions, shocked those who had to overcome them.

The Japanese did not want to be taken prisoners, and in every battle they fought to the death, or at the last moment killed themselves to avoid capture. They wouldn't surrender. A wounded Japanese would wait until someone came up to examine him, and then kill himself and the other fellow with a hand grenade.

Charlie, busy caring for the injured was hurrying back and forth, helping them as they lay on the battlefield, dead and dying, and others in pain—trying not to cry out.

The shells and machine-gun fire whizzed all around them, but Charlie kept at his job. He had fought and seen the bloody aftermath of the battles with the Japs on the fields of the Solomon Islands and later Gudacanal.

There were so many wounded who sometimes had to wait because medical supplies were short. This angered Charlie too. His job as a Medic was to help people. Seeing all the suffering was affecting Charlie.

He had come off the field for a much deserved rest, but, instead, he refilled his supply paraphernalia and went out again. There were soldiers out there who needed what little he could do for them.

Charlie had lost so many of his friends—had seen them lying there—bloodied, in the mud and the relentless rain. He had come upon them when the fighting left a battle field and seen Allied soldiers lying close together where the Japs had left them decapitated or with multiple bayonet wounds. His anger filled his heart and head and anguished, he cried to himself.

He and the others arrived on the now deserted battlefield to look for more wounded. The Japanese had cleaned up there on the island and moved their troops elsewhere. Charlie's men checked systematically; they took the rifles from the dead soldiers and stood them up in the dirt and mud, butt side up, with the soldier's helmet set on top.

There were so many dead. They found the wounded—giving them aid and drugs for pain. Charlie gave them words of encouragement. Some were frightened but tried to be brave. Charlie hurried, trying to help as many as he could. Some were already being taken off the field.

A medic called to Charlie. There was a wounded Japanese soldier in a fox hole left there by the Japanese who thought he was dead.

Charlie and the other medic approached him with caution. This could be a trap. Charlie's flashlight beamed on a very young soldier. He was suffering greatly for his Emperor. His eyes were wide open with fear in them. Charlie checked his wounds. The soldier was mortally wounded. The young man would be dead in an hour or so.

Charlie put the boy's (that's what he was a boy) knapsack under his head so he could rest, lit a cigarette for him, and put it in his mouth. Then he gave him a shot of morphine. Charlie told him, "You're okay," and smiled at him. He then took the cigarette from his mouth. The Jap didn't understand. His eyes closed. He died quietly. Then Charlie took the sword from his side, planted it in the earth above his head, and put his helmet on it. Charlie stood there for a second, then continued to check the field.

So many times Charlie, seeing the death and destruction, had thought about the "evil ones" who start wars. He criss-crossed the battlefield and found more dead and wounded. *Young—what a tragic waste*! he thought. He blamed himself for the death of a soldier. "I should have gotten here to help him!"

Very tired he made it back to camp. Sometimes on the islands, supplies were short. There were the C-rations and the men were happy when small coastal freighters would make it past the Japanese bringing these and small ammunitions.

Often Charlie and a few others would cast out a huge net into the sea and stand there waist deep in water working the nets to haul in fish. They had to hike back through the jungle to their camp; so tired by then, they fell into their cots that stood with their legs in the filthy water of the swamp all around them.

When the sun went down, the deadly malaria-bearing mosquitoes swarmed around the nets, draped over the canvas cots. Many of the soldiers were bitten and became very ill. Charlie treated them with quinine and dealt with the illness that took such a toll of the men. Charlie got it, too. His net, like many, had a small hole in it but "a smart mosquito found it," Charlie wrote.

Many nights before he fell asleep—he looked at the picture of his daughter. *She's beautiful,* he thought. *I hope I get to see her.*

Charlie's thoughts of Carole and his family, and his friends, Max and Serena and their son, and Bill and Lainie helped him through so many days and nights that were hard to deal with.

In his mind's eye, he pictured how it would be when they were all together again. There would be happy carefree times again. He often said quiet—calming prayers to himself—sometimes doing his work, with the pain of wounded all about him. Often after he left the fields where death was everywhere, there were more prayers.

He was opening mail from Carole, anxious to hear about her and little Judy. One paragraph near the end of the page told of Bill being seriously hurt. They didn't know what the injuries were. Lainie was waiting to hear when and where she could see Bill. "I'll write more later," Carole promised. She sent her love and "please take care, Charlie. We love you!" Charlie read the letter over two more times, then put the letter in his shirt pocket.

In the morning they would receive further orders—on which islands they would be sent to—to fight the invading Japanese.

Charlie had hoped, "If we keep going, this will end. It has to!" He kept telling himself.

XV
Human Strengths and Weaknesses

Sundays in London had been lonesome for Max until he met Leslie and her parents. They were gracious enough to have him to dinner. He had gone and enjoyed himself, being with a family. It was like home with his parents and Serena. Sundays at the Hodges became a regular part of his life. He had written Serena and his parents about them. The Kellers and Serena had sent letters thanking the Hodges and Leslie for being so kind to Max and invited them to come after the war to visit them in St. Louis.

Max had made several trips to Europe with the officers and men in his company. They had come through some rough ordeals. When he got back, he found mail from Serena about the birth of their son, Robert, born July 1, 1943. There were pictures of Serena and the baby.

Max, so happy and proud, showed the pictures around to his friends. That night—after "lights out," Max lay there wide-eyed in the dark, thinking of the miracle of his son and Serena. He grappled with his loneliness for them and turned on his stomach, his face down in his pillow. Sometimes it was almost more than he could bear. He wanted so to be home with them.

Letters from his parents and Serena's family only confirmed all that Serena had written about little Robert. Of course, from them he learned a first grandchild was something special.

During the week, he called Leslie, saying he was back. He wanted to know if it was okay for him to come. He told her about the baby and that he was bringing pictures. She relayed the news to her parents. "He's really excited!" and they understood. Leslie met him at the bus station. She was happy to see him and said, "How much we all had missed you."

Max, looking at her, realized how much he had missed his time with them. The visits to her home had become important to him. *What is it*? he thought. *Is that strange*? *We're good friends*! He asked that of himself, then answered it with that plausible excuse; *We're just friends*!

At the Hodges at dinner, they celebrated the birth of his son. They drank a toast with wine, and the picture was passed around and around again; Max, proud as a peacock of all the nice things said about Serena and the baby.

Leslie spoke up; "There's a dance tonight at the canteen. Would you like to go?" For a second he hesitated. It wasn't what he really wanted to do. He could see on Leslie's face that she wanted to go. "Okay, that sounds good," he said, trying to sound a bit enthusiastic.

At the bus stop, they had a few minutes wait. There were quite a few people, mostly couples, soldiers and young ladies queued up talking about the dance. They were lucky to get on the crowded two-decker and made it to Trafalgar Square. They had been here a few times with Leslie's cousin, Allison, who worked at the canteen.

Inside, Leslie saw Max's eyes wandering around the room. He was looking for Allison. "No!" Leslie answered Max's question about her cousin. "She's gone for the weekend visiting her parents in Edinburgh."

The music was good—a small band—soldiers and girls dancing—some sitting at tables set up around the dance floor. Some were being served refreshments. The band was in high gear, just finished playing "Don't Sit Under the Apple Tree." Max and Leslie had danced the fast fox trot and came off the dance floor laughing and out of breath.

They sought out a bench back against the wall. There they sat resting and relaxing, Max quietly listening as Leslie told about happenings at the hospital. "I'm concerned," she said. "There are so many wounded coming across from Europe. Our hospitals are filled to overflowing. So many wounded are in beds in the hallways until room can be found for them."

"Please, Leslie," Max pleaded, "let's not talk about that tonight." His thoughts went to the battlefields where he had been that week. He didn't tell anyone about the hundreds of men, women, and children the Allies had found murdered in the towns the Germans had left. It had been difficult to see and hard to believe. He knew he wasn't dealing with it very well.

"Max! Max!" He heard Leslie's voice bringing him back to here and now. "You were far away, Max." Her voice was a bit reproachful. "Let's get out, Leslie." They decided to walk back.

Outside the spotlights criss-crossed the heaven—on alert for the German Luftwaffe. A cool mist was dripping out of the sky, bone-chilling as only it can be in London. They were both silent as they turned onto the Strand, Allison's neighborhood.

Suddenly the sirens began their wailing—warning them to seek shelter. The German planes were coming. They came at night when the English, tired from the bombings during the day, wanted desperately to rest.

"Those German devils won't let anyone sleep." The English, exhausted from these raids every night, were voicing the thoughts of every Englishman.

They had a long walk before them. Buses would not be running for a while—there was the blackout and the sirens, and soon there would be the bombs. "We're near Allison's. I know where her key is. I think we ought to go there," Leslie said. "I know she wouldn't mind." Max didn't think that was such a good idea, but Leslie said, "We ought to get out of the cool damp air, and it would be safer." So, he agreed.

Off in the distance, they could hear the bombs exploding, hitting their targets—then see the fires lighting up the different parts of the city.

"We have to get off the street before we're caught disobeying the curfew when planes are overhead!"

They hurried for another block, Max holding Leslie's arm as she tried to grope her way to Allison's flat in the dark. She unlatched the hook on the gate and stopped. "There are two steps here," she warned Max. Searching around she found the key hung on a nail hidden by the bushes. A little nervous, she couldn't unlock the door. Exasperated, she gave it to Max. "You try it!"

Max had no trouble and they went in. Leslie found the switch and turned on the lights—then hurried to pull the blackout shades and close the curtains on the two windows in the living room.

They took off their raincoats and hung them on the chairs. There was a heater in the fireplace and Leslie lit it—then went to the cabinet, retrieved two glasses, and poured them each a glass of wine.

It would take awhile before the warmth of the small heater would penetrate the chill in the room. Leslie brought a blanket, and Max covered them both. They sat on the couch quietly watching the heater's red-hot elements, with their own thoughts—slowly sipping their glasses of wine. Leslie leaned toward Max's shoulder, then pulled herself away. She had scolded herself many times in the past few weeks. "Leslie, you're falling in love with this American and he's married."

She got up, walking toward the fireplace where it was warmer. Max asked if she would like another glass of wine. "Yes, please. I'm still cold."

They could still hear the bombs and the droning of the planes battling in the air. Max observed, "There must be more German planes coming. The bombs are hitting different areas." He had his head turned a little—listening.

Leslie worried about her parents, "I hope they got safely to a shelter. It's getting quite late and we'll have to stay until the 'all clear' sounds. That may be quite awhile."

Max had to be back before morning. While he was contemplating a decision, Leslie brought two more glasses of wine.

"Leslie, you sleep in the bedroom. I'll stay here on the couch." To Max it was an awkward situation.

They were settling in their respective places. Leslie found one of her cousin's gowns, and Max was trying to get to the bathroom in the dark when a bomb exploded on their block. Leslie jumped out of bed and Max came out—she ran to Max so frightened. Cautiously, they lifted the curtain and saw buildings blown up and the raging fires, and they heard the fire engines already clanging down the street.

Max held Leslie, who was crying. He was trying to console her, and then suddenly he couldn't say how it happened. It seemed right, with all the chaos around them and the loneliness. They were sitting on the bed. Leslie had her arms around his neck and was kissing him, and he was returning her passionate kisses.

"Oh, Max!" Leslie was crying. "You do love me! You do love me!"

Max did have feelings for her—had them for a long time. "I tried to fight them," he said.

"I know, darling. It's been so hard to be with you and love you, and you not even know I was around," Leslie saying the things she had been feeling.

They were together—caution thrown to the wind—there was no turning back. They clung to each other, he fulfilling her hunger for him, and she taking away the loneliness and anguish of the war that was deep, deep in his heart and mind.

Later, Leslie had fallen asleep. He couldn't sleep, had overwhelming feelings of remorse—of guilt. Dragging himself off the couch, he shaved and dressed. Leslie was up. She had made a pot of tea and found a few scones, and a bit of ginger preserve. Max couldn't eat, and didn't say too much to her.

"What are we going to do?" she asked. Max looked at her. He didn't know what his response would be. He was sick inside of himself. "I have Serena and the baby. I love them. Last night shouldn't have happened, but it did. I love Serena, but I've grown to care for you too." He turned away. "I have to get back. I'll call you during the week." She walked to the door with him, but she wasn't going to leave with him. She felt this way was best.

She put her arms about him and kissed him on the mouth. Max returned the kiss on her forehead. He felt badly as he kissed her that way, for he knew he cared about her. He didn't want to hurt her. He knew she was the kind of young woman who was serious about her love for him. She was a fine person. All the way back to camp, his mind was in a turmoil.

At the base, he found a letter from Serena. As he read it, he became depressed. Serena, there with their baby, waiting for him to come home. He felt unworthy of Serena and little Robert. How could he have done this?

He had talked with his friends, and heard others—married—discussing their affairs, but there were many who went to the canteens, met other women, but they were true to their girlfriends or wives.

His days were filled with misery and self-reproach. He would never tell Serena. It would break her heart. How could he tell her he had been unfaithful to her, their child, and to their marriage vows? This was something he had vowed he would never do.

Max started a letter to Serena but couldn't finish it. He set it aside in his locker. He tried to forget it all in his work. Leslie waited for the call from him, but he couldn't talk to her. He thought about it—felt like a heel.

All that week he suffered recrimination upon recrimination. He wished life could go back to the day before "that night." He wished so many things—"he shouldn't have gone to Leslie's, and they shouldn't have stopped at Allison's." He kept saying over and over, "If only—but it was too late. He knew that. He blamed himself. Was he weak that he succumbed to temptation?

Max finally finished the letter to Serena. He knew she would be waiting to hear from him. He poured his anguished heart out—how lonesome he was for them, how much he missed her, and loved her. He had been driven—thinking if Serena knew she would leave him, and in some parts of his letter he sounded depressed.

Serena received the mail that she had anxiously waited for, Max's reaction to the birth of their son, and the pictures she sent. As she read on, she became concerned. This wasn't the usual letter she received from Max. It had a bit of a tone of something. She couldn't say what exactly. Was it desperation in between the lines? It worried her. Something had happened. She didn't know what. She was sure it was the war horrors he was in, that she caught only glimpses of in the movie newsreels. *He might be injured,* she thought.

Little Robert began to whimper, and Serena went to him. She cradled him close to her breast. "Oh, Max," she prayed, "please take care and come safely home to us." She hoped somehow her prayer had reached Max.

That night she wrote to him telling him about their son. She wanted to make him happy. "He looks more like his dad every day and he is good. I tell him about you. What a wonderful man you are and how proud we are, and how much we love you."

She mentioned his parents and friends. "Everyone sends best wishes and their love." She ended it with "Good night, Max. Take care, my love."

A few weeks passed and Max didn't visit Leslie and her parents. It was difficult for him. He didn't want to hurt them. They had been wonderful to him. He cared for Leslie, knowing in his heart it was wrong for both of them.

Max managed to make a call to Leslie. He could hear in her voice that she had missed him, which only made him feel worse. He explained he hadn't called because they had been very busy. He couldn't give her any further explanation.

Leslie said she understood. Deep down she wondered if Max's feelings for her had changed. She knew hers had only grown stronger. She thought of him so many times during the day—nights were worse. He was always on her mind. She waited for his calls. "Did he think of her? Did he know how much she missed him? No, he's too busy—he doesn't have time. It's the war." She answered her own questions with excuses she made for him.

In great pain, she acknowledged the excuses were partly true. "If he had wanted to, he could have given me a ring up on the phone. That was it—he hadn't wanted to." She felt ill—couldn't eat or sleep. It was difficult to keep focused on her work at the hospital. Sometimes it was torture to try to make it through the day. It took weeks, and finally she found the strength to do her job—she was needed. The day-to-day encounter with the brave wounded men found her absorbed again with their problems. Hers had been inconsequential.

The scoldings she gave herself were complex. She had been selfish thinking of herself. England was at war in a life struggle, and she was helping in the ways she could. For a while she was sidetracked. This thing between Max and her would have to wait. It would take its course no matter how they felt about each other. Where would it lead to? What would happen? Leslie fought with herself to set it aside.

The warnings sounded—the German Luftwaffe would soon be bombing London again. Lights were dimmed and patients moved in wheelchairs and in their beds to a safe part of the hospital. Leslie and the staff rushed to get them there. They talked in soft, soothing voices—trying to calm the frightened patients. Then the sound of exploding bombs filled the air, then noise of falling debris—then came the wailing of sirens of the fire engines and ambulances. Leslie waited in the middle of the room—whispering words of comfort. They called her from different parts of the room. She looked around, glad she was there—there where she belonged!

XVI
D-Day—Max in Normandy

All during the war, the Allied leaders, Roosevelt, Churchill, and Stalin of Russia, met at many conferences for discussions vital to the life and death struggles of their countries. It was at the conference held in Teheran, Iran, that the discussions were of a "cross-channel" invasion of Normandy, France—"strategic if the war in Europe was to be won." Generals and military officers of the countries, with reasoning and argumentation, sought answers to the critical situations that lay before them. Hitler and his officers knew that Allies would strike, but there was much debate where on the continent that would take place.

The war, for the Allies, for a long time had not gone well. They had been drawn into it by treachery, and they were woefully unprepared.

Germany had used planes most effectively in the war in Europe. The German Luftwaffe was sent in first to bomb the country they planned to take. The bombs destroyed fortifications and all vital points—preparing it for the tanks and army that would come in and take over control. Governments of the countries had to surrender—their people were being killed in the air raids.

England had been hit by the German Luftwaffe day and night. The Royal Air Force battled them over the English Channel and over England. The casualties on both sides were high. So many planes and pilots were lost. "The situation was most serious," as Churchill wrote President Roosevelt.

Planes had proved to be one of the most important weapons in this war. Firms and plants all over the country were participating in the war effort. In St. Louis, there were many plane factories producing them and sending them to England, where they were desperately needed. The news became more encouraging. The planes were helping turn the tide for the Allies, and the optimism bolstered the spirits in America and England.

Serena, attending the early morning important discussions and meetings at work, listened, and remembered, all worried at the many problems that were discussed, hoping to find answers. She couldn't discuss what had gone on at the meetings with anyone outside the office. It all weighed heavily on her mind. The daily reports were thought-provoking and there were many opinions to listen to. New reports came from England daily—and the newspaper morning meetings were held more frequently with fever-pitch discussions about what America and the Allies were doing. It was a harrowing time to deal with—to listen to. Serena had security clearance and was in on all of it.

General Dwight Eisenhower was made "Supreme Commander" to head the cross-channel attack. With the help of many generals in the Allied Command, the planning of this great task progressed secretly. Preparations had been going on for almost two years. The United States was sending over a million men to England—and more would be coming when needed to supply the various war fronts.

At this time, there was the problem of finding enough shelters—or more would have to be built to accommodate all the soldiers coming in. Many English people took soldiers into their homes. Hospitals had to be set up for future casualties, and more training areas had to be prepared.

In preparation for the invasion, there were also great quantities of supplies coming in, needed for the men when they arrived from America. There were different fields in areas where ammunitions of all types and sizes were stored. From St. Louis manufacturers came grenades, and grenade launchers, shells, bombs, and torpedoes, and so much more. They were kept in what looked like huge supply parks. Max was kept busy working with a unit whose job it was to see that the area and supplies were well camouflaged.

Max welcomed the work. It helped keep his mind off his problems concerning Leslie. In London, he volunteered his time off, first to keep busy, to keep track of the inventory of thousands of tanks, jeeps, trucks, and the supplies needed for maintenance. Max felt proud when he saw the labels on the different supplies coming in that read, "Made in St. Louis." He remembered to mention it to his father. Everything the Army needed was being shipped in. It was a massive commitment of resources being supplied by America.

There was much debating and discussions with top military minds as to where the most strategic area for the invasion would take place.

Churchill wanted it in French Northwest Africa where German and British troops were locked in battle, with enormous numbers of casualties.

Roosevelt and the American generals thought the coast of France would be the best for the Allied landings—specifically Normandy.

Churchill received a report of bad news—the German General Rommel, who was called "the Desert Fox," had captured important British facilities and forced the retreat of the British Army. This helped decide—the invasion of Europe would begin in Normandy, not Africa.

D-Day was planned for June 1944. The men had already received their orders. Max and his buddies, Jim and Jerry, were among those going. They spent the evening writing letters home—but nothing could be said about their going. They had been forewarned. It was all "top secret."

The invasion had to be postponed because of bad weather across the channel. This worried the Allied Command. It wasn't a good beginning. The bright side of this predicament was bad weather kept almost all the German Air Force grounded. Their commanders were sure there would be no Allied invasion in bad weather.

On June 5th, hundreds of British bombers hit German installations. At midnight, British soldiers landed in areas where specific beaches would soon receive Allied forces. That night was the beginning of the "Invasion Across the Channel."

In England, small Navy vessels took the men to the bigger ships waiting nearby. Nervous and anxious, they came by the thousands. It was a secretive but wonderful sight to see as the invasion fleet sailed out of the English harbor. They were unaware that President Roosevelt, speaking from the White House on June 6th, announced to America—the invasion they had all been waiting for had begun at last. In thousands of towns all over the country, church bells rang. People there, in Canada, and in England, went to churches and synagogues to pray for the men—wishing them victories in battle and praying for the horrible conflict to end.

During the night, paratroopers were dropped in the different areas. Their job was to prepare the beach for safe landings for the troops. They were to knock out lines of communications and blow up bridges and rail stations to hamper the German supply routes. It had gone well in some areas; the Germans had been completely surprised, but in one beach area, German aircraft fire hit some of the Allied planes dropping the paratroopers. The parachutes coming down were hit by German machine gun fire and rifle fire from the ground. So many young lives sacrificed. They never had a chance.

Max, Jim, and Jerry stood up with the others—crowded together—jostled back and forth as their craft sped toward the shore. Coming closer, they saw the lifeless bodies entangled in the parachute cords and ropes, floating near the surface. It was an unnverving sight. A few of the men got sick and tried to make it to the side of the craft.

They were nearing the beach in Normandy. Then the craft stopped with a jerk and dropped its gate, and the men were hurried off, carrying heavy equipment on their backs. They held their rifles up near their chests as they attempted to wade through waist-high water. The craft couldn't get closer to shore, and the men disembarked in water quite deep.

A machine gun chattered its shells away, exploding around the soldiers everywhere. Several were hit. Max saw Jim fall. He turned, his instinct was to stop and help his friend, but the captain's deep voice bellowed at them all—"Move it! Move it!"

On the beach they struggled ahead as German guns fired at them from behind thick hedges of bushes. The soldiers had orders to get to the woods; their eventual destination would be Cherbourg on the northern coastline of France.

They pushed on—German gunfire continuous—and their comrades falling all around them. A soldier, in shock, stood there beside a fallen friend. Their captain leading them yelled again, "Move it! C'mon, move it!" They started to run faster toward their objective, the gun nest up on a hill.

Daylight was slowly fading and the men were down now, crawling forward. Some slid into what looked like foxholes for cover. A few were digging furiously in the sand with whatever they had handy. It didn't take long to hurriedly displace the sand and dirt to make a foxhole. They weren't deep enough. There wasn't time, but still they afforded some protection.

A German gun in the concrete-enclosed pillbox was shelling the area. Max moved slowly—crawling—pushing himself ahead, the equipment on his back, moving a little from side to side. He lowered himself into another foxhole a few yards forward. There was another soldier in it. Max knew he was dead, lying on his back looking up seeing nothing. It was a soldier who had gotten off the ship with him just a short while ago. Max felt sick, cold, and shaky. His head pounded and he pushed his helmet up a bit, then quickly pushed it back. His thoughts were of Jim lying out there.

Just then Captain O'Rourke slithered in beside him. He said something to Max, but just then the gun fired shells, and Max couldn't hear what the captain said. At times the gun was quiet, but not for long. If there was the slightest sound on the field, the gun would start up again—the gunfire fanning out over a large area. There would be an explosion followed by many others. Soldiers cried out when hit, but many didn't—suffering in silence, not to give their positions away. With authority in his voice, the captain spoke to Max again. "We've got to put those 'Krauts' out of commission. We can't stay here!"

The gun nest had them bogged down, hindering their advance. It was serious. O'Rourke explained his plan to Max. Then he crawled out to the other soldiers nearby. They were to start firing to the right to distract the Germans and give the captain time to get to the hill to send grenades into the gun nest. The soldiers had three minutes, after their leader was back with Max, to begin shooting. They synchronized their watches.

He made it back. Max was to follow closely with his flame-thrower. The few minutes passed and the soldiers began firing. The machine gunners from the nest began working their gun. It swiveled to the left for a while. The captain made a run for it. The gunners began shooting to the right. The captain was a few feet away from his objective when he was hit several times. He went down. He didn't get up again.

Max scrambled forward and made it up the hill, withdrew the grenade pin, and threw it in—then stood there with his flame-thrower spewing its long trail of fire at those in the gun nest. They came out running. Some came with their guns blazing, some with their clothes on fire screaming in pain.

Max, angry at the enemy, responsible for the deaths of so many of his friends and his "captain," kept the flame-thrower on them yelling, "Take that! And take that!" until the last one was down and the guns were quiet.

Another officer took over the command, took Captain O'Rourke's place, and was now in charge of the survivors of the onslaught. They were led forward—they encountered the enemy everywhere—battles raged and several other gun nests were destroyed. Casualties on both sides were high, and the Americans had taken several hundred German prisoners. The area was now Allied-secured, and the information reported to headquarters, relieved to be getting some news of positive results.

The medics came to tend the wounded and later the Grave Detail came covering the field, finishing their jobs, like automatons, their feelings trying to stay buried as they went on performing the sad duty.

Military tanks and jeeps loaded with soldiers left the area and would join other soldiers on foot, later. They headed toward Cherbourg, on the northwestern coast of France. The port was of utmost importance to both sides. It was now in the hands of the Germans, who had it heavily barricaded, protected like a fortress.

The Allies were to capture it, as supplies and reinforcements would have to come through it to support the Allied armies. The

Allied forces reached Cherbourg on June 25th. Their leaders had figured the taking of Cherbourg would be accomplished in a few days, but it took several weeks. The Battle of Cherbourg was fierce and brutal. Every battle took its toll—hundreds and hundreds—into the thousands, causing great concern for Americans at home.

The German general in command had asked his superiors for permission to surrender. He was trying to defend the port with his wounded soldiers. Hitler sent in more reinforcements, and he informed his generals in no uncertain terms—"Cherbourg was to be held at all costs. They were to hold to the last!" German high command still did not believe the Allies would invade at Normandy. They were sure what was going on there was a trick—a diversion, and then still believed the true invasion would be elsewhere.

In America, President Roosevelt kept warning, "There would be large casualty lists—dead, wounded, and missing." The men were tired, exhausted from battle. The Allies kept fighting for Cherbourg. Finally most of it was Allied-controlled.

Still the Germans fought on—attacked at other points, and there was sporadic firing and battles. As the Allies advanced from different directions of France, heading toward Paris, they were retaking cities, towns, and villages along the way.

Max, Jerry, and the troops were waiting for reinforcements. They had a little time for relaxation. Their time together was good. Eagerly, they waited for mail call that day. Max received three letters that had been held up somewhere before reaching him.

He began opening one before he got back to his place. The letter from Serena told him "we are all fine." A number of times she told him, "I miss you and love you. Little Robert knows his dad is the one in the picture on the radio. We hear some news about the war on the radio and in the papers. We worry. Please take care of yourself. We send our love and prayers."

Max's eyes were misty. He couldn't help it. He tried to swallow the lump in his throat. *God,* he thought, *I miss them.*

He didn't read the next letter for a while, just kept reading Serena's over and over. Then he folded it carefully and put it in his pocket.

Max read the next letter from his mother. They all missed him, waiting for him to come home. They were saddened by Uncle Dave's passing, talked about little Robert, how much they loved their grandchild and sent their love. The last letter was from Saul also telling about Dave's death. Saul wrote, "I didn't want to write sad news, but I was sure you would want to know." He knew he would be reading them many times.

That night the fellows talked about home as they finished dinner and prepared to rest. Jerry sat next to Max. There hadn't been time to talk, but Jim had been on their minds. They missed him. They had trained and prepared, were toughened up, but in the happenings of the last few weeks, they had seen such hate in human beings. The shock of what they had been through and seen affected them all.

Max spoke, his voice strangely subdued. "On the way coming over, Jim wrote a letter to his wife. He asked me, if anything happened to him, would I get it to her." Max took out a ring he had on his dog chain. It was Jim's. "I told him nothing would happen, Jerry." His voice broke. "But it did. He died!"

"You couldn't help that, Max. It happened! It just happened!"

Max turned his head away. He didn't want Jerry to see his face. Jerry had his left elbow on the table, his hand supporting his head. His face was turned away from Max. For a few minutes, they were together, but alone, their thoughts far away to their homes and families.

Jerry spoke, "If we both get back, let's go see Peggy and little Timmie." He paused, "If one gets back, let's promise he will see her, to give her the letter and ring, and tell her what a great guy Jim was, and how much he loved her and their son, always talking about his family." Max touched Jerry's shoulder, and they made the promise, one to the other.

XVII
Max's French Connection—Paris

Before Ressel died, she asked Dave to keep looking for Nedda's daughter, Tova. The family had been in contact with the Red Cross and various other immigration organizations trying to find out what had happened to her since the Partisans had rescued her and escaped from the Warsaw Ghetto during the uprising there. There were many reports from people who professed to have some knowledge. The welcome information was checked, but it eventually led to a dead end.

Dave made contacts again and again. The last one led to a man named Francois Duvall, presumed to be living somewhere in France. No one knew too much about him and the trail went cold. Dave was disheartened and anguished, but he knew he had tried to fulfill his sister's dying wish, even though the outcome had been unsuccessful.

Time had passed, and Dave had remarked often, "It seems as we get older, the days, weeks, months, and even years get shorter—go more quickly. Do you find it so?" he would ask his friends. They agreed. It seemed there wasn't enough time to do things one really wanted to.

Dave's time was growing short. He had become ill and knew he was dying. He asked only one thing of the family—to keep looking for Tova. He had so many sleepless nights, and so often the same nightmares tormented him. It was of a child crying piteously, frightened by angry German soldiers, with drawn bayonets, coming at her and the family. He would awaken covered in perspiration and shaking. He was relieved to find it a hideous dream. Exhausted, he would fall back on the pillow, unable to sleep for hours. He wondered why he had this unnerving, recurring dream. Could it be trying to tell him something? It hurt not knowing if she was alive or where she was. "What, dear God," he asked, "what happened to her?"

Max was in Europe. Saul had written about Tova. "If you get to France, please keep in mind we're looking for her. There might be something, someone there can help us with." So far, Max had been unable to follow up on that request from home. Mail to folks back home was heavily censored. Max could tell them nothing of where he was or what he was involved in.

They didn't know he and his company with the Allied Command were engaged in ferocious battles with the Germans. They were retaking French towns and forcing retreat of the Germans, pushing them into Germany. Before the Germans retreated, however, they destroyed the towns. Most of the civilians and slave workers in factories were sent to concentration camps to be killed before the Allied Armies came in.

As always, their priorities were to round up the Jews. They had been deported from other countries—Holland, Belgium, Italy, and sent to concentration camps where they were murdered by the thousands. Even though every day brought liberation to towns, the killings had gone on. It was death to those who helped the Resistance fighters.

The Allies, marching in on liberated French towns, had many opportunities to see the brutal handiwork of the retreating German army. Sometimes, Max could inquire of a few townspeople, trying to get whatever information he could, but there were always those around who were infiltrators, sympathetic to the German cause. Max had learned to be extremely careful not to put any of the friends of the Allies in danger. There had been so few contacts for Max. After meetings held secretly, he felt discouraged. They never gave him much hope. "It had happened many years ago," they told him.

Almost twenty-seven years had passed, but they had never stopped looking, always optimistic. She could have survived—by some miracle—she could have survived! She could also have died with millions of others. She was an infant. That would have been sad, but it would at least be a closure to that horrible pain of not knowing they carried in their hearts.

If she were alive, who was she now? Would she be happy to meet them? Did she know about them? Would they be causing her any trouble if they found her? So many questions and no answers.

By August, the Allies had retaken the towns of Caen and Rouen, the towns along the Seine, and other small villages and towns. They were then to join others for the march to Paris. Their goal: to recapture Paris.

It was while in the town of Rouen that Max's inquiries brought a glimmer of hope. A meeting was set up. Max had unknowingly undergone extensive scrutiny by two Frenchmen before he was put in touch with a Phillipe Le Roux.

There was no conversation as they drove off together into the countryside Le Roux turned off the main road and entered a dirt road to a small house set back, almost hidden by trees. Le Roux took his rifle, got out, and checked around. He motioned for Max to follow. Inside they waited to meet the man called "Duvall." "He might not be the right man," Le Roux forewarned him. Le Roux spoke English, but with a slight French accent. "There were many 'Duvalls' living in France." He didn't want to raise false hopes in this young man. He had seen too many disappointments of people trying to locate lost relatives.

They sat having a glass of wine. Le Roux heard a car stopping. He hurried to the window, "That's Francois Duvall." Max got up and looked out at the man headed toward the house. He was a man about fifty with hair brown and gray; not too tall, and of a stocky build. He walked with firm steps.

Le Roux opened the door. They greeted each other, kissing first on one side of the face and then the other. Duvall sat down studying the American. His eyes searched Max's. He wore a worried look. Max could see the man had gone through much. Life had drawn its deep lines on his face.

His accent definitely French, he began questioning Max. "How are you related to this person you are looking for?" He evidently knew some of the story from Le Roux. "That was a long time ago. What did you call her?"

"Tova," Max answered.

"What do you know about her?" Duvall questioned further.

Max told all he knew about the Varners in Warsaw and what had happened to them. The Frenchman listened intently. Francois spoke, "Do you have a picture of anybody in the family?" Max took out the picture of Serena and Little Robert. Francois took the picture and Max watched his eyes widen, and he had a little difficulty trying to catch his breath. "Who does the child look like?" he asked. He looked a little like Serena. There was a definite resemblance.

"He looks mostly like his grandfather, Robert, and would be a cousin to Tova," Max explained. He pointed to Serena in the picture, "My wife would be a second cousin."

Francois produced a picture of his Michelle. Max looked at it; his heart began racing. Michelle looked like the Varners. Francois took back the picture of his daughter. No one at the table spoke. For a few minutes, they were trying to cope with the shock of what this could mean. In disbelief, Max spoke, "She's alive!" he said in wonderment. "She's alive! Grandma Ressel and Uncle Dave would have been so happy to know she survived and is all right."

Duvall was shaken. "We never told her she wasn't our child. We thought it safer for her." He looked quite upset.

"Please know, we don't want to hurt you, or her. You saved her life and took care of her. The family discussed this so many times over the years. They worried whether she was safe, being taken care of, and loved. They prayed. Francois, you answered all their prayers. So many tears were shed for her," said Max.

Duvall spoke, "I'll have to talk to my wife, and then we will have to decide what would be best for Michelle."

Max answered, "I'll leave it to you to tell her the truth, that she has more family who love her. However, if you decide to leave things as they are, I'll understand. Still, I would like to see her, if at all possible, so I can tell the family."

"We had a great compassion for what the Jewish people were going through here in this war. Michelle worried about what was happening to them. We lost friends and we know it isn't safe here yet. We hate the German Nazis—what they stand for and what they've done.

"So many times I found myself wanting to tell her she was Jewish, but it would not have been good for her if they knew she wasn't French. She was our child. We loved her." Francois shook his head. "I don't know if that was the right thing to do. It bothered me—was on my mind constantly. We didn't have the right to take away her birthright. No one has that right!"

He got up to leave. His shoulders seemed to have the weight of the world on them. He promised to let Max know through Le Roux what had been decided. It would be awhile. He didn't know how long he would be away. He was going to be busy. He didn't explain further. They shook hands. Le Roux took his rifle, opened the door, stood there for a few minutes, his eyes searching the area. Max could see him through the window checking around the house. Then he came in, said something in French to Duvall, and hurriedly Duvall left.

Le Roux said to Max, "We'll have to wait at least twenty minutes to be sure we weren't followed. If they heard shooting, they were to leave for another route through the woods," Le Roux explained.

They waited. Le Roux was nervous. Then they left. As they were leaving, Le Roux cautioned Max again, "The Germans are still here. That makes it dangerous for Francois and his family." It was dangerous for Le Roux too, if he were seen by a German sympathizer with an American soldier. "Be careful. Say nothing to anyone!"

"I know. Don't worry," Max tried to assure Le Roux. Before reaching town, they parted, Le Roux promising to get in touch with him as soon as he had any news.

Max and his troop met with other Allied troops and left on their drive toward Paris. The troops were coming from all directions in France, from Italy liberating French towns along the southeastern route, all headed toward Paris. The Germans were set for a long struggle; their aim to hold onto Paris as ordered by their high command.

The French Resistance helped the Allies battle the aggressor in so many ways. They blew up bridges, factories, and fuel dumps important to the German war machine. Daily they risked their lives to save Allied pilots and soldiers to get them to safety, back to England. When they were caught, they were tortured, often rounded up, taken to the center of town, hanged or shot, and left there—a warning to others. Wherever they were needed, they came to help the fight. The Germans could kill them, but they came by the thousands joining up, willing to die for freedom.

Duvall and a group of twelve fighters were on their way to accomplish a mission of great importance to the Allied effort. Duvall knew the area well. He had carefully watched and observed, and he knew what the buildings and warehouses contained. His orders were to demolish as many as they could within the time table allotted them. It had to be carried out with great precision and be successful in order for the Allies to come in to complete their assignment. The warehouses contained fuel for German tanks and other vehicles. There were munitions for their machine guns and everything needed to supply their troops. The success of Duvall's mission meant the Germans would be stopped and the Allies could advance to complete their plan to end the war.

Duvall led the group that night, experts in dynamiting. It was important for each one to carry out his assignment. It was a team effort and had to be perfectly timed. They came in the dark, working in teams of two. Synchronizing their watches with Duvall, they left in different directions. Duvall and his partner headed for the main building and saw two guards unexpectedly headed their way. They hid. The German guards would have to be disposed of before they could give any kind of alarm.

Duvall came around with his partner on the other side. Each pounced on one guard and strangled him. The Germans were young, strong, and it took awhile to subdue them. Duvall worried his timing would be off, but there often were unforeseen problems. They hurried to do their job, working feverishly, then lit the fuses and stayed a second to be sure they were working.

The others had finished their jobs before Duvall and his partner had gotten to safety, then waited for them. The explosions had begun. Every few seconds another could be heard. The earth shook, and fires could be seen for blocks. Germans in some barracks ran out, but the explosions caused heavy machinery, burning materials, and collapsing buildings to fall everywhere. There was devastation all around.

The mission was a success, and the report was sent to headquarters, waiting to hear whether the troops could advance. The Allied Command was jubilant. It was a job well done, dangerous, but the French Resistance had come through again for the Allies. There was prayer the war would end sooner with fewer casualties.

Duvall and his partner, trying to get away, had been hit by the flying, burning debris. They made it back to safety, but they were kept hidden as the Gestapo was hunting those responsible. They searched street to street, house to house, took hostages into custody for the sabotage. They pushed them, beating them with their rifles, and yelling, "*Mach schnell*! *Mach schnell*! (Hurry! Hurry!)"

They were marched to fields, made to dig trenches (their own graves). Now they were ordered to undress, the clothing set aside. They were forced to jump into the pits. Some were pushed when they hesitated. The Germans set up their machine guns and mowed them down. Some began running in the pit, others scratched trying to make it to the top, but they soon fell in agonizing death. One woman had tried to shield her child and was shot again to be sure she was dead. The child whimpered and the guard shot its head, and brain matter splattered all around. The German soldiers talking, laughing, gathered up their guns and left the massacre there for all to see.

The Allied troops coming through saw the handiwork of the Germans. The troops were told to bury the poor, defenseless ones killed in this brutal manner. When the news reached Duvall and the Resistance, they wept. It made them more determined to fight the enemy, to end the war. Their mission had caused many reprisals like this one, but they had to go on.

Hearing about the child, Duvall remembered how he had managed to save Tova (his Michelle). He was most anxious to get back to his family. When he was away, he was acutely aware of the danger his family was in. He prayed they were safe.

Duvall would discuss the situation that had arisen with the American, with his wife, Monique. He knew what a shock it would be to all of them, and it worried him. His concern was how Michelle would feel now, on learning they were not her birth parents.

Duvall had been badly injured the night of the explosion, and the Gestapo was still searching for those responsible. For a whole week, every day, they came—armed German guards—to take by brute force innocent civilians, women and their children, lined them up against walls of houses and shot dead. Sometimes they were collected, put in boxcars to be carted off to the crematoriums.

Only one person knew the whereabouts of Duvall—another Frenchman Anton. He could be trusted. Anton's wife and two young children had been rounded up and shot with other civilians in reprisal for an attack on two German soldiers. This, in the village of Boulogne where Anton lived. He had been away and when he returned and learned of the massacre, his hate for the Boche almost consumed him. He became one of the French Freedom Fighters—volunteering for every mission he could. The killing of Germans became his goal in life. Anton's hate for the Nazis doubly ensured the safety of Duvall—Duvall, who was key to many of the successful undertakings of sabotage. Those in the Resistance knew if captured, under the worst torture, they would never reveal names to put anyone in danger. Thousands died keeping the promise. Dying, they shouted "Vive la France!"

As the weeks of recuperation passed, there was plenty of time for Duvall to think. The days were restless ones for him, knowing he should be helping, but stopped because of his injury. His thoughts were of his family. He had pondered long and hard, and he made a decision. He and his wife together would tell Michelle. His heart was heavy. They might lose this daughter they loved so much. She had been their life. Now she would learn the secret they had carried fearfully all these years in their hearts.

Would she be angry with them? Hate them? He didn't know. It was a torment thinking about it, but it had to be faced. For him, it was the only way, the right way. She had to be told, no matter what the outcome or consequence would be.

Good news came; he could be going home in a week. His spirits greatly lifted, he began planning. "First, I'll get in touch with Le Roux, then the American." He hesitated. News from the different fronts of the Allies advancing, and the battles being fought, death struggles, made Duvall pause. *In this war,* he thought, *who knows where they are*! He hoped to see them well. He prayed Le Roux and the American were safe—wherever they were. It was important to him and his family.

Francois Duvall was back home for just a week. It was a quiet reunion with Monique and Michelle. At the French Forces Headquarters, he learned Le Roux was with those advancing on Paris. They were less than thirty miles from the capital—all the way encountering heavily armed German troops and patrols attacking. The Germans were to hold Paris at all costs.

The Allies from all parts of France were headed toward Paris. The Germans were a strong, vicious, ruthless enemy, but the Allies hung on. Resistance groups, Allied troops, and civilians by the thousands were killed. Casualties were high on both sides, but finally the German commander of Paris surrendered on August 25th.

Paris was free at last!

It was a day to remember. Thousands lined the streets of Paris to welcome their liberators with flags waving, food, flowers, and wine. Max and his friend Jerry were in the troops marching in, being mobbed by the crowds of well-wishers. Women of all ages grabbed the soldiers, hugging and kissing them on both cheeks. The soldiers had never encountered anything like this before—bewildered and weary—soon they were all smiling.

Max and Jerry, like the other soldiers, were passing out chocolate bars to the children. A few hours later, General DeGaulle made his way through the crowds and marched in triumph down "Champs Elysees." Church bells were ringing all over the city. Paris was jubilant!

There was sadness, too. The Allies discovered that before the Germans surrendered Paris, they had taken French political prisoners from the Gestapo prisons and loaded them on trains—and they sent them to concentration camps where they were killed.

The American and British troops were now fighting across France, retaking cities from the Germans. Max and Jerry, there with the Americans, were now nearing the western border of Germany.

As the Allies advanced, the German soldiers fought savagely to hold out as long as they could. Before they retreated behind the lines, the "S.S." killing squads rounded up civilians, prisoners of war, and slave laborers, crowded them into buildings, shut them in, then fired on them until there was only devastation and death. In places they were made to stand near huge pits that were dug. They were shot, petrol poured over their bodies and set ablaze. The Allies coming in found the graves not yet finished. There they saw bodies piled in, or around, buildings—stacked like wood. Survivors who had miraculously escaped came out and told of the torture and killings.

As always, in the madman Hitler's war, Jews especially were victims. In city after city, the story was the same. As Allies were gaining control of the countries once held by the Germans, they found thousands of Jews from Holland, Belgium, Estonia, Hungary, Yugoslavia, and the rest of the countries had been deported. They were sent by railway to Auschwitz and other camps to be gassed.

The Germans previously had kept records and files of torturous medical experiments with thousands of false death records. Now, they were losing the war, and the evidence of their madness was being destroyed, the corpses burned, and then camps were to be dismantled and eliminated.

As late as fall that November of 1944, in Budapest, Hungary, over forty thousand Jews were driven on a death march. For about a week, they traveled on foot towards Austria—over 150 miles away. There was no resting. They were beaten, and those falling, unable to go on, were shot by the "S.S." guards. About one-fifth died on the march.

Trains and trucks were busy daily bringing in the Jews who were told they were being relocated. They were crowded into the cars, starved, ill with disease, in torn, dirty clothing. They were freezing. They came, men, women, and children sent to Auschwitz and the other camps and crematoriums all over Poland and Germany. Many died before they reached their destination.

The bodies were thrown off and collected by slave laborers picked for this job, many of them Jews. They were sickened by their duties. Those still alive in the trains and trucks were sent to the showers (the gassing stations), then thrown into the ovens. When the slave laborers were finished, they were lined up and shot or gassed, and others threw their bodies in the ovens, disposing of them as evidence.

There were plenty of dead bodies stacked everywhere, ready for the ovens. This happened because at times so many came in going through the showers (gassing chambers), there hadn't been time to burn them, even though the ovens were going full blast twenty-four hours a day, consuming tens of thousands of souls, victims of the madman Hitler and his armies.

The killings were done systematically before the Germans retreated from a town or city. The Allied soldiers and their officers could not believe what they were finding. They took photos. Death from the war was one thing, but these killings were another. The enormity of the situation was incomprehensible to them. It was hard to look at. Many were angered, filled with hate, some said prayers. They set about the sorrowful task of burying the dead, hoping they were at peace.

XVIII
Losses and Victories

The liberation of Paris was welcome news, indeed, to America and her Allies. The war in Europe, for a long time, had been one with many setbacks. Now, every success was viewed with optimism.

People hoped that Germany would surrender and the war would end. Then it became apparent the war was far from over. Hitler wouldn't listen to his generals and commanders. Those who spoke of losing the war were immediately replaced. Some were even killed, charged with being traitors to the German cause. His orders were to keep fighting. There was to be no surrender!

For a long time, there had been rumors of the Germans working on secret weapons. From Churchill, in Britain, came the dreaded news—the Germans were attacking England from across the channel with these new weapons carrying tons of explosives. They were called "V-1's and V-2's, Flying Bombs, and Rocket Bombs!"

The hits came regularly. Wherever they landed, there was mass destruction, and the death toll kept rising. British bombers attacked some of the weapon factories and plants, but the V-1's and V-2's then came from other sites and continued the frightening raids on England. Courageous though the British were, there were times when morale wavered.

In America, there was great concern. The losses in planes and pilots were very high, as the Royal Air Force made its raids on the German weapon factories. In St. Louis, and other parts of the country, aircraft plants were working full shifts and overtime to supply the Allies with the planes so desperately needed.

St. Louis reflected what the country was dealing with in the war—trying on so many different levels to help in the war effort. There were food shortages. Young farmers who could get deferments from the war chose to leave the farms and work in defense plants to help the war effort in that way. The women and children were left to manage the farms. Some did a fair job of it, but they couldn't keep up with the demand. The first priority for America was to see that the soldiers had enough food. Civilians were urged to grow gardens of vegetables to help the war effort.

Serena and Carole, like families in St. Louis and around the country, started what was known as "Victory Gardens." Tony, the caretaker, gave them a little plot of ground in back of the building. The plots were roped off with rope and sticks.

The girls, like most of the other new gardeners, knew absolutely nothing about gardening, but they got the packets of seeds, and under Tony's tutelage and direction, they planted carrots, lettuce, radishes, and two tomato plants. Then half-inch wooden poles were stuck in the ground where it was hoped peas and beans might climb. The empty packets were nailed to the sticks so the new gardeners would know what was coming up.

Gardens sprouted on boulevards around the city, and on plots between buildings. Everywhere civilians could be seen weeding, hoeing, and watering. People chatted, became friends, giving garden tips, and sharing glimpses of their lives. It was wonderful to see and be a part of.

Serena and Carole took care of their garden. After a few weeks, their efforts were coming to fruition—green shoots appeared. The gardeners stood there smiling, so happy with their results. They learned to respect the farmers, as Serena said, "Just think how hard they work to bring the food we get at the store, and we never gave it a thought. Now we'll know different."

They shared their bounty with Tony and Lainie, and with some of the neighbors in the next building. It was exciting to write Max about what families on the home front were doing to help the war effort. The Victory Gardens were a huge success! President Roosevelt commended the country for its efforts, working together—assuring it "Victory would come!"

President Roosevelt had taken the country through troubled times, and his health seemed to be failing, but on November 7,

1944, he was elected for another four-year term. He chose as his vice president, the senator from Missouri, Harry S. Truman. Carole and Serena had voted the Democratic ticket, and they were so proud to have voted for Roosevelt. They had faith in him, believed he would see the war to its end, and their men would be home soon.

The months of war continued, with casualty lists ever mounting. Serena, Carole, and Lainie had gotten small flags that hung in the windows of families who had soldiers in the war. The flags had embroidered stars in the middle. Gold stars showed the family had a soldier who would not be coming home; the silver star was for a wounded soldier. Walking down the street, one became aware that almost every house in a block had a flag in its window.

Carole, Serena, and Lainie had silver stars in their flags. There were so many families with "gold stars" in their windows; the mothers were known as "Gold Star Mothers." They were a sad, heartbroken group, but proud. Their husbands or sons had died fighting—believing in freedom—and the price of freedom was high!

Carole, after putting Judy to bed, often came down to listen to the evening news with Serena. Sometimes, after Lainie had gotten Bill to bed, she would join them. Lainie was having a difficult time caring for Bill, but she never complained. Many times she dozed off, very tired, and Serena and Carole let her rest.

They listened quietly as the newscaster reported the Germans fighting in Russia—at one time victorious, now retreating. This was bad news for the German High Command. Serena worried, turned the radio off. "We really don't know for sure what's happening. We're not being told all because of security reasons."

"Yes, I know. I think about it all the time."

"I do, too," Serena agreed, "I wonder when it will end."

Gently, they wakened Lainie, who apologized for having fallen asleep. They hugged each other and said their "good nights," and returned to their respective apartments to cope with their worlds.

Carole and Serena often took their youngsters to the playground. As the children played, they discussed how life would be when their men came home. To pass the time, they made plans—some very serious—about their futures. Some plans were frivolous. Sometimes they discussed Bill and Lainie. Bill wasn't improving too much. Lainie didn't discuss the situation with Carole and Serena, but they could see things were not good. They visited, but Bill was not himself. The visits became uncomfortable. Lainie tried to keep conversation going. Serena talked about Max, Carole about Charlie. Serena had written Max to write to Bill. "It might help him," she had said.

Taking the children back to their apartments, Serena suggested they might take turns keeping Bill company so Lainie could get away for a few hours. They decided to talk to Bill and Lainie. The rest of the way back they walked in silence, each lost in private thoughts.

That night Serena put her son to bed with wishes and prayers that Max would be home soon. Sometimes she was strong and full of courage. Max would want her to be that way. It took strength and courage to care for her son, to watch him grow, with his father far off in harm's way. That worry hung over her head. She wrote Max, but it wasn't the same as if he were there sharing in his child's accomplishments. Before she went to bed, she tiptoed into her son's room and watched as he slept, so wonderful, so innocent. She kissed him gently on the cheek and slipped out quietly.

The nights, the long nights were lonely. Serena lay there tossing and turning, worried, fear in her heart for what the next day would bring. So many times there were tears for the loneliness she felt for Max. She wanted him home, there beside her, holding her, loving her. She closed her eyes. In her mind, she pictured him with her, his kisses and hers mingling in the ecstasy of their lovemaking.

She didn't want to open her eyes for fear the mind dream would disappear, but she did. Then taking Max's pillow in her arms, burying her head in it, she sobbed, "Oh, Max, I miss you so!" She hugged the pillow until merciful sleep took over. Another long day passed, but there were the tomorrows.

Sometimes in the quiet of the night, Serena could hear through the opened windows Carole crying in the bedroom upstairs. She wanted to go up to comfort her friend, but she felt it was a private time for Carole. She respected her friend's privacy, and she couldn't interfere. They had confided and shared many things, these two close friends, but this now was Carole's need for her own space. It was the same for Serena, and she understood her friend's pain, the fear for her loved one's well-being, and a loving wife, lonesome for her mate.

Carole hadn't received any mail from Charlie for almost two weeks, which was unusual, in a sense, since he wrote regularly. Then she consoled herself with the fact the news on the radio and newspapers told of several campaigns on the islands in the Pacific. Charlie had told her, "Don't worry. I'm kept pretty busy." She knew what that meant, soldiers injured, and she worried about Charlie. In spite of what he said, she worried.

Two days later, Carole, terribly upset, came running down to Serena. She had been notified Charlie was being flown to a hospital. She would be contacted when he arrived. The information was meager. Serena put an arm around her friend, who was visibly shaken, crying. Serena gently guided her to a chair in the kitchen. Serena, too, became worried, *What does this mean*? she wondered.

Over and over, when the tears stopped for a few minutes, Carol questioned, "Where is he hurt? How bad is it? Oh, God, is he going to be all right?" She thought about Bill downstairs. All these questions she had and didn't know when she would get answers. She felt ill.

It was early morning and the apartment was warm. The weatherman on the radio was forecasting another hot, humid day in St. Louis. Serena turned on the fan and poured Carole a glass of iced tea. Then she brought a wet washcloth with a few ice cubes wrapped in it, soothingly wiping Carole's perspiring brow. Carole closed her eyes and heaved a deep sigh.

"I can't do this, Serena." She took the cloth from her forehead. "I can't fall apart. I have to be strong for Charlie and Judy. There is so much I have to do." She hugged Serena and thanked her friend for being there for her. She saw Serena as being stronger than she was. She always seemed to be calmer. Carole greatly admired her for that. Upstairs she called Charlie's mother and then her father. He was coming over to see what information he could get. Then there would be the awful waiting—the waiting and uncertainty!

From an island in the Pacific, Charlie was flown back home to St. Louis, to a military hospital there. Carole had been notified and made arrangements to visit him. At the hospital, she first had a meeting with the doctor in charge, Dr. Wheeler. He explained she would find Charlie a little changed. *He's preparing me,* she thought.

She asked, "Is he going to be all right?"

"It will take time," was Dr. Wheeler's answer. The doctor walked her down the hall. They stopped at the door marked 420. "For the first visit we recommend about a half hour," he told her. Putting his hand on her shoulder, he wished her "Good luck, Mrs. Schwartz."

Carole opened the door and went in. Her heart was pounding, not knowing what she was going to see. At the first sight of Charlie, she was shocked. He looked thin, very pale and ill. She knew he had malaria. She thought, *that's what wrong with Charlie.* He was sitting in a chair near the window. He got up and she rushed to embrace him. He had his arms about her and she was kissing him. She sensed something different, but didn't know what it was, or how to explain it.

She talked and took out newer pictures of Judy. Charlie didn't say too much. The time went quickly, and a nurse came in to say visiting time was over. Carole assured Charlie she would come every weekend. He seemed pleased, nodding his head.

The doctor met her as she was leaving. He wanted to discuss Charlie's illness. "It is a new disability," he explained. The government named it "Battle Fatigue." They weren't sure how to treat it. There were thousands of soldiers afflicted with this new illness. The doctor explained the patients were being given medications. They had deep bouts of depression that came from seeing too much of the horror of this war—the extreme cruelty was almost unbearable. They had nightmares and the patients suffered grief and guilt. Charlie blamed himself for not having sufficient supplies of drugs for the injured, and he saw them suffer and die.

Carole asked what the prognosis was for this illness. The doctor told her, "Truthfully, we don't know to what extent Charlie, or the others will recover."

Carole turned her head away, tears were starting. Regaining her composure, she looked at Dr. Wheeler, "You don't sound very hopeful."

"We're doing all we can," he assured her, "and there's always hope."

"When I come next week, will it be all right to bring our child?"

"I think that will help a great deal. Yes, that will help." He took her hand and said, "We'll see you next weekend." Then he said, "Good-bye."

Riding back, Carole thought about her conversation with Dr. Wheeler that day. She had just met him, but she felt he was sincere—and Charlie liked him. Her mind was comforted in that she had confidence in the man and put her trust in him—he would try to help Charlie.

Carole came every weekend. Some visits were better than others. If he had no flashbacks, or nightmares, and his week had been a good one, Charlie progressed and things went well.

There was talk, then, of Charlie coming home. Carole was greatly encouraged, and even Dr. Wheeler was optimistic. Carole would start to say, "Charlie was like his old self." Then she would stop short, for she knew Charlie had gone through too much and would never be like "the old Charlie." She would have to get used to that.

Carole brought Judy, and some weekends were good for the child to be with her father. She looked forward to seeing him. Then there were a few experiences—Charlie wasn't well—and she had to stop bringing Judy.

It went like that for almost four months, and then Dr. Wheeler discharged Charlie. There wasn't any more they could do for him. "Now, you have to go home and adjust to civilian life again," Dr. Wheeler told him. "You'll do just fine," he assured

Charlie, who was a little apprehensive. Charlie had to check in with Dr. Wheeler once every two months.

Charlie came home and as they drove up, he became excited. "Carole, you don't know how many times I wished—I wished I could see that '707 Westgate' address on our building!" He flew up the stairs and he waited at the door for Carole to get there. He opened the door, then turned to Carole and picked her up.

"What are you doing?"

"I'm carrying you over the threshold. We're beginning again—you and I!" She began to cry.

"Oh, Charlie, I'm so glad you're home!"

Carole's father brought Charlie's mother over to see her son. They all sat and talked. Serena came up with Judy, who had been playing with Robert. Charlie and Robert became friends. Judy wanted to sit on her father's lap, and Robert wanted to sit there, too.

Carole said, "We love you all to be here, but it's been a long day, and we're going to bed early." She laughed. "I know you'll excuse us for sending you home."

They all got up. "Okay, we're going." It was lots of hugs and kisses. They all agreed. "It's wonderful to have you home, Charlie."

Later when Judy was asleep, Charlie and Carole listened to the news for just a little while. Charlie was home with her. How many times she had visualized this, and she said to Charlie as he held her. "Oh, Charlie, I dreamed of this so many times. I was so lonesome for you."

"I know! I know!" Charlie told her with so much emotion in his voice. "I dreamed of you almost every night. No matter how bad it was, I thought of you. You were my hope. Out there, you were my hope."

They were together, and Carole said, "We'll be all right, Charlie. We're together!" He smothered her with kisses on her forehead, face, and lips, again and again, as if he were taking inventory of her.

Charlie went to work in the drug store and was doing well. Everyone was glad to see him back, and life seemed to be on an even keel. Every once in a while, he had the nightmares and would be calling out in his sleep, terrified by the demons that had taken over. Carole would wake him gently, and he would be shaking. She tried to calm him, as Dr. Wheeler had suggested she could help Charlie through the nightmares.

For a few days after an episode, Charlie would have mood swings. Carole would try to keep him busy discussing plans for their future. They made plans to buy a house, and Charlie would seem better. Carole's father, too, would talk to Charlie about expanding the business. They made contacts with other companies in other cities around St. Louis. It was decided Charlie would stay in the drug store, and Carole's father would make the trips selling pharmaceutical supplies to doctors' offices and to other drug stores. Carole's father thought the travel would be too much pressure for Charlie.

At Charlie's next visit to Dr. Wheeler, the doctor listened to Charlie's plans and approved. Charlie was cheerful, full of plans for the future, and he seemed to have made a good adjustment. The one thing he worried about with Charlie was his mood swings, sometimes high, and sometimes low. He voiced this to Carole, for her to keep track of them or make note of them. Now, Charlie was home. Bill was home, and they were waiting to hear that Max would soon be home.

America and its Allies were receiving better news about the Germans in Europe. Hitler's Armies were engaged in battle on so many fronts, and their casualties were very high according to messages intercepted by British Intelligence. There was a desperate need for more soldiers—the situation was acute.

The spring of 1945 saw the German Army taking all boys born in 1929—this was before their sixteenth birthday. These new soldiers were taken from Hitler's Youth Groups. They had been in the groups training from their early ages and learned the tactics of war—how to fight, to show no mercy to the enemy, and hate for Jews. Above all, they were to fight to the death—no surrender.

Then the Allies were dealt a devastating blow. President Roosevelt died on April 12, 1945, and Vice-President Truman became president. April 14th was declared a day of mourning. Memorial services were held over the country and in so many parts of the world. St. Louis held services in Soldier Memorial. The day was cold, and even Heaven cried. It rained all day. Churches and synagogues held services. All day radios told the sad news. People stood solemn, hearts broken and crying, at the loss of a great leader. Everyone loved and respected President Roosevelt.

This wasn't true, of course, with America's enemies. Nazi leaders rejoiced—sure this was a turning point in their favor, but they were wrong. Most of Germany's ammunition factories and plants had been secured by the Allies as they advanced through Germany. They were retaking cities on the way to Berlin. Hitler's orders were—German troops were to defend Berlin at all costs. He had been receiving reports that angered him. All he had worked for all his life for Germany was being destroyed by the Allies.

Hitler was in his bunker fifty feet underground celebrating his birthday on April 20th. Bombers were attacking Berlin. Hitler came up to inspect his new teenage soldiers and the older men in the S.S. Division. They were to defend the capital. He came up to wish them success, then returned for his birthday celebration.

Reports were brought to him telling him how the Germans were celebrating his birthday—the Gestapo and S.S. troops were killing, by hanging, prisoners of war, Jews in camps, and slave laborers, who were mostly Jews—their bodies taken and cremated. They boasted to their leader—thousands were being killed. In the bunker, the celebration continued with laughter, toasts with liquor, and food.

The Americans and other Allied troops were nearing Berlin. The fighting was fierce; the Germans determined to hold their ground and not to surrender Berlin. Thousands on both sides were being killed.

The Allies reached camps, liberated thousands, who didn't come out at first. They couldn't believe they were free from the horrors they had been subjected to. They were found in the most deplorable conditions with no food—they were starved. They slept on straw mattresses that had no straw, so they slept on the filthy boards or the floor. They were locked in with no water, no facilities for washing, not enough buckets used for latrines that overran the floor. The smells were horrible and soldiers came out ill and retching, to see the people so degraded, so dehumanized.

Some survivors tried to get off the beds to get the food being brought in. They were so emaciated, they looked like death with their skeletal bodies and sunken eyes. They tried to walk, but very weak, fell, and didn't get up. The soldiers came to help them, but they couldn't get up. They were dead. For them, liberation had come too late. Those who were there and saw it would never forget it. It would haunt them always.

In every country in Europe the Germans had occupied, the story was the same.

Hitler began making plans, finally accepting Germany was losing the war. His mistress, Eva Braun, and he were married underground in his bunker. There was a celebration with some of his friends. The honeymoon was a short one—for on April 30th, Eva was given poison and died. Then Hitler with one shot in the mouth committed suicide. Their bodies were taken from the bunker, sprayed with gasoline, and set on fire.

In that last week, wherever they could round up slave laborers who were Jews from factories, they were killed in camps, killing gas vans, or shot and stacked in mass graves. The killings went on.

German officers surrendered their forces in different parts of Germany. Some engaged the Allies in brutal battles, but they surrendered as the Allies continued in their costly victories—costly in casualties! Some German generals tried to negotiate to end the fighting, but General Eisenhower made it clear—there would have to be a complete surrender of all German forces wherever they were fighting.

Finally, Germany surrendered. It happened on May 7th, 1945, signed by generals from Germany, Russia, France, and the Allied Expeditionary Force. The war with Germany was ended! VE-Day (Victory in Europe Day) was celebrated in Great Britain and America on May 8, 1945. The war in Europe was ended. Church bells rang out, and there were prayers in synagogues and churches. The toll in lives was millions upon millions, cities destroyed, families torn apart, and millions of lives ruined.

Hitler had promised the Germans "A Thousand Year Reich." They would be masters of the world. It ended after twelve years of hate—evil—and innocent bloodshed.

The Germans let a madman take control of them with lies, deceit, and hate. A hate so vile, a hate that consumed them to a point that was unbelievable and incomprehensible. They followed, and they became perpetrators of the evil themselves.

As the countries were liberated, the American commanders took pictures and filmed the Nazi atrocities. These films later were shown all over the country, every two hours day in and day out. It was hoped everyone over sixteen years of age would see and learn—and never let it happen again!

Part Four
Coming Home

XIX
Farewells

Weary Allied troops were now preparing to leave the continent for home. Thousands were converging on the port of Le Havre on the Seine River in France. They were to embark on troop ships that would take them across the English Channel to England first, and then to their countries. Max and his company were headed that way. The soldiers were noisy, boisterous, and deliriously happy at the prospect of finally going home. Max's company was to leave in a week.

At mail call, Max had received letters from the family, and from Le Roux. Max shared the information that he would be leaving soon, and if possible, he wanted to see Duvall. Le Roux shared the news with Duvall as soon as he could. When the war with Germany ended, Duvall came home. He had heard of the attack on a village near his home. He had traveled, heavy-hearted, anxious to get home; not knowing if he would find his family alive. He told Monique, "I prayed, I prayed constantly!"

Monique, in detail, told what happened. As the Germans retreated, their trucks came lumbering in noisily on the cobblestone streets. The German soldiers poured out with their rifles ready, striking fear into the hearts of all. They rushed into homes, dragging and pushing out the occupants—adults and children of all ages. They prodded them with the rifles, lined them up facing the walls. The soldiers shot them in the back of their heads, and left them where they fell. Back they rushed into their conveyances and set off for another street to continue the slaughter.

Some French, who were German sympathizers, had informed to the Gestapo that the villagers had hidden Jewish children from the Nazis and cared for them. Monique told how they had not been time to warn the villagers, and they died needlessly with "freedom" almost within their grasp. Fearing they would be next, Monique and Michelle went into hiding. Monique's voice trembled, "It was the worst week of my life!" With her Francois away, she worried constantly that the Germans had somehow discovered their secret that their daughter, Michelle, was Jewish and not French.

Now, Monique listened as Duvall told her about the American going home and wanting to meet with them. They discussed the situation while Monique prepared dinner. When Michelle came in, there was a happy reunion of father and daughter. At the table there was laughter and prayers. Duvall lifted his glass of wine saying, "It is good to be home with my family!"

His eyes were on Michelle and his thoughts were of Max and the task before him—the information he had to impart to his Michelle. He and Monique had decided to tell her that evening. Then, for fear of how Michelle would react to learning that he and Monique were not her parents, he hesitated. He was almost ready to put it all off until the following day, but he decided to tell her. It would give her a few more days to get used to the news.

The family went into the main room of the house. Duvall, nervous, got up several times. Michelle noticed and said, "Dad, are you all right?"

He looked stricken. "What's wrong, Father?" Monique went over and put her arm in his. He seemed to have picked up a bit more courage then.

He spoke to his daughter. "Michelle, have we been good parents to you?"

A surprised Michelle looked at them—from one to the other—"The best in the whole world! What is it?"

Something quite serious was going on, and she was greatly perturbed. What was going on? Were her parents ill?

Worried about how she would take the news that they were not her parents, they were quite concerned about the shock of learning this. Would she be angry with them? Would her love turn to hate? They didn't know, but this they knew, she had to be told.

Duvall sat across from her, looking straight at her. He began. "I have something important to tell you. I joined a Resistance group at age twenty-three. Your mother and I had been married for a short time. The Germans had come to Poland to kill Jews and had killed all those in a ghetto in Warsaw, among them your mother and grandparents."

The Germans, sure all were dead, set them on fire and left, but her mother's body had protected her. He had found her, and with help from the women in the Resistance, he brought her home and they raised her as their child. They loved her as their own. Duvall was silent for a few minutes. Michelle was quiet too, trying to absorb what she had just been told. "Why are you telling me this now?" she wanted to know.

Duvall told her then of Max, the American soldier, who had come to help in the war. He was a relative. The family had been trying all these years to find her. They loved her, too. Through the Resistance, Max had come in contact with Duvall. They were both sure from pictures that Michelle was the lost relative, the child named "Tova."

The young man was leaving for America, but he wanted to meet her, only if she wanted to. He didn't want to disrupt her life here. She had a few days to think about it, to let them know if she was interested in the meeting. "You will always be our daughter. We love you," both Monique and Duvall assured her. Michelle came over and they embraced together. They were all in tears.

Then Michelle wanted to know more, what he could tell her about her mother. "You look a lot like her," he told her. They discussed much until late night.

"I'm going to bed," Michelle said. "I'm tired. So much is new to think about." At the door, she paused and looked at them both. "You're saying I'm Jewish." She smiled. "I'm glad I'm French and Jewish!"

Duvall made arrangements for the family to travel to a village near Le Havre. They were to meet Max that Monday at noon for lunch at a café, away from the crowds milling around in the bustling port city.

On Monday, Max tried to find his way. There were deep craters everywhere, and the narrow streets were choked with debris from buildings that were destroyed by the many German bombings. He found the café, one window boarded up. A sign with the name "Lyon Café" hung there, held up by two rusty chains that rattled in the wind. Max sat down in one of the chairs and waited in anticipation. He was glad he would get a chance to meet Duvall's wife and Michelle. He thought of her as "Tova." It was almost eleven o'clock. He got up a few times and walked around, hoping to see Duvall. He wondered how this meeting would go, and what he would say to Michelle. He hoped he would have something positive to bring back to the family after meeting Michelle.

Max looked around. The area was a reminder of the war, but slowly changes were progressing. He glanced at his watch. It was just past twelve. Max studied the area. Not too many weeks ago, he knew there must have been fear here because of the large presence of German soldiers. Now it was a place of French luncheon patrons filing in, smiling and talking as they filled the empty chairs at the small round tables.

Max glanced at his watch again. It was one o'clock. He got up slowly, disappointed at the prospect of not having made connections with Duvall. Then he saw him coming with two women. Duvall was walking faster, a little ahead of the women who were trying to keep up with him.

Duvall greeted Max as the French did—the touching of their faces, first one side and then the other. He introduced Monique, then Michelle. "My daughter," he said. Max kept looking at Michelle. He saw the definite resemblance to Serena's family even more defined than he had seen in the photograph Duvall had shown him at their first meeting.

Michelle, too, studied this American, this relative who was changing her life. Duvall began telling that he had explained the circumstances of their life together to Michelle. He was rubbing his hands together, and he looked down at them. He shook his head, and a deep sigh escaped him. He was thinking of how he had found her, protected by her dead mother's body. Duvall looked up at them all, then in a voice hoarse with emotion, he questioned, "Max, I hope you brought the pictures of your family. I'm sure Michelle would like to see them."

Max nodded and brought out Serena's picture with little Robert. Monique and Michelle studied the pictures. They could see the resemblance to Michelle. Max promised to have Serena's family look through pictures to see if they had any of Michelle's mother or father, and he'd send them. Michelle glanced at Monique and Duvall. She didn't want to hurt them in any way. They nodded—they assured her they wanted her to have them.

Lunch was good, and there was talk and many questions from Max, from Michelle and from Monique. Max had to get back. He said the family would write and keep in touch. He hoped they could come to visit in America. "Some day," they promised. At the parting, Duvall put his arms around Max's shoulders. Monique embraced him. Then Michelle, a little hesitant at first, came over and they said their "goodbyes". Everyone seemed happy with the outcome of the meeting. They were all family. When Max got back to Le Havre, he sent a letter off to Serena telling about meeting Michelle. "You'll like her," he wrote.

On Wednesday, Max left with hundreds of other soldiers on an old troop ship. There was great commotion with shouting and orders barked at the waiting troops. Officers with lists checked them aboard as they marched up the gangplanks. The boarding finally ended, and the ship set sail.

It was a stormy night, and the ship was buffeted by the high waves. They landed early the next morning in a thick-hung fog with a cold, dripping mist. None of that mattered to the crowded, weary men.

"It was good to be in England again," was heard over and over. Max felt that way, too. Soon, very soon, he would be on the last leg of his journey, bound for America and home!

London was crowded with thousands of returning soldiers. Disembarkation was slow—there were so many troop ships waiting to dislodge their cargoes of men. Max made it back to the base, and after a few hours, he was successful in locating his friend, Jerry. They had been separated several times on the continent, and now there was much to talk about. First they each voiced their concerns they had for each other as soldiers, and as friends.

"You son-of-a-gun," Max grabbed Jerry's shoulder in a big arm squeeze. They were laughing, and Jerry buried his head against Max's. "We made it! Damn it, we made it!" They were so relieved to find each other.

They didn't know exactly when they would be leaving London. They were to have a briefing the next day or two. They decided to go shopping for gifts for their families. They had been laughing and enjoying their shopping spree, talking about going home. Jerry, a bit nostalgic and serious, said, "Max, I can't wait to see my folks, and Mary, and the farm. When I get home, I think I'll sleep for a year in my bed, nice and warm. Yes, sir, It'll be hard to get me up!"

They both laughed. Max said, "Talking about going home, I was thinking how wonderful it would have been if only Jim were here with us. I'll always have good feelings whenever I think of him, and I am so glad to have had him for a friend. I'll be sad, too, because I was there when he died. That I won't ever forget. It will be a hurt I'll always have."

They stopped to shop for Jim's wife, Peggy, and for his son, Timmie. Max reminded Jerry, "We're going to make that trip on a weekend to see them." They queued up in a line at the corner waiting for the double-decker bus that would take them back.

Several times that evening, Max had gone to phone Leslie. He had pondered that move, then finally put his call through. Mrs. Hodges answered the phone. "I'm so happy you are back, Max, and thankful you're all right." She sounded so sincere and was speaking from her heart when she said with a little break in her voice, "We all missed you and prayed you were safe."

Max thought how much he cared about "The Hodges" as he called them. They had been there for him through his loneliness, accepted him like family. Max accepted the invitation to dinner and thanked her. He asked to be remembered to Mr. Hodges and Leslie.

The next morning Max had taken a few hours to shop at Harrod's. He had gotten flowers for Leslie, a wonderful box of chocolates for Mrs. Hodges, and a bottle of wine for Leslie's father. He waited for a cabbie, and he made it to the Hodges. Leslie opened the door, smiling. "So good to see you, Max."

He handed her the flowers and kissed her on the cheek. Mr. Hodges took the bottle of wine Max held out. "You shouldn't have done that, son," and then he warmly embraced Max.

Mrs. Hodges got her chocolates and exclaimed, "My favorites!" Then she, too, added, "You shouldn't have, Max, but you know I'll enjoy them."

Leslie had taken the flowers to the kitchen and appeared again, her face quite flushed.

Mr. Hodges opened the wine, and at dinner, he proposed a toast. "Happy to have Max back, thankful the war is over, and God bless England and America. You Yanks were there with us, side-by-side. We, in England, will never forget that," he said, and he then had to take out his handkerchief to wipe away a tear and blow his nose.

Mr. Hodges engaged Max in conversation about the war. Max didn't say too much, and Mr. Hodges guessed Max didn't care to talk about it, so he changed the subject. Max said he was anxious to get back home to his family and parents, and he talked about his plans for the future. Max thought his life would be in one of the shoe stores, hoped he could buy a home, and "get back to life as it was," was how he put it. The words were no sooner out of his mouth and his mind told him, "You know that will never happen. Life will never be the same."

After dinner, he and Leslie went for a walk, silence between them. Then she asked, she had wondered, if he had ever thought about her while away. It hurt her terribly to ask. She had tried to be busy, not to think about him, but when she saw him tonight, she knew she still loved him, and there wasn't much she could do about that. She might go with others, but it would never ever be like the feelings she had for Max. She wondered—in time, would some of it be forgotten? When Max was back with his family, she'd have to begin the forgetting process as she had tried to do so many times when he was away. Then he came back. She loved him, and told him that before he pushed off for Europe.

Max's thoughts were of Leslie as they walked. He had heard her question and was torn. He felt the attraction between them again. "Leslie," he began, "I've thought of you—how wonderful and caring and loving you were to me. I know no matter what will be in my life, you will always be a part of me."

"I know, I feel the same, but I don't know if I can deal with it. You are stronger than I am, Max." She started to cry. He took her arm and they went on in silence, each with their own thoughts, of the many things said, and those left unspoken.

There were so many things different about this walk. Max didn't know exactly what it was. Then he realized and said to her, "It's the quiet. There are no planes droning overhead, no guns going off near the coast, and no sirens wailing. People are not rushing to shelters." His mind had been busy with other things, and he hadn't realized. It was his first experience of a quiet night in London. It was a little eerie.

"I know. It took a little getting used to," Leslie told him.

Just before they came to the Hodges' home, Leslie said she hoped everything would go well for him and his family, and he wished her the same.

At the door, before they entered, Max took her in his arms and kissed her. He knew he couldn't leave her without embracing her once more. She clung to him, hungering for him, loving him, heartbroken at his going from her life. There they stood, enclosed in each other's arms, neither one wanting to let go. Then Max slowly, gently released her. Leslie straightened her hair a bit, and they went in after a few minutes of trying to compose themselves.

Max had to get back, and the farewells with the Hodges was difficult with Mr. Hodges telling Max to take care of himself and keep in touch. They all wished him "Good Luck!"

"You know my family has invited you all to come to the States. I hope someday you will come. It would make us all happy."

Max left with a multitude of feelings and thoughts. Some were of Leslie, and some of Serena. His mixed thoughts began to formulate.

I love Serena! No matter what I feel here, I love Serena!

Still he knew Leslie would always own a part of his heart. She would be interwoven and strongly connected to all that had happened to him here in England, and all they had shared with his injuries.

Max got back to find there was mail from Serena, and even though it was late, he decided to answer it right away and mail it the next morning. He felt a little uneasy; perhaps it was the guilt of thinking of both Serena and Leslie in the same time frame. He sat down to concentrate on his letter to Serena, but that contained news of the Hodges, too.

"I was at the Hodges for dinner, and I thanked them for all their kindnesses. It was a little tough to say good-bye," he wrote. "I'll miss England, but am so glad to be coming home to you and Robert. You've been on my mind. I'll call you when we land in New York and give you the date and time of my arrival at Union Station. I've missed you and love you." He signed it, "Love, Max."

He had spent so many sleep-deprived nights and was weary to the bone, but he couldn't sleep. Serena, and his son, were on his mind. Part of him so happy to be going home, and part full of anxiety. He had been away almost three years. How would it be for Serena and for him? In her many letters, it was always how much she missed him, loved him. "We are waiting for you to come home so we can resume a normal life again," she had written.

What would she think when she saw him? He had changed inwardly in so many ways, and she would see the ugly red scar on his cheek. It had always bothered him. Leslie had kept impressing on him that wasn't important. When he read Serena's letters telling about Bill's injuries and Charlie's problems, he accepted compared to that, and what he had seen in the war, Leslie was right. Still he wondered how Serena would feel. How would she accept that change in him? He felt guilt again thinking of Leslie, but there she was, an interlude on his mind. He couldn't stop the intrusion of her. He didn't know how he was going to deal with that.

The next morning the troops were notified they were to leave the next day. Max and hundreds of others were to board a train that would take them to Southampton. There they would embark on a ship for the trip home across the Atlantic to New York

Harbor. Excitement was at fever pitch at camp. There was much to pack and get ready for departure the next morning.

Later many of the fellows went out on the town, but Max and Jerry had decided to visit a small neighborhood pub. They ordered "lemon squash," an English soda pop drink, which Max said was "quite refreshing." Leslie had introduced him to it on a warm day one summer. It met with Jerry's approval.

The two sat and reminisced, exchanged addresses and telephone numbers, and would make plans to visit Jim's family soon. That was a priority that had to be dealt with. They remembered friends they had lost and talked a bit about their experiences in the war—what they had seen. Then Max said, "I'm not going to talk about the war anymore when I get home. I'm going to leave it here." They promised each other, "Let's try to go on from here." They finished their drinks and came back to get to bed early.

Wake-up call was early. After breakfast they were taken to the train station for Southampton. From there, they embarked on a large troopship crossing the Atlantic to New York. The crossing was uneventful. They didn't have to worry about German U-boats. A few days later, it was announced the ship would be docking in the New York Harbor.

When the ship landed in American waters, everyone was singing, happy to see America. The soldiers stood crowded against the ship's rails as the ship docked. Streamers fell, and bands were playing, "God Bless America." Some soldiers were crying unashamedly, crying to see America and home. The troops disembarked, they had their orders, and there were "M.P's" standing by to answer soldiers' questions.

Some were taken to New York Grand Central to get their trains home. They were crowded, spilling over inside, hanging out of windows, waving at friends and civilians alike on the platform as the trains pulled out.

Max had stopped to call Serena. He and Jerry had decided to take a train to Sioux Falls, South Dakota, to see Jim's wife. This was the only time they would be together for a long while. Max was anxious to get home to see Serena and Robert, but this was something Max had promised Jim. He would be back two days later. He wanted to know if this was okay with her. Serena understood. She had put herself in Peggy's place; she would have wanted someone to do that for her. The train stopped in Chicago, and they got tickets to Sioux Falls. From there, they had tickets to their homes.

The train pulled into Sioux Falls. Max called Jim's home and explained to his wife, Peggy, that Jerry and he had a letter for her from Jim. They arrived in a cab and were welcomed by Peggy and Timmie. Peggy was an attractive young woman, and they could see why Jim talked about her. She was a charming person and loving, the way she held Timmie, who was four years old.

They gave her the gifts they had brought for them, and they gave Peggy the letter. Max gave her Jim's ring that he had kept on his finger so as not to lose it. Peggy, overcome, cried, "It's so good of you to take the time to do this. It means a great deal to me."

They talked for a long while telling her about Jim. "He spoke of you very often. He loved you and Timmie!"

Before they left, they promised to keep in touch. Peggy drove them to the station. Jerry took the train to Iowa, and Max the one to St. Louis. Their parting was sad and happy. "Let's not lose track of each other, buddy," Jerry warned him. They hugged and they kidded each other with lots of back-slapping.

On the train, Max sat back and tried to relax. He put his cap forward over his eyes, and tried to concentrate on home. He had wanted to get there a few days ago, but the promise to Jim was important to him, and Serena had agreed he should do it. He began speculating on who would meet him at Union Station. He wanted to see Serena, the son he didn't know, and his parents. His mind began working overtime. There were so many things he began thinking about. Bill and Lainie, Charlie and Carole. He felt a concern for them more now that he was going home.

The ride was long—too long for a guy anxious to get home. The train stopped at many cities, and many soldiers had gotten off. Max welcomed the announcement of the conductor, "Next stop St. Louis!" Huge crowds of soldiers and civilians and families were milling around, waiting anxiously to meet and greet the returning veterans. Those with crutches, with arm or leg casts were getting off first. They were a little slower. The conductor helped them off. Max followed the line moving slowly ahead. On the platform, his eyes swept over the crowd—then he saw his parents and Serena waving and smiling at him.

Serena ran to him and he watched her glance at his face. It was as if she didn't see it; she just hugged him. He put his arms about her. She felt so good. He covered her with kisses, *God,* he thought, *I missed her so*!

His parents stood by, then he embraced his mother and his father. They were going to their home, to let Max and Serena go home. Max asked, "Where is Robert?"

Serena said, "I thought we'd see him at home where there wasn't too much commotion." Max agreed with her that was probably better. Serena asked if he wanted to drive. He was "glad to get started in civilian life duties," he said.

Serena wanted to know about the train ride. "Was it all right?" She was nervous. Max saw this and didn't feel like talking, but when he was home, he started to ask about Carole and Charlie, and Bill and Lainie. He listened as Serena talked. He had missed her—her voice and everything she was to him, *Lord,* he thought, *how I've missed her*!

Upstairs, Carole was waiting with Judy and Robert. She just kissed Max and said, "We'll see you another day." There were tears in her eyes. She was happy for Serena and Max to be together again. As she went upstairs, she said, "Thank you, God, for bringing all of them home."

XX
Max's Confession

The war in Europe had ended and millions of veterans were returning. The brutality of the war and the horrors of the combat experiences made it difficult for many to adjust to civilian life. Franklin Roosevelt, in early 1942, began to formulate plans for soldiers coming home. Before the war, the economy was in good shape and unemployment was low. Most veterans had grown up during the Depression years, and were called into service. They had grown up in families that didn't own their homes.

Roosevelt didn't want them coming home to inflation and unemployment, and he introduced the "Servicemen's Readjustment Act." He signed it into law in June 1944. In it there were four postwar benefits for all veterans. They received readjustment allowances when unemployed. There was vocational education and on-the-job training, and they got twenty dollars a week to help them. They now had educational opportunities in colleges and universities. Loans were available to them for homes, businesses, and farms. Help was there to find jobs, get medical benefits, and hospitalization.

Returning veterans were now in different colleges they had chosen. The Veterans Administration sent the necessary checks to the schools every month for tuition, books, and supplies. The single veterans got fifty dollars a month, seventy-five dollars if married, and fifteen dollars for one or more children. Many lived in makeshift quarters, as rentals were scarce. They had new opportunities, worked hard, and they could soon own homes of their own. The country cared about them, and they were proud to be Americans.

There were other problems, too. Women hadn't worked out of their homes before the war. Now, some husbands came back to find their wives, having worked in defense plants, had become quite independent, having their own money, and not willing to surrender their independence. Many had new men friends, and there was a high rate of divorce.

Many veterans returned married, with their wives from different countries, and many veterans came back to find their girls had married other young men at home. To thousands, the homecoming was a rude awakening of what had happened to their families.

Most women who had worked in defense plants or outside the home, settled into being full-time wives, and those families, with returning veterans, adapted to civilian life with few problems.

For Max and Serena, their reunion was wonderful, filled with joy and "thanks for our blessings," as Serena put it. Max was overwhelmed with his son. The child accepted him, knew him as his "daddy" from the photograph Serena had repeatedly shown him. Max thought about that—she had taught their son with her love, to love and know his father. Serena had been faithful in her love.

With a twinge in his heart and a pounding in his head, Max thought of Leslie and the circumstances that led to the affair. He couldn't forgive himself, and he worried how it would be for Serena when he confessed his infidelity to her. He hated the secret—the lie—he was burdened with.

So many times he had heard men discussing their sweethearts and wives, talking about the numerous times they had been unfaithful. It didn't bother them at all. He remembered in a discussion, a sergeant saying "What the little woman don't know, won't hurt her!" Max had listened and was surprised that many agreed with that.

But to Max, the affair with Leslie had marked him. He couldn't live with this between them. Serena noticed. Max, who had been so even-tempered, was easily provoked. It was little inconsequential things, and she tried hard to avoid the provocations. At these times, conversation became minimal, especially as they prepared for bed. Late in the night, Serena would be awakened by Max's thrashing around, moaning, agitated at something. Gently, she would put her arm around him and he would waken, get out of bed, and sit in the living room.

She lay there wondering what was troubling her Max. When she came down and tried to talk to him, he would say, "It's nothing, Serena."

Later, when he came back to bed, she tried to soothe him. "It's all right, Max," she would say, "I understand." She was thinking it was the terrible things in the war he didn't want to talk about. This only made him feel worse. He knew he was coming to the point where he would have to tell Serena. It was the only way to rid himself of the guilt, and he would have to take the consequences for what he had done. He tried to muster up his courage, but when he looked at Serena, knowing how it was going to hurt her, breaking her trust and faith in him, he lost his nerve and set it aside.

Problems in the relationship were surfacing. It made Serena angry, and she was in a constant state of nervousness—not knowing when he would lose his temper. She worried about this taking place in front of their son, who would cry. When she tried to discuss the situation with Max, he wouldn't explain—he just said, "I'm sorry. It won't happen again."

That didn't help—just created a bit of animosity. It happened again and frequently. Serena decided she would have to say what was on her mind, but concerned and not wanting a confrontation, she kept putting it off. The strain between them grew, creating a greater chasm. "We have to do something about this. This can't go on." They both knew it.

The first week when Max was home, Charlie had come to welcome his friend. Serena had invited them to spend Saturday evening with them. She hoped it would help the strain between Max and herself.

"Oh, no," Charlie answered. "You need time together." Charlie knew it would take "awhile" for Max and Serena to adjust. He hoped it would be a "little while," since he and Carole were still having problems, which made their life together complicated.

Charlie had told Max, "You look good." Max ran his fingers along the scar on his face—still very self-conscious about it—only because he felt it made a difference to Serena. Max wanted to talk to his friend, but Carole insisted they leave. They got up to go, and Charlie put his arm around Max's shoulder. His eyes looked deep into his friend's and he saw pain. "We're so glad to have you back home, Max."

"Yeah, me too, Charlie, you don't know how good it is to see you."

What he saw was that Charlie was not well, pale and thinner, and his eyes, the windows into his soul, had seen and recorded much. Max had worried about Charlie, and he was deeply affected by what he saw.

In the weeks that followed, the two couples went out once for dinner to the Park Plaza, the place that held wonderful memories for both. They seemed to be having a good time. The women laughed and talked. *Max's conversation was a bit stinted,* Charlie thought. Max knew the camaraderie, as they knew it, had escaped them that evening, try as they might to recapture it. Everything was changed. They were changed.

They left early, and at the apartments stopped to say "good night" to Serena and Max on second floor. Charlie said, "It was good to be together." They climbed the two flights of stairs to their apartment. Charlie drove the sitter home, and Carole went to bed. She was thinking about the evening and had a deep concern for Serena and Max. She couldn't say exactly what it was that made her uneasy, but something wasn't right.

Serena had not said anything to her, so she had to just be there—not say anything that might be construed as "meddling." When Charlie returned, they talked about it, not in a gossipy manner, but friends concerned about good friends.

Charlie "had noticed it, too, with Max," he told Carole. "No, Max hadn't said anything to him either," Charlie said.

So, if they both felt it, they were sure there was a problem. They were downhearted. It hurt to see friends in pain! Charlie, usually the pessimist, said in an optimistic tone, "I know whatever it is, Serena and Max will work it out." He had great faith in both of them.

Carole ended it with, "From your mouth to God's ears!"

The next few weeks were long ones for Charlie in the drug store. Carole's father, concerned with his son-in-law's bouts of depression, was thinking of changes that might help Charlie, might relieve him of the pressures he felt. Mr. Schwartz had worried about the welfare of his daughter and granddaughter, and Charlie, too. He planned to make things easier for Charlie at the store.

Max was back at the store. His attitude had not escaped his father who suspected the couple was having problems. Max's parents wanted to help, but they knew interference from parents often did more harm than good. They wanted to help, but suffered along with their children. The Kellers invited them for Sunday dinner. Sometimes they came, and the grandparents fussed over their grandson. Max often went with his father, and there was discussion about the stores.

Serena helped her mother-in-law with the cleanup, and they discussed little Robert. Later Max's mother would have very little to say about what was wrong. "Serena is in pain. I wanted to take her in my arms. She didn't talk about anything except Robert."

Mr. Keller, talking business to Max, had little to offer except to say, "Max said nothing." They worried about the situation. Weeks were passing with no apparent resolve in sight. They kept speculating on what the problem could be. They prayed for a happy ending to the problem. Maybe they would never know what caused the situation, and that was fine, too. They just wanted it ended, and their children happy, but life is a mystery. "There is no way to know or predict what decisions are made, and what will happen," said Mr. Keller, speaking in a philosophical manner to his wife. "We will have to be patient and wait."

The Keller stores were doing well. Vets had become civilians with jobs and families. The Sunday paper had a large ad about an area where new homes for veterans were going up. There was a model home for the veterans and their spouses to see. They were encouraged to come out and pick their lots, to make arrangements for their G.I. Loans. The government was anxious to help them.

Carole and Charlie were discussing the prospect of owning their own home. Serena was quite excited about the idea. Max didn't say anything. Charlie questioned his friend, "Max, what do you think about this?" "Sounds wonderful," was Max's answer. Serena noted there wasn't a real enthusiasm in Max's reply. Charlie suggested they go together—pick their lots in the same area. As so often happens, when suggestions are bandied about, the conversation turned to other things—Charlie and his work, and Max's about the new store for children. Carole spoke up. She was going to bring Judy down to get a new pair of shoes, and she was excited about seeing the new store.

Getting ready for bed, Max decided he was going to tell Serena about Leslie. The talk of homes made him realize he couldn't plan his life too far ahead. He didn't know how Serena would feel. Maybe she wouldn't want to get a home with him, and he couldn't blame her. Serena was going to ask Max why he wasn't more enthused at the prospect of owning their own home. They had talked about it many times before. She emerged from the shower and was towel-drying her hair. She looked lovely. Max was remembering how many times he had thought about her when he was away, and how much he had missed her.

From the bedroom he called, "Siri, let's go into the living room. I have something to tell you." His voice was a bit tremulous. They would be away from their son's room. He sounded not quite like himself. Coming out of the bedroom, she asked, "Max, are you all right?"

On the sofa, they sat a little apart, and she moved closer. He was looking at her intensely, and his heart was racing. He started to speak, and his breath and voice were interrupted by a troubled sigh that had to be released. "This is something I've thought about and wanted to tell you for a long time, but I couldn't because I knew it would hurt you. I'm sorry, because by not telling you, my actions since I've been home have hurt you," and again he said, "I'm sorry."

He paused. "I want you to know I love you. I've always loved you, and I always will."

"What is it, Max?" Serena looked at him and became frightened. He sounded so sad. She was totally unprepared for what followed.

It was plain to see he was expending much effort to say the words she heard pass from his mouth.

"While in London, I had an affair with Leslie Hodges. It was a stupid mistake. I was lonesome and depressed, and scared." He looked at her pleadingly. "I know that's no excuse. It happened."

Max stopped as he saw the disbelief in her eyes. She didn't say anything. She put one hand on her stomach, one over her mouth, and made a dash for the bathroom, and he could hear her throwing up. She had become physically ill. Max had hurt her in the worst way a husband can hurt his wife.

Max, worried, was at the door turning the knob, but Serena had locked the door. He pleaded with her, "Siri, please open the door."

He heard her then, crying, and from deep within her well of pain came the heart-rending sobs. He kept asking her to open the door.

Serena sat there on the edge of the tub and wished she could die. In one moment, her whole world was overturned, topsy-turvy. Her marriage that was everything to her was gone. Everything she believed in was gone. The shock of what he had said had sunk in all too quickly. She felt so alone, and her mind was whirling. She felt anger, a great anger and hate—yes, hate. How could he do this to her? Tears welled up. She had worried so when he was away, when he was hurt. Every night she had prayed for his safe return. Slowly the tears began again rolling down her cheeks. She tried to stop, but when she thought about Robert, her son, the tears came again.

She unlocked the bathroom door and Max got up. He tried to put his arm around her, but she shrugged it off. Over and over to herself, she said, "Oh, Max, how could you?"

She went to bed, but she couldn't fall asleep. Max fixed a place for himself on the sofa for which she was glad. Most of the night she spent thinking and talking to herself. "Oh, Max, how could you? I wish it hadn't happened." She saw it as a deep rejection of her.

"I know," she thought with a deep sorrow, *I won't forget it. Our life as we knew it is finished*! That was the saddest heart-breaking declaration she had to accept.

The night for her was long. She caught snatches of sleep, but woke troubled—the pain reminded her, and then the tears again. She didn't know how she would make it through the day.

The days that followed were difficult for both. Max's suffering was deep, too. He wished the earth would have opened up and swallowed him before he hurt his Serena. He couldn't blame her for the hurt she felt.

He thought about himself. He hadn't felt like a good person for a long time. He had gone off to war—thinking he knew what to expect after the long training. He came up against the dreadful unexpected. He had shot and killed, blown up the enemy, and spewed his flame-thrower. He had seen what the enemy had done. No matter how many times those in charge kept enforcing, "The job has to be done, and you can do it," it didn't help how he felt inside after the bloody encounters.

Max wasn't at ease in the civilian world when he first came back. He had been in a murdering world. He tried not to think of Leslie and himself. All that had happened was now a part of him. He couldn't blame the war! It was his fault alone! He was responsible. He could have avoided the situation, the decision was his. Now he lived with a great inner torment.

He had finally told Serena, and whatever would happen, he knew he was the cause of her great pain. He wished, as he had so many times before, that he could change things—go back to the day before it all happened.

"Oh, God," he prayed. "I don't deserve it, but please help me!"

They were together, but living as strangers. The weeks slipped by. Max made several overtures, attempting to talk to her. Serena spoke very little to him, only when it was really necessary. Max left for work, his thoughts always of her. Mr. Keller worried the situation was going on too long. He suggested they talk to someone who could help them.

This was one thing Serena and Max discussed together—talking was a good sign. Infidelity in a marriage is between a husband and wife and God. It takes all three to work the problem out. It's always difficult, and there are many scars, but with months, or however long it would take, meeting the challenges every day, they could work it out. They loved each other and wanted to save their marriage.

They thought about it seriously—they would try together to make a decision. At first, when Max tried to talk to Serena, she would get very angry. For months she had worried his actions and behavior resulted from the war. She had been such a fool defending him, making excuses for him. He had known the reason for his behavior and thinking about it made her seem so foolish.

Max, unable to talk to her, wrote her letters trying to explain, but always reminding her that he loved her and missed her. She remembered that Max was always kind and loving and caring. She struggled with her feelings—vacillating as they did. She saw how miserable he was when he got home. He played with his son, had dinner, and would always thank her for the wonderful dinner. The conversations were always cool and polite. The changes in their lives were big and the hardships greater. This went on for months.

Serena read and reread the letters he had sent from London and Europe. He had gone through much. She realized Max really loved her. So many nights she thought about the two of them in the early days of their marriage and wondered if it were possible for her to forgive him.

Sometimes when she began thinking that way, she became quite angry with herself. She remembered conversation with her friends—when the talk came to husbands, they all voiced some approvals, but mostly disapprovals, telling things about their husbands. Serena never spoke or said anything derogatory about Max. She had loved him so. Her friends knew how she felt when she said, "Trust is the sum and substance for a good marriage." She believed it with all her heart, that she had this in her marriage, until that fateful night when Max told her about Leslie.

She wondered, *What do I do now*? *I can't live with anyone I don't trust. I can't live with Max anymore*!

She felt mortally wounded, but she was not dead. Her life with Max was dead! She wondered in self-doubt if there was something wrong with her to feel this utter devastation. There must be millions of women who are hurt this way. What do they do? Are they the ones getting divorces? Is that why the divorce rate, a serious topic lately for discussion, was climbing? It frightened her to be thinking along these lines. She felt alone, isolated from the rest of the world. With words, she fought herself back and forth.

Max had come back, not the same person she knew. They didn't discuss problems fully anymore. She had attributed that to a problem in the business, or the war, which he was reluctant to talk about. It seemed wives were always making excuses for their husbands, but Serena began to think the excuses were really for the wives. She remembered hearing Carole with her excuses for Charlie's moods. She thought about Carole once saying when trouble started with Charlie, "It must be me. Charlie must be right. I'm getting too sensitive. I'll have to try harder if we're to have a marriage."

Serena began to wonder, "What were the things I did that were contributing factors to the problem?" She knew she wasn't perfect. No one is. She spent endless hours in dissecting her thoughts and actions over the past few years, and there were the sleepless nights trying to find answers to the many questions she had. Serena came to several conclusions—they could be right, or they could be wrong—she didn't know. Desperately, she sought a solution.

"People go to churches and synagogues, listen to services and sermons, and prayed to God to make them better human beings, to forgive them," she reminded herself. She had gone and done that matter-of-factly. Now she was sure she was part of the blame. How big a part, she didn't know. It was difficult for her to acknowledge that, but she accepted she must be part of the problem in her marriage.

Serena thought about that and knew staying in a marriage, to make it work, is hard. There had to be love and mutual respect for each other. Many times when hearing of divorce, she thought, *What could be so insurmountable that it couldn't be worked out in a marriage? It's the way marriage partners face and cope with the problems that can save, or destroy, a marriage,* her heart told her.

Serena knew she and Max would have to find the way. They had been together, but remote from each other, and it was at these times they could delve into their innermost feelings. Serena remembered the goodness of Max before he went off to war. There were so many happy times in their marriage to recall. He had gone through much, but he didn't want to discuss it. It had been hard for him to deal with.

In so many sermons the Rabbi had given in the Temple, Serena had heard always, "We shouldn't judge each other, but forgive. In order to be forgiven, we must first forgive!" She wondered if she could forgive him. "Maybe," she thought, but she didn't know about "forgetting!"

The talks between Serena and Max began with serious thoughts about their feelings. When Serena poured her soul out, Max listened. She had much to say. When Max bared his feelings of guilt, Serena listened. At different times there were tears. They came to a deeper understanding of each other. They were uncovering their hearts with truth, for they loved one another. Max had always said to her, "Siri, I love you!" There were many questions that Serena needed answers to, to quell the uncertainties in her mind. Discussions often continued late into the evening when Robert was asleep. The child sensed the situations that were not right, and he had asked, "Is Daddy going to sleep on the couch forever?" Serena had answered, "I don't think so," and the questioning had stopped.

The store was open late on Thursday night, but Max left early. There were things he wanted to discuss with Serena. At dinner, he asked what she thought about the idea of taking time out of their busy schedule to attend Friday night services at Temple Israel.

"Oh, Max, that would be wonderful." She had missed that with Max away. This would be important to both of them, so it was agreed.

Serena's turn in the discussion came when she tried to explain to Max that she felt part of the blame was hers. He tried to convince her that wasn't so, but Serena's mind couldn't be changed in that regard, and she was asking for his forgiveness and said so earnestly from her heart, "I forgive you, Max!"

He looked at her, almost not believing that she could forgive him for the torment he had caused her. He told her again, "It's all my fault!" His voice full of the deep emotion he felt, he said, "Siri, I'm such a lucky person to have you." He shook his head in wonderment.

Unsure of how she would feel if he embraced her, he stood before her with his arms outstretched. She came into them willingly. They closed tightly around her. He kissed her then, his lips touching her gently on the forehead and eyelids, then hungrily he kissed her longer and passionately. She clung to him, feeling safe again!

That night, Serena took Max's pillow and blanket from the sofa, and returned them to their bedroom. Coming from his shower in robe and slippers, he saw her full forgiveness and acceptance of him.

In the process of dealing with everyday living, some days went better than others. It couldn't be obliterated from each of their minds. It would take time and endless patience to work things out. There was no going back to the way things once were. They weren't the same people. They had been tested!

In the healing, they learned how fragile marriages are. There is no guarantee, no matter how many years there are in a marriage, that it can be taken for granted. Every day is an important one in a marriage, which needs love and careful nurturing to survive.

The days that followed became brighter for both of them. The heaviness in Serena's heart was slowly dissipating. For Max, Serena's forgiveness had given him a second chance in their marriage. So many times at the store, driving home, that thought came to him. He considered himself a most fortunate person. *How many people,* he wondered, *get a second chance in life*?

Max remembered Serena saying, "We're just human beings with faults. We think we know it all, but we don't. There are always new things to learn to make us better, but only if we allow our minds to do it."

How wise my Siri is! He felt, once again, how lucky he was.

XXI
New Decisions–New Changes

On the battlefields of the Pacific, the Allied troops were engaged in fierce fighting with the Japanese. Casualties were extremely high on both sides. The enemy fought relentlessly, never surrendering. They had been indoctrinated into believing capture would bring dishonor on their Emperor Hirohito, and on themselves, and their families. Thousands committed suicide by killing themselves with their swords or blowing themselves up with grenades.

President Truman, after consultation with his advisers and generals, made the decision to use the atomic bomb in hopes of putting an end to the dreadful war. The Japanese War ushered in the "Atomic Age." On August 6th, 1945, an American plane, the *Enola Gay,* left with a huge bomb weighing over 8,000 pounds that was dropped on Hiroshima in Japan. It hit the city causing fire, devastation, over 60,000 deaths, and almost as many injured. The Japanese did not surrender, and another bomb was dropped on Nagasaki on August 9th. This time the Japanese surrendered, but the news was not received on all fronts, and the execution of prisoners-of-war and battles continued into the middle of August.

For the first time ever, the Japanese heard the voice of their emperor, considered to be "divine," come over the radio, informing the people of Japan of "the cruel bomb being used against them by the enemy, causing much damage, and the loss of innocent lives." It took almost the end of the month before hundreds of thousands of Allied prisoners-of-war, who had gone through the cruelty of the enemy's torture systems, learned of the Japanese surrender.

On September 2nd, the chief of staff of the Japanese Army came aboard the *Missouri* battleship in Tokyo Bay and signed the documents witnessed by General MacArthur who signed in the name of the Allies, and the war ended. That weekend was one of prayer at churches and synagogues all over America. It was almost four years since the cowardly attack on Pearl Harbor. The rest of the months of September and October saw the Japanese forces surrendering on different islands in the Pacific.

Allied warships were liberating prisoners-of-war who had survived battles on Formosa, Guadacanal, the "Death March" of Bataan, and the others they remembered, but wanted to forget, of friends killed or captured, then murdered by their captors. Details of deliberate cruelty they suffered while in captivity were being documented and would be used later in war crime trials.

Charlie, on hearing the news of the Japanese surrender, was jubilant and called Max. "Did you hear the good news?" Max was happy, too. All the customers coming in had expressed their relief that, finally, the war was ended.

"I got a bottle of wine to celebrate with the customers," Max said. "They were glad it was over."

Charlie asked if the two of them could go out that evening for a little while to celebrate. His voice, excited at first, broke, and Max knew Charlie was in pain again—not physical pain, the other kind, as Charlie had explained. "It came when pictures flashed quickly of the many I had seen dead, bayoneted in the fields, and on the beaches. It came when I remembered the harsh treatment, the deprivation, the illnesses without medical supplies, and the tortures executed by the drunken guards." It all came rushing back, time and time again since Charlie had come home. There were the bouts of depression he battled, and the fever of the islands. After dinner, Charlie came down to get Max, and they were off.

In the last few months, Carole and Serena hadn't spent much time together. Carole knew there were problems, but she didn't know the nature of them. Serena had not said too much to her, and Carole didn't ask. If Serena wanted her to know, she would have told her. They were good friends, and most good friends know when not to cross the "privacy" line.

A half hour later, Carole came and plopped herself down comfortably in one corner of the sofa. Serena joined her, bringing in a tray with two glasses of lemonade. Serena had taken a pillow and placed it in the other corner of the sofa. They sat facing each other.

"I'm glad Charlie and Max went out. Charlie's been 'antsy' all day. I guess they needed their talk, probably about the war. A man's thing," Carole called it.

Serena, looking at Carole, noticed she looked pale and thinner. She felt guilt; she had been so engrossed in her own problems, there hadn't been time for her friend. She began by saying, "Carole, I'm so sorry. I've been so neglectful."

"It's all right, Serena. I just want to know you're okay." Carole went on, "I know you've had your share of things to deal with. Charlie and I thought about you two and hoped things would work out."

Serena didn't answer.

Carole began talking about Charlie. "Charlie is getting worse. Some days he can't make it to the drug store. Dad wants us to move back. He thinks it will be less for Charlie to worry about. Charlie doesn't seem to be able to handle any kind of pressure and gets very depressed.

"How do you feel about moving back?"

"I'm not sure. It's not what I planned to do, but Charlie is my primary concern. I want to do what is best for him. I've gone to the Department of Education to see about teaching again. Dad can't handle all the expenses. It isn't fair to him."

"What about Judy?" Serena asked in a worried tone. Judy and Robert would not be ready for school for another few years.

"Between Dad and Charlie, Judy will be looked after. I think it will work out." If she was concerned, she didn't show it.

She and Carole had been together for a long time. Serena moved closer to Carole and took her hand. Carole was trying to wipe away the tears. "I'm so sorry, Carole. We won't let these changes make things different between us." Carole just nodded and wiped some of the tears again. She had kept them inside—here with Serena, they came.

"I don't know how things will work out, but we had to decide. We gave Tony notice, and he was going to put the "for rent" sign up at the end of the month. We wanted to tell you and Max first."

Serena left the room and came back with a handkerchief, wiping her eyes. She and Carole had been together for a long time. It hurt her to think Carole was going through this terrible time with Charlie, and it was getting worse. "What's going to happen? What are the doctors saying?" Serena, troubled, questioned.

"There were times when they made us feel optimistic about the future, but not lately. The prognosis was discouraging, but we have to have faith, and hope for the best."

They talked about the children being in school the following year, and life was going ahead. They even began laughing, remembering how they had wanted Serena to come to St. Louis. "We've had some wonderful times together." They both agreed, felt good. Carole said, "It's getting late, I better go up."

Serena hugged her friend. "I love you, Carole, and please know Max and I are here for you.,"

"I know, Serena, I know!" Then Carole left.

At the Park Plaza, Max and Charlie were having their one drink each, which they nursed as they talked. They kept refilling their glasses with ginger ale from a bottle on the bar near them. Charlie couldn't drink a lot, taking medication, and Max usually had one sometimes, two drinks. That was his limit. They had discussed the war a bit, not too much. Max had heard some of what Charlie had been through.

Charlie wanted to know a little of what Max had seen in Europe. Max told the story of losing Jim and O'Rourke. He was tense then, sat up against the bar, rolling the glass in both hands. He didn't want to talk about it anymore. Charlie didn't either. "It's late, Charlie. I think we should go!" Driving home, they felt better, having gotten some of the war off their chests to someone who understood, but still there was a frustration and anger deep within both of them.

Opening the door at 707 Westgate, they climbed slowly upward. Charlie thanked Max for coming out. "Don't thank me. I enjoyed being with you, Charlie. We'll do it again." Max opened his door and called up to his friend. "Have a good night, Charlie!"

"You, too," came back Charlie's voice, he was stifling a yawn.

Serena saw Max more relaxed, thought the meeting between Charlie and Max had been beneficial in some respects, was glad the men had been together. She mentioned it to Max, then said, "What do you think of Charlie and Carole moving?"

"What do you mean?" Max questioned.

"Didn't Charlie tell you?"

"Tell me what?" Serena explained what Carole had told her.

"No, Charlie hadn't mentioned it. Evidently, it's something Charlie isn't happy about." Max thought about the evening with Charlie. He knew his friend was suffering deeply, not just about the war he had been through, but dealing with the serious health problems it had left him with.

Max said, "Think how lousy he must feel to have to move back to Carole's home, and not be able to work full time.

"We were going to buy our lots together and build our homes, be neighbors. I hope it's just for awhile that their plans are set aside."

"I don't think so, not the way Carole talked. It'll be for a long time, maybe forever."

Max was disturbed and saddened. It had been a happy day, the war had ended, but reminders of its toll on survivors were everywhere.

Serena and Carole were returning from grocery shopping at Schenberg's market on Delmar Boulevard. They enjoyed walking the few blocks and meeting neighbors for a friendly chat. Coming up the walk at 707, they noticed the "For Rent" sign—"apartment on 1st floor," it read. "Okay," Carole said. Tony made a mistake. "Our sign isn't to be put up 'til the end of the month. I'll call him tonight."

"No," it was no mistake. "Bill and Lainie had given their notice!"

They had visited Bill and Lainie just a week ago, and they had seen the serious health problems Bill had. Lainie, usually fun-loving and laughing, was quite tense and nervous. Bill tried to converse, but a stroke had made it almost impossible to understand him. When Lainie tried to interpret and help, but couldn't make out what he wanted to say, he would become so frustrated and angry.

The apartment was rented, and Lainie was preparing to move. Joe, Bill's brother, was to help. Max and Serena, and

Charlie and Carole called, offering any help they needed, and they wanted to know where they were moving.

Lainie told them of a house they had purchased. It wasn't a new house, but it would suit their needs. It was a duplex—two separate apartments; one on the first floor, the other directly above on the second floor. "We were going to tell you first. Tony wasn't going to put up the signs; then decided to put it up. He had two apartments to rent." Of course, apartments were at a premium, and they were rented almost immediately. Rents had been frozen during the war, but would-be renters paid bonuses to the landlords in cash, or getting things that were hard to get because of the war.

Lainie didn't offer too much more information. There clearly was serious tension between Lainie and Bill that their friends could see.

Max asked again, "If you need help, let us know."

Lainie answered back. "Thanks! You're such good friends! Isn't that right, Bill?" He didn't speak, just nodded his head, but his eyes gave him away. There was a troubled, haunted look in them.

One night Serena and Max, Charlie and Carole brought dinner and set it up at Bill's and Lainie's apartment. They talked about their friendship and how they would miss not being close to them. It was a fun evening—"one they would remember," several said.

Back in their own apartment, Serena and Max discussed the moving of their friends, the sad circumstances, and the unhappiness they were witness to. Serena thought out loud, "Everyone was changed. They weren't the light-hearted innocents they were before the war!"

At the end of the month, Lainie and Bill moved. It was difficult to see them go. Max had taken Bill in his wheelchair to the new place. Serena and Carole helped Lainie with the moving and unpacking. By the weekend, they were pretty well settled in the first floor apartment.

A few weeks later, Charlie and Carole moved. Max and Serena helped a little, but Carole and Charlie had things pretty well organized, and the moving wasn't as hectic as Lainie's and Bill's. Carole was using some of their furniture, and some was put into the garage. It wasn't the way Carole and Charlie wanted it, but it would do. Carole had hope in her heart that some day they could move into their own place again.

Max and Serena came back to 707. It was strange to come into the building that seemed so empty now. The new neighbors were moving in, in another few weeks.

Little Robert missed Judy, and he couldn't understand if everyone was moving, why they didn't. Max broached the subject of getting their own home. He could see Serena missing her friends. He hoped the idea would meet with Serena's approval. That weekend they went to a new suburb under construction and selected a wonderful lot near a small stream that ran through the back part of their lot.

Every lot where homes were being built, or those where owners were already residing in their homes, had a beautiful willow tree out in front and one in back near the stream. These were gifts of the contractor and developer. The area was called "Willow Ridge." It was one of the things that drew Serena and Max here. She loved the idea and couldn't wait to plant their trees.

The contractor promised their home would be ready for occupancy in the spring. Every few weeks they would take a ride to check on the progress of their place. The contractor always met them, telling them their lot was large and they could add on to their home if needed. To Max and Serena, the home would be wonderful when finished. They were happy living in anticipation of the day when they could move in.

On the day Serena and Max were called that their trees were there, they came anxious to see them. Max dug, and a workman came over to help Serena hold the tree so it was set in straight. The one in front went in first, then they worked on the one in the back near the stream. They stepped aside to view their handiwork, and they were so proud. They came away feeling good. Max came two or three times a week to water the trees. When Serena saw them, she just beamed. She loved Willow Ridge.

Max vowed again never to make her unhappy. She had forgiven him. The wonderment of her was with him constantly. So many times thinking to himself, he was thankful, "God has been good to me!" Looking at the tree, he said, "When we can, we'll get a bench so you can sit near your tree."

"That will be so wonderful, Max." She was full of plans for a flower garden and the house. They brought and set out two lawn chairs that would suffice for the time being, and enjoyed the warm summer evenings near the willow, near the stream.

Some nights they watched the sun go down. It was quiet, and they listened and heard the gurgle of the stream as it flowed gently over small stones and rocks, and there were the sounds of frogs and crickets blending. The day had ended into darkness, and there were the bright dots of stars in the heavens. The heart and mind were calmed. Then it was time to go, but they would be back soon, to stay.

On the way back to the apartment, Serena was thinking of the choice that she and Max had made. It had made possible another wonderful day to put in the memory bank. She prayed the decisions made by Charlie and Carole, and Bill and Lainie would do the same for them. They were notified that they could move in March.

"Oh, Max," Serena affirmed so many times, "I love it! I can't wait!"

"I know. I feel the same way, Siri. It will be so good being in our own place. I think about it so many times." Max said, "It will be wonderful."

Serena put her arm through his, and they walked slowly to the car, the sidewalks were not in yet. The new streetlights were in on the new streets, and everything was moving along.

They wondered who their new neighbors were. There was much to look forward to. Serena's thoughts were of Max. "We're lucky. God has been good!"

The anger, hate, and bitterness were gone from her heart. *How good to know,* she thought, *our love grows stronger.*

XXII
Lainie and Bill

Late in the summer, Max and Serena planned a housewarming with family and friends. Charlie and Carole, Bill and Lainie were invited. Serena's mother and Saul, Jenny, and Rachel were coming for the weekend. For some reason, when Bill and Lainie moved away, the relationship seemed to falter. Lainie was always busy, and it seemed difficult to get together.

Serena's family came in on Friday and were excited about the lovely home, and to see Serena and Max happy. There had been concern in reading Serena's letters. Now they were here and could see for themselves how things looked. They came with a letter and a picture of Michelle, Monique, and Francois. Serena and Max brought out two letters they had received from the Duvalls; the last letter in answer to Max's inviting them to come to America.

The second letter contained a picture of Michelle and her young man, Paul Renee. They were to be married on Christmas. Serena and Max had written they wouldn't be able to make it and were so sorry, but they had just gotten into their home. They hoped they could all be together soon. The correspondence came regularly on both sides of the ocean. Michelle had written "She loved to get the mail from America." It was the same for Max, Serena, and her family.

On Saturday evening, Carole and Charlie came. Lainie came alone. "Bill," she said "wasn't up to it. He doesn't go out much." Of course, Serena and Max were quite disappointed. They had wanted their friends to celebrate with them.

"Maybe he can come another time," Serena hoped.

The party was fun. It was good to have the chance to connect again with Serena's family, to see Jennie, Saul, and Rachel. The families hadn't visited too much during the war. Of course, there were the phone calls and letters, but it wasn't the same as seeing each other.

It was getting late and the party was beginning to break up. Serena fixed a bag of goodies for Bill and elicited a promise from Lainie to come again. Saul and his family left with the Kellers. They had enjoyed the party, and were leaving a bit regretfully, it seemed.

After everyone left, Max helped Serena straighten up as they discussed the party. "I missed Bill. I think I'll stop over to see him tomorrow night after work, Siri. I'll be a little late."

"That will be nice. I know Bill will like that." Max had always been so caring about both of his friends, Charlie and Bill.

Max left work a little earlier than usual, and soon he was ringing the doorbell at Bill's. Joe, Bill's brother, came to the door. Max had called ahead so was expected. "Gosh, it's good to see you, Max!" He took Max's jacket and showed him into the living room where Bill was sitting in his wheelchair.

Max didn't see Lainie, so he asked, "Is Lainie out?"

"Yes, she's working tonight. We have a man who comes in to care for Bill. I come to stay when Lainie's going to be late," Joe explained. He invited Max to stay for dinner.

Max was hesitant, but something about the way Joe asked him to stay made him answer, "Oh, I'd love to have dinner with you."

Max got up, "Do you mind if I use your phone? I'll call Siri." In the kitchen, making the call, he said, "It's important I stay for dinner. I'll explain later." His voice sounded troubled.

She asked, "Is it Bill?"

Max answered, "Yes." He came into the dining room. "It's okay." He tried to sound cheerful. He pulled up a chair and talked to Bill while Joe was busy in the kitchen. "We missed you at the housewarming, Bill!" Bill didn't answer. He thought he saw Bill's lip tremble, but then Bill looked at him and smiled. His eyes were troubled, but he managed a smile.

Joe called, "Dinner is on!" Max got up to help Bill with the wheelchair. They sat and Max commented on the food Joe brought in. "Boy, Joe, you do okay in the kitchen. I could never do this." Then he added, "It looks wonderful, and I'm starved!" At the table, Max asked questions of Bill, but Joe answered. Max forgot speaking was difficult for Bill. Joe and Bill discussed things about the business they were working in. Max included Bill in the discussions by directing remarks to him. Bill didn't speak, but he listened intently and seemed quite interested in what was going on in the world.

It was getting late and Max got up. "It's time to go," he said.

Bill shook his head. "No." He was enjoying the visit with his friend.

Joe pleaded, "Please stay a little longer." He felt good; he hadn't seen Bill looking so enlivened for a long while. It lifted Joe's spirits. "You can help me get Bill to bed. He'll like that. You know how he feels about you, Max."

Joe got Bill in the wheelchair into the bedroom. Max was shocked to see Bill was almost helpless. Bill was a tall, strapping fellow. Joe was not. Max saw what a strain getting Bill into bed was. Max held Bill under the armpits while Joe got him undressed and got his pajamas on. They worked together getting him washed up in the bathroom, then finally lifting him into bed. Then Joe put the sides of the bed up so Bill would not fall out. Now he was ready for the night.

Max was deeply affected by what he had just seen transpire. In a voice he hoped sounded cheerful, he held Bill's hand, "It was good to see you, old buddy. Have a good night. I'll see you again soon."

Bill just nodded. He had been embarrassed having Max help get him to bed. Max left the room. Joe was busy fixing an electric cord around one of the adjustable bed rails. It had a handy button that Bill could push with very little effort. It rang a bell that sounded throughout the house. "A contraption," Joe called it, "that Lainie's friend, Phil, had rigged up for Bill if he needed help." Max heard Joe saying "good night" to his brother.

Joe came into the living room and flopped down on the sofa. He looked exhausted. Max could see Joe was helping out in a big way. Bill had always been close to his younger brother, but Max wondered how long Joe could do this for Bill. He asked Joe, "How do you manage this by yourself? It took the two of us tonight, and, of course, I wasn't too much help; you carried most of the load."

"You were a big help and I appreciated having you here. It's okay. I'm glad we have him home. We were lucky."

Joe knew Max was a close friend of Bill's, and he felt a need to confide his brother's problems, what he had been through. He thought it would help Max understand some of the changes in Bill. He began with, "You know, Max, Bill was seriously injured in the war. He was in the hospital for a long time, and Lainie was almost crazy with worry about him. She was there all the time, but there was something bothering her. It seemed she was driven and quite nervous. That wasn't like Lainie. I chalked it up to Bill's condition. When he came home, she tried to manage him by herself. Bill didn't want anyone else to see him that way.

"Bill wasn't the best of patients. He was angry all the time. Then he had the stroke, and his condition worsened. He couldn't use his arms or legs, and now he couldn't talk. He babbled, but couldn't be understood. When Lainie tried so hard to make out what he was saying, he became angrier, and was mad at the world." Joe lowered his voice for a minute so Bill wouldn't hear. "Before Bill went to war," he said, "Lainie and Bill had an active sexual relationship in their marriage. It was a good marriage and you know how happy they were together, but there was something more going on here."

Joe stopped speaking for a second to take a sip of water, then continued. "I think the trouble for Lainie started when she began working while Bill was away. She used to tell me about the different guys she met through work. Lainie wasn't used to guys like that; drinking, dancing, and who knows what else? She started talking about this Phil. They were just friends. He was different from the other guys. At one point, I thought she might be sleeping around, but I couldn't believe Lainie would do that to Bill. Then Bill came home with his physical injuries, and psychological ones, too.

"The doctors discussed his disabilities with both of them, and they were told Bill couldn't be a husband sexually to Lainie because of some injuries he had sustained. That was a hard blow to both of them, and they couldn't deal with it. He didn't feel like a man, and a deep depression set in.

"Lainie had missed Bill, and now she couldn't be with him. I think that's when she and Phil became lovers. He came over a few times to spend time with Lainie and Bill. I was there one night. I knew then by the way they looked at each other they were lovers. I went home feeling sad and angry, hating both Lainie and Phil." Max didn't say anything. Joe needed to talk, and he wanted Max to listen. Max could see Bill's problems were a deep concern to his brother, so didn't interrupt.

"You can imagine, Max," he said, "how Bill felt when he found out. He felt betrayed and couldn't forgive her, and the hate and anger were consuming him. They were in the same house, but both miserable with each other. Bill was helpless, and she felt an obligation to care for him. She said, 'Joe, I had feelings for him. He had been a good husband before he went away to war, and I loved him.'

"Lainie felt guilty. She had broken her marriage vows. She made excuses to herself that satisfied her—she needed Phil. Bill couldn't accept that she had found someone else, and he added to her guilt by his attitude towards her. No matter what she did for him, it was as if he didn't know her—was a stranger caring for him. He resented the fact that he was helpless. He resented her, blaming her for everything that was wrong.

"It made him feel loathing for himself and her. He sat there, unable to walk or talk, but he could think. There were many confrontations, if you could call them that. He would be stubborn and make it difficult to try to handle him. Many times she did it with such frustration—almost ready to explode.

"Lainie, full of anguish, discussed this with us. She was in pain, and her concern was for Bill. She wouldn't leave him. We met her friend, Phil Mills, a fellow in his mid-forties. He's an engineer—couldn't get into the military. He was classified 4-F because of a disability, and he had worked in a defense plant for the duration. He's a decent chap and loves her. It isn't difficult to understand why she fell in love with him.

"Lainie and Bill were going to divorce, and Phil and Lainie would be married and move into the apartment upstairs. The family at first was angry with Lainie, and she couldn't blame them, but she felt it was something she and Bill had to work out. She felt a responsibility to him, maybe her guilt, but she wanted to be friends and take care of him. Lainie wanted just one thing, she needed to be forgiven by Bill for her infidelity in their marriage. It weighed heavily on her mind," Joe remembered.

"In the months that followed, the family saw the devotion Lainie had for Bill. She had someone coming in every day. Lainie never complained no matter how tough my brother made it. Outwardly, she never got angry, but you can imagine it was taking its toll of her. It wasn't good, and I tried to reason with him. Lainie was infinitely patient with him. He had plenty of time to think, and I don't know how it came about, but I noticed a few efforts he seemed to be putting forth.

"His anger seemed to be subsiding when Lainie was trying to help him. Whenever I tried to help, she waved me aside. She was there for him. She felt the need to do it. Then things began to change. Bill realized Lainie had always been a good wife and he had been wrong directing all his anger at her. For a long time, he had been feeling sorry for himself. Bill is a good-hearted guy. You know that, Max, as well as I do. I guess he realized he had been selfish, denying her the right to happiness—to a full life again. Their circumstance wasn't Lainie's fault, I told Bill, trying to resolve the problem.

"It was the damn war that interrupted their lives as it had done for so many others. Bill came to the conclusion that it was time to change things. He had been too difficult for a long time to Lainie, who cared for him. Plans went ahead, and Bill and Lainie were divorced. Then Lainie and Phil were married—just family. I know friends couldn't understand that, but it was decided that way was best. I think, you'll understand why there were no wedding invitations and lots of questions from friends unanswered. There was still more to work through. Lainie, knowing she had hurt Bill, prayed for his forgiveness."

Joe took a deep breath, then continued on. "Bill was still undergoing medical treatment, and then was in speech therapy, learning to speak all over again. His progress was slow. He wanted to learn to speak one sentence to Lainie. That was his first priority. It took time, but one day he spoke slowly and managed to say to her, 'Lainie, I forgive you!'

"The sentence wasn't too distinguishable, but Lainie understood. She went to him where he sat in his wheelchair, put her arms around his shoulders, and embraced him. This time he didn't shrink away from her, as he had done so many times before. The forgiving was good for both of them. Bill's anger kept slipping away, and he was more pleasant, more like the Bill we knew. It would have been impossible for him to smile then as he did a few times tonight, Max. Lainie was so happy. She had asked for Bill's forgiveness for her infidelity. After that she could at least forgive herself.

"Lainie and Phil have made provisions for Bill to be taken care of as long as he lives. They would not hear of any help from us, the family. This was of great importance to them. Isn't that a wonderful thing when you think of it?" Joe said in admiration. "You know, Max," Joe ended by saying, "the understanding that Lainie and Phil have, to care for Bill the way they do."

Then he added, "It was Bill's deep love and forgiveness for Lainie that gave her another chance for happiness. We're human and flawed, but we can make choices. My brother Bill did!" He said it with such pride, "My brother Bill."

Max had listened for a long time as Joe told of Bill's situation, and he didn't interrupt. Joe was reaching out to him and needed someone close to listen. Max was a friend, and he was glad that he could be there. He had so many mixed feelings hearing it all. Max got up to go and made a mental note to talk to Charlie and make arrangements to visit Bill more often.

Driving home, his thoughts were of Bill, Lainie, and Phil. It saddened him to see his friend, the robust, strong, handsome specimen of manhood, reduced to this helpless human being. Joe had said, "The speech therapy wasn't going too well, so Bill chose not to speak until it was greatly improved. You saw he didn't talk tonight, Max. Maybe he will do better next time."

I hope so, Max thought to himself. Max became angry and hit the steering wheel with his fist. "Damn that war! Damn that war!" He hated the changes it had made in Bill's life, in Charlie's life, and in millions of others. Joe had talked about it and made it sound like a problem resolved, but Max wondered, "People hide their innermost thoughts. How did Bill really feel in his heart? He must be in such pain and suffering at the changes in his life." He thought, *Oh, God give Bill peace in his heart*!

Max drove along Delmar Boulevard on his way home. It was late and most shops were closed. There were some late nighters walking arm-in-arm Max saw, then stop at the corner stop sign. He thought, *You're one of the lucky pairs—you're together*!

He turned into the driveway of his home. Serena had left the porch light on. It was comforting and welcoming. He turned off the motor and sat there for a few minutes, his head resting on the steering wheel. His thoughts were of his good life with Serena, Robert, and family. He had so much to be thankful for, and he had come close to losing it.

I've been such a fool, he thought.

Serena was in bed reading. She had waited up for Max. He bent to kiss her and she saw he had things on his mind, so asked no questions. He came to bed and moved closer, put his arms around her, feeling the warmth and wonderful smell of her. Nuzzling her with gentle kisses, he murmured in her ear, "I love you, Siri!" His voice became a bit husky as it usually did when he became emotional, and he said again, "I love you and need you!" Serena responded with her love, giving of herself to her Max—her love—their paradise! They lay there relaxed, arm-in-arm, tired but contented; their heads close together on one of the pillows. The last thing Serena remembered hearing were the 2:00 A.M. chimes of the clock downstairs.

Max tossed around. His mood was fretful, irritated with himself because he was tired but couldn't fall asleep. His thoughts kept reverting to Bill. It was almost morning before he closed his eyes and drifted into a deep sleep, when the shrill alarm woke him.

He was slow this morning, but he made it out of bed. However, his vigor and energy were still asleep. He felt tired. At breakfast, he gulped down a cup of strong coffee, kissed Serena, saying, "I'm late. I'll call you later." He started out the door, then came back.

She looked surprised and questioned, "What did you forget?"

He came over, embraced her and gave her a long kiss. "I forgot this, I love you, Siri!" He smiled at her as he opened the door again and left hurriedly.

Serena walked to the opened window and waited for him to make it out of the door. She called to him, and he turned and looked up. He saw her standing there, so fresh, so lovely; his breath caught in his throat. She smiled and waved, and he waved back as he turned into the garage.

Turning from the window, Serena began humming along with the song playing on the radio. This was a wonderful morning. She poured herself a cup of coffee and walked out the back door to the lawn chair near the willow tree. It was early, but the weather was warm. She smiled to herself. She loved this space, it was so peaceful and calm. She loved the water.

Her thoughts went to family. It had been wonderful to have them here with friends. Friends whom she cared about, and she was saddened by Carole's and Charlie's problems. It hurt so much to see and know their unhappiness. She looked at the tree, it stood there like a good friend, and she spoke out loud. "Oh, God, let things be good for Carole and Charlie." She sat there awhile longer, then went in.

Max called at noon. He would be home early to spend time with little Robert, and they would have the evening together. "I want to tell you about Bill and Lainie."

When he hung up, she thought about Bill and Lainie. *Whatever Max wanted to tell her,* she thought, *must be important.*

Throughout the day, Max's thoughts were interrupted with different pieces of Bill and Lainie. To Max, their lives seemed to be greatly complicated. Later, on his way home, Max once more wondered about the decisions Bill and Lainie had made that changed their lives. Were they right? Were they wrong? Only time would make that determination. Max prayed it would be good for all of them.

XXIII
Celebrations—Charlie and Carole

As Serena's position required, she came to early morning meetings and discussions at the newspaper office. There she learned the news of the latest happenings and problems.

By 1950, in St. Louis as well as the rest of the country, the baby boomers were almost doubling the population. This phenomenon meant new residential construction. As communities grew, more schools, more hospitals, more shopping centers, and all services needed to support them had to be made available.

The Kellers' shoe businesses had flourished with the opening of stores in the new centers. The new stores catered to children and were doing extremely well. Max was kept pretty busy.

Robert and Judy were at Delmar-Harvard School where Carole taught second grade. Serena made it a point to be home early afternoon before Robert was out of school.

Max and Serena were nearing their tenth anniversary. They had planned an elaborate affair in celebration, but because of the situation of Bill and Charlie, they changed it to a party at home with family and their friends. Charlie, especially, had not been doing well.

Max was surprising Serena with a marble bench. He had it inscribed in gold lettering, "My Love Forever," and the date July 1, 1951. It was to be delivered Friday while Serena was at work, and it was to be placed near the willow tree by the stream.

The tree was special to both of them, but to Serena it was more. It became a private space where she could come with a problem to unravel, or a care to reflect upon. The time spent there was important to her, and she sometimes sat for long periods of time in silence, only with her thoughts. She found herself many times arguing out loud, presenting both sides of a question, heard only by the tree. After a while, satisfied in her mind what she had come to contemplate had been reasoned and dealt with, she could then leave with satisfaction. She would get up from the lawn chair.

For these reasons, Max had wanted to get her something special to relax in. He had given much thought to the gift for her. He was anxious to know how she would like it. The tree they loved had been doing well and was in full foliage for the summer. It was an amazingly lovely-shaped one with its graceful branches.

When Serena came home, there was a card from Max telling her to go down to the tree. At the window, she could see part of the bench. She ran down and when she saw the inscription, she was deeply moved by the lovely gift. She wanted to tell him that. Serena tried to call, but he was already on his way home.

That special Sunday came and guests were arriving. Carole, Charlie and family, Lainie, Bill, Phil, and Joe came, and of course, Max's family, and Serena's. Serena had arranged an afternoon buffet with an array of delicious dishes with everyone's favorite. Of course, they brought gifts, and all went out to see the bench with the cascading willow branches back-dropping it. They all agreed with Serena and Max, "this was a special place."

The evening was filled with laughter and good wishes, and it was wonderful to have family and friends there. Serena and Max were especially happy that Charlie and Bill could come. Everyone, it seemed, made a special effort to spend time with Bill and Charlie, and they expressed pleasure in seeing them. All in all, it had been an incredible day with wonderful things to remember.

The ladies helped with the clean-up, and after the guests left, Serena and Max went out to the bench. It was a perfect summer evening. Max had his arm around Serena, and they sat watching the twinkling stars in the sky. "We had a wonderful party, Siri. You made it such a happy time. I'm so proud to have been married to you for all these special ten years." He kissed her and held her closer. The whole day meant so much to both of them. They talked about Charlie, voicing concern, and Max said he was going to try to see both Charlie and Bill a little more often.

Carole's father had expanded the business now called Berg and Schwartz Drug Supplier. Charlie was now a partner. Mr. Berg went out of town calling on drug stores and doctors' offices, selling pharmaceutical supplies. He did very well.

Charlie was in charge of the drug store, and he had another pharmacist and clerk assisting him. He seemed to be doing okay. Carole, always vigilant about Charlie's behavior, noticed a change taking place. He was becoming more morose and depressed. The two visited his doctors. Sometimes his medications were changed. They helped for a while; however, that status quo was short-lived.

Max, visiting Charlie often, noted the changes. He called Charlie one day telling him they needed to visit Bill. Charlie wasn't too enthusiastic, but Max insisted saying, "Charlie, Bill always asks about you. He'll really appreciate seeing you!"

The visit to Bill was difficult to deal with. Seeing Bill with all his problems, and not complaining, trying hard to help himself—to cope—made Charlie feel really inadequate. Bill had so many problems to overcome.

Charlie came home feeling sorry for his friend, Bill, and he mentioned that to Carole. For a few weeks, the visit seemed to have reaped some benefits for Charlie. There were high and low periods in Charlie's life. They always worried Carole. Before he visited Bill, he was in a low period, and after the visit, he was in a better mood. To him, "his problems weren't major," that's what he told Carole.

Charlie wanted to see Bill again, and Max was glad to go with him, thinking it might help Charlie.

Mr. Berg, seeing what this was doing to his daughter, spoke to her about his concern for his son-in-law. It might help if Charlie took the trip out of town to see how he liked it. "Getting away for a few days, the change might be good for him," Mr. Berg thought.

Before Carole talked to Charlie, she wanted to check with his doctor. He thought Charlie could try it, impressing upon her the importance of Charlie taking his medications regularly. At home, she could remind him; away, he would have to take care of it. The following week the subject was broached to Charlie. "Think about it. Don't have to decide right now. You can do it later, if you like." Mr. Berg didn't want Charlie to feel pressured.

Almost a month later, Charlie, after giving the idea much thought, decided he would like to take the business trip. He had been feeling better, and Carole was pleased with his decision. The break in his daily routine at the drug store might prove to be beneficial. Still, her mind would not be at ease while he was away.

Carole tried her best to be cheerful around Charlie, and there were times when it was almost impossible to do because of the pressure she felt. The doctors were not very encouraging. They didn't know how Charlie's situation would be resolved. It was a day-to-day process with "ups and downs"; then there were the explosions of temper, and the violent streaks when he had to be hospitalized.

Those were periods that took their toll on them, Carole, her father, Judy, and yes, Charlie, too. He had been in therapy—a one-on-one with different doctors. They tried group therapy at different hospitals. This was a new thing, this "mental fatigue" that happened to so many soldiers from this war. There were so many different opinions to listen to; some helped and some did not. Carole tried everything they suggested. In the end, it was still the same for Charlie. He had the disturbing nightmares. In his sleep, he heard the injured calling for the medical corps. Charlie would start running—racing to get to them. Sometimes he saw himself running in slow motion, other times like on a treadmill—running, running, but never reaching the injured calling him.

Sometimes when he reached the men, he found he didn't have the medical supplies, and he saw the men die. Many times he heard their cries for help, but couldn't get to them—he was being held back by Japanese guards.

Then there were the times when he found them, but the Japs had gotten there first, and killed them with their bayonets. The images of the mutilated dead didn't leave him, and he blamed himself for their deaths because he didn't have enough medical supplies, or he didn't get to them in time. He felt responsible—that he had failed them, and he couldn't forgive himself.

Charlie went on one trip to St. Charles, Vandalia, and Hannibal. He promised Carole he would call home to let her know how things were going. He was gone for three days; he had called—was doing fine. He came home very up-beat. At dinner, he talked about the people he met and was positive he was going to like it.

The next visit to the doctor was good. Charlie was doing well. He had been on the job a little over two months. He was getting tired, and Carole wanted her father to take the trip for a while, then Charlie could rest or be in the drug store. He wouldn't hear of it. He would be "okay," is what he said.

Charlie was a difficult patient. A few days later, he called from Springfield. Carole could tell by his voice things were not going well. She asked, "Charlie, did you take your medication?" No, he would take it when he got home. He arrived home in a pitiful state. He hadn't shaved for a few days. When she tried to get him to take his medication, he became angry, abusive, and violent as he had done a few times before.

Carole called the doctor. An ambulance came and took Charlie to the hospital. He was in the psychiatric ward, and Carole came every day. The doctor told her Charlie had stopped taking the medication. With the nightmares recurring, Charlie gave up on the medications, which worsened his mental state.

He was in a special area in the hospital. When Carole came to see him, she was saddened to see him huddled in a corner of the room. She stayed with him and spoke quietly, lovingly to him. He stared at her with vacant eyes that put fear in her heart for Charlie. She hugged him and said, "good-bye." There was no answer. She left full of despair.

That night Carole was called back to the hospital. Charlie had tried to commit suicide. There had been one thing after another with him. Her nerves were as taut as strings on a violin. Carole rushed to the hospital, near collapse herself. Her face was pale with dark-circled eyes from sleepless nights.

She didn't know how she would find Charlie. The sides of his bed were up, and the wrists on both hands bandaged and taped. The doctor was there waiting for her. Charlie, under a "suicide watch," had managed to get a piece of sharp metal, and had worked on his wrists; first on one, then the other, and cut into his veins.

One of the nurses found Charlie on the floor near his bed. He had lost quite a lot of blood and had already received blood transfusions. Carole looked at Charlie, so pitiful lying there. It was almost more than she could bear. Why did Charlie do it? No matter what had been done to try to help him, nothing could take from his brain the nightmares that were enslaving him. She sat beside him, gently pushing his hair back from his forehead. He looked so lost, it tore at her heart. One of the nurses came in and gave him a hypodermic of medication that made him more comfortable.

Terribly upset, Carole left when he closed his eyes wearily, and fell asleep. She took a leave of absence again and stayed with Charlie. Over and over she repeated how much she and Judy loved and needed him. Charlie seemed to be listening, but he didn't say much. She wondered if he understood. "Do you understand what I'm saying?"

On medication, he could now nod "yes."

Weeks later, Charlie was able to come home. Serena and Max came often to spend time with them. They had dinner together, and Charlie seemed to be improving.

"Charlie," Max said, "we're planning to go out New Year's Eve to the Park Plaza. So take care, Old Buddy!"

A few months passed and Charlie wanted to help in the drug store. Everyone's spirits were lifted. It seemed to be a good sign that Charlie was recovering. Mr. Berg made the trips out of town, and day-to-day living was returning to normalcy. Carole planned to return to school in the spring of the year.

Carole was in the drug store. Charlie was helping a customer. It was almost five o'clock. "I'm going in to fix dinner," she announced and left.

At home, she was bustling about the kitchen, humming, and making Charlie's favorites. An hour later, she heard her father's car out front. Usually he stopped into the drug store. She called to tell them dinner would be ready in fifteen minutes. "Dad," she said, "send Charlie in."

"Charlie's not here," he told her. "He didn't say he was going out."

"One minute he was here, and the next he wasn't," one of the clerks offered. "He'll be back soon."

This wasn't like Charlie to leave and not say he was leaving, Carole thought. Worried, she went to see if the car was in the garage. The garage door was locked, and there was the odor of gas fumes around the garage. Looking in the window, she saw the smoke-filled garage. She ran calling for help, "Call the police! Call an ambulance!"

Her father came and broke the garage window, then opened the garage and shut the motor off. Charlie was slumped over the steering wheel. Gently, Mr. Berg moved Charlie back in his seat. Carole came to Charlie. She was coughing and Mr. Berg led her out, both coughing, trying to get some air. Mr. Berg was shaking. He knew Charlie was dead.

Help came, their sirens screaming, and jumped out quickly. A crowd was gathering. The ambulance took Charlie. Carole went with them. She sat in front crying hysterically, "Oh, Charlie, why did you do it? Why did you do it?"

Charlie left a letter to Carole. It was on the cash register. "I can't go on this way. I love you and Judy. I can't hurt you anymore. Forgive me, I love you." He signed it "Charlie." The year was 1952.

She had called Serena and had seen her come and take Judy. *Thank God,* she thought, *for Serena; Serena is always there.* Carole put her hands over her face to stifle the sobs, thinking about her child. *Judy*, she thought, *how will it be for her? She loved her father so.* Carole was shocked and saddened, but an anger crept in, too. She was angry that Charlie would do this—kill himself!

It took the rest of the week to get doctors' reports on Charlie's problems, and the death certificate. Funeral arrangements were made. Carole and Charlie had never discussed them. The services were not lengthy. The Rabbi spoke of Charlie's life. He had known him as a youngster, losing his father, and caring for his mother.

He talked of Charlie's married life. He spoke of his love for Carole and Judy, and of his going to war, innocent of the hate and evil he found that later consumed his life. "He died," Rabbi said, "because his heart with its goodness could not comprehend the evil he had seen, and couldn't forget. He left a legacy of love."

Max gave the eulogy for his friend. He was heartbroken. He remembered what a wonderful friend Charlie was; how kind and good. He had gone off to war and had seen the evil of it that remained with him. He could not understand the hatred of the enemy he saw in the Pacific. He spoke about it. "What makes men so evil?" That was the question he put to his doctors and friends. He didn't find answers. Max asked God "to give him peace so his tortured brain could rest." Max broke down at the end when he said, "Good-bye, dear friend."

Lainie came with Phil and brought Bill in his wheelchair. Mrs. Keller and Serena had taken care of lunch. Afterwards as guests left, Serena asked if Carole wanted her to stay. Carole thanked her, but wanted to be with her family. Serena and Max understood. As they were leaving, they promised to call in the morning. In the car, Max said again, "It was that damn war. There was hate enough there to remember for thousands of years!"

Carole didn't go back to school for the rest of the year. She was home caring for Judy. There was Charlie's mother to take care of. After Charlie committed suicide, his mother had a massive heart attack. Two months later, she died. Her grief over losing Charlie was more than her heart could take. Carole saw to it that she was buried next to her husband and close to Charlie.

Ever since the day Carole had found Charlie dead, she thought about him in anger. She loved him, but she could not forgive him for taking his own life. She wondered what made him do this to himself, knowing it would hurt her and Judy. She didn't know the answer, and was tormented beyond belief.

For a long time, she turned herself inside out asking questions of herself. She blamed herself—feeling a great guilt. Had she been the cause? Moving back home when Charlie didn't want to? She had made the decision, she thought, to help them all, to be able to care for Charlie, and this is what happened! Charlie had hated it so that he killed himself. For months she carried this in her heart, making excuses not to go out. She didn't even want to see Serena.

Serena spoke to Jenny about this. Jenny, a psychologist, was seeking a way to help Carole. Serena knew her friend couldn't go on this way. Judy needed her mother, and Carole wasn't there for her. Mr. Berg had called Serena; he was terribly concerned. After quite a few discussions, Serena got Carole to see a therapist to help her. She went once a week. After months of therapy, she began to understand it wasn't her. Charlie had had his moods when she first met him, and they were contributing factors to what happened to him in the war.

He believed he was there in the medical corps to help save lives. He felt he was at fault—had failed. No matter how many times the doctors or Carole tried to impress upon him it wasn't so, he believed otherwise. He didn't have the medical supplies needed, because at that time the supplies coming in ships were sunk by Japanese submarines; still he blamed himself. Charlie, the idealist, expected too much of himself. He was trying to fight the war alone and couldn't. He felt responsible for most of the deaths on his battlefields.

Carole was in therapy for almost a year. She was back in school at the start of the new semester, and life at home with her father and Judy was more conducive to working at their relationships, which had suffered so from the tragedy and its' aftermath.

Serena and Max tried to coax her out to dinner or a movie, but she wasn't ready to go. While Carole was struggling to put her life together, America had gone through the Korean War, and Dwight D. Eisenhower, who had been the Allied commander in World War II, became America's thirty-fourth president in 1953.

President Eisenhower promised to deal with America's problems, and most Americans felt this war hero was the man to do it. They put their hope and faith in him. Max and Serena had many discussions about America's problems. They set them aside in the competent hands of the new president. Then they turned to the problems of their friend Carole. They invited her out to dinner, then told her about David Miller, a friend of Max's. David owned the jewelry store in the shopping center; David and Max had become good friends.

At first Carole was hesitant and didn't want to come. She said, "I don't want any match-making!" She was still an angry Carole; she had not forgotten her anger at Charlie. Carole, still very attractive, met David. He was about fifty, a little older than Charlie, soft spoken, nice looking, a most pleasant individual. He was attentive to Carole in a gentlemanly fashion. The evening went well, and when it was over, David asked if he could take her home. Max had picked her up. On the way, he answered some of her questions. "Yes," he had been married. His wife had died in a car crash a few years back. Carole liked the way he said quite simply, "I've missed her."

At Carole's, they sat in the car talking in a pleasant manner, both at ease with each other. When she said, "It's getting late," David helped her out of the car. She didn't ask him in. She didn't want to encourage him. Talking to Serena about David that week, Carole said, "I won't ever get married again!"

David had enjoyed being with Carole, and he told Max that. He wanted to ask her out. Max suggested he wait. Carole would come along in a foursome, but he didn't think she was ready to be asked out on a date. Serena invited Carole to join them for dinner the following Saturday. "It will be fun," she said. "David is coming along, too."

During the week, Carole thought about seeing David. She was pleasantly surprised to acknowledge to herself that she was looking forward to seeing him. Dressing for school, she had always been conservative in her taste with skirts and blouses, and she always looked nice. For Saturday, she had purchased a lovely aqua silk dress. It looked fantastic on her. Her hair had been done, and while she turned this way and that, she blushed at the image of the young woman looking back at her from the mirror.

"I haven't done this for a long while!" She felt happy. For a minute, she wondered if it was right for her to be happy. She came into the living room to wait for Serena and Max to pick her up. Her father looked up from his newspaper and nodded his approval, "You look lovely, Carole." It made her feel good inside.

"Thanks, Dad." She came over to peck him on the cheek with a kiss.

Max was at the door and came in to say "Hi" to Mr. Berg, then they left. They drove to the hotel where they were to meet David. They were all in a cheerful mood, talking and laughing. David had such a delightful sense of humor. That was another thing Carole liked about him.

The evening progressed with dinner and dancing, and every once in a while, Serena would catch Max's eye, and he winked at her, nodding his head toward Carole and David. The chemistry of geniality between those two was unmistakable. They wondered where it would lead to.

David always drove her home. They sat in the car on the porch swing talking, but she still hadn't asked him in. He was quite understanding. He remembered how it had been for him when well-meaning friends wanted to invite him to meet a young lady. It was quite difficult for him. He had made many excuses, then he remembered he had almost excused himself from the dinner date to meet Carole.

Max had been persistent. *Thank God for that*! David thought. His heart skipped a beat when he reflected how close he had come to not meeting Carole. At the last moment, he had changed his mind and made the decision to come.

He had not been disappointed when he saw Carole. She was lovely, and she said, "It's so nice to meet you," and she said it with a smile. She entered into the conversation lady-like and with knowledge, but not an all-knowing like some he met. She looked right at him. He liked that she was straightforward.

They became friends. It was a good place to be, and love was making inroads into their lives. On the day of their first month anniversary, David sent a bouquet of pink roses. He had learned they were her favorite flowers. Carole was touched by his remembering. Three months went by. David was now calling Carole. They went on long rides, had long talks, and the process of learning about each other was evolving. They were good together.

Always the gentleman, he held her arm firmly when they walked. It made her feel safe. He was someone she felt she could trust. She was overwhelmed with the many wonderful things he did. Every month he sent flowers with a touching card that professed his love for her. When they were together and she thanked him, he would ask, "Are you happy, Carole, honey?"

David always brought something for Judy that he thought she would like, and he spent time with her. Judy had become quite fond of him, and called him "Uncle David." That delighted him as he felt "to be part of the family."

Charlie was gone for over three years, and Carole's pain was slowly subsiding. Try as she might not to think about the suicide, it would trespass on her mind, upsetting her. It remained deep inside, not forgotten, and she couldn't forgive him.

Carole and David were to meet Serena and Max for dinner. David had come earlier. He wanted to discuss something with her. It had been raining, and Carole was helping David out of his raincoat. She went to hang it up. David, meanwhile, was pacing back and forth. He was nervous and his stomach felt queasy.

He sat down on the sofa just as Carole came back. She came to sit near him and was about to say something when David began, "Carole, honey," and nervous, he had to clear his throat. "I've known you for a while and you know I love you. I want the chance to prove my love for you and make you and Judy happy." He stopped and took a deep breath. He had said what he wanted to say thus far. "Carole," he was holding her hands in his, "will you do me the honor of being my wife?" He looked so serious, pouring out his love.

Carole was taken by surprise. She loved David and was sure at one point he would propose. Then sometimes she had doubts and didn't know if he would. Women never know what to expect. *Life is full of the unexpected,* she thought, lost in the moment of the proposal from David.

He was still baring his heart. "I'll make you happy, you'll see." He was having a little difficulty getting something out of his suit pocket. "There," he said with a sigh of relief, as he held onto a small box. He opened it and showed Carole the beautiful marquise-cut diamond ring resting there in all its glory. David put it on her finger. She turned her hand this way and that, and the lights reflected its brilliance.

"Oh, David, it's so beautiful." Carole was thrilled. She had not answered his proposal for a moment. There was a flashback to the night she and Charlie were engaged. That seemed so long ago. Dave, sensing her hesitancy, asked, "You do care for me?"

She recovered quickly and answered, "Yes, I do, David. I'll be proud to be your wife."

They embraced and he held her close. They had been honest with each other, and she added, "I don't know if I am doing the right thing. Sometimes I'm not sure."

David held her. "I understand your feelings. We'll do this together. I'll always be there for you." He spoke, as he always did to her, with sincerity. She thought, *What a wonderful person David is,* and she had told him that numerous times. Out loud she said, "David, I'll try to be a good wife to you." David knew her pretty well—the kind of caring person she was. He knew they would be in a good marriage.

Carole's father had taken Judy to the movies, and they weren't back yet. Carole wanted to share the exciting news of the engagement. They deliberated about waiting, then decided to leave. "We'll see them later," David said. "It's getting late to meet Serena and Max." It was still raining as they ran to David's car, but that didn't dampen their spirits. They were on "cloud nine," and they couldn't wait to tell Max and Serena.

The friends celebrated, Serena and Max rejoicing with them in their happiness. They talked all through dinner about plans for the future. They had all learned you can plan for the future, but live your life one day at a time. There were happy toasts with champagne, and dancing—changing partners. Max telling Carole how pleased he was for her. "Be happy, Carole. Be happy." He said it twice.

Serena, dancing with David, was expressing her pleasure and happiness for him and Carole. "She's a wonderful person, David. We love her." She, too, told him, "Be happy."

Carole and David were leaving a little earlier than usual. They wanted to see Carole's father and Judy. The ride home was wonderful too. Carole had her head on David's shoulder. They weren't talking, savoring these special moments.

David spoke up. "I love you, Carole. For a long time, I didn't seem to know where I belonged. Now, I am where I want to be—with you, and that's a wonderful feeling!"

Carole squeezed his arm, "You know, David, before you came into my life, it was muddled, unsure. With you now, I feel I'm home. Safe!"

Driving home, Max and Serena were mulling over the evening's happy event. "Max, you did a good thing getting David to come that night to meet Carole."

"Well, it was lucky he decided to come. You know he wouldn't come for a long time."

"Yes," Serena agreed. "It was lucky Carole decided to come that same night, too. She had not been too receptive about meeting anyone for a long time either. I guess it was the right time for both of them, and tonight was the happy result."

"They're both good people, and suffered such tragedies." Max's voice was solemn. He was remembering the grim, heartbreaking ordeals they had both endured. "I'm sure they will be all right. Guess what, Siri, we're pretty good matchmakers."

They laughed together, pleased as punch with themselves, happy for their good friends.

Carole's father was overwhelmed at the news when Carole and David showed him the ring. He said it was beautiful, then kissed her. "I'm so glad for you, dear." Then he shook hands with David. "I'll be proud to call you my son-in-law," he said. He knew David was a fine person, and in his heart he was thankful for the happiness David had brought to Carole.

Judy, too, was overcome with joy. She liked David. "Gosh, mom, that's good. I'm glad for both of you." Then there were hugs all around for Judy.

Carole's father said to both of them, "I know you love each other and you'll be happy."

Carole knew her father had suffered much pain watching her cope with Charlie's problems. He never said anything, just tried to help in any way he could. He had always been there for her. She put her arm around her father. She realized with a shocked feeling, she had been too busy with her problems and had neglected her dad. She should have taken time for him. She saw the worry had taken its toll. The hair was more white than gray, and the lines on his face more defined. He was thinner, and it tugged at her heart to see it and know it was because of her and her troubles.

"Dad," she said, "you know how much I love you. I could never ever thank you enough for all you've done. Now, I hope you will take it easier. We want to take care of you. We need you." They sat there on the sofa close together.

"That's all right, dear," he said, his voice always calm. "I'm glad I was here for you."

The next few weeks were busy. David and Carole purchased a home near Max and Serena. It was being redecorated. Carole and David would stay in her home until it was ready. They were so excited to be going soon into their own place. Both Carole and David told her father there was a special place for him in their home whenever he was ready to come. They assured him he was wholeheartedly welcome. Dave especially said, "We want you with us. We're family."

The weeks flew by and it was the night before the wedding. Dave got up to leave. He kissed Carole and whispered in her ear, "See you tomorrow."

They were up late discussing a few last-minute details. Then Carole reminded her dad and Judy, "We better get to bed. Tomorrow will be a wonderful day." Then she added, "Dad, I'm glad you're here for my wedding,"

Judy came over and kissed her mother "good night." Carole was so proud of her daughter, almost twelve, and quite a young lady.

The wedding day dawned bright and clear that June morning. The household was up early and bustling about. The wedding was to be held in the living room, beautifully decorated with small bouquets of pink and white roses. The morning sped along, and soon it was almost two o'clock, the magical hour. David came earlier so the photographer could take the precious pictures.

It was to be a small wedding, just their closest friends, Serena's family, Max's family, Lainie, Bill and Phil. Serena was matron of honor, and Max best man. Judy was her mother's junior bridesmaid and looked so grown up in a lovely pale pink dress. She was escorted down by Robert, dressed in a tuxedo. Robert was tall for his age, and they made a "handsome couple," friends remarked.

David was escorted down by Serena and Max, and he waited nervously for his bride. Carole, on her father's arm, was beautiful in an off-white gown, and her father couldn't have looked happier. David, at the sight of his lovely Carole, began to tremble.

The ceremony was a simple one, and though everyone was happy for these two, there were tears. At weddings, there are always tears. After getting so many good wishes for happiness, there was a reception. It all went quite well.

Guests began leaving, and Serena and Max stayed to help the bride and groom leave on their one-week honeymoon. They flew down to Miami and embarked on a huge cruise ship, the S.S. *Emerald Seas.* Carole was so excited at all these new adventures with David.

They had a most pleasurable voyage. Passengers were most obliging to the honeymoon couple, taking their pictures whenever they asked. "Everyone was nice," Carole said later. They visited many islands in the Caribbean, one named Paradise Island. "That's exactly what it was," David said. "It was paradise!"

The honeymooning couple called a few times to see how Judy and her grandfather were. They were fine. The new couple had a spectacular time and came back looking "wonderfully happy" was the comment from most of their friends.

After five months, in November, they moved into their new home. Everything the newlyweds received as wedding gifts was unpacked carefully with "oohs and aahs," and handled most gingerly.

They shopped for new things and took great delight in putting them in "just the right place." This was all special to them, an adventure with much laughter and happiness.

For Judy, too, this was exciting, and they let her help, which made it special for her. When they were somewhat finished, they agreed "it looked wonderful." They sat together and admired their handiwork.

It was well into the evening. Judy kissed her mother and Uncle David "good night," then went to bed.

Carole turned down one of the lamps and left the room. Comfortable against a large pillow sat David, a contentment in his heart that had been missing for a long time. Just then Carole came back with a small tray, "I brought us some hot chocolate, David."

"Sounds good."

They talked and sipped, looking around in wonderment, so proud. Carole making pleasurable comments about the gifts. David saw it all, too. "You know, Carole, honey, it's you and Judy here, that makes this our home." David thought a lot about that.

"It's you, too, David. Without you there would be none of this." In her heart, she hoped she could make him as happy as he had made her. He brought his gift of stability to her and Judy. She couldn't help but love this man. It had taken time, with uncertainties and misgivings, then faith and hope, to take this step, which they did. Day by day with optimism, they would meet their unfolding tomorrows.

XXIV
Another Generation!

In life, there are always changes, and this was true for Mr. Berg. At the urging of David, Carole, and Judy, he came to live with them. He had been there a little over two years, his steadily failing health a concern to the family. One evening he was rushed to the hospital, terribly ill. The doctors did their best, but he died that night. His valiant heart had taken its last beat.

The chapel where the funeral was held was overflowing with so many friends of the family. The death of her father was most difficult for Carole to deal with; she missed having him in her everyday life. Judy was inconsolable, and Robert came every day to be with her. David, too, missed this man who had become like a father to him. "Time," everyone said, "would be the healer."

The new seasons changed to other seasons, and one by one the years were passing. America's papers told of Hawaii becoming the fiftieth State of the Union. The new flags now boasted fifty stars on their blue fields.

While everybody was busy with the living of each day, it had escaped them that it wasn't just the parents and grandparents getting older, it was happening almost unnoticed to the young folk, too. The summer of 1960 saw Judy and Robert graduating high school. The years had swallowed their birthdays. They were now all of seventeen. Family and friends attended the graduation, and when the ceremonies were over, they left for a celebration that Carole and David had planned for the graduates.

It was a fun evening, and time flies when you're having a good time. Guests began to depart, all except Serena and Max. They thanked Carol and David for the spectacular evening, and they stayed awhile longer to talk.

It was quite late when they got home. Max turned on the television for the late, late news and found he had missed most of it, so he turned it off. Serena, already in her robe, was going down to her "space" for a little while. Max headed for his shower. "Siri, it's late. Don't be too long," he said.

The lights were still on in the backyard. Serena walked slowly, gazing at the dark blue heaven with a crescent moon hanging suspended there. Her coming had disturbed the birds nesting in the tree. The quiet was interrupted by the flutter of wings. They took sleepy-eyed note of her, knowing she was no danger, settled back in, and soon all was still.

Today was a "happy time" day that she could talk about to her willow. Going over the magical happenings of the day, the thrill of seeing Robert get his diploma made her happy. She thought of Judy. Out loud she spoke softly. "There are so many things to be grateful for. Thank you, God, for all your blessings." Her faith was strong. She paused, then nodded her head, affirming all she had just said. It was late, she didn't stay down too long.

Upstairs at the bedroom door, she called to Max. There was no answer. He was asleep. After a quick shower, she got into bed and snuggled up to Max's back. She sighed a sigh of contentment; her life was full on so many levels. She tossed a bit, then finally, finally fell asleep.

The middle of the week brought anxiously awaited mail from Francois and Monique. Michelle always sent pictures of her husband Paul and her daughter Nedda, who resembled Ressel. The family in America reciprocated, sending pictures of everyone, and their parents. It was good—the families came to know each other. To the American family that Michelle was alive, and safe, and loved, was a miracle! When they pondered the circumstances that made it possible for Max to find her, it was truly a miracle!

The rest of the summer skipped along, and for the young adults, it went rather swiftly. It was fall, the first week in September, and Washington U was bracing itself for the onslaught of thousands of students. Robert and Judy were two of them. Robert was hoping to get his degree in business management, and Judy was eager to pursue her degree in psychology. The psychologist, who had helped her mother and her, had made quite an impression on Judy. She wanted to do something, too, that helped people. Her family was supportive, and she set that as her goal.

The relationship between Judy and Robert had grown. They were going to school and giving thought to their future, a future together, with dreams and plans.

The Second World War had ended. The peace came with problems that were soon apparent. Berlin was divided between the three governments of America, Great Britain, and Russia, which left fertile ground for misunderstandings. Ideas took hold, and communism was a problem in the Eastern European countries. They were known as the countries behind the "Iron Curtain." Eisenhower was President, attempting to deal with communism.

John F. Kennedy became the next president at a time when these many problems were confronting America. Serena had come home from a work meeting. All the papers carried the news the next day. President Kennedy spoke to America saying we were in grave danger. The year was 1962.

Russia was setting up missile sites in Cuba, aimed at the United States. Kennedy imposed an arms embargo on Cuba. The president stood firm; they were to be dismantled or we would be at war with Russia.

As always, there were dissenters, those against what the president was doing. However, most Americans were with him. Those were anxious days for America, and the world. Max remembered, after Pearl Harbor, he went to war. If this was war again, Robert and millions of other young men would go. The patriotic young, full of life and adventure, were ready to go to war. While the world was in turmoil, Robert and Judy were finishing up two years at Washington.

Serena and Max, and thousands of worried parents, could breathe a bit easier when the blockade was imposed, and U.S. warships were stopping ships carrying arms to Cuba. Russia backed off, and dismantled their sites.

A year later, November 23, 1963, President Kennedy was assassinated—killed by a sniper, as he rode in a car in Dallas.

The infamous killer was Lee Harvey Oswald, a marine who had defected to Russia.

It was one of the saddest days in America to learn of the violent death of their young president. He was only forty-six years old. People in St. Louis, and around the world, could not believe the news when they heard it. Men and women wept openly and were saddened and angered.

St. Louis and cities all around the country went dark—in mourning. Theatres and restaurants closed, electric signs were turned off, and flags flew at half-mast. America and the whole world were grief-stricken.

Lyndon Johnson, Vice President, became the thirty-sixth president. He inherited and promised to continue giving aid to the South Vietnamese in their war against communism with the North Vietnamese. The U.S. had a commitment to the security of Southeast Asia, and was stressing it would fight to defend its commitment, as President Kennedy had done.

North Vietnam attacked two U.S. destroyers in the Gulf of Tonkin. America responded with planes, attacking North Vietnamese bases. The North Vietnamese retaliated with P.T. boats, attacking two U.S. destroyers with torpedoes.

Americans considered this open aggression on the high seas, and America was at war. By lottery, Americans were being called into service, and sent to Vietnam, and the war escalated. American homes were again suffering huge, huge numbers of casualties as more and more troops were called up to duty.

The war news once again superimposed itself on television, radio, in the papers, and theatre newsreels. Congress, the president, and his cabinet, were in constant solemn discussions. There didn't seem to be a solution to the problem. Americans listened, voiced opinions, and tried to lead their interrupted lives with some degree of normalcy amidst the chaos in the country.

The New Year was approaching, and Max and Serena, and Carole and David, were planning to attend the celebration at the Park Plaza. Robert and Judy were to join them a bit later. Robert was giving Judy a ring. They were to become engaged.

They were graduating that June of 1964. Robert would work at one of the shoe stores, and Judy hoped to get a job. The big night arrived. Robert went to pick up Judy. He came in. There was something of importance he wanted to discuss with her. He was so nervous, he had to ask for some water. "What's wrong, Rob?" Judy asked. "Are you all right?" Robert nodded as he gulped some of the water. It had always been easy for these two to talk to each other. Tonight, with all the rehearsing he had done at home, wasn't simple.

"Judy," he began, "you know I love you." He held out the precious small package with both hands, as if in prayer and asked, "Judy, will you marry me?" He had twisted and turned the package until the ribbon was a crumpled mess. "Open it, Judy." he couldn't wait any longer to see if she liked it.

When it was opened and she saw it, she gasped, "Oh, Robert, it's just beautiful!" She handed it to him and held out her hand for him to put in on her finger. He held onto her hands and asked again, "Will you marry me?"

"Yes, oh yes! Oh, Robert." Almost in tears, she said, "I love you." This was their moment as they sat together on the kitchen chairs, she looking at the ring, and then at him; he looking at her—love struck, kissing her, forgetting they were due at the Plaza.

The two lovebirds walked in all smiles. Judy put out her hand to her mother, dangling her fingers up and down until Carole saw the ring. The family gathered around, embracing and congratulating them.

At midnight, they rang in the new year. Robert and Judy left first. David and Carole were taking Max and Serena home, and they were invited in. They stayed just a little while, and talked of the wonderful thing that had happened that night.

"Now," Max said, "we're not only friends but will be in-laws."

After they had gone, Max again went over the evening's events. "We have a lot to look forward to—the graduation, then the kids' getting married the following year. Gosh, the years are flying. Then we'll be one year away from our twenty-fifth anniversary. Can you believe it?"

He wanted to talk about that, but she was tired. "Okay, beautiful!" He turned off the lamp near his side of the bed.

Serena turned to face him. Max put his arm around her and kissed her. They touched with warmth and love, and soon they were in the throes of ecstasy of their love, beginning another New Year.

Serena and Max gave the graduation party. The year of the graduation, countries in Europe were dealing with serious problems that had begun almost from the end of WWII. They had been liberated from Nazism, and were working towards becoming democracies, but there were those who opposed it with communism, backed by the Soviets.

Countries now became "policed states" under the eye of the KGB. "Secret Police." People were watched, hounded, harassed, their human rights violated. Those thought to be enemies of the government were arrested, tortured, and sent to prison, lost to their families, or killed. This growing climate of violence was escalating and worrisome to the Free World.

Robert and Judy, young and so in love, were impatient to enter into marriage, and into a happy life together. The year passed, and plans for their wedding went forward. In April, they found an apartment and experienced the joy of shopping together. Momentous decisions were made that weren't always easy, and there had to be compromise by each of them.

Carole and David were planning the wedding. Carole, caught up in this new experience, expressed her feelings. "I want this to be perfect for them!" Robert, they knew as a fine young man, the two had grown up together. Their future looked bright!

Letters and invitations were mailed to Francois and family. Max wrote he was making arrangements for them all to come for this wedding, or the twenty-fifth wedding anniversary the following year, 1966. It was their choice, whichever date would be more convenient for them.

The family in France sent congratulations, but Michelle was sorry, Paul couldn't come now. There were problems in some of the countries his company did business with. "The following year would be better, if that was all right," Michelle wrote. They thanked Max for doing this wonderful thing for them. They so wanted to come to see America and Michelle's family here.

Max wrote, "We are looking forward to your coming. That will be something special for us."

The days on the calendar moved along, but for Judy and Robert, at a snail's pace. Spring buzzed in and out, like the bees in the garden. Finally, it was June. The wedding was two weeks away.

Rachel was one of the bridesmaids, and the family from Madison was coming the week before the wedding. Peggy and her family, and Jerry and Mary, had answered their invitations, so eager to come. The wedding was to be held at two o'clock, Sunday, June 15th, at Temple Israel. Rabbi Golden from Madison was officiating.

The night before the wedding, Judy and her parents had time together in her room, then each spent time alone with her. They told her how much they loved her and wanted her to be happy. Later Judy wrote a letter to them thanking them for so many things, but most of all for their love and being wonderful parents. She slipped it under their bedroom door. Leisurely, she readied for bed and turned the lights off, all except the small lamp on the table beside her bed.

Slowly her eyes followed the few pictures on the wall. There was one of her father, Charlie. She had wanted it there. Tonight, as on many other nights, she thought about him. She wasn't angered or saddened about him anymore. She hoped he knew how happy she was. She knew he would be happy for her. Her thoughts went to Robert again. She was thinking of him and hoped he was thinking of her.

The day of the wedding dawned bright and clear, a perfect day. The wedding group had finally gathered early at the Temple for the photographer. Everyone seemed to be rushing about.

Carole and Serena came out to check the sanctuary again to be sure all was in readiness. A basket of pink roses waited at the altar on each side of the canopy, and wide ribbons connected the pews on each side of the aisle. Serena and Carole embraced. "Oh, Carole," Serena was misty-eyed. "It's so beautiful!"

Guests were arriving. Bill, Lainie, Phil, and Joe came early. They had places set aside out front, as there was room for Bill's wheelchair. Serena and Carole went up to greet them. Bill looked wonderful in a tuxedo.

Serena and Carole embraced them, “We’re so glad to see you.”

When everyone seemed to be in place, the violinist began playing music that settled the guests, and little by little, the murmuring ceased. There was a quiet, a hush in the sanctuary—a few coughs, and a few sneezes, then the “Wedding March” began.

Mr. and Mrs. Keller, the grandparents, came in all smiles as they walked up the aisle and were seated. Then Saul escorted his mother to her seat, where she sat so proud, looking wonderful.

Rachel, in a soft rose gown, came down on the arm of Timothy, Peggy’s son. He, Robert and Judy had become good friends. They looked a little nervous, but they made it down to the altar, and stood. Rachel on one side, Tim on the other.

Serena and Max came in with Robert, handsome in his tuxedo, and walked down to the altar. He kissed his mother and was hugged by his father.

Parents love and care for their children, and with faith and hope, look forward to this day when their offspring love and leave to build their own lives—a new generation. The parents watch them go and pray in their hearts that all will be well.

The music began again for the bride. Everyone turned in their seats to see Carole and David looking so wonderfully happy walking Judy down the aisle. Judy was beautiful in a gown of white, embroidered with hundreds of tiny pearls, and a tiara of tiny pearls that held her veil.

You could hear the ‘oh’s’ as they came; Robert, seeing his beautiful Judy, felt his eyes get misty. He wiped that away and waited for his bride. Carole and David took her to his side, but first she was kissed by her parents. Then Judy and Robert came up the steps to where Rabbi was waiting under the canopy with the bridesmaid Rachel. The parents went up one set on each side. Max was Robert’s best man.

The wedding ceremony began with the rabbi leading them with the exchange of marriage vows and exchange of wedding rings. Then the Rabbi spoke of the commitment each partner brings to the marriage. Robert broke the glass, and the ceremony was over. They were now "man and wife."

The ceremony ended with music, and the newlyweds hurried down the aisle. Guests were congratulating parents, family and friends as they were leaving for the Park Plaza for the reception, dinner and dancing.

After dinner, friends and family visited with each other, catching up on their lives. Max and Serena spent time with Jerry and Mary, who were running a small farm. Mary confided to Serena and Max that Jerry, who still had nightmares about the war, and saw his doctor often, was on medication. "There were times when things got pretty bad. We decided not to have children," Mary told them. "We've both missed that in our lives."

Peggy and her husband, Richard, spent time with Max and Serena. They liked Richard. Max was glad, it seemed to be a happy family. Timothy was the spitting image of Jim. He had a degree in engineering, and liked his work with roads and bridges. They were a challenge to him. He had a girlfriend, Jeanne, and they were planning to be engaged on her birthday in August.

That Timothy, Robert, and Judy had become good friends pleased Peggy and Max. Max knew that would have pleased Jim, too. He thought about the circumstances that brought Jim in his life—the war! Then the sad circumstances under which he met Peggy and Timothy. He remembered how he had dreaded meeting her. Now, she was important to Max, to his family—extended family close!

It was late when the bride and groom said their "good-byes" to guests, parents, and grandparents. They left in a car; the family had decorated with a big sign that read, "Just Married. Watch St. Louis grow!" Max and Serena said their farewells to Jerry and Mary, and Peggy and family; then headed home with the family from Madison. They were leaving early the next morning.

Carole and David drove home later. Carole had her head on David's shoulder; they rode in silence. "Are you asleep, Carole?""

"No." She was just tired. The excitement was wearing off. She was happy, but a little sad inside. Why? She didn't know. There hadn't been time to ponder it really, but it was there.

David told her what a wonderful job she had done on the wedding. "Everyone said it was so nice. You looked so beautiful, Carole. I was bursting with pride. I still think you did a terrific job."

They drove along in silence. David saw Carole shut her eyes. He knew she must have been thinking of Charlie many times during the past few weeks, and he wondered what she was feeling inside. He wanted to ask her so many times, but he didn't as long as she didn't say anything. She was pained, and he was concerned.

"I've been thinking," David said. "We should take a vacation—go somewhere where you've always wanted to go. You've worked so hard; last year graduation, this year the wedding. What do you think?"

"Well, where would you like to go?" She turned the question to him.

He wanted to say Hawaii, but knowing it would bring back Charlie and all they had been through said, "Well, I'll leave that up to you."

"I know," she volunteered. "What about Paradise Island where we spent our honeymoon?"

"Gosh, Carole, I've been thinking of that place, too."

"What do you say?" she asked.

"I say, yes. Let's go there. We had a wonderful time." He was so happy that she wanted to go back there. He hoped he had made her happy. He loved her.

It was decided. After the honeymooners got back, they would leave. Carole had a thought, "What do you think about asking Serena and Max to join us?"

David, silent for a few minutes, questioned, "Honestly? I'll tell you how I feel. I think this should just be our time, just the two of us. I'll leave it up to all of you. If they want to come, that will be fine with me. We'll ask them and see how they feel."

When they got home, they readied for bed, both exhausted. David was in bed and dozed off for a few minutes. He awakened to find Carole had not come to bed. Concerned, he went to find her. He called, but she didn't answer. He thought he knew where she was.

He saw the light coming through the space beneath the closed door to Judy's room. He knocked and asked, "Carole, are you all right?"

He heard her sobbing and went in. She was sitting on the edge of Judy's bed. He sat beside her with his arm about her.

"I miss her," she said.

"I know, honey. I miss her, too, but Carole, she's gone for a wonderful reason, her honeymoon. She's married to Robert. She'll be fine! I talked to Rabbi about this, the empty nest syndrome." David had anticipated something like this, knowing the closeness of mother and daughter.

Rabbi had said, "All parents have to deal with it when children leave, but you've done a good job of bringing up your children if they are capable of going out into the world to make their way as fine young adults."

"We'll deal with this adjustment together," David, comforting her, said. "That's why we're going to Paradise Island, honey."

XXV
Almost Full Circle

For David and Carole, the other life, just the two of them, "the togetherness life" had its beginning. The house was quiet that morning, no music or radio coming from Judy's room. David turned on the radio in the kitchen. He poured coffee while Carole was getting the eggs and toast.

Having their breakfast, David spoke to a silent Carole, "It will be different for a while, but we'll manage, honey."

He took her hand across the table and smiled at her. Carole felt better.

"I know, you're right, David. I'll be okay. It'll just take a little time."

She voiced what she'd been thinking. "Serena and Max must be feeling this way. Don't you think we ought to ask them to go with us?"

David agreed, and the invitation to Paradise Island was extended to their friends. "It's a good thought." Both Serena and Max thanked them for that, but had to decline. They were going to be busy with plans for the anniversary party and the preparations necessary to bring the relatives from France to America. Then they were going on a second honeymoon when the party was over. They thought, too, that Carole and David should go off, just the two of them, entering into this new phase of their lives.

"It'll be like a second honeymoon for you. It'll be wonderful." Serena's enthusiasm made Carole feel better about all of it.

Judy and Robert returned after a whirlwind week of honeymoon bliss, with the belief of most newlyweds that they were in control of their "perfect world" and had embarked on a "happy everafter" life's journey.

Seeing their happiness, Carole and David left for Paradise Island. They were as excited as newlyweds. Their cards came, sounding wonderfully happy. Max and Serena read and reread them. One card came, saying, "We hate to leave here. It is paradise!" They decided to stay another week.

They came back looking rested, well-tanned, and happy; ready to resume their lives with the changes. David and Carole had discussed them at length and had arrived at the conclusion that life has no permanency. There were always new things to deal with, and as David said, "Good changes make life interesting."

In retrospect, they knew they were two lucky people. At this point in their lives, there were two alternatives—either embracing life and living, or shutting one's self off from life, and slowly dying. They chose to cope with it as they had done so many times in their lives before, embracing life.

If the days in the week were busy ones, Serena and Carole managed to have phone talk fests a few evenings. Max and David saw each other in their shopping center stores and so were kept up-to-date on what was happening with each family. Judy and Robert, busy with work, tried to spend one Sunday a month with Carole and David for lunch or dinner, and one Sunday with Max and Serena. They had their friends, and their lives seemed to be on an even keel. It was clear to everyone they were happy.

The fall of the year with its holidays was fast approaching. It was always a very festive time for friends and family. They had gotten together in Madison for the celebrations. During the week of the holidays it had snowed. The dinners were special, and later, dressed warmly, they found the walks at night most invigorating and found time to go down hills on an old toboggan. Then they came in for hot chocolate and reminiscing until they couldn't stifle their yawns and reluctantly went to bed. The next morning on the train back to St. Louis, they talked about the wonderful weekend, so special, set aside in their memory bank to be happily recalled time and time again.

The old year was departing and the New Year, 1966, was almost upon them. The group had been thinking of going to the Park Plaza, but settled for a house get-together at Serena and Max's home. It was always pleasurable to be with family. All came with their contributions to the food and drinks; everyone wanted to be a part of it, and Serena let them. It made them happy, and there was fun and laughter at the unwrapping and setting up each one's gift. Max poured the champagne, and made the "toast," thankful they could "all be together this New Year's Eve."

They sat in a semi-circle, each telling stories. Lainie and Phil told some. Lainie wasn't as bubbly as she once was. She was a more subdued Lainie. She still looked wonderful with that engaging smile of hers. When the smile left her face, Serena saw the sadness in her eyes and it worried her.

Bill could speak better. His speech was still slow and stilted, but he spoke without embarrassment. He told of some things he heard on television, would speak just a few sentences, then would stop. Max and David, listening to him, would then enter into the conversation to help Bill along, but they did it in a very subtle manner.

Joe told stories of when he and Bill were younger, some of the pranks they played on each other. Everyone laughed, and it was good to hear Bill laugh again. The countdown to midnight came, and soon they were shouting, "Happy New Year" to each other. They continued with the story-telling. Serena told of escapades with her brother, Saul, and Max told some stories of his friends when they were young. Serena and Max had started to talk of college days, but they changed the subject because they would remember them with Charlie and didn't want Carole feeling badly.

If Carole ever mentioned Charlie, they could talk about him, but she never did. Carole told of things that happened at school with the children. The stories were funny; the children in their innocence would tell some pretty personal stories. Carole had them all laughing. David, too, talked of different things in his family, about his parents, that had them laughing. It was an enjoyable experience, and they learned more about each other. Joe got up to remind them it was late, and he thought they should go. Max and Serena exacted a promise from Bill, Lainie, Phil and Joe, that they would get together soon.

Max and Serena had been making arrangements, helping Francois get passports for the family. Francois had written they had a few problems concerning Michelle when she and Paul were getting married. She had no birth certificate or any papers. Francois, having been in the Resistance, had to move his family hurriedly so many times, the papers had been lost. He couldn't tell the authorities he was in the Resistance. He had worried Michelle would have trouble. There were more questions, but finally new papers were issued to Francois' family.

Now getting the passports, she had these papers and her marriage license, and she received the passport. There had been some anxious moments on both sides of the ocean.

"We are so proud to have our passports," Francois wrote. They lived the next months in great anticipation. They were coming a month before the party. Saul was to meet them in New York, to bring them to Madison. They would spend a week there, then come to St. Louis where Max would meet them. Serena had written, "We can't wait to see you!"

In spring, the clocks sprang ahead one hour for Daylight Savings Time, and the next few months raced ahead. The American family counted the days off the calendar until the last week in May. They, too, were eagerly anticipating the visit of their family from France. The family arrived in New York. Saul was there to meet them and helped them through Customs. "All a learning experience," Francois told Saul.

At dinner, they talked excitedly about the big plane, interrupting each other, telling about the huge ocean they flew over. They had some anxious moments, they confessed. They were all so excited to see the Statue of Liberty they always heard so much about. Saul wanted to take them to see some of New York. They would have liked to have gone, but Francois and Monique were tired. They decided to get to bed as they had an early call leaving for Madison. Saul agreed that was probably better. He saw them settled in their rooms, and he would be in the room next to theirs if they needed him. Francois, Paul, and Saul said their "good nights," because Francois said, "We are in America." They didn't do the cheek-kissing.

Jennifer met them in Madison and took Francois and Monique to Ann's. Saul took a cab with Michelle and her family. They were all meeting at Ann's for brunch. It was a late, late brunch.

There was talk and pictures of Ressel and Dave taken at different holidays that were passed back and forth. Michelle wanted to see them over and over again. Then Saul took them to the cemetery where Ressel, Dave, and Robert were buried. These were highly emotional moments for Michelle, and there were tears remembering how her mother had died, and how Francois had rescued her. She wished she could have known her mother. Francois and Monique wept, too, at the sadness that brought Michelle into their lives.

They spent such a warm, loving week in Madison. They had spent time with Jennifer and Rachel, family was family, getting to know each other was no problem. Their hearts felt the bonds. It was a miracle to be together. The farewells were emotional, but they were looking forward to seeing each other soon at Max and Serena's anniversary.

On the train to St. Louis, Francois and the family talked about how wonderful the family and friends were to them. He remembered as a Resistance fighter all the terrible crimes he had witnessed done to innocent, good people like these who were now part of his family. It saddened him to think it could have happened to his Michelle. He shuddered. The evil had not disappeared. It was here in different hideous forms. *Where would it lead to*? Francois wondered.

The ride was long, but they enjoyed seeing America through the windows of the train. They arrived in St. Louis. Before venturing out, they checked to see if they had their belongings. People on the train were helpful and kind. When they came out, Francois saw Max waiting there. David had come with his car to help with the passengers. He took Michelle and family, and Max took Francois and Monique. They were all going to Max's. Serena and Carole were waiting there.

The meeting was exciting for all of them. They were happy to finally meet Serena, and Serena told them, "It was good to see you after the writing and pictures." They met Carole. Everyone talking, asking questions. Serena showed them pictures she had. After much talk again, Serena said, "I know you are tired. I'll show you to your rooms. You can rest or unpack, or come down to have something to eat."

Carole and David were leaving so the families could be together. Francois and Monique thanked them. "We're family," Carole and David answered. Max and Serena embraced them with big hugs for their help.

About an hour later, Francois came down; the others soon followed, not wanting to miss anything. Serena had food on the table. They were enjoying some of it while talking to Serena and Max. They were too excited to rest; they wanted to go out to see the garden. They had seen part of it from the window upstairs. Serena told them about her favorite spot and gladly took them there. They fell in love with the garden, the bench, the tree, and the stream. They took turns sitting on the bench, admiring it. "Come out whenever you like." Serena had Max bring a few folding chairs.

They sat down, enjoying Serena's "space," not wanting to move anywhere. This they all enjoyed, sitting together, talking, learning about each other.

Francois, a little tired, rested on the bench, enjoying the garden. Monique and Michelle strolled in the yard and around the beautiful neighborhood. After dinner, Robert and Judy came and met the family. They stayed a little while; tomorrow was a work day. Everyone was tired. It had been a long day with so many wonderful things to see, people to meet. They went up to bed. Tomorrow they would have another full day of excitement.

Carole came to pick up Serena, Nedda, Michelle, and Monique. The ladies were going shopping in the special shops in the shopping center.

Max took Francois and Paul to see the shoe stores and the shoe manufacturing plants in St. Louis. They were fascinated, seeing how shoes were made. They visited the factory where boots were made for the Army. Francois spoke to one of the men operating a machine that sewed on the thick soles. "They were good shoes. We were lucky to have them. I still have mine. They were wonderful in all kinds of weather!" He said, "Thank you," and he vigorously shook the man's hand.

Serena and Carole had enjoyed every minute with the visitors. They were so impressed with the beautiful stores. They had lunch out and then tired, came home. The men were there, and then there was talk about America. They were impressed how friendly people were and happy. Americans were happy people!

That evening, they went to dinner at the Shanghai Restaurant on Delmar Boulevard. The Chinese food was a fine treat and another new experience. During the week, they visited the Forest Park Zoo. Max and his father took them to see a baseball game. The Cardinals, the home team, were playing, which was always exciting. Francois and Paul enjoyed it, even though the game had to be explained to them. Francois had been too busy in the Resistance, with no time to learn about baseball. They came home so invigorated. They became baseball fans that afternoon. It was one of the highlights of their visit.

For a few weeks, the tourists had been kept busy seeing St. Louis. Max drove them to towns and interesting places in areas around St. Louis. They were so pleased to meet the people who were always so helpful. They wanted to see as much of America as they could.

The weekend of the party, much anticipated, had arrived. Peggy and her family, and Mary and Jerry were comfortably ensconced at the Park Plaza Hotel. Both Serena and Max had called several times to see if the accommodations they had arranged were okay. Because Serena's home was being readied for the "big bash," as Max called it, Francois and Monique were enjoying their stay with the Kellers.

Serena, on this, her "day of days," had come out quite a few hours earlier to sit on the bench under the tree. In just a few hours, she had gone through her whole life, a lifetime, thus far, reviewed in a couple of hours.

There had been times during the remembering when she felt great pain. There had been tragedy and sadness for family and friends, but there had been a multitude of happy times, too. She felt relaxed and happy. This was the gift "her space" gave her.

From the house, she heard Maude, the maid, calling, looking for her. If her car was in the garage and she wasn't in the house, they knew where to find her. Maude came down to tell her Carole called and would be there in a few minutes. They were going to lunch and then to the beauty salon.

Serena got up to go to the house just as Carole drove up. In the car, talking, they decided to forego lunch, just a quick stop at the coffee shop. Serena was quite calm. Carole noted, "Gosh, Serena," Carole questioned, "aren't you nervous?"

"No, I'm fine. I'm excited, but I'm fine."

"I'm so happy for you and Max. David and I were saying this morning, "It's such a wonderful thing, a twenty-fifth anniversary!"

At the beauty salon, the girls congratulated Serena and gathered around her to give her their gift. She thanked them and said, "You're all so wonderful. We've been friends for a long time." Then they got to work, and Carole and Serena were on their way home in less than two hours.

Carole dropped Serena off and left to get Michelle's family to the party. Before Serena went up to dress, she went out to check on the preparations. Everything looked grand. The decorations were done in sky blue and white. The three-tiered wedding cake sat majestically on a round table. It was beautifully decorated with blue frosting festoons, and blue and white flowers outlining each tier.

The bridal table and all the other tables were covered with blue cloths and silver vases, with blue and white flowers as the dramatic centerpieces. When the guests would enter the main tent, they would be treated to a truly wondrous sight to behold.

The time was advancing to the magical hour. Serena was finishing up her dressing when Max came in. He saw Serena in the lovely ecru lace gown. He came over and pinned a corsage of blue flowers on her. "They're lovely, Max." She kissed him. "Happy Anniversary." Then said it once more, "They're lovely."

He took her hands and held them. "You're so beautiful, Siri. Happy Anniversary." He said it again, "Happy Anniversary. I love you!"

Serena waited as he hurried to get dressed. They could see the guests arriving, and then went down. They met Maude on the steps. She had come to tell them the Rabbi was waiting in the den. Rabbi congratulated them. They talked a bit—signed important papers, and heard the violinist begin his lovely music. It was almost five o'clock. The wedding procession began.

Rachel and Nedda in blue gowns were bridesmaids and walked down together. Then Judy, who was matron of honor, came down escorted by Robert, who was best man.

The Kellers walked with Max. Saul, and his mother, walking slowly, came proudly down with Serena. Max took her arm, and they walked together where the Rabbi waited under the canopy.

Rabbi welcomed the guests to this important occasion, the couple renewing their wedding vows. He spoke of "True love in a marriage where partners go through many things, illness, sadness, and many others. There are also the good things. They don't always balance out, for life is not easy. Having faith, and love, and respect for each other. God, under this canopy, gives his blessings to Max and Serena." The Rabbi blessed them, and Max stomped on the cloth-covered glass so hard that everyone heard it shatter. "You may kiss the bride." A beaming Rabbi congratulated them.

Max embraced her, "Happy Anniversary, beautiful." He kissed her gently on the lips.

The music began again, and they walked back down the aisle to the end of the room where the family was waiting in a reception line. Serena and Max joined them, then were shown to the tables in the huge main tent. The waiters poured champagne and waited for the bride and groom to come to the head table where members of the family were seated. Saul and David gave toasts, and there was a murmuring of voices talking and laughing.

Robert and Judy got up to make a speech. The buzz in the room stopped. Judy spoke, wishing them all good things in life. "I'm so happy to be part of this family."

Then Robert spoke, "We wanted to give you a special gift for your special anniversary. We have one, but it won't be delivered until December. With God's help, we hope to present you with your first grandchild."

Serena and Max came over to embrace them and to congratulate them. Carole and David came over. They had been told that morning. They all sat down to eat and visit, and to take part in this wonderful evening. The party went its fast pace, but was slowing down in the late, late hours. Max and Serena had made attempts to spend a bit of time with each of their guests. Max spoke to Peggy and her husband, Richard. They were worried about Timothy and the Vietnam War. "It'll be some time before they call Tim or Robert." Max attempted to alleviate their fears. "There are so many ahead of them, the war could be over by then."

Serena and Max continued making the rounds, thanking the guests for coming. It had taken quite awhile, and by that time, some were leaving. Peggy and her family, and Jerry and Mary left for their hotel. They were taking off early the next morning. Francois and family were going with the Kellers. The Madison women were getting to the airport with Mr. Keller. Saul was going with Francois and family to New York to see them off.

Serena and Max were going away for a week after all the guests had gone. They were so looking forward to that time to unwind, to talk about things important to the two of them. That night, Serena helped Monique and Michelle pack, and then they all sat talking. There was so much they wanted to say to each other, and the time was growing short.

Francois and Monique thanked them again and again. Everyone had been so wonderful. Michelle and family felt a very strong connection to them, and were "so happy to be part of this family." Serena and Max voiced the same, and as they said so often, "It was a miracle that in that chaotic world we had connected with Francois and family to Michelle.

Serena and Max drove them to the airport. They had taken both cars to accommodate the luggage and passengers. At the airport, they were early enough to talk more. They talked about the new baby coming. "Send pictures right away," Michelle shook her finger to make her point.

They promised, "Right away!"

Soon it was time to board, and they embraced and cried. Serena waved at them as they walked to get into their plane. Saul would remain with them until they were safely aboard their plane for France and he would fly home to Madison.

Max didn't go to the store. He stayed home to be with Serena. There hadn't been time to really talk to each other. There was much each wanted to say. They were both physically and emotionally exhausted.

Max said, "Siri, why don't we go out to lunch, come home, and shower, and get some rest."

Serena thought that was a brilliant idea and said so. They drove to the Shanghai, and had some of their favorite Chinese food. They ate leisurely, talking about the wonderful surprise that Judy and Robert had for their anniversary. They couldn't get over it, saying again and again, "Can you believe it? We're going to be grandparents!" They were ecstatic. They hadn't really had a chance to discuss it with Carole and David. They had just congratulated each other at the party. Serena said, "We'll talk to them tomorrow."

They showered together and got into their robes, but they were too wide awake to go to sleep. It was lovely out, and Serena's idea was to go out to the yard, to the bench. She led the way and he followed. They sat there just looking at the flowers in the garden, at the butterflies fluttering about, and the water in the stream flowing fresh and clear.

"It's beautiful here, Max. I just love our home and everything!"

"I'm glad, Siri." He had put his heart and soul into loving her and making her happy. "Have you been happy, Siri?" he questioned.

They had been looking at each other when she answered, "Yes, Max, you know I've been happy. What about you, Max? Have you been happy?" He took her hands and his closed over hers, held them; then said, "Siri, my life here with you has been my heaven!"

Max took her in his arms and kissed her. They sat there, her head leaning against his shoulder, and talked about the ceremony, how moving it was. "I looked out in the chapel and saw the family and friends who were there with us, and it was such a wonderful feeling. I remember Rabbi once telling us, 'Living our lives, we round a circle.' Sometimes events occur that interfere, interrupt the circle from going forward, overcoming them adds to the circle, bit by bit."

"We've made a good advance with our twenty-fifth anniversary, and looking forward to our first grandchild will add more. I pray there are no further interruptions as we go forward to our full circle. I see our friends moving forward in their circles," Serena added.

"Yes," Max was enthusiastic. "You saw Bill and Joe, and Lainie and Phil, all together. Later when I talked to them, Bill's speech is improving, and he seems happier with the arrangement. Thank God. I hope the pain in their lives subsides even more, and they continue to be happy."

Serena interrupted, "Look at Carole and David's world, once so chaotic, is now good. They're happy together and looking forward to their first grandchild." Serena pointed out all the wonderful things that had happened to her best friend.

"I don't know if she's forgiven Charlie yet. She doesn't talk about it. I'm happy with how I see her now. There's so much to be thankful for where she and David are concerned." Serena said, "I hope their life will continue to be good, adding to their 'circle' as you call it, Max."

Max thought it was truly wonderful of Saul to see Francois and family safely to New York, and to put them on the plane to France. Saul felt he had to do it for his father and Grandmother Ressel, and for himself.

Serena had enjoyed having her mom, and Saul and his family. "They're a happy little family group, all taking care of each other. Jennifer and Mom love that Rachel, and she is such a nice young lady. Saul told me she has lots of friends, and a boyfriend. It won't be long before she gets married, and their little family will grow. Gosh, it's hard to believe how life goes on."

It had been wonderfully satisfying to meet Francois and Monique and Michelle, Paul and Nedda. "I worry about Francois," Max said, "I told him I was glad to see him relaxed and not so worried about conditions in some of the European countries."

Francois had said, "There's much to worry about, but we are always ready."

Max said, "I told him, he should stop, he's done enough. He's older and should take care of himself."

Francois had replied, "We can't stop. Wherever there is trouble, we do whatever needs to be done. War is still on in so many countries—new problems."

"I know," Max had told him, "I'll worry about you!"

Francois had said, "Don't worry, I'll be all right."

Max said, "Francois can say that, but I know Monique and Michelle are worried. Monique voiced her fear to me."

Serena changed the subject. She didn't want to think about the problems in Europe—not tonight.

"We have so much to be thankful for—to look forward to the future." She felt good about it.

Yes, the coming of their first grandchild was mentioned again. They were both so pleased. Now they understood more of how their parents felt when Robert was born.

"Yes," Serena said again, "we have much to be thankful for." She said it slowly—thoughtfully.

Refreshed, relaxed, sitting under the willow, they saw their future bright. The "tomorrows" in their world would be good! They had plans to leave the following morning for their vacation, so excited to be going to Hawaii. They were ready—finished packing, and David and Carole were driving them to the airport quite early.

That night, a terribly upset Peggy called Max. Timothy was to report immediately for service. Max tried to console her. What could he say? Peggy, crying, would try to talk, saying over and over, "They took Jim, they can't take his son, too." Then the crying would resume once more. Max heard Richard trying to soothe her. He got on the phone, talked to Max for a few minutes, then hung up.

Max came away from the phone, sick at heart. Serena had heard some of his conversation with a distraught Peggy, who couldn't talk to Serena. Max relayed Peggy's problem and worry. Serena's first question was, "What about Robert?" Now that Timothy was called for the war in Vietnam, that war didn't seem so far away. A cold shiver went through her.

"Robert's number won't come up for some time," Max said. He said it with such confidence, as if that was a certainty. In his heart, he wasn't so sure. Serena wanted to postpone their trip, but Max knew she would worry at home or in Hawaii. Being away for a week was better. "We don't want to upset Judy and Robert," he told her, and she agreed with that.

They left the next morning, flew to the West Coast, then across the Pacific to Hawaii. It was beautiful there. They swam in the ocean and rested on the wonderful beaches. Max, trying to engage her in conversation on so many levels—their anniversary, meeting the family from France, their friends, and the wonderful news of a coming grandchild.

They had delicious dinners out, in beautiful places. Serena saw Max's attempts to be cheerful, and she tried, too, for his sake. They were brave for each other. Still, Serena had to get the newspaper to read the bits of news about Vietnam. Their hearts were not fully into this vacation thing, but there were some good moments. They had their love for each other and, being optimists, there was always eternal hope!

Back home, Robert, coming in from work, stopped to pick up the mail and entered the apartment. He deposited the mail on the table near the door. Judy wasn't home yet, but he knew she would be along soon. He always felt better when she was there with him. He was thinking of her as he took off his tie and suit coat. Robert got the mail and sat down to open it while waiting for Judy.

He opened the first, an electric bill, and set it aside. He opened the next one, an official-looking letter, which began, "Greetings!" It was one he knew would be coming, but still it startled him. He read on. He was being called into the military service and was to report to the induction center on the date given. He realized the men weren't given too much time, as the date was coming up soon.

With each other, and with friends, Robert and Judy had discussed the situation. Robert had wanted to enlist. It wasn't something they could discuss with their parents. Their parents had always stressed their love of country. Judy and Robert had been taken to the parades on holidays, waving their flags. Patriotism had been instilled in them all their lives. Their parents, they knew, worried when they heard talk of the war, but they were somewhat prepared. There was fear, but a burning patriotism in theirs, and in the hearts of their eager young.

Robert's thoughts were interrupted when he heard Judy at the door and got up to meet her. How would she take the news now that it was here? She had been very supportive, but he worried. They would be separated, far away. That would be difficult for both of them. He would wait until after dinner to tell her, but Judy was well attuned to her Robert and knew something had come up. She questioned and couldn't be put off. He showed her the letter. She read it and then looked at him. "We knew it would come. We just didn't know when," she said it matter-of-factly. She hoped she sounded calm, but her heart was racing.

Judy tried to keep the conversation going at dinner. Robert could see the worry already in her eyes. He tried to deal with it. "We don't have too much to do, to put our affairs in order. Everything will be okay," he told her, "it will all work out." He made her feel better as he held her. The impact of what this meant, separation from Robert, caused the tears to come. She would miss his not being there with her.

Max and Serena arrived home, happy to be back. The next day they spoke with Judy and Robert, and invited them for Sunday dinner. Judy and Robert had pondered the question of when to tell them Robert was leaving soon. They decided to tell their parents Sunday after dinner. At the dinner table, there was talk of so many things. Serena remarked how well Judy looked and wanted to know how she was feeling.

Serena talked glowingly about the beauty of the island. Judy wanted to know more about Hawaii. Max talked about visiting the Pearl Harbor Memorial, where the *Arizona* had gone down. He talked of the many tourists who were there. They had such a pleasant time and hoped someday Judy and Robert could go visit there.

Later in the living room, Robert told his parents he had been called into service and would be leaving soon. Serena, shocked and upset, tried to be calm for the sake of Judy and Robert, who were talking about their plans and the baby.

Serena made an attempt at easing a little of the tension, talked to Judy about a baby shower, and soon all were laughing, happy to be together, masking the nagging fear. Robert and Judy were about to leave, saying they had much to do and were going to stop to tell Carole and David.

After they had gone, Serena burst into tears that had been so near the surface, that she had tried to control in front of Judy and Robert. Max held her tight, close to his breast, trying to soothe her. She wept the tears of the pent-up worry she had kept inside for weeks. For Max, there was the knowing of the country's desperate need of its young men. He also knew the gods of war have voracious appetites with needs to be satisfied. Max knew war!

It was late, but Serena wanted to go out to her space. She had a great need for it tonight. Max went with her, and they sat together, his arm about her, both silent. Serena spoke up with a sadness in her voice, "There are always wars. Will it ever end?" That was the question she posed to Max, and he had no answer for her.

For Max and Serena, and their friends, life had almost come "full circle." Now, there again was a war, the aftermath of other wars, interfering in their lives once again. Max was thinking. "It's beginning again, a new circle with another generation—his son's generation, full of honor, courage, and willing sacrifice—going off to war." He wondered, "Would this at last be the one, the one war to end all wars?"

The world would have to wait for the answer, for the consequences to evolve from the choices that its leaders would make.

Epilogue

The Great War, WWII, also known as the "Holocaust War," in which six million Jews and millions of others were killed by the evil-doers, those filled with a maniacal hate, jealousy, and greed, was the war of Nazism. It was to be the war to end all wars. It didn't do that!

The effects of its Peace Treaty resounded in the subsequent wars with "isms" in their names. In the Vietnam and Korean Wars, it was communism, where thousands of Americans and others were captured, tortured, and brutally murdered. Thousands are still listed as "M.I.A.'s," Missing in Action, and the effects continue into the twenty-first century.

In America, on September 11, 2001, we and our country were betrayed with an attack by terrorists, the Al-Qaeda. We are now fighting terrorism. Its goal to destroy us and our civilization.

We, like the characters in the book, were lulled into a complacency, and then we discovered nothing can be taken for granted. We are at war, and our military answers the call with courage, and strength in spirit and faith.

We've learned, we must be ever vigilant, ready to do all that is best for our country.

"Eternal Vigilance Is the Price of Liberty." Together we stand united, for our world, our liberties, and our freedoms are in grave danger.

This book is a tribute to those who fought in the past wars, to those who fight now, and to those who are committed to preserving our freedom in the future.

In all that has gone before, decisions were made with much thought, and there were consequences affecting so many. What is happening in the present requires decisions to be made with consequences far-reaching and yet unknown.

We pray for our leaders in their awesome tasks to be wise and strong and resolute. Ever-present are the decisions to be made, and hope in the "Consequence of Choice" that good will triumph over evil!

Bibliography

I. Burnett, Betty. *St. Louis at War.* Patrice Press: Tucson, AZ, 1987.

II. Costello, John. *The Pacific War, 1941–1945.* William Morrow and Co: New York, NY, 1981.

III. Don Passos, John. *Mr. Wilson's War.* Doubleday and Co., Inc.: Garden City, N.Y. 1962.

IV. Gilbert, Martin. *The Second World War.* Henry Holt and Co.: New York, N.Y., 1981, or Atlantic Communications, 1981.

V. Goldhagen, Daniel Jonah. *Hitler's Willing Executioners.* A division of Random House: New York, N.Y., 1963.

VI Lawson, Don. *The United States of World War I.* Scholastic Book Services: New York, N.Y., 1963.

VII. Marrin, Albert. *The Yanks are Coming.* Atheneum, Macmillan Publishing Co.: New York, N.Y., 1986.

VIII. Reeder, Colonel Red. *The Story of the First World War.* Duell-Sloan and Pearce: An affiliate of Meredith Press: New York, N.Y., 1962.

IX. Reeder, Colonel Red, 1942–1945. *The Story of the Second World War.* Hawthorne Books, Inc.: New York, N.,Y., 1970.